SMALL TOWN DREAMS

First Impressions

and

Less of a Stranger

Sign of Seven Trilogy
Blood Brothers • The Hollow • The Pagan Stone

Bride Quartet
*Vision in White • Bed of Roses • Savor the Moment • Happy
Ever After*

The Inn Boonsboro Trilogy
The Next Always • The Last Boyfriend • The Perfect Hope

The Cousins O'Dwyer Trilogy
Dark Witch • Shadow Spell • Blood Magick

The Guardians Trilogy
Stars of Fortune • Bay of Sighs • Island of Glass

Chronicles of The One
Year One • Of Blood and Bone • The Rise of Magicks

The Dragon Heart Legacy
The Awakening

EBOOKS BY NORA ROBERTS

Cordina's Royal Family
*Affaire Royale • Command Performance • The Playboy
Prince • Cordina's Crown Jewel*

The Donovan Legacy
Captivated • Entranced • Charmed • Enchanted

The O'Hurleys
*The Last Honest Woman • Dance to the Piper •
Skin Deep • Without a Trace*

Night Tales
*Night Shift • Night Shadow • Nightshade • Night Smoke •
Night Shield*

• *Portrait in Death* • *Imitation in Death* • *Divided in Death*
• *Visions in Death* • *Survivor in Death* • *Origin in Death*
• *Memory in Death* • *Born in Death* • *Innocent in Death*
• *Creation in Death* • *Strangers in Death* • *Salvation in Death*
• *Promises in Death* • *Kindred in Death* • *Fantasy in Death* •
Indulgence in Death • *Treachery in Death* • *New York to Dallas*
• *Celebrity in Death* • *Delusion in Death* • *Calculated in Death*
• *Thankless in Death* • *Concealed in Death* • *Festive in Death* •
Obsession in Death • *Devoted in Death* • *Brotherhood in Death*
• *Apprentice in Death* • *Echoes in Death* • *Secrets in Death* •
Dark in Death • *Leverage in Death* • *Connections in Death* •
Vendetta in Death • *Golden in Death* • *Shadows in Death*
• *Faithless in Death*

ANTHOLOGIES

From the Heart • *A Little Magic* • *A Little Fate*

Moon Shadows
(with Jill Gregory, Ruth Ryan Langan, and Marianne Willman)

The Once Upon Series
(with Jill Gregory, Ruth Ryan Langan, and Marianne Willman)
Once Upon a Castle • *Once Upon a Star* • *Once Upon a
Dream* • *Once Upon a Rose* • *Once Upon a Kiss* • *Once Upon
a Midnight*

Silent Night
(with Susan Plunkett, Dee Holmes, and Claire Cross)

Out of This World
(with Laurell K. Hamilton, Susan Krinard, and Maggie Shayne)

Bump in the Night
(with Mary Blayney, Ruth Ryan Langan, and Mary Kay McComas)

Dead of Night
(with Mary Blayney, Ruth Ryan Langan, and Mary Kay McComas)

Three in Death

SMALL TOWN DREAMS

First Impressions

and

Less of a Stranger

TWO NOVELS IN ONE

NORA ROBERTS

St. Martin's Paperbacks

This is a work of fiction. All of the characters, organizations, and events portrayed in this book are either products of the author's imagination or are used fictitiously.

First published in the United States by St. Martin's Paperbacks, an imprint of St. Martin's Publishing Group

SMALL TOWN DREAMS: FIRST IMPRESSIONS copyright © 1984 by Nora Roberts and LESS OF A STRANGER copyright © 1984 by Nora Roberts.

All rights reserved.

For information, address St. Martin's Publishing Group, 120 Broadway, New York, NY 10271.

www.stmartins.com

ISBN: 978-1-250-79646-2

Our books may be purchased in bulk for promotional, educational, or business use. Please contact your local bookseller or the Macmillan Corporate and Premium Sales Department at 1-800-221-7945, ext. 5442, or by email at MacmillanSpecialMarkets@macmillan.com.

Printed in the United States of America

St. Martin's Paperbacks edition 2021

10 9 8 7 6 5 4 3 2 1

First Impressions

To Georgeann, neighbor and friend

CHAPTER 1

The morning sun shot shafts of light over the mountains. It picked up the hints of red and gold among the deep green leaves and had them glowing. From somewhere in the woods came a rustling as a rabbit darted back to its burrow, while overhead a bird chirped with an insistent cheerfulness. Clinging to the line of fences along the road were clumps of honeysuckle. The light scent from the few lingering blossoms wafted in the air. In a distant field a farmer and his son harvested the last of the summer hay. The rumble of the baler was steady and distinct.

Over the mile trek to town only one car passed. Its driver lifted his hand in a salute. Shane waved back. It was good to be home.

Walking on the grassy shoulder of the road, she plucked a blossom of honeysuckle and, as she had as a child, drew in the fleetingly sweet aroma. When she crushed the flower between her fingers, its fragrance briefly intensified. It was a scent she associated with summer, like barbecue smoke and new grass. But this was summer's end.

Shane looked forward to fall eagerly, when the mountains would be at their best. Then the colors were breathtaking, and the air was clean and crisp. When the wind came, the world would be full of sound and flying leaves. It was the time of woodsmoke and fallen acorns.

Curiously, she felt as though she'd never been away. She might still have been twenty-one, walking from her grand-mother's to Sharpsburg to buy a gallon of milk or a loaf of bread. The busy Baltimore streets, the sidewalks and crowds of the last four years might have been a dream. She might never have spent those four years teaching in an inner-city school, correcting exams and attending faculty meetings.

Yet four years had passed. Her grandmother's narrow two-story house was now Shane's. The uneven, wooded three acres of land were hers as well. And while the mountains and woods were the same, Shane was not.

Physically, she looked almost as she had when she had left western Maryland for the job in a Baltimore high school. She was small in height and frame, with a slender figure that had never developed the curves and roundness she'd hoped for. Her face was subtly triangular with its creamy skin touched with warm color. It had been called peaches and cream of-ten enough to make Shane wince. There were dimples that flashed when she smiled, rather than the elegant cheekbones she had wished for. Her nose was small, dusted with freck-les, tilted up at the end. Pert. Shane had suffered the word throughout her life.

Under thin arched brows, her eyes were large and dark. Whatever emotion she felt was mirrored in them. They were rarely cool. Habitually, she wore her hair short, and it curled naturally to frame her face in a deep honey blond. As her temperament was almost invariably happy, her face was usu-ally animated, her small, sculpted mouth tilted up. The ad-jective used most to describe her was *cute*. Shane had grown to detest the word but lived with it. Nothing could be done to alter sharp, vital attractiveness into sultry beauty.

As she rounded the last curve in the road before coming

into town, she had a sudden flash of having done so be-fore—as a child, as a teenager, as a girl on the brink of womanhood. It gave her a sense of security and belonging. Nothing in the city had ever given her the simple pleasure of being part of the whole.

Laughing, she took the final yards at a run, then burst through the door of the general store. The bells jingled fiercely before it slammed shut.

"Hi!"

"Hi, yourself." The woman behind the counter grinned at her. "You're out early this morning."

"When I woke up, I discovered I was out of coffee." Spot-ting the box of fresh doughnuts on the counter, Shane rolled her eyes and headed for them. "Oh, Donna, cream filled?"

"Yeah." Donna watched with an envious sigh as Shane chose one and bit into it. For the better part of twenty years, she'd seen Shane eat like a linebacker without gaining an ounce of fat.

Though they had grown up together, they were as different as night and day. Where Shane was fair, Donna was dark. Shane was small; Donna was tall and well rounded. For most of their lives, Donna had been content to play follower to Shane's leader. Shane was the adventurer. Donna had liked nothing better than to point out all the flaws in whatever plans Shane was hatching, then wholeheartedly fall in with it.

"So, how are you settling in?"

"Pretty well," Shane answered with her mouth full.

"You've hardly been in since you got back in town."

"There's been so much to do. Gran couldn't keep the place up the last few years." Both affection and grief came through in her voice. "She was always more interested in her gardening than a leaky roof. Maybe if I had stayed—"

"Oh, now don't start blaming yourself again." Donna cut her off, drawing her straight dark brows together. "You know she wanted you to take that teaching job. Faye Abbott lived to be ninety-four. That's more than a lot of people can hope for. And she was a feisty old devil right to the end."

Shane laughed. "You're absolutely right. Sometimes I'm sure she's sitting in her kitchen rocker making certain I wash up my dishes at night." The thought made her want to sigh for the childhood that was gone, but she pushed the mood away. "I saw Amos Messner out in the field with his son haying." After finishing off the doughnut, Shane dusted her hands on the seat of her pants. "I thought Bob was in the army."

"Got discharged last week. He's going to marry a girl he met in North Carolina."

"No kidding?"

Donna smiled smugly. It always pleased her, as proprietor of the general store, to be the ears and eyes of the town. "She's coming to visit next month. She's a legal secretary."

"How old is she?" Shane demanded, testing.

"Twenty-two."

Throwing back her head, Shane laughed in delight. "Oh, Donna, you're terrific. I feel as though I've never been away."

The familiar unrestricted laugh made Donna grin. "I'm glad you're back. We missed you."

Shane settled a hip against the counter. "Where's Benji?"

"Dave's got him upstairs." Donna preened a bit, thinking of her husband and son. "Letting that little devil loose down here's only asking for trouble. We'll switch off after lunch."

"That's the beauty of living on top of your business."

Finding the opening she had hoped for, Donna pounced on it. "Shane, are you still thinking about converting the house?"

"Not thinking," Shane corrected. "I'm going to do it." She hurried on, knowing what was about to follow. "There's always room for another small antique shop, and with the museum attached, it'll be distinctive."

"But it's such a risk," Donna pointed out. The excited gleam in Shane's eyes had her worrying all the more. She'd seen the same gleam before the beginning of any number of outrageous and wonderful plots. "The expense—"

"I have enough to set things up." Shane shrugged off the pessimism. "And most of my stock can come straight out of the house for now. I want to do it, Donna," she went on as her friend frowned at her. "My own place, my own business." She glanced around the compact, well-stocked store. "You should know what I mean."

"Yes, but I have Dave to help out, to lean on. I don't think I could face starting or managing a business all on my own."

"It's going to work." Her eyes drifted beyond Donna, fixed on their own vision. "I can already see how it's going to look when I'm finished."

"All the remodeling."

"The basic structure of the house will stay the same," Shane countered. "Modifications, repairs." She brushed them away with the back of her hand. "A great deal of it would have to be done if I were simply going to live there."

"Licenses, permits."

"I've applied for everything."

"Taxes."

"I've already seen an accountant." She grinned as Donna sighed. "I have a good location, a solid knowledge of antiques, and I can re-create every battle of the Civil War."

"And do at the least provocation."

"Be careful," Shane warned her, "or I'll give you another rundown on the Battle of Antietam."

When the bells on the door jingled again, Donna heaved an exaggerated sigh of relief. "Hi, Stu."

The next ten minutes were spent in light gossiping as Donna rang up and bagged dry goods. It would take little time to catch up on the news Shane had missed over the last four years.

Shane was accepted as an oddity—the hometown girl who had gone to the city and come back with big ideas. She knew that to the older residents of the town and countryside she would always be Faye Abbott's granddaughter. They were a proprietary people, and she was one of their own. She hadn't settled down and married Cy Trainer's boy as predicted, but she was back now.

"Stu never changes," Donna said when she was alone with Shane again. "Remember in high school when we were sophomores and he was a senior, captain of the football team and the best-looking hunk in a sweaty jersey?"

"And nothing much upstairs," Shane added dryly.

"You always did go for the intellectual type. Hey," she continued before Shane could retort, "I might just have one for you."

"Have one what?"

"An intellectual. At least that's how he strikes me. He's your neighbor too," she added with a growing smile.

"*My* neighbor?"

"He bought the old Farley place. Moved in early last week."

"The Farley place?" Shane's brows arched, giving Donna the satisfaction of knowing she was announcing fresh news. "The house was all but gutted by the fire. Who'd be fool enough to buy that ramshackle barn of a place?"

"Vance Banning," Donna told her. "He's from Washington, D.C."

After considering the implications of this, Shane shrugged. "Well, I suppose it's a choice piece of land even if the house should be condemned." Wandering to a shelf, she selected a pound can of coffee then set it on the counter without checking the price. "I guess he bought it for a tax shelter or something."

"I don't think so." Donna rang up the coffee and waited while Shane dug bills out of her back pocket. "He's fixing it up."

"The courageous type." Absently, she pocketed the loose change.

"All by himself too," Donna added, fussing with the display of candy bars on the counter. "I don't think he has a lot of money to spare. No job."

"Oh." Shane's sympathies were immediately aroused. The spreading problem of unemployment could hit anyone, she knew. Just the year before, the teaching staff at her school had been cut by three percent.

"I heard he's pretty handy though," Donna went on. "Archie Moler went by there a few days ago to take him some lumber. He said he's already replaced the old porch. But the guy's got practically no furniture. Boxes of books, but not much else." Shane was already wondering what she could spare from her own collection. She had a few extra chairs . . .

"And," Donna added warmly, "he's wonderful to look at."

"You're a married woman," Shane reminded her, clucking her tongue.

"I still like to look. He's tall." Donna sighed. At five foot eight, she appreciated tall men. "And dark with a sort of lived-in face. You know, creases, lots of bone. And shoulders."

"You always did go for shoulders."

Donna only grinned. "He's a little lean for my taste, but the face makes up for it. He keeps to himself, hardly says a word."

"It's hard being a stranger." She spoke from her own experience. "And being out of work too. What do you think—"

Her question was cut off by the jingle of bells. Glancing over, Shane forgot what she had been about to ask.

He was tall, as Donna had said. In the few seconds they stared at each other, Shane absorbed every aspect of his physical appearance. Lean, yes, but his shoulders were broad, and the arms exposed by the rolled-up shirtsleeves were corded with muscle. His face was tanned, and it narrowed down to a trim, clipped jaw. Thick and straight, his black hair fell carelessly over a high forehead.

His mouth was beautiful. It was full and sharply sculpted, but she knew instinctively it could be cruel. And his eyes, a clear deep blue, were cool. She was certain they could turn to ice. She wouldn't have called it a lived-in face, but a remote one. There was an air of arrogant distance about him. Aloofness seemed to vie with an inner charge of energy.

The spontaneous physical pull was unexpected. In the past, Shane had been attracted to easygoing, good-natured men. This man was neither, she knew, but what she felt was undeniable. For a flash, all that was inside her leaned toward him in a knowledge that was as basic as chemistry and as insubstantial as dreams. Five seconds, it could have been no longer. It didn't need to be.

Shane smiled. He gave her the briefest of acknowledging nods, then walked to the back of the store.

"So, how soon do you think you'll have the place ready to open?" Donna asked Shane brightly with one eye trained toward the rear of the store.

"What?" Shane's mind was still on the man.

"Your place," Donna said meaningfully.

"Oh, three months, I suppose." She glanced blankly around the store as if she had just come in. "There's a lot of work to do."

He came back with a quart of milk and set it on the counter, then reached for his wallet. Donna rang it up, shooting Shane a look from under her lashes before she gave him his change. He left the store without having spoken a word.

"That," Donna announced grandly, "was Vance Banning."

"Yes." Shane exhaled. "So I gathered."

"You see what I mean. Great to look at, but not exactly the friendly sort."

"No." Shane walked toward the door. "I'll see you later, Donna."

"Shane!" With a half laugh, Donna called after her. "You forgot your coffee."

"Hmm? Oh, no thanks," she murmured absently. "I'll have a cup later."

When the door swung shut, Donna stared at it, then at the can of coffee in her hand. "Now what got into her?" she wondered aloud.

As she walked home, Shane felt confused. Though emotional by nature, she could, when necessary, be very analytical. At the moment, she was dealing with the shock of what had happened to her in a few fleeting seconds. It had been much more than a feminine response to an attractive man.

She had felt, inexplicably, as though her whole life had been a waiting period for that quick, silent meeting. Recognition. The word came to her out of nowhere. She had recognized him, not from Donna's description, but from some deep inner knowledge of her own needs. *This was the man.*

Ridiculous, she told herself. Idiotic. She didn't know him, hadn't even heard him speak. No sensible person felt so strongly about a total stranger. More likely, her response had stemmed from the fact that she and Donna had been speaking of him as he had walked in.

Turning off the main road, she began to climb the steep lane that led to her house. He certainly hadn't been friendly, she thought. He hadn't answered her smile or made the slightest attempt at common courtesy. Something in the cool blue eyes had demanded distance. Shane didn't think he was the kind of man she usually liked. Then again, her reaction had been far removed from the calm emotion of liking.

As always when she saw the house, Shane felt a rush of

pleasure. This was hers. The woods, thick and touched with the first breath of autumn; the narrow struggling creek; the rocks that worked their way through the ground everywhere—they were all hers.

Shane stood on the wooden bridge over the creek and looked at the house. It did need work. Some of the boards on the porch needed replacing, and the roof was a big problem. Still, it was a lovely little place, nestled comfortably before woods, rolling hills and distant blue mountains. It was more than a century old, fashioned from local stone. In the rain, the colors would burst out of the old rock and gleam like new. Now, in the sunlight, it was comfortably gray.

The architecture was simple—straight lines for durability rather than style. The walkway ran to the porch, where the first step sagged a bit. Shane's problem wouldn't be with the stone, but with the wood. She overlooked the rough edges to take in the beauty of the familiar.

The last of the summer flowers were fading. The roses were brown and withered, while the first fall blooms were coming to life. Shane could hear the hiss of water traveling over rocks, the faint whisper of wind through leaves, and the lazy drone of bees.

Her grandmother had guarded her privacy. Shane could turn a full circle without seeing a sign of another house. She had only to walk a quarter mile if she wanted company, or stay at home if she didn't. After four years of crowded classrooms and daily confinement, Shane was ready for solitude.

And with luck, she thought as she continued walking, she could have her shop open and ready for business before Christmas. Antietam Antiques and Museum. Very dignified and to the point, she decided. Once the outside repairs were accomplished, work could start on the interior. The picture was clear in her mind.

The first floor would be structured in two informal sections. The museum would be free, an inducement to lure people into the antique shop. Shane had enough from her family collection to begin stocking the museum and six rooms of antique furniture to sort and list. She would have to go to a few auctions and estate sales to increase her inventory, but she felt her inheritance and savings would hold her for a while.

The house and land were hers free and clear, with only the yearly taxes to pay. Her car, for what it was worth, was paid for. Every spare penny could go into her projected business. She was going to be successful and independent—and the last was more important than the first.

As she walked toward the house, Shane paused and glanced down the overgrown logging trail, which led to the Farley property. She was curious to see what this Vance Banning was doing with the old place. And, she admitted, she wanted to see him again when she was prepared.

After all, they were going to be neighbors, she told herself as she hesitated. The least she could do was to introduce herself and start things off on the right foot. Shane set off into the woods.

She knew the trees intimately. Since childhood she had raced or walked among them. Some had fallen and lay aging and rotting on the ground among layers of old leaves. Overhead, branches arched together to form an intermittent roof pierced by streams of morning sunlight. Confidently she followed the narrow, winding path. She was still yards from the house when she heard the muffled echo of hammering.

Though it disturbed the stillness of the woods, Shane liked the sound. It meant work and progress. Quickening her pace, she headed toward it.

She was still in the cover of the trees when she saw him. He stood on the newly built porch of the old Farley place, hammering the supports for the railing. He'd stripped off his shirt, and his brown skin glistened with a light film of sweat. The dark hair on his chest tapered down, then disappeared into the waistband of worn, snug jeans.

As he lifted the heavy top rail into place, the muscles of his back and shoulders rippled. Totally intent on his work, Vance was unaware of the woman who stood at the edge of the woods and watched. For all his physical exertion, he was relaxed. There was no hardness around his mouth now or frost in his eyes.

When she stepped into the clearing, Vance's head shot up. His eyes instantly filled with annoyance and suspicion. Overlooking it, Shane went to him.

"Hi." Her quick friendly smile had her dimples flashing. "I'm Shane Abbott. I own the house at the other end of the path."

His brow lifted in acknowledgment as he watched her. What the hell does she want? he wondered, and set his hammer on the rail.

Shane smiled again, then took a long, thorough look at the house. "You've got your work cut out for you," she commented amiably, sticking her hands into the back pockets of her jeans. "Such a big place. They say it was beautiful once. I think there used to be a balcony around the second story."

She glanced up. "It's a shame the fire did so much damage to the inside—and then all the years of neglect." She looked at him then with dark, interested eyes. "Are you a carpenter?"

Vance hesitated briefly, then shrugged. It was close to the truth. "Yes."

"That's handy, then." Shane accepted the answer, attributing his hesitation to embarrassment at being out of work. "After D.C. you must find the mountains a change." His mobile brow lifted again and Shane grinned. "I'm sorry. It's the curse of small towns. Word gets around quickly, especially when a flatlander moves in."

"Flatlander?" Vance leaned against the post of the railing.

"You're from the city, so that's what you are." She laughed, a quick bubbling sound. "If you stay for twenty years, you'll still be a flatlander, and this will always be the old Farley place."

"It hardly matters what it's called," he said coldly.

The faintest of frowns shadowed her eyes at his response. Looking at the proud, set face, Shane decided he would never accept open charity. "I'm doing some work on my place too," she began. "My grandmother loved clutter. I don't suppose you could use a couple of chairs? I'm going to have to haul them up to the attic unless someone takes them off my hands."

His eyes stayed level on hers with no change of expression. "I have all I need for now."

Because it was the answer she had expected, Shane treated it lightly. "If you change your mind, they'll be gathering dust in the attic. You've got a good piece of land," she commented, gazing over at the section of pasture in the distance. There were several outbuildings, though most were in desperate need of repair. She wondered if he would see to them before winter set in. "Are you going to have livestock?"

Vance frowned, watching her eyes roam over his property. "Why?"

The question was cold and unfriendly. Shane tried to overlook that. "I can remember when I was a kid, before the fire. I used to lie in bed at night in the summer with the windows open. I could hear the Farley cows as clearly as if they were in my grandmother's garden. It was nice."

"I don't have any plans for livestock," he told her shortly, and picked up his hammer again. The gesture of dismissal was crystal clear.

Puzzled, Shane studied him. Not shy, she concluded. Rude. He was plainly and simply rude. "I'm sorry I disturbed your work," she said coolly. "Since you're a flatlander, I'll give you some advice. You should post your property lines if you don't want trespassers."

Indignantly, Shane strode back to the path to disappear among the trees.

CHAPTER 2

Little twit, Vance thought as he gently tapped the hammer against his palm. He knew he'd been rude, but felt no particular regret. He hadn't bought an isolated plot of land on the outskirts of a dot on the map because he wanted to entertain. Company he could do without, particularly the blond cheerleader type with big brown eyes and dimples.

What the hell had she been after? he wondered as he drew a nail from the pouch on his hip. A cozy chat? A tour of the house? He gave a quick, mirthless laugh. Very neighborly. Vance pounded the nail through the wood in three sure strokes. He didn't want neighbors. What he wanted, what he intended to have, was time to himself. It had been too many years since he had taken that luxury.

Drawing another nail out of the pouch, he moved down the rail. He set it, then hammered it swiftly into place. In particular, he hadn't cared for the one moment of attraction he had felt when he had seen her in the general store. Women, he thought grimly, had an uncanny habit of taking advantage of a weakness like that. He didn't intend for it to happen to him again. He had plenty of scars to remind him what went on behind big, guileless eyes.

So now I'm a carpenter, he mused. With a sardonic grin,

Vance turned his hands palms up and examined them. They were hard and calloused. For too many years, he mused, they had been smooth, used to signing contracts or writing checks. Now, for a time, he was back where he had started—with wood. Yes, until he was ready to sit behind a desk again, he was a carpenter.

The house, and the very fact that it was falling to pieces, gave him the sense of purpose that had slipped from him over the last couple of years. He understood pressure, success, duty, but the meaning of simple enjoyment had become lost somewhere beneath the rest.

Let the vice president of Riverton Construction, Inc., run the show for a few months, he mused. He was on vacation. And let the little blonde with her puppy-dog eyes keep on her own land, he added, pounding in another nail. He didn't want any part of the good-neighbor policy.

When he heard leaves rustling underfoot, Vance turned. Seeing Shane striding back up the path, he muttered a long stream of curses in a low voice. With the exaggerated care of a man greatly aggravated, he set down his hammer.

"Well?" He aimed cold blue eyes and waited.

Shane didn't pause until she had reached the foot of the steps. She was through being intimidated. "I realize you're *extremely* busy," she began, matching his coolness ice for ice, "but I thought you might be interested in knowing there's a nest of copperheads very close to the footpath. On *your* edge of the property," she added.

Vance gave her a narrowed glance, weighing the possibility of her fabricating the snakes to annoy him. She didn't budge under the scrutiny, but paused just long enough to let the silence hang before she turned. She'd gone no more than two more yards when Vance let out an impatient breath and called her back.

"Just a minute. You'll have to show me."

"I don't *have* to do anything," Shane began, but found herself impotently talking to the swinging screen door. Briefly, she wished that she'd never seen the nest, or had simply ignored it and continued down the path to her own home. Then, of course, if he'd been bitten, she would have blamed herself.

Well, you'll do your good deed, she told herself, and that will be that. She kicked a rock with the toe of her shoe and thought how simple it would have been if she'd stayed home that morning.

The screen door shut with a bang. Looking up, Shane watched Vance come down the steps with a well-oiled rifle in his hands. The sleek, elegant weapon suited him. "Let's go," he said shortly, starting off without her. Gritting her teeth, Shane followed.

The light dappled over them once they moved under the cover of trees. The scent of earth and sun-warmed leaves warred with the gun oil. Without a word, Shane skirted around him to take the lead. Pausing, she pointed to a pile of rocks and brown, dried leaves.

"There."

After taking a step closer, Vance spotted the hourglass-shaped crossbands on the snakes. If she hadn't shown him the exact spot, he never would have noticed the nest . . . unless, of course, he'd stepped right on it. An unpleasant thought, he mused, calculating its proximity to the footpath. Shane said nothing, watching as he found a thick stick and overturned the rocks. Immediately the hissing sounded.

With her eyes trained on the angry snakes, she didn't see Vance heft the rifle to his shoulder. The first shot jolted her. Her heart hammered during the ensuing four, her eyes riveted to the scene.

"That should do it," Vance muttered, lowering the gun. After switching on the safety, he turned to Shane. She'd turned a light shade of green. "What's the matter?"

"You might have warned me," she said shakily. "I wish I'd looked away."

Vance glanced back to the gruesome mess on the side of the path. That, he told himself grimly, had been incredibly stupid. Silently, he cursed her, then himself, before he took her arm.

"Come back and sit down."

"I'll be all right in a minute." Embarrassed and annoyed, Shane tried to pull away. "I don't want your gracious hospitality."

"I don't want you fainting on my land," he returned, drawing her into the clearing. "You didn't have to stay once you'd shown me the nest."

"Oh, you're very welcome," she managed as she placed a hand on her rolling stomach. "You are the most ill-mannered, unfriendly man I've ever met."

"And I thought I was on my best behavior," he murmured, opening the screen door. After pulling Shane inside, Vance led her through the huge empty room toward the kitchen.

After a glance at the dingy walls and uncovered floor, Shane sent him what passed as a smile. "You must give me the name of your decorator."

She thought he laughed, but she could have been mistaken.

The kitchen, in direct contrast to the rest of the house, was bright and clean. The walls had been papered, the counters and cabinets refinished.

"Well, this is nice," she said as he nudged her into a chair. "You do good work."

Without responding, Vance set a kettle on the stove. "I'll fix you some coffee."

"Thank you."

Shane concentrated on the kitchen, determined to forget what she'd just seen. The windows had been reframed, the wood stained and lacquered to match the grooved trim along the floor and ceiling. He had left the beams exposed and polished the wood to a dull gleam. The original oak floor had been sanded and sealed and waxed. Vance Banning knew how to use wood, Shane decided. The porch was basic mechanics, but the kitchen showed a sense of style and an appreciation for fine detail.

It seemed unfair to her that a man with such talent should be out of work. Shane concluded that he had used his savings to put a down payment on the property. Even if the house had sold cheaply, the land was prime. Remembering the barrenness of the rest of the first floor, she couldn't prevent her sympathies from being aroused again. Her eyes wandered to his.

"This really is a lovely room," she said, smiling. The faintest hint of color had seeped back into her cheeks. Vance turned his back to her to take a mug from a hook.

"You'll have to settle for instant," he told her.

Shane sighed. "Mr. Banning . . . Vance," she decided, and waited for him to turn. "Maybe we got off on the wrong foot. I'm not a nosy, prying neighbor—at least not obnoxiously so. I was curious to see what you were doing to the house and what you were like. I know everyone within three miles of here." With a shrug, she rose. "I didn't mean to bother you."

As she started to brush by him, Vance took her arm. Her skin was still chilled. "Sit down . . . Shane," he said.

For a moment, she studied his face. It was cool and unyielding, but she sensed some glimmer of suppressed kindness. In response to it, her eyes warmed. "I disguise my coffee with milk and sugar," she warned. "Three spoonfuls."

A reluctant smile tugged at his mouth. "That's disgusting."

"Yes, I know. Do you have any?"

"On the counter."

Vance poured the boiling water, and after a moment's hesitation, took down a second mug for himself. Carrying them both, he joined Shane at the drop leaf table.

"This really is a lovely piece." Before reaching for the milk, she ran her fingers over the table's surface. "Once it's refinished, you'll have a real gem." Shane added three generous spoons of sugar to her mug. Wincing a little, Vance sipped his own black coffee. "Do you know anything about antiques?"

"Not really."

"They're a passion of mine. In fact, I'm planning on opening a shop." Shane brushed absently at the hair that fell over her forehead, then leaned back. "As it turns out, we're both settling in at the same time. I've been living in Baltimore for the last four years, teaching U.S. history."

"You're giving up teaching?" Her hands, Vance noted, were small like the rest of her. The light trail of blue veins under the pale skin made her seem very delicate. Her wrists were narrow, her fingers slender.

"Too many rules and regulations," Shane claimed, gesturing with the hands that had captured his attention.

"You don't like rules and regulations?"

"Only when they're mine." Laughing, she shook her head. "I was a pretty good teacher, really. My problem was discipline." She gave him a rueful grin as she reached for her coffee. "I'm the worst disciplinarian on record."

"And your students took advantage of that?"

Shane rolled her eyes. "Whenever possible."

"But you stuck with it for four years?"

"I had to give it my best shot." Leaning her elbow on the table, Shane rested her chin on her palm. "Like a lot of people who grow up in a small, rural town, I thought the city was my pot of gold. Bright lights, crowds, hustle-bustle. I wanted excitement with a capital *E*. I had four years of it. That was enough." She picked up her coffee again. "Then there are people from the city who think their answer is to move to the country and raise a few goats and can some tomatoes." She laughed into her cup. "The grass is always greener."

"I've heard it said," he murmured, watching her. There were tiny gold flecks in her eyes. How had he missed them before?

"Why did you choose Sharpsburg?"

Vance shrugged negligently. Questions about himself were to be evaded. "I've done some work in Hagerstown. I like the area."

"Living this far back from the main road can be inconvenient, especially in the winter, but I've never minded being snowed in. We lost power once for thirty-two hours. Gran and I kept the woodstove going, taking shifts, and we cooked soup on top of it. The phone lines were down too. We might have been the only two people in the world."

"You enjoyed that?"

"For thirty-two hours," she told him with a friendly grin. "I'm not a hermit. Some people are city people, some are beach people."

"And you're a mountain person."

Shane brought her eyes back to him. "Yes."

The smile she had started to give him never formed. Something in the meeting of their eyes was reminiscent of the moment in the store. It was only an echo, but somehow more disturbing. Shane understood it was bound to happen again and again. She needed time to decide just what she was going to do about it. Rising, she walked to the sink to rinse out her mug.

Intrigued by her reaction, Vance decided to test her.

"You're a very attractive woman." He knew how to make his voice softly flattering.

Laughing, Shane turned back to him. "The perfect face for advertising granola bars, right?" Her smile was devilish and appealing. "I'd rather be sexy, but I settled for wholesome." She gave the word a pained emphasis as she came back to the table.

There was no guile in her manner or her expression. What, Vance wondered again, was her angle? Shane was involved in studying the details of the kitchen and didn't see him frown at her.

"I do admire your work." Inspired, she turned back to him. "Hey, listen, I've got a lot of remodeling and renovating to do before I can open. I can paint and do some of the minor stuff myself, but there's a lot of carpentry work."

Here it is, Vance reflected coolly. What she wanted was some free labor. She would pull the helpless-female routine and count on his ego to take over.

"I have my own house to renovate," he reminded her coolly as he stood and turned toward the sink.

"Oh, I know you wouldn't be able to give me a lot of time, but we might be able to work something out." Excited by the idea, she followed him. Her thoughts were already racing ahead. "I wouldn't be able to pay what you could make in the city," she continued. "Maybe five dollars an hour. If you could manage ten or fifteen hours a week . . ." She chewed on her bottom lip. It seemed a paltry amount to offer, but it was all she could spare at the moment.

Incredulous, Vance turned off the water he had been running, then faced her. "Are you offering me a job?"

Shane flushed a bit, afraid she'd embarrassed him. "Well, only part-time, if you're interested. I know you can make more somewhere else, and if you find something, I wouldn't expect you to keep on, but in the meantime . . ." She trailed off, not certain how he would react to her knowing he was out of work.

"You're serious?" Vance demanded after a moment.

"Well . . . yes."

"Why?"

"I need a carpenter. You're a carpenter. There's a lot of work. You might decide you don't want any part of it. But why don't you think about it, drop by tomorrow and take a look?" She turned to leave, but paused for an instant with her hand on the knob. "Thanks for the coffee."

For several minutes, Vance stared at the door she had closed behind her. Abruptly, he burst into deep, appreciative laughter. This, he thought, was one for the books.

* * *

Shane rose early the next morning. She had plans and was determined to begin systematically. Organization didn't come naturally to her. It was one more reason why teaching hadn't suited her. If she was to plan a business, however, Shane knew an inventory was a primary factor—what she had, what she could bear to sell, what she should pack away for the museum.

Having decided to start downstairs and work her way up, Shane stood in the center of the living room and took stock of the situation. There was a good Chippendale fireplace seat in mahogany and a gateleg table that needed no refinishing, a ladderback chair that needed new caning in the seat, a pair of Aladdin lamps, and a tufted sofa that would require upholstering. On a Sheridan coffee table was a porcelain pitcher, circa 1830, that held a spray of flowers Shane's grandmother had dried. She touched them once briefly before she picked up her clipboard. There was too much of her childhood there to allow herself the luxury of thinking of any of it. If her grandmother had been alive, she would have told Shane to be certain what she did was right, then do it. Shane was certain she was right.

Systematically, she listed items in two columns: one for items that would need repairs; one for stock she could sell as it was. Everything would have to be priced, which would be a huge job in itself. Already she was spending her evenings poring through catalogs and making notations. There wasn't an antique shop within a radius of thirty miles she hadn't visited. Shane had taken careful account of pricing and procedure. She would incorporate what appealed to her and disregard what didn't. Whatever else her shop would be, she was determined it would be her own.

On one wall of the living room was a catchall shelf that had been built before she'd been born. Moving to it, Shane began a fresh sheet of items she designated for the museum.

An ancestor's Civil War cap and belt buckle, a glass jar filled with spent shells, a dented bugle, a cavalry officer's sabre, a canteen with the initials JDA scratched into the metal—these were only a few pieces of the memorabilia that had been passed down to her. Shane knew there was a trunk in the attic filled with uniforms and old dresses. There was a scrawled journal that had been kept by one of her great-great-uncles during the three years he fought for the South, and letters written to an ancestral aunt by her father, who had served the North. Every item would be listed, dated, then put behind glass.

Shane might have inherited her grandmother's fascination for the relics of history, but not her casualness. It was time the old photos and objects came down from the shelf. But as always when she examined or handled the pieces, Shane became caught up in them.

What had the man been like who had first blown that

bugle? It would have been shiny then, and undented. A boy, she thought, with peach fuzz on his face. Had he been frightened? Exhilarated? Fresh off the farm, she imagined, and sure his cause was the right one. Whichever side he had fought for, he had blown the bugle into battle.

With a sigh, she took it down and set it in a packing box. Carefully, Shane wrapped and packed until the shelves were clear, but for the highest one. Standing back, she calculated how she would reach the pieces that sat several feet above her head. Not bothering to move the heavy ladder from across the room, she dragged over a nearby chair. As she stood on the seat, a knock sounded at the back door.

"Yes, come in," she called, stretching one arm up while balancing herself with a hand on one of the lower shelves. She swore and muttered as her reach still fell short. Just as she stood on tiptoe, teetering, someone grabbed her arm. Gasping as she overbalanced, Shane found herself gripped firmly by Vance Banning. "You scared me to death!" she accused.

"Don't you know better than to use a chair like that?" He kept his hands firmly at her waist as he lifted her down. Then, though he'd had every intention of doing so, he didn't release her. There was a smudge of dust on her cheek, and her hair was tousled. Her small, narrow hands rested on his arms while she smiled up at him. Without thinking, Vance lowered his mouth to hers.

Shane didn't struggle, but felt a jolt of surprise. Then she relaxed. Though she hadn't expected the kiss then, she had known the time would come. She let the first stream of pure pleasure run its course.

His mouth was hard on hers, with no gentleness, no trace of what kissing meant to her—a gesture of affection, love or comfort. Yet instinct told her he was capable of tenderness.

Lifting a hand to his cheek, Shane sought to soothe the turbulence she sensed. Immediately, he released her. The touch
of her hand had been too intimate.

Something told Shane to treat it lightly no matter how her
body ached to be held again. Tilting her head, she gave him
a mischievous smile. "Good morning."

"Good morning," he said carefully.

"I'm taking inventory," she told him with a sweeping gesture of the room. "I want to list everything before I haul it
upstairs for storage. I plan to use this room for the museum
and the rest of the first floor for the shop. Could you get
those things off the top shelf for me?" she asked, looking
around for her clipboard.

In silence, Vance moved the ladder and complied. The
fact that she'd made no mention of the turbulent kiss discon-
certed him.

"Most of the work will be gutting the kitchen and putting one in upstairs," Shane went on, giving her lists another
glance. She knew Vance was watching her for some sort of
reaction. She was just as determined to give him none. "Of
course, some walls will have to be taken out, doorways widened. But I don't want to lose the flavor of the house in the
remodeling."

"You seem to have it all plotted out." Was she really so
cool? he wondered.

"I hope so." Shane pressed the clipboard to her breasts as
she looked around the room. "I've applied for all the necessary permits. What a headache. I don't have any natural business sense, so I'll have to work twice as hard learning. It's a
big chance." Then her voice changed, became firm and determined. "I'm going to make it work."

"When do you plan to open?"

"I'm shooting for the first part of December, but . . ." Shane shrugged. "It depends on how the work goes and how soon I can beef up my inventory. I'll show you the rest of the place. Then you can decide if you want to take it on."

Without waiting for his consent, Shane walked to the rear of the house. "The kitchen's a fairly good size, particularly if you include the pantry." Opening a door, she revealed a large shelved closet. "Taking out the counters and appliances should give me plenty of room. Then if this doorway is widened," she continued as she pushed open a swinging door, "and left as an archway, it would give more space in the main showroom."

They entered the dining room with its long diamond-paned windows. She moved quickly, he noted, and knew precisely what she wanted.

"The fireplace hasn't been used in years. I don't know whether it still works." Walking over, Shane ran a finger down the surface of the dining table. "This was my grand-mother's prize. It was brought over from England more than a hundred years ago." The cherrywood, stroked by sunlight, gleamed under her fingers. "The chairs are from the original set. Hepplewhite." Shane caressed the heart-shaped back of one of the remaining six chairs. "I hate to sell this, she loved it so, but . . ." Her voice was wistful as she unnecessarily straightened a chair. "I won't have anywhere to keep it, and I can't afford the luxury of storing it for myself." Shane turned away. "The china cabinet is from the same period," she continued.

"You could keep this and leave the house as it is if you took a job in the local high school," Vance interrupted. There was something valiant and touching in the way she kept her shoulders straight while her voice trembled.

"No." Shane shook her head, then turned back to him. "I haven't the character for it. It wouldn't take long before

I'd be cutting classes just like my students. They deserve a better example than that. I love history." Her face brightened again. "*This* kind of history," she said as she walked back to the table. "Who first sat in this chair? What did she talk about over dinner? What kind of dress did she wear? Did they discuss politics and the upstart colonies? Maybe one of them knew Ben Franklin and was a secret sympathizer of the Revolution." She broke off laughing. "That's not the sort of thing you're supposed to teach in second-period eleventh-grade history."

"It sounds more interesting than reciting names and dates."

"Maybe. Anyway, I'm not going back to that." Pausing, Shane watched Vance steadily. "Did you ever find yourself caught up in something you were good at, something you'd been certain was the right thing for you, then woke up one morning with the feeling you were locked in a cage?"

The words hit home, and he nodded affirmatively.

"Then you know why I have to choose between something I love and my sanity." She touched the table again. After a deep breath, Shane took a circle around the room. "I don't want to change the architecture of this room except for the doorways. My great-grandfather built the chair rail." She watched Vance walk over to examine it. "He was a mason by trade," she told him, "but he must have been handy with wood as well."

"It's a beautiful job," Vance agreed, admiring the workmanship and detail. "I'd have a hard time duplicating this quality with modern tools. You wouldn't want to touch this or any of the woodwork in this room."

In spite of himself he was becoming interested in the project. It would be a challenge—a different sort than the house he had chosen to test himself on. Sensing his change of attitude, Shane pressed her advantage.

"There's a small summer parlor through there." Indicating

another door, she took Vance's arm to draw him with her. "It adjoins the living room, so I plan to make it the entrance to the shop, with the dining room as the main showroom."

The parlor was no more than twelve by twelve with faded wallpaper and a scarred wooden floor. Still, Vance recognized a few good pieces of Duncan Phyfe and a Morris chair. On the brief tour, he had seen no furniture less than a hundred years old and, unless they were excellent copies, a few pieces of Wedgwood. The furniture's worth a small fortune, he mused, and the back door's coming off the hinges.

"There's a lot of work here," Shane commented, moving over to open a window and dispel the faint mustiness. "This room's taken a beating over the years. I suppose you'd have a better idea than I would exactly what it needs to whip it into shape."

She watched his frowning survey of chipped floorboards and cracked trim. It was obvious to her that his professional eye missed little. It was also obvious the state of disrepair annoyed him. And, she thought, faintly amused, he hadn't seen anything yet.

"Maybe I shouldn't press my luck and take you upstairs just yet," she commented.

A quizzical brow shot up as he turned to her. "Why?"

"Because the second floor needs twice the attention this does, and I really want you to take the job."

"You sure as hell need somebody to do it," he muttered. His own place needed a major overhaul. Heavy physical work and a lot of time. This, on the other hand, needed a shrewd craftsman who could work with what was already there. Again, he felt the pull of the challenge.

"Vance . . ." After a moment's hesitation, Shane decided to take a chance. "I could make it six dollars an hour, throw in your lunches and all the coffee you can drink. The people who come in here will see the quality of your work. It could lead to bigger jobs."

He surprised her by grinning. Her heart leaped into her throat. More than the tempestuous kiss, the quick boyish grin drew her to him.

"All right, Shane," Vance agreed on impulse. "You've got a deal."

CHAPTER 3

Pleased with herself and Vance's abrupt good humor, Shane decided to show him the second floor. Taking his hand, she led him up the straight, steep stairway. Though she had no notion of what had prompted the amused gleam or sudden grin, Shane wanted to keep him with her while his mood lasted.

Against his work-hardened hand, her palm was baby soft. It made Vance wonder how the rest of her would feel—the slope of her shoulder, the length of her thigh, the underside of her breast. She wasn't his type, he reminded himself, and glanced at the hairline crack in the wall to his left.

"There are three bedrooms," Shane told him as they came to the top landing. "I want to keep my own room, and turn the master into a sitting room and the third into my kitchen. I can handle the painting and papering after the initial work is done." With her hand on the knob of the master bedroom door, she turned to him. "Do you know anything about drywall?"

"A bit." Without thinking, Vance lifted a finger and ran it down her nose. Their eyes met in mutual surprise. "You've dust on your face," he mumbled.

"Oh." Laughing, Shane brushed at it herself.

"Here." Vance traced the rough skin of his thumb down her cheekbone. Her skin felt as it looked: soft, creamy. It would taste the same, he mused, allowing his thumb to linger. "And here," he said, caught up in his own imagination. Lightly he ran a fingertip along her jawline. He felt her slight tremor as his gaze swept over her lips.

Her eyes were wide and fixed unblinkingly on his. Abruptly, Vance dropped his hand, shattering the mood but not the tension. Clearing her throat, Shane pushed open the door.

"This—umm . . ." Frantically, Shane gathered her scattered thoughts. "This is the master," she continued, combing nervous fingers through her hair. "I know the floor's in bad shape, and I'd like to skin whoever painted that oak trim." She let out a long breath as her pulse began to level. "I'm going to see if it can be refinished." Idly, she touched a section of peeling wallpaper. "My grandmother didn't like changes. This room hasn't altered one bit in thirty years. That's when her husband died," she added softly. "The windows stick, the roof leaks, the fireplace smokes. Basically, the house, except for the dining room, is in a general state of disrepair. She never had the inclination to do more than a patch job here and there."

"When did she die?"

"Three months ago." Shane lifted a corner of the patchwork coverlet, then let it fall. "She just didn't wake up one morning. I was committed to teaching a summer course and couldn't move back permanently until last week."

Clearly, he heard the sting of guilt in her words. "Could you have changed anything if you had?" he asked.

"No." Shane wandered to a window. "But she wouldn't have died alone."

Vance opened his mouth, then closed it again. It wasn't

wise to offer personal advice to strangers. Framed against the window, she looked very small and defenseless.

"What about the walls in here?" he asked.

"What?" Years and miles away, Shane turned back to him.

"The walls," he repeated. "Do you want any of them taken down?"

For a moment, she stared blankly at the faded roses on the wallpaper. "No . . . No," she repeated more firmly. "I'd thought to take out the door and enlarge the entrance." Vance nodded, noting she had won what must be a continuing battle with her emotions. "If the woodwork cleans off well," she continued, "the entrance could be framed in oak to match."

Vance walked over to examine it. "Is this a bearing wall?"

Shane made a face at him. "I haven't the slightest idea. How do—" She broke off, hearing a knock at the front door. "Damn. Well, can you look around up here for a few minutes? You'll probably get the lay of things just as well without me." With this, Shane was dashing down the steps. Shrugging, Vance took a rule out of his back pocket and began to take measurements.

Shane's instinctively friendly smile faded instantly when she opened the door.

"Shane."

"Cy."

His expression became faintly censorious. "Aren't you going to ask me in?"

"Of course." With a restraint unnatural to her, Shane stepped back. Very carefully, she shut the door behind him but moved no farther into the room. "How are you, Cy?"

"Fine, just fine."

Of course he was, Shane thought, annoyed. Cy Trainer Jr., was always fine—permanent-pressed and groomed. And prosperous now, she added, giving his smart-but-discreet suit a glance.

"And you, Shane?"

"Fine, just fine," she said, knowing the sarcasm was both petty and wasted. He'd never notice.

"I'm sorry I didn't get by last week. Things have been hectic."

"Business is good?" she asked without any intonation of interest. He failed to notice that too.

"Money's loosening up." He straightened his tie unnecessarily. "People are buying houses. Country property's always a good investment." He gave her a quick nod. "The real estate business is solid."

Money was still first, Shane noticed with irony. "And your father?"

"Doing well. Semiretired now, you know."

"No," she said mildly. "I didn't." If Cy Trainer Sr. relinquished the reins to Trainer Real Estate six months after he was dead, it would have surprised Shane. The old man would always run the show, no matter what his son liked to think.

"He likes to keep busy," Cy told her. "He'd love to see you though. You'll have to drop by the office." Shane said nothing to that. "So . . ." Cy paused as he was wont to do before a big statement. "You're settling in."

Shane lifted a brow as she watched him glance around at her packing cases. "Slowly," she agreed. Though she knew it was deliberately rude, she didn't ask him to sit. They remained standing, just inside the door.

"You know, Shane, this house isn't in the best of shape, but it is a prime location." He gave her a light, condescending smile that set her teeth on edge. "I'm sure I could get you a good price for it."

"I'm not interested in selling, Cy. Is that why you came by? To do an appraisal?"

He looked suitably shocked. "Shane!"

"Was there something else?" she asked evenly.

"I just dropped by to see how you were." The distress in both his voice and eyes had an apology forming on her lips. "I heard some crazy story about your trying to start an antique shop."

The apology slipped away. "It's not a story, crazy or otherwise, Cy. I am going to start one."

He sighed and gave her what she termed his paternal look. She gritted her teeth. "Shane, have you any idea how difficult, how risky it is to start a business in today's economy?"

"I'm sure you'll tell me," she muttered.

"My dear," he said in calm tones, making her blood pressure rise alarmingly. "You're a certified teacher with four years' experience. It's just nonsense to toss away a good career for a fanciful little fling."

"I've always been good at nonsense, haven't I, Cy?" Her eyes chilled. "You never hesitated to point it out to me even when we were supposed to be madly in love."

"Now, Shane, it was because I cared that I tried to curb your . . . impulses."

"Curb my impulses!" More astonished than angry, Shane ran her fingers through her hair. Later, she told herself, later she would be able to laugh. Now she wanted to scream. "You haven't changed. You haven't changed a whit. I bet you still roll your socks into those neat little balls and carry an extra handkerchief."

He stiffened a bit. "If you'd ever learned the value of practicality—" he began.

"You wouldn't have dumped me two months before the wedding?" she finished furiously.

"Really, Shane, you can hardly call it that. You know I was only thinking of what was best for you."

"Best for me," she muttered between clenched teeth. "Well,

let me tell you something." She poked a dusty finger at his muted striped tie. "You can stuff your practicality, Cy, right along with your balanced checkbook and shoe trees. I might have thought you hurt me at the time, but you did me a big favor. I *hate* practicality and rooms that smell like pine and toothpaste tubes that are rolled up from the bottom."

"I hardly see what that has to do with this discussion."

"It has *everything* to do with this discussion," she flared back. "You don't see anything unless it's listed in neat columns and balanced. And I'll tell you something else," she continued when he would have spoken. "I'm going to have my shop, and even if it doesn't make me a fortune, it's going to be fun."

"Fun?" Cy shook his head hopelessly. "That's a poor basis for starting a business."

"It's mine," she retorted. "I don't need a six-digit income to be happy."

He gave her a small, deprecating smile. "You haven't changed."

Flinging open the door, Shane glared at him. "Go sell a house," she suggested. With a dignity she envied and despised, Cy walked through the door. She slammed it after him, then gave in to temper and slammed her hand against the wall.

"*Damn!*" Putting her wounded knuckles to her mouth, she whirled. It was then she spotted Vance at the foot of the stairs. His face was still and serious as their eyes met. With angry embarrassment, Shane's cheeks flamed. "Enjoy the show?" she demanded, then stormed back to the kitchen.

She gave vent to her frustration by banging through the cupboards. She didn't hear Vance follow her. When he touched her shoulder, she spun around, ready to rage.

"Let me see your hand," he said quietly. Ignoring her jerk of protest, he took it in both of his.

"It's nothing."

Gently, he flexed it, then pressed down on her knuckles with his fingers. Involuntarily, she caught her breath at the quick pain. "You didn't manage to break it," he murmured, "but you'll have a bruise." He was forced to control a sudden rage that she had damaged that small, soft hand.

"Just don't say anything," she ordered through gritted teeth. "I'm not stupid. I *know* when I've made a fool of my-self."

He took a moment to bend and straighten her fingers again. "I apologize," he said. "I should have let you know I was there."

After letting out a deep breath, Shane drew her hand from his slackened hold. The light throbbing gave her a perverse pleasure. "It doesn't matter," she muttered as she turned to make tea.

He frowned at her averted face. "I don't enjoy embarrass-ing you."

"If you live here for any amount of time, you'll hear about Cy and me anyway." She tried to make a casual shrug, but the quick jerkiness of the movement showed only more agi-tation. "This way you just got the picture quicker."

But he didn't have the full picture. Vance realized, with some discomfort, that he wanted to know. Before he could speak, Shane slammed the lid onto the kettle.

"He always makes me feel like a fool!"

"Why?"

"He always dots his i's and crosses his t's." With an angry tug, she pulled open a cabinet. "He carries an umbrella in the trunk of his car," she said wrathfully.

"That should do it," Vance murmured, watching her quick, jerky movements.

"He never, never, *never* makes a mistake. He's always rea-sonable," she added witheringly as she slammed two cups down on the counter. "Did he shout at me just now?" she demanded as she whirled on Vance. "Did he swear or lose his temper? He doesn't *have* a temper!" she shouted in frustration. "I swear, the man doesn't even sweat."

"Did you love him?"

For a moment, Shane merely stared; then she let out a small broken sigh. "Yes. Yes, I really did. I was sixteen when we started dating." As she went to the refrigerator, Vance turned the gas on under the kettle, which she had forgotten to do. "He was so perfect, so smart and, oh . . . so articulate." Pulling out the milk, Shane smiled a little. "Cy's a born salesman. He can talk about anything."

Vance felt a quick, unreasonable dislike for him. As Shane set a large ceramic sugar bowl on the table, sunlight shot into her hair. The curls and waves of her hair shimmered briefly in the brilliance before she moved away. With an odd tingling at the base of his spine, Vance found himself staring after her.

"I was crazy about him," Shane continued, and Vance had to shake himself mentally to concentrate on her words. The subtle movements of her body beneath the snug T-shirt had begun to distract him. "When I turned eighteen, he asked me to marry him. We were both going to college, and Cy thought a year's engagement was proper. He's very proper," she added ruefully.

Or a cold-blooded fool, Vance thought, glancing at the faint outline of her nipples against the thin cotton. Annoyed, he brought his eyes back to her face. But the warmth in his own blood remained.

"I wanted to get married right away, but he told me, as always, that I was too impulsive. Marriage was a big step. Things had to be planned out. When I suggested we live together for a while, he was shocked." Shane set the milk on the table with a little bang. "I was young and in love, and

I wanted him. He felt it his duty to control my more . . . primitive urges."

"He's a damn fool," Vance muttered under the hissing of the kettle.

"Through that last year, he molded me, and I tried to be what he wanted: dignified, sensible. I was a complete failure." Shane shook her head at the memory of that long, frustrating year. "If I wanted to go out for pizza with a bunch of other students, he'd remind me we had to watch our pennies. He already had his eye on this little house outside of Boonsboro. His father said it was a good investment."

"And you hated it," Vance commented.

Surprised, Shane looked back at him. "I despised it. It was the perfect little rancher with white aluminum siding and a hedge. When I told Cy I'd smother there, he laughed and patted my head."

"Why didn't you tell him to get lost?" he demanded.

Shane shot him a brief look. "Haven't you ever been in love?" she murmured. It was her answer, not a question, and Vance remained silent. "We were constantly at odds that year," she went on. "I kept thinking it was just the jitters of a long engagement, but more and more, the basic personality conflicts came up. He'd always say I'd feel differently once we were settled. Usually, I'd believe him."

"He sounds like a boring jackass."

Though the icy contempt in Vance's voice surprised her, Shane smiled. "Maybe, but he could be gentle and sweet." When Vance gave a derisive snort, she only shrugged. "I'd forget how rigid he was. Then he'd get more critical. I'd get angry, but I could never win a fight because he never lost control. The final break came over the plans for the honeymoon. I wanted to go to Fiji."

"Fiji?" Vance repeated.

"Yes," she said defiantly. "It's different, exotic, romantic.

I was barely nineteen." On a fresh wave of fury, Shane slammed down her spoon. "He had plans for this—this plastic little resort hotel in Pennsylvania. The kind of place where they plan your activities, have contests and an indoor pool. Shuffleboard." She rolled her eyes before she gulped down tea. "It was a package deal—three days, two nights, meals included. He'd inherited a substantial sum from his mother, and I had some savings, but he didn't want to waste money. He'd already outlined a retirement plan. I couldn't stand it!"

Vance sipped his own tea where he stood and studied her. "So you called off the wedding." He wondered if she would take the opportunity he was giving her to claim the break had been her idea.

"No." Shane pushed her cup aside. "We had a terrible fight, and I stormed off to spend the rest of the evening with friends at this little club near the college. I had told Cy I wouldn't spend my first night as a married woman watching a tacky floor show or playing bingo."

Vance's lips twitched but he managed to control his grin. "That sounds remarkably sensible," he murmured.

On a weak laugh, Shane shook her head. "After I'd calmed down, I decided where we went wasn't important, but that we'd finally be together. I told myself Cy was right. I was immature and irresponsible. We needed to save money. I still had two more years of college, and he was just starting in his father's firm. I was being frivolous. That was one of his favorite adjectives for me."

Shane frowned down at her cup but didn't drink. "I went by his house ready to apologize. That's when he very reasonably, very calmly jilted me."

There was a long moment of silence before Vance came to the table to join her. "I thought you told me he never made mistakes."

Shane stared at him a moment, then laughed. It was a quick, pure sound of appreciation. "I needed that." Impulsively, she leaned her head against his shoulder. The anger had vanished in the telling, the self-pity with the laugh.

The tenderness that invaded him made Vance cautious. Still, he didn't resist the urge to stroke his hand down her disordered cap of hair. The texture of her hair was thick and unruly. And incredibly soft. He wasn't even aware that he twisted a curl around his finger.

"Do you still love him?" he heard himself ask.

"No," Shane answered before he could retract the question. "But he still makes me feel like an irresponsible romantic."

"Are you?"

She shrugged. "Most of the time."

"What you said to him out there was right, you know." Forgetting caution in simple wanting, he drew her closer.

"I said a lot of things."

"That he'd done you a favor," Vance murmured as his fingers roamed to the back of her neck. Shane sighed, but he couldn't tell if the sound came from pleasure or agreement. "You'd have gone crazy rolling up his socks in those little balls."

Shane was laughing as she tilted her head back to look at his face. She kissed him lightly in gratitude, then again for herself.

Her mouth was small and very tempting. Wanting his fill, Vance cupped his hand firmly on the back of her neck to keep her there. There was nothing shy or hesitant in her response to the increased pressure. She parted her lips and invited.

On a tiny moan of pleasure, her tongue met his. Suddenly hot, suddenly urgent, his mouth moved over hers. He needed her sweetness, her uncomplicated generosity. He wanted to saturate himself with the fresh, clean passion she offered so willingly. When his mouth crushed down harder, she only yielded; when his teeth nipped painfully at her lip, she only drew him closer.

"Vance," she murmured, leaning toward him.

He rose quickly, leaving her blinking in surprise. "I've got work to do," he said shortly. "I'll make a list of the materials I'll need to start. I'll be in touch." He was out the back door before Shane could form any response.

For several moments, she stared at the screen door. What had she done to cause that anger in his eyes? How was it possible that he could passionately kiss her one second and turn his back on her the next? Miserably, she looked down at her clenched hands. She had always made too much of things, she reminded herself. A romantic? Yes, and a dreamer, her grandmother had called her. For too long she'd been waiting for the right man to come into her life, to complete it. She wanted to be cherished, respected, adored.

Perhaps, she mused, she was looking for the impossible—to keep her independence and to share her dreams, to stand on her own and have a strong hand to hold. Over and over she had warned herself to stop looking for that one perfect love. But her spirit defied her mind.

From the first instant, she had sensed something different about Vance. For the flash of a second when their eyes had first held, her heart had opened and shouted. *Here he is!* But that was nonsense, Shane reminded herself. Love meant understanding, knowledge. She neither knew nor understood Vance Banning.

With a jolt, she realized she might have offended him. She was going to be his employer, and the way she had kissed him . . . he might think she wanted more than carpentry for her money. He might think she intended to seduce him while dangling a few much-needed dollars under his nose.

Abruptly, she burst into laughter. As her mirth grew, she

threw back her head and pounded both fists on the table. Shane Abbott, seductress. Oh Lord! she thought, wiping tears of hilarity from her eyes. That was rich. After all, what red-blooded man could withstand a woman with dirt on her face who tries to punch holes in walls?

She sighed with the effort of laughing. Her imagination, she decided, needed a rest. Shane went back to her inventory.

CHAPTER 4

Vance couldn't sleep. He had worked until late in the evening, sweating off anger and frustrated desire. The anger didn't worry him. He knew that emotion too well to lose sleep over it. Neither was he a stranger to desire, but having to acknowledge he felt it for a snippy little history buff infuriated him . . . and made him restless.

He should never have agreed to take the job, he told himself yet again. What devil had provoked him into doing it? Annoyed with himself, Vance wandered outside to stand on the porch.

The air had cooled considerably with nightfall. Overhead, the stars were spread in a wide, brilliant pattern around a white half-moon. Venus was as clear as he'd ever seen it. An army of crickets sent out their high, monotonous signal while fireflies danced, tiny yellow lights, over the fallow field to his right. When he looked straight ahead, he could see to the edge of the trees but no farther. The woods were dark, mysterious, secret. Shane slept on the other side in a room with faded wallpaper and a Jenny Lind bed.

He imagined her cuddled under the wedding ring quilt he'd seen on the bed. Her window would be open to let in the sounds and scents of night. Did she sleep in one of those fussy cotton nightgowns that would cover her from neck to feet, he wondered, or would she slip under the quilt in solitary nakedness?

Furious with the direction of his thoughts, Vance cursed himself. No, he should never have taken the damn job. It had appealed to his ego and his humor. Six dollars an hour. He laughed shortly, startling an owl in a nearby tree. Leaning on a post, he continued to stare into the woods, seeing nothing but silhouettes and shadows.

When was the last time he'd worked for an hourly wage? To answer his own question, Vance looked back, trying to remember. Fifteen years? Good God, he thought with a shake of his head. Had so much time passed?

He'd been a teenager starting out at the bottom of his mother's highly successful construction firm. "Learn the ropes," she had told him, and he'd eagerly agreed. Vance had wanted nothing more than to work with his hands, and with wood. He'd had his share of youthful confidence—and youthful arrogance. Administration was for old men in business suits who wouldn't know how to miter a corner. He'd wanted no part of their stuffy business meetings or complicated contract negotiations. Shuffle papers? No, he was too clever to fall into that trap.

How long had it taken before he had been pulled in—chained behind a desk? Five years? he thought. Six? With a shrug, he decided it didn't matter. He'd gone beyond the time when a year made much difference.

Sighing, Vance walked the length of the porch. Under his hand, the rail he had built himself was rough and sturdy. What choice had there been? he asked himself. There had been his mother's sudden stroke and long painful recovery. She had begged him to take over as president of Riverton. As a widow with only one child, she had been desperate not to see her business run by strangers. It had mattered to her, perhaps too much, that the firm she had inherited, had struggled to keep during the lean years, stay in the family. Vance knew that she had fought prejudices, taken chances and worked nearly half her life to turn a mediocre firm into an exemplary one. Then she had been all but helpless, and asking him.

If he had been a failure at it, he could have delegated the responsibilities and stayed a figurehead without a qualm. He could have picked up his tools again. But he hadn't been a failure—there was too much of his mother in him.

Riverton Construction had thrived and expanded under his leadership. It had grown beyond the prestigious Washington concern into a national conglomerate. It was his own misfortune that he had the same knack with administration that he had with a hammer. He had bolted the lock on his own cage.

Then there had been Amelia. Vance's mouth tightened into a cynical smile. Soft, sexy Amelia, he mused, with hair like a sunset and a quiet Virginia drawl. She had kept him yapping at her heels for months, drawing him in, holding him off, until he had been mad to have her. Mad, Vance thought again. A very apt word. If he had been sane, he would have seen through that beautiful, cultured mask to the calculating scrambler she had been—before he had put the ring on her finger.

Not for the first time, he wondered how many men had envied him his lovely, dignified wife. But they hadn't seen the face unmasked—the perfect face with a rotted shell beneath. Cold. In all of his experience, Vance had known no one as cold as Amelia Ryce Banning.

The owl in the oak to his left set up a steady hooting: two short calls, then a long—two short, then a long. Vance listened to the monotonous sound as he thought over the years of his marriage.

Amelia had spent his money lavishly those first months—clothes, furs, cars. That had mattered little to him as he had felt her unearthly beauty demanded the finest. And he had loved her—or the woman he had thought she'd been. He had thought she was a woman made for diamonds, for soft, exotic furs and silks. It had pleased him to surround her with them, to see her sulky beauty glow. For the most part, he had ignored the excessive bills, paying them without a murmur. Once or twice he had commented on her extravagance and had received her sweet distress and apologies. He'd hardly noticed that the bills had continued to flow in.

Then he had discovered she was draining his bank account to feed her brother's teetering construction firm in Richmond. Amelia had been tearful and helpless when confronted with it. She had pleaded prettily for her brother. She had claimed she couldn't bear to have him almost facing bankruptcy while she lived so well.

Because he'd believed her familial concern, Vance had agreed to a personal loan, but he'd refused to siphon money from Riverton into an unstable and mishandled company. Amelia had been far from satisfied, had pouted and cajoled. Then when he'd remained adamant, she had attacked him like a crazed tigress, raking his face with her well-manicured nails, spewing out obscenities through her tinted Cupid's bow mouth. Her anger had driven her to strike out and tell him why she had married him—for his money and position, and what both could do for her and her own family business. Then Vance had looked beneath the beauty and the careful charm to see what she was. It had been only the first of many shocks and disillusionments.

Her warm passion had become frigidity; her adoring smiles had become sneers. She had refused to consider having children. It would have spoiled her figure and restricted her freedom. For more than two years Vance had struggled to save his failing marriage, to salvage something of the life he had planned to have with Amelia. But he had come to know that the woman he thought he had married was an illusion.

Ultimately, he'd demanded a divorce, and Amelia had laughed and agreed. She would happily give him his freedom for half of everything he owned—including his share of Riverton. She had promised him an ugly court battle and plenty of publicity. After pointing out that she would be the injured party, Amelia had vowed to play her part of the cast-off wife to the hilt.

Trapped, Vance had lived with her for another year, keeping up the pretense of marriage in public, avoiding her privately. When he had discovered Amelia was taking lovers, he'd seen the first ray of hope.

He had felt no pain on being betrayed, for there had been no emotion in him for her. Slowly, discreetly, Vance had begun to compile the evidence that would give him his freedom. He was willing to face the humiliation and publicity of a messy court battle to free himself and his company. Then there had been no more need. One of Amelia's discarded lovers put a bullet through her heart and ended it.

It had been due to Vance's wealth and influence that the publicity hadn't been worse than it had been. Still, the whispers and speculation had been ugly enough. Yet there had been a staggering relief in him rather than grief. The guilt this had brought had caused him to bury himself even more in his work. There were condominiums to be built in Florida, a large medical complex in Minnesota, an addition to a university in Texas. But there had been no peace for him.

Determined to find Vance Banning again, he'd bought the dilapidated house in the mountains and had taken an extended leave of absence. Time, solitude and the work he loved had been his prescription. Then, just when he had thought he had found the answer, he had met Shane Abbott.

She was no smoldering hothouse beauty as Amelia had been, no poised sophisticate as were the women he had taken to his bed over the last two years. She was fresh and vital. Instinctively, he was attracted to her good-natured generosity. But his wife's legacy to him had been cynicism and distrust. Vance knew that only a fool fell for the innocent act twice. And he was no fool.

He had taken the job with Shane on impulse, and now he would see it through. It would be a challenge to learn if he was still capable of the fine precision work she required. And he knew how to be cautious with a woman now. It was true her fresh looks and artless charm had appealed to him. He admired her way of dealing with her former fiancé. She'd been hurt, yet she had held her own and booted Cy out the door.

It might be interesting, he decided, to spend his vacation remodeling Shane's house and learning what she hid under her mask. Everyone wore masks, he thought grimly. Life was one long masquerade. It wouldn't take long to discover what went on behind her big brown eyes and bubbling laugh.

With a sound of disgust, Vance hurled himself back into the house. He wasn't going to lose any sleep over a woman. Nevertheless, he tossed and turned much of the night.

* * *

It was a perfect morning. In the west, the mountains rose into a paintbrush blue sky. Birds chattered in noisy jubilation as Shane tossed open the windows. The air that rushed in was warm, laced with the scent of zinnias. It was all but impossible for one of her nature to remain inside on such a day, cooped up with dust and a clipboard. But there were

ways, Shane decided as she leaned on the windowsill, of doing her duty *and* having fun.

After dressing in an old T-shirt and faded red shorts, she
rummaged through the basement storage closet and unearthed
a can of white paint and a roller. The front porch, she knew,
needed more repair than her meager talents could provide,
but the back was still sturdy enough. All it required was a
coat or two of paint to make it bright and cheerful again.

Picking up a portable radio on her way, Shane headed
outside. She fiddled with the tuner until she found a station
that matched her mood; then, after turning the volume up, she
went to work.

In thirty minutes, the porch was swept clean and hosed
down. In the bright sun, it dried quickly while Shane pried
the lid off the paint can. She stirred it, enjoying the day and
the prospect of work. Once or twice, she glanced toward the
old logging path, wondering when Vance would "keep in
touch." She would have liked to have seen him coming down
the path toward her. He had a long, loose-limbed stride she
admired, and a way of looking as though he were in complete command of himself and anything that might get in
his way. Shane liked that—the confidence, the hint of controlled power.

She had always admired people of strength. Her grandmother, through all her hardships and disappointments, had
remained a strong woman right to the end. Shane would have
admitted, for all their disagreements, that Cy was a strong
man. What he lacked, in her opinion, was the underlying
kindness that balanced strength and kept it from being hard.
She sensed there was kindness in Vance, though he was far
from easy with it. But the fact that the trait existed at all
made the difference for Shane.

Turning away from the path, she took her bucket, roller

and pan to the end of the porch. She poured, knelt, then took a deep breath and began to paint.

When Vance came to the end of the path, he stopped to watch her. She had nearly a third of the porch done. Her arms were splattered with tiny specks of white. The radio blared, and she sang exuberantly along with it. Her hips kept the beat. As she moved, the thin, faded material of her shorts strained over her bottom. That she was having a marvelous time with the homey chore was as obvious as her lack of skill. A smile tugged at his mouth when Shane leaned over for the bucket and rested her palm on the wet paint. Cheerfully, she swore, then wiped her hand haphazardly on the back of her shorts.

"I thought you said you could paint," Vance commented.

Shane started, nearly upsetting the contents of the bucket as she turned. Still on all fours, she smiled at him. "I said I could paint. I didn't say I was neat." Lifting her hand, she shielded her eyes against the sun and watched him walk to her. "Did you come to supervise?"

He looked down at her and shook his head. "No, I think it's already too late for that."

Shane lifted a brow. "It's going to be just fine when I've finished."

Vance made a noncommittal sound. "I've got a list of materials for you, but I need to make a few more measurements."

"That was quick." Shane sat back on her haunches. Vance shrugged, not wanting to admit he'd written it out in the middle of the night when sleep had eluded him. "There was something else," she continued, stretching her back muscles. Leaning over, she turned down the volume on the radio so that it was only a soft murmur. "The front porch."

Vance glanced down at her handiwork. "Have you painted that too?"

Correctly reading his impression of her talents, Shane made a face. "No, I didn't paint that too."

"That's a blessing. What stopped you?"

"It's falling apart. Maybe you can suggest what I should do about it. Oh, look!" Shane grabbed his hand, forgetting the paint as she spotted a family of quail bobbing single file across the path behind them. "They're the first I've seen since I've been home." Captivated, she watched them until they were out of sight. "There's deer too. I've seen the signs, but I haven't been able to catch sight of any yet." She gave a contented sigh as the quail rustled in the woods. All at once, she remembered the condition of her hand.

"Oh, Vance, I'm sorry!" Releasing him, she jumped to her feet. "Did I get any on you?"

For an answer, he turned his palm up, studying the white smear ironically.

"I really am sorry," she managed, choking on a giggle. He shot her a look as she struggled to swallow the irrepressible laughter. "No, really I am. Here." Taking the hem of her T-shirt, Shane lifted it to rub unsuccessfully at his palm. Her stab at assistance exposed the pale, smooth skin of her midriff.

"You're rubbing it in," Vance said mildly, trying not to be affected by the flash of skin or the glimpse of her narrow waist.

"It'll come off," she assured him while she fought a desperate battle with laughter. "I must have some turpentine or something." Though Shane pressed the back of her hand against her mouth, the giggle escaped. "I *am* sorry," she claimed, then dropped her forehead on his chest. "And I wouldn't laugh if you'd stop looking at me that way."

"What way?"

"Patiently."

"Does patience usually send you into uncontrollable laughter?" he asked. Her hair carried the scent of her shampoo, a faint tang of lemon. It was odd that he would think just then of the honey-sweetness of her mouth.

"Too many things do," she admitted in a strangled voice. "It's a curse." She drew a deep breath but left her hand on his chest as she tried to compose herself. "One of my students drew a deadly caricature of his biology teacher. When I saw it, I had to leave the room for fifteen minutes before I could pretend I disapproved."

Vance drew her away, unnerved by his unwanted, unreasonable response to her. "Didn't you?"

"Disapprove?" Grinning, Shane shook her head. "I wanted to, but it was so good. I took it home and framed it."

Suddenly, she became aware that he was holding her arms, that his thumbs were caressing her bare skin while his eyes watched her in the deep, guarded way he had. Looking at him, Shane was certain he was unaware of the gentle, intimate gesture. There was nothing gentle in his eyes. If she had followed her first instinct, she would have risen to her toes and kissed him. It was what she wanted—what she sensed he wanted as well. Something warned her against making the move. Instead, she stood still. Her eyes met his calmly, with no secrets to be seen in them. All of the secrets were his, and at that moment, they both knew it.

Vance would have been more comfortable with secrets than candor. When he realized that he was holding her, that he wanted to go on holding her, he released her.

"You'd better get back to your painting," he said. "I'll take those measurements."

"All right." Shane watched him walk to the door. "There's hot water in the kitchen if you want some tea."

What a strange man, she thought, frowning after him.

Unconsciously, she lifted a finger to the warm spot on her arm where his flesh had touched hers. What had he been looking for, she wondered, when he had searched her eyes so deeply? What did he expect to find? It would be so much simpler if he would only ask her the questions he had. Shrugging, Shane went back to her painting.

Vance paused by the foot of the stairs and glanced at the living room. Surprised, he walked in for a closer look. It was clean as a whistle, with every vase, lamp and knickknack packed away in labeled boxes.

She must have really worked, he thought. That compact little body stored a heavyweight energy. She had ambition, he concluded, and the guts to carry it through. Whatever her former fiancé termed her, Vance would hardly characterize Shane Abbott as frivolous. Not from what he had seen so far, he reminded himself. He felt another flash of admiration for her as he mounted the stairs.

She'd been at work on the second floor as well, Vance discovered. She must move like a whirlwind, he concluded as he looked at the labeled boxes in the master bedroom. After taking his measurements and notations, he moved into Shane's room.

It was a beehive of activity, with none of the meticulous organization he had found in the other rooms. Papers, lists, notes, scrawled tablets and bills sat heaped on the open slant top of a Governor Winthrop desk. They fluttered a bit from the breeze through the open windows. On the floor beside it were dozens of catalogs on antiques. A nightgown—not the one he had envisioned her in, but a thigh-length chemise—was tossed inside out over a chair. A pair of worn sneakers sat propped against the closet as if they had been kicked there then forgotten.

In the center of the room was a large box of books, which

he remembered seeing the day before. Then they had been in the third bedroom. Obviously, Shane had dragged them into her own room the night before to sort through them. Several were piled precariously on the floor; others littered her nightstand. It was apparent that her style of working and style of living were completely at variance.

Oddly, Vance thought of Amelia and the elegant order of her private rooms. They had been decorated in pinks and ivories, without the barest trace of dust or clutter. Even the army of bottles of creams and scents on her vanity had been carefully arranged. Shane had no vanity at all, and the bureau top held only a small enameled box, a framed photo and a single bottle of scent. He noted the photo was a color snapshot of a teenaged Shane beside a very erect, white-haired woman.

So this is the grandmother, Vance mused. She had a prim, proper smile on her face, but he was certain her eyes were laughing out of the lined face. He observed none of the softness of old age about her, but a rather leathery toughness that contrasted well with the girl beside her.

They stood on the summer grass, their backs to the creek. The grandmother wore a flowered housedress, the girl a yellow T-shirt and cut-off jeans. This Shane was hardly different from the woman outside. Her hair was longer, her frame thinner, but the look of unbridled amusement was there. Though her arm was hooked through the old woman's, the impression was of camaraderie, not of support.

She was more attractive with her hair short, Vance decided as he studied her. The way it curled and clung to the shape of her face accented the smoothness of her skin, and the way her jaw tapered . . .

He found himself wondering if Cy had taken the picture and was immediately annoyed with the idea. He disliked Cy on principle, though he'd certainly employed a good many men like him over the years. They plotted their way through life as though it were a tax return.

What the hell had she seen in him? Vance thought in disgust as he turned away to take more measurements. If she had tied herself up with Cy, she would be living in some stuffy house in the suburbs with 2.3 children, the ladies auxiliary on Wednesdays and a two-week vacation in a rented beach cottage every year. Fine for some, he thought, but not for a woman who liked to paint porches and wanted to see Fiji.

That buttoned-down jerk would have picked on her for the rest of her life, Vance concluded before he headed back downstairs. She'd had a lucky escape. Vance thought it was a pity he hadn't had one himself. Instead he had spent an intolerable four years wishing his wife out of existence and another two dealing with the guilt of having his wish come true.

Shaking off the mood, Vance walked outside to take a look at Shane's front porch.

Later, when he was measuring and muttering, Shane came out with a mug of tea in each hand. "Pretty bad, huh?"

Vance looked up with an expression of disgust. "It's a wonder someone hasn't broken a leg on this thing."

"No one uses it much." Shane shrugged as she worked her way expertly around the uncertain boards. "Gran always used the back door. So does anyone who comes to visit."

"Your boyfriend didn't."

Shane shot him a dry look. "Cy wouldn't use the back door, and he's not my boyfriend. What do you think I should do about it?"

"I thought you'd already done it," he returned, and pocketed his rule. "And very well."

Shane eyed him a moment, then laughed. "No, not about Cy, about the porch."

"Tear the damn thing down."

"Oh." Gingerly, Shane sat on the top step. "All of it? I was hoping to replace the worst boards, and—"

"The whole thing's going to collapse if three people stand on it at the same time," Vance cut in, frowning at the sagging wood. "I can't understand how anyone could let something get into this condition."

"All right, don't get riled up," she advised as she held out a mug of tea. "How much do you think it'll cost me?"

Vance calculated a moment, then named a price. He saw the flicker of dismay before Shane sighed.

"Okay." It killed her last hope of holding on to her grandmother's dining room set. "If it has to be done. I suppose it's first priority. The weather might turn cold anytime." She managed a halfhearted smile. "I wouldn't want my first customer to fall through the porch and sue me."

"Shane." Vance stood in front of her. As she sat on the top step, their faces were almost level. Her look was direct and open, yet still he hesitated before speaking. "How much do you have? Money," he added bluntly when she gave him a blank look.

She drew her brows together at the question. "Enough to get by," she said, then made a sound of annoyance as he continued to stare at her. "Barely," she admitted. "But it'll hold until my business makes a few dollars. I've got so much budgeted for the house, so much for buying stock. Gran left me a nest egg, and I had my own savings."

Vance hesitated again. He had promised himself not to become involved, yet he was being drawn in every time he saw her. "I hate to sound like your boyfriend," he began.

"Then don't," Shane said quickly. "And he's not."

"All right." Vance frowned down at his mug. It was one thing to take on a job as a lark, and another to take money from a woman who was obviously counting her pennies.

He sipped, trying to find a reasonable way out of his hourly wage. "Shane, about my salary—"

"Oh, Vance, I can't make it any more right now." Distress flew into her eyes. "Later, after I've gotten started . . ."

"No." Embarrassed and annoyed, he put a hand on hers to stop her. "No, I wasn't going to ask you to raise it."

"But—" Shane stopped. Realization filled her eyes. Tears followed it. Swiftly, she set down the mug and rose. Shaking her head, she descended the stairs. "No, no, that's very kind of you," she managed as she walked away from him. "I—I appreciate it, really, but it's not necessary. I didn't mean to make it sound as though—" Breaking off, she stared at the surrounding mountains. For a moment there was only the sound of the creek bubbling on its way behind them.

Cursing himself, Vance went to her. After a brief hesitation, he put his hands on her shoulders. "Shane, listen—"

"No, please." Swiftly, she turned to face him. Though the tears hadn't brimmed over, her eyes still swam with them. When she lifted her hands to his forearms, he found her fingers surprisingly strong. "It's very kind of you to offer."

"No, it's not," Vance snapped. Frustration, guilt and something more ran through him. He resented all of it. "Damn it, Shane, you don't understand. The money isn't—"

"I understand you're a very sweet man," she interrupted. Vance felt himself become tangled deeper when she put her arms around him, pressing her cheek to his chest.

"No, I'm not," he muttered. Intending to push her away and find a way out of the mess he'd gotten himself into, Vance put his hands back on her shoulders. The last thing he wanted was misplaced gratitude. But his hands found their way into her hair.

He didn't want to push her away, he realized. No, by God, he didn't. Not when her small, firm breasts were pressed against him. Not when her hair curled riotously around his fingers. It was soft, so soft, and the color of wild honey. Her mouth was soft, he remembered, aching. Surrendering to need, Vance buried his face in her hair, murmuring her name.

Something in the tone, the hint of desperation, made Shane long to comfort him. She didn't yet sense his desire for her, only his trouble. She pressed closer, wanting to ease it while she ran soothing hands over his back. At her touch, his blood leaped. In a swift, almost brutal move, Vance pulled her head back to savage her mouth with his.

Shane's instinctive cry of alarm was silenced. Her struggles went unnoticed. A fire consumed him—so great, so unbearably hot, he had no thought but to quench it. She felt fear, then, greater than fear, passion. The fire spread, engulfing her until her mouth answered his wildly.

No one, nothing had ever brought her to this—this madness of need, terror of desire. She moaned in panicked excitement as his teeth nipped into her bottom lip. Along her skin, quick thrills raced to confuse and inflame. There was never a thought to deny him. She knew she was already his.

He thought he would go mad if he didn't touch her, learn just one of the secrets of her small, slim body. For countless hours the night before, his imagination had tormented him. Now, he had to satisfy it. Never stopping his assault on her mouth, he reached beneath her shirt to find her breast. Her heart pounded beneath his hand. She was firm and small. His appetite only increased, making him groan while his thumb and finger worked the already erect peak.

Colors exploded inside her head like a blinding, brilliant rainbow. Shane clutched at him, afraid, enthralled, while her lips and tongue continued with a demand equal to his. Against her smooth skin his palm was rough and calloused. His thumb scraped her, lifting her to a delirium of excitement. There was no smoothness, no softness in him. His mouth was hard and hot with the stormy taste of anger.

Crushed to hers, his body was taut and tense. Some raw, turbulent passion seemed to pour out of him, to dare her to match it.

She felt his arms tighten around her convulsively; then she was free so quickly she staggered, grabbing his arm to steady herself.

In her eyes, Vance saw the clouds of passion, the lights of fear. Her mouth was bruised and swollen from the fierceness of his. He frowned at it. Never before had he been rough with a woman. For the most part, he was a considerate lover, perhaps indifferent at times but never ungentle. He took a step back from her. "I'm sorry," he said stiffly.

Shane lifted her fingers to her still-tender lips in a nervous gesture. Her reaction, much more than Vance's technique, had left her shaken. Where had all that fire and feeling been hiding all this time? she wondered. "I don't . . ." Shane had to clear her throat to manage more than a whisper. "I don't want you to be sorry."

Vance studied her steadily for a moment. "It would be better all around if you did." Reaching in his back pocket, he drew out a list. "Here are the materials you'll need. Let me know when they're delivered."

"All right." Shane accepted the list. When he started to walk away, she drew up all of her courage. "Vance . . ." He paused and turned back to her. "I'm not sorry," she told him quietly.

He didn't answer, but walked around the side of the house and disappeared.

CHAPTER 5

Shane decided she had worked harder over the previous three days than she had ever worked in her life. The spare bedroom and dining room were loaded with packing boxes, labeled and listed and sealed. The house had been scrubbed and swept and dusted from top to bottom. She had pored through catalogs on antiques until the words ran together. Every item she owned was listed systematically. The dating and pricing was more grueling for her than the manual work and often kept her up until the early hours of the morning. She would be up to start again the moment the sunlight woke her. Yet her energy never flagged. With each step of progress she made, the excitement grew, pushing her to make more.

As the time passed, she became more convinced, and more confident, that what she was doing was right. It *felt* right. She needed to find her own way—the sacrifices and the financial risk were necessary. She didn't intend to fail.

For her, the shop would be not only a business but an adventure. Though Shane was impatient for the adventure to begin, as always, the planning and anticipation were just as stimulating to her. She had contracted with a roofer and a plumber, and had chosen her paints and stains. Just that afternoon, in a torrent of rain, the materials she had ordered from Vance's list had been delivered. The mundane, practical occurrence had given her a thrill of accomplishment. Somehow, the lumber, nails and bolts had been tangible evidence that she was on her way. Shane told herself that Antietam Antiques and Museum would become a reality when the first board was set in place.

Excited, she had phoned Vance, and if he were true to his word, he would begin work the next morning.

Over a solitary cup of cocoa in the kitchen, Shane listened to the constant drumming rain and thought of him. He had been brief and businesslike on the phone. She hadn't been offended. She had come to realize that moodiness was part of his character. This made him only more attractive.

The windows were dark as she stared out, with a ghostly reflection of the kitchen light on the wet panes. She thought idly about starting a fire to chase away the damp chill, but she had little inclination to move. Instead, she rubbed the bottom of one bare foot over the top of the other and decided it was too bad her socks were all the way upstairs.

Sluggishly, a drip fell from the ceiling into a pot on the floor. It gave a surprising ping now and again. There were several other pots set at strategic places throughout the house. Shane didn't mind the rain or the isolation. The sensation of true loneliness was almost foreign to her. Content with her own company, the activity of her own mind, she craved no companionship at that moment, nor would she have shunned it. Yet she thought of Vance, wondering if he sat watching the rain through a darkened window.

Yes, she admitted, she was very much attracted to him. And it was more than a physical response when he held her, when he kissed her in that sudden, terrifyingly exciting way. Just being in his presence was stimulating—sensing the storm beneath the calm. There was an amazing drive in him. The drive of a man uncomfortable, even impatient, with idleness. The lack of a job, she thought with a sympathetic sigh, must frustrate him terribly.

Shane understood his need to produce, to be active, although her own spurts of frantic energy were patchworked with periods of unapologetic laziness. She moved fast but didn't rush. She could work for hours without tiring, or sleep until noon without the least blush of guilt. Whichever she did, she did wholeheartedly. It was vital to her to find some way to enjoy the most menial or exhausting task. She concluded that while Vance would work tirelessly, he would find the enjoyment unnecessary.

The basic difference in their temperaments didn't trouble her. Her interest in history, plus her teaching experience, had given her insight into the variety of human nature. It wasn't necessary to her that Vance's thoughts and moods flow along the same stream as hers. Such comfortable compatibility would offer little excitement and no surprises at all. Absolute harmony, she mused, could be lovely, rather sweet and very bland. There were more . . . interesting things.

She'd seen a spark of humor in him, perhaps an almost forgotten sense of the ridiculous. And he was far from cold. While she accepted his faults and their differences, these qualities caused her to accept her own attraction to him.

What she had felt from the first meeting had only intensified. There was no logic in it, no sense, but her heart had known instantly that he was the man she'd waited for. Though she'd told herself it was impossible, Shane knew the impossible had an uncanny habit of happening just the same. Love at first sight? Ridiculous. But . . .

Impossible or not, ridiculous or not, Shane's heart was set. It was true she gave her affections easily, but she didn't give them lightly. The love she had felt for Cy had been a young, impressionable love, but it had been very real. It had taken her a long time to get over it.

Shane had no illusions about Vance Banning. He was a difficult man. Even with spurts of kindness and humor, he would never be anything else. There was too much anger in him, too much drive. And while Shane could accept the phenomenon of love at first sight on her part, she was practical enough to know it wasn't being reciprocated.

He desired her. She might puzzle over this, never having thought of herself as a woman to attract desire, but she recognized it. Yet, though he wanted her, he kept his distance. This was the reserve in him, she decided, the studied caution that warred with the passion.

Idly, she sipped her drink and stared out into the rain. The problem as Shane saw it was to work her way through the barrier. She had loved before, and faced pain and emptiness. She could accept pain again, but she was determined not to face emptiness a second time. She wanted Vance Banning. Now all she had to do was to make him want her. Smiling a little, Shane set down her cup. She'd been raised to succeed.

The glare of headlights against the window surprised her. Rising, Shane went to the back door to see who'd come visiting in the rain. Cupping her hands on either side of her face, she peered through the wet glass. She recognized the car and immediately threw open the door. Cold rain hurled itself into her face, but she laughed, watching Donna scramble around puddles with her head lowered.

"Hi!" Still laughing, Shane stepped back as her friend dashed through the door. "You got a little wet," she observed.

"Very funny." Donna stripped off her raincoat to hang it on a peg near the back door. With the casualness of an old friend, she stepped out of her wet loafers. "I figured you were hibernating. Here." She handed Shane a pound can of coffee.

"A welcome home present?" Shane asked, turning the can over curiously. "Or a hint that you'd like some?"

"Neither." Shaking her head, Donna ran her fingers through her wet hair. "You bought it the other day, then left it at the store."

"I did?" Shane thought about it a moment, then laughed. "Oh, that's right. Thanks. Who's minding the store while you're out making deliveries?" Turning, she popped the can into a cupboard.

"Dave." With a sigh, Donna plopped onto a kitchen chair. "His sister's babysitting, so he kicked me out."

"Aw, out in the storm."

"He knew I was restless." She glanced out the window. "It doesn't seem as though this rain's ever going to let up." With a shiver, she frowned at Shane's bare feet. "Aren't you cold?"

"I thought about starting a fire," she said absently, then grinned. "It seemed like an awful lot of trouble."

"So's the flu."

"The cocoa's still warm," Shane told her, automatically reaching for another cup. "Want some?"

"Yes, thanks." Donna ran her fingers through her hair again, then folded her hands, but she couldn't keep them still. Suddenly, she gave Shane a glowing smile. "I have to tell you before I burst."

Mildly curious, Shane looked over her shoulder. "Tell me what?"

"I'm having another baby."

"Oh, Donna, that's wonderful!" Shane felt a twinge of envy. Hurriedly dismissing it, she went to hug her friend. "When?"

"Not for another seven months." Laughing, Donna wiped the rain from her face. "I'm just as excited as I was the first time. Dave is too, though he's trying to be very nonchalant." She sent Shane a beaming look. "He's managed to mention it, very casually, to everyone who came into the store this afternoon."

Shane gave her another quick hug. "You know how lucky you are?"

"Yes, I do." A little sheepishly, she grinned. "I've spent all day thinking up names. What do you think of Charlotte and Samuel?"

"Very distinguished." Shane moved back to the stove. After pouring cocoa, she brought two cups to the table. "Here's to little Charlotte or Samuel."

"Or Andrew or Justine," Donna said as they touched rims.

"How many kids are you planning to have?" Shane asked wryly.

"Just one at a time." Donna gave her stomach a proud little pat.

The gesture made Shane smile. "Did you say Dave's sister was watching Benji? Isn't she still in school?"

"No, she graduated this summer. Right now she's hunting for a new job." With a contented sigh, Donna sat back. "She was planning to go to college part-time, but money's tight and the hours she's working right now make it next to impossible." Her brow creased in sympathy. "The best she can manage this term is a couple of night classes twice a week. At that rate it's going to take her a long time to earn a degree."

"Hmm." Shane stared into her cocoa. "Pat was a very bright girl as I remember."

"Bright and pretty as a picture."

Shane nodded. "Tell her to come see me."

"You?"

"After the shop's set up, I'm going to need some part-time help." She glanced over absently as the wind hurled rain at the windows. "I wouldn't be able to do anything for her for a month or so, but if she's still interested, we should be able to work something out."

"Shane, she'll be thrilled. But are you sure you can afford to hire someone?"

With a toss of her head, Shane lifted her drink. "I'll know within the first six months if I'm going to make it." As she considered, she twisted a curl around her finger—a gesture Donna recognized as nerves. She drew her brows together but said nothing. "I want to keep the place open seven days a week," Shane continued. "Weekends are bound to be the busiest time if I manage to lure in any tourists. Between sales and bookkeeping, inventory and the buying I have to do, I won't be able to manage alone. If I'm going down," she murmured, "I'm going down big."

"I've never known you to do anything halfway," Donna observed with a trace of admiration vying with concern. "I'd be scared to death."

"I am a little scared," Shane admitted. "Sometimes I imagine this place the way it's going to look, and I see customers coming in to handle merchandise. I see all the rooms and records I'm going to have to keep . . ." She rolled her eyes to the ceiling. "What makes me think I can handle all that?"

"As long as I can remember, you've handled everything that came your way." Donna paused a moment as she considered Shane carefully. "You're going to try this no matter how many pitfalls I point out?"

A grin had Shane's dimples deepening. "Yes."

"Then I won't point out any," Donna said with a wry smile. "What I will say is that if anyone can make it work, you can."

After frowning into her cocoa, Shane raised her eyes to Donna's. "Why?"

"Because you'll give it everything you've got."

The simplicity of the answer made Shane laugh. "You're sure that'll be enough?"

"Yes," Donna said so seriously that Shane sobered.

"I hope you're right," Shane murmured, then shook off the doubts. "It's a little late in the game to start worrying about it now. So," she continued in a lighter tone, "what's new besides Justine or Samuel?"

After a moment's hesitation, Donna plunged ahead. "Shane, I saw Cy the other day."

"Did you?" Shane lifted a brow as she sipped. "So did I."

Donna moistened her lips. "He seemed very . . . ah, concerned about your plans."

"Critical and concerned are entirely different things," Shane pointed out, then smiled as the color in Donna's cheeks deepened. "Oh, don't worry about it, Donna. Cy's never approved of any of my ideas. It doesn't bother me anymore. In fact, the less he approves," she continued slowly, "the more I'm sure it's the right thing to do. I don't think he's ever taken a chance in his entire life." Noting that Donna was busy gnawing on her bottom lip, Shane fixed her with a straight look. "Okay, what else?"

"Shane." Donna paused, then began running her fingertip around and around the rim of her cup. Shane recognized the stalling gesture and kept silent. "I think I should tell you before—well, before you hear it from someone else. Cy . . ."

Shane waited patiently for a few seconds. "Cy what?" she demanded. Miserably, Donna looked up.

"He's been seeing quite a lot of Laurie MacAfee." Seeing Shane's eyes widen, Donna continued in a rush. "I'm sorry, Shane, so sorry, but I did think you should know. And I figured it might be easier hearing it from me. I think . . . well, I'm afraid it's serious."

"Laurie . . ." Shane broke off and seemed to stare, fascinated, at the water dripping into the pot. "*Laurie MacAfee?*" she managed after a strangled moment.

"Yes," Donna said quietly, and she stared down at the

table. "Rumor is they'll be married next summer." Donna waited, unhappily, for Shane's reaction. When she heard the burst of wild laughter, she looked up, fearing hysterics.

"Laurie MacAfee!" Shane pounded her palms on the table and laughed until she thought she would burst. "Oh, it's wonderful; it's perfect! Oh God. Oh God, what an *admirable* couple!"

"Shane . . ." Concerned with the damp eyes and rollicking laughter, Donna searched for the right thing to say.

"Oh, I wish I had known before so I could have congratulated him." Almost beside herself with delight, Shane laid her forehead on the table. Taking this as a sign of a broken heart, Donna put a comforting hand on her hair.

"Shane, you mustn't take on so." Her own eyes filled as she gently stroked Shane's hair. "Cy isn't for you. You deserve better."

The statement sent Shane into a fresh peal of laughter. "*Oh, Donna!* Oh, Donna, do you remember how she always wore those neat little coordinates to school? And she got straight As in home economics." Shane was forced to take deep breaths before she could continue. "She did a term paper on planning household budgets."

"Please, darling, don't think about it." Donna cast her eyes around the kitchen, wondering if there were any medicinal brandy in the house.

"She'll have her own shoe trees," Shane said weakly. "I just know it. And she'll label them so they don't get them mixed up. Oh, Cy!" On a new round of giggles, she pounded a fist on the table. "Laurie. Laurie MacAfee!"

Almost frantic with concern, Donna gently lifted Shane's face. "Shane, I . . ." With a jolt she saw that rather than being devastated, her friend was simply overcome with amusement. For a moment, Donna stared into round dancing eyes. "Well," she said dryly, "I knew you'd be upset."

Shane howled with laughter. "I'm going to give them a Victorian whatnot as a wedding present. Donna," she added with grinning gratitude, "you've made my day. Absolutely made it."

"I knew you'd take it badly," Donna said with a baffled smile. "Just try not to weep in public."

"I'll keep my chin up," Shane promised, then smiled. "You're sweet. Did you really think I was carrying a torch for Cy?"

"I wasn't sure," Donna admitted. "You were . . . well, an item for so long, and I knew how crushed you were when the two of you broke up. You'd never talk about it after that."

"I needed some time to lick my wounds," Shane told her. "They've been healed over for a long while. I was in love with him, but I got over it. He put a large dent in my pride. I survived."

"I could have killed him at the time," Donna muttered darkly. "Two months before the wedding."

"Better than two months after," Shane pointed out logically. "We would never have made a go of it. But now, Cy and Laurie MacAfee . . ."

This time they both broke out into laughter.

"Shane." Donna gave her a sudden sober look. "A lot of people are going to be thinking you still care for Cy."

Shane shrugged it off. "You can't do anything about what people think."

"Or what they say," Donna murmured.

"They'll find something more interesting to talk about before long," Shane returned carelessly. "Besides, I have too much to do to be worried about it."

"So I noticed from the pile of stuff on the porch. What's under that tarp?"

"Lumber and materials."

"Just what are you going to do with it?"

"Nothing. Vance Banning's going to do it. Want some more cocoa."

"Vance Banning!" Stunned, then fascinated, Donna leaned forward. "Tell me."

"There's not much to tell. You didn't answer me," Shane reminded her.

"What? No, no, I don't want any more." Impatiently, she brushed the offer away. "Shane, what is Vance Banning going to do with your lumber and materials?"

"The carpentry work."

"Why?"

"I hired him to do it."

Donna gritted her teeth. "Why?"

"Because he's a carpenter."

"Shane!"

Valiantly, Shane controlled a grin. "Look, he's out of work, he's talented, I needed someone who'd work under union scale, so . . ." She spread her hands.

"What have you found out about him?" Donna demanded the right to fresh news.

"Not much." Shane wrinkled her nose. "Nothing, really. He doesn't say much."

Donna gave her a knowing smirk. "I already knew that."

A quick grin was Shane's response. "Well, he can be downright rude when he wants to. He has a lot of pride and a marvelous smile that he doesn't use nearly enough. Strong hands," she murmured, then brought herself back. "And a streak of reluctant kindness. I think he can laugh at himself, but he's forgotten how. I know he's a workhorse because when the wind's right, I can hear him hammering and sawing at all hours." She glanced out the window in the direction of the path. "I'm in love with him."

"Yes, but what—" Donna caught her breath and choked on it. "*What!*"

"I'm in love with him," Shane repeated with an amused smile. "Would you like some water?"

For nearly a full minute, Donna only stared at her. She's joking, she told herself. But by Shane's expression, she saw her friend was perfectly serious. It was her duty, Donna decided, as a married woman starting on her second child, to point out the dangers of this kind of thinking.

"Shane," she began in a patient, maternal tone, "you only just met the man. Now—"

"I knew it the minute I set my eyes on him," Shane interrupted calmly. "I'm going to marry him."

"Marry him!" Beyond words, Donna could only come up with sputters. Indulgently, Shane rose to pour her some water. "He—he asked you to marry him?"

"No, of course not." Shane chuckled at the idea as she handed Donna a glass. "He only just met me."

In an attempt to understand Shane's logic, Donna closed her eyes and concentrated. "I'm confused," she said at length.

"I said I was going to marry him," Shane explained, taking her seat again. "He doesn't know it yet. First I have to wait for him to fall in love with me."

After setting the untouched water aside, Donna gave her a stern look. "Shane, I think you're under more strain than you realize."

"I've been giving this a lot of thought," Shane answered, ignoring Donna's comment. "Number one, why would I have fallen in love with him in the blink of an eye if it wasn't right? It must be right, so number two, sooner or later he's going to fall in love with me."

Donna followed the pattern of thought and found it filled with snags. "And how are you going to make him do that?"

"Oh, I can't make him," Shane said reasonably. Her voice was both serene and confident. "He'll have to fall in love with me just as I am and in his own time—the same way I fell in love with him."

"Well, you've had some nutty ideas before, Shane Abbott, but this is the top." Donna folded her arms over her chest. "You're planning on marrying a man you've known barely a week who doesn't know he's going to marry you, and you're just going to sit patiently by until he gets the idea."

Shane thought for a moment, then nodded. "That's about it."

"It's the most ridiculous thing I've ever heard," Donna stated, then let out a surprised laugh. "And knowing you, it'll probably work."

"I'm counting on it."

Leaning forward, Donna took Shane's hands in hers. "Why do you love him, Shane?"

"I don't know," she answered immediately. "That's another reason I'm sure it's right. I know almost nothing about him except he's not a comfortable man. He'll hurt me and make me cry."

"Then why—"

"He'll make me laugh too," Shane interrupted. "And make me furious." She smiled a little, but her eyes were very serious. "I don't think he'll ever make me feel—inadequate. And when I'm near him, I *know*. That's enough for me."

"Yes." Donna nodded, giving Shane's hands a squeeze. "It would be. You're the most loving person I've ever known. And the most trusting. Those are wonderful traits, Shane, and—well, dangerous. I only wish we knew more about him," she added in a mutter.

"He has secrets," Shane murmured, and Donna's eyes sharpened. "They're his until he's ready to tell me about them."

"Shane . . ." Donna's fingers tightened on hers. "Be careful, please."

A little surprised by the tone, Shane smiled. "I will. Don't worry. Maybe I am more trusting than most, but I have my defenses. I'm not going to make a fool of myself." Unconsciously, she glanced out the window again, seeing the path to his house in her mind's eye. "He's not a simple man, Donna, but he is a good one. That much I'm sure of."

"All right," Donna agreed. Silently, she vowed to keep a close eye on Vance Banning.

For a long time after Donna left, Shane sat in the kitchen. The rain continued to pound. The steady drip from the ceiling plopped musically into the pan. She was aware of how reckless her words to Donna had been, yet she felt better having said them out loud.

No, she wasn't as blindly confident as she appeared. Inside, she was terrified by the knowledge that she loved so irrationally. She was trusting, yes, but not naive. She understood there was a price to pay for trust, and that often it was a dear one. Yet she knew her choice had already been made—or perhaps she'd never had one.

Rising, Shane switched off the lights and began to wander through the darkened house. She knew its every twist and turn, every board that creaked. It was everything familiar and comforting to her. She loved it. She knew none of Vance's twists and turns, none of his secret corners. He was everything strange and disturbing. She loved him.

If it had been a quiet, gentle love, she could have accepted it easily. But there was nothing quiet in the storm churning inside her. For all her energy and love of adventure, Shane had grown up in a slow, peaceful world where excitement was a run through the woods or a ride on the back of a tractor at haymaking. To fall suddenly in love with a stranger might seem romantic and wonderful in a story, but when it happened in real life, it was simply terrifying.

Shane walked upstairs, habitually avoiding the steps that

creaked or groaned. The rain was a hollow, drumming sound all around her, whipped up occasionally by the wind to fly at the windows. Her bare feet met bare wood with a quiet patter. A small bucket caught the drip in the center of the hall. Expertly, she skirted around it.

Who was she to think all she had to do was to sit patiently by until Vance fell in love with her? she asked herself. After flipping on the light in her room, she went to stare at herself in the mirror. Was she beautiful? Shane asked her reflection. Alluring? With a half laugh, she rested her elbows on the dresser to look closer.

She saw the dash of freckles, the large dark eyes and cap of hair. She didn't see the stunning vitality, the temptingly smooth skin, the surprisingly sensual mouth.

Was that a face to send a man into raptures? she asked herself. The thought amused her so, that the reflection grinned back with quick good humor. Hardly, Shane decided, but she wouldn't want a man who looked only for a perfect face. No, she hadn't the face or figure to lure a man into love had she wanted to. She had only herself and the love in her heart.

Shane flashed the mirror a smile before she turned away to prepare for bed. She'd always thought love the ultimate adventure.

CHAPTER 6

Weak sunlight filtered through the bad-tempered clouds. The creek was swollen from the rainfall so that it ran its course noisily, hissing and complaining as it rounded the bend at the side of Shane's house. Shane was doing some complaining of her own.

The day before, she had moved her car out of the narrow driveway so that the delivery truck could have easy access to the back porch. Not wanting to ruin the grass, she had parked in the small square of dirt her grandmother had used as a vegetable garden. Once the car had been moved, Shane had become involved with the unloading of lumber and had promptly forgotten it. Now, it was sunk deep in mud, firmly resisting all efforts to get it out.

She pressed the gas lightly, tried forward, then reverse. She gunned the engine and swore. Slamming out of the driver's side, Shane sloshed ankle-deep in mire as she stomped back to the rear tire. She gave it an accusing stare, then kicked it.

"That's not going to help," Vance commented. He had been watching her for the last few minutes, torn somewhere between amusement and exasperation. And pleasure. There was a simple pleasure in just seeing her. He'd stopped counting the times over the last few days that he'd thought of her.

Out of patience, Shane turned to him, hands on hips. Her predicament was annoying enough without the added benefit of an audience. "You might have let me know you were there."

"You were . . . involved," he said, glancing pointedly at her mired car.

She sent him a cool look. "You've got a better idea, I suppose."

"A few," he agreed, moving across the lawn to join her. Her eyes snapped with temper while her mouth pouted. Her boots were caked with mud past the ankle. Her jeans, rolled up to the calf, had fared little better. She looked ready to boil over at the first wrong word. A cautious man would have said nothing.

"Who the hell parked it in this mud hole?" Vance demanded.

"*I* parked it in this mud hole." Shane gave the tire another fierce kick. "And it wasn't a mud hole when I did."

He lifted a brow. "I suppose you noticed it rained all night."

"Oh, get out of my way." Incensed, Shane pushed him aside and stomped back to the driver's seat. She turned on the ignition, shoved the shift into first, then stepped heavily on the gas. Mud flew like rain. The car groaned and sank deeper.

For a moment, Shane could only pound on the steering wheel in enraged impotence. She would have dearly loved to tell Vance that she didn't require any assistance. There was nothing more infuriating than an amused, superior male . . . especially when you needed one. Forcing herself to take a deep breath, she climbed back out of the car to meet Vance's grin with icy composure. "What's the first of your few ideas?" she asked coolly.

"Got a couple of planks?"

Even more annoyed that she hadn't thought of it herself,

Shane went to the shed and found two long, thin boards. Without fuss or conversation, Vance took them and secured them just under the front wheels, Shane folded her arms and tapped one muddy boot as she watched him.

"I'd have thought of that in a minute," she muttered.

"Maybe." Vance stood again to walk to the rear of the car. "But you wouldn't get anywhere the way your back wheels are stuck."

Shane waited for him to make some comment on feminine stupidity. Then she would have an excuse to give him the full force of her temper. He merely studied her flushed face and furious eyes. "So?" she said at length.

Something suspiciously like a smile tugged at his mouth. Shane's eyes narrowed. "So, get back in and I'll push," he said, then put a restraining hand on her arm. "Gentle on the gas this time, hot rod. Just put it in drive and easy does it."

"It's a four-speed," she told him with dignity.

"I beg your pardon." Vance waited until she had waded her way back to the front of the car. For the first time in months, perhaps years, he had to make a concentrated effort to control laughter. "Let the clutch out slow," he instructed after clearing his throat.

"I know how to drive," she snapped, and slammed the door smartly. Frowning into the rearview mirror, Shane watched him until he gave her a nod. With meticulous care, she engaged the clutch and gently pressed on the gas. The front wheels crept slowly onto the planks. The back tires slid, then stuck, then ponderously moved again. Shane kept the speed slow and even. It was humiliating, she thought, glaring straight ahead, absolutely humiliating that he was going to get her out without a hitch.

"Just a little more," Vance called to her, shifting his weight. "Keep it slow."

"What?" Shane rolled down the window, then stuck her

head out to hear his answer. As she did, her foot slipped and fell heavily on the gas. The car shot out of the mud like a banana squeezed from its peel. With a gasp, Shane hit the brake, rocking to an abrupt halt.

Closing her eyes, she sat for a moment and considered making a run for it. She didn't dare glance in the rearview mirror now. It wouldn't be difficult, she reflected, to make a U-turn, then keep right on going. But cowardice wasn't her way. She swallowed, bit her lip, then climbed out of the car to face the music.

Vance was kneeling in the mud. He was thoroughly splattered and hopping mad. *"You idiot!"* he shouted before Shane could say a word. Even as she started to agree with him, he continued. "What the hell did you think you were doing? Pea-brained little twit, I told you to take it *slow*."

He didn't stop there. He swore at length, and fluently, but Shane lost track of the content. It was enough to know he was in a justifiable high rage, while she was fighting a desperate battle with laughter. She did her best, her very best, to keep her face composed and penitent. Feeling it would be unwise, as well as useless, to interrupt with apologies, she folded her lips, bit the bottom one and swallowed repeatedly.

At first she concentrated on keeping her eyes directly on his, hoping the fury there would kill the urge to giggle. But the sight of his mud-splattered face had her sides aching with restrained mirth. She hung her head, ostensibly from shame.

"I'd like to know who the hell told you you could drive," Vance went on furiously. "And what person with a brain cell working would have parked the car in a swamp to begin with?"

"It was my grandmother's garden," Shane managed in a strangled voice. "But you're right. You're absolutely right. I'm so sorry, really . . ." She broke off here as a gurgle of laughter rose dangerously. Clearing her throat, she hurried on. "Sorry, Vance. It was very"—she had to look over his head in order to compose herself—"careless of me."

"Careless!"

"Stupid," she amended quickly, thinking that might placate him. "Absolutely stupid. I'm really sorry." Helplessly, she pressed both hands to her mouth, but the giggles came through. "I *am* sorry," she insisted, giving up as he glared at her. "I don't mean to laugh. It's terrible." Dizzy with the effort of trying to hold back, Shane bent over double. "Really awful," she added on a howl of laughter.

"Since you think it looks like fun . . ." he muttered grimly, and grabbed her hand. Shane landed on her seat with a gentle splash and kept on laughing.

"I didn't—I didn't thank you," she said on a peal of giggles, "for getting my car out."

"Think nothing of it." Most women, he mused, would have been infuriated to find themselves sitting in a pile of mud. Shane was laughing just as hard at herself as she had at him. His grin was completely unexpected and spontaneous. "Brat," he accused, but Shane shook her head.

"Oh no, no I'm not, really." She pressed the back of her hand to her mouth. "It's just this terrible habit of laughing at the wrong time. Because I really am sorry." The last word was drowned in a flood of laughter.

"I can see you are."

"Anyway, I didn't get it *all* over you." Scooping up some mud, she wiped it across his cheek. "I missed that part right there." She made a little choking sound in her throat. "That's much better," she approved.

"You aren't wearing nearly enough," Vance returned. He trailed both muddy palms down her face. Trying to avoid him, Shane slid, ending up flat on her back. Vance's boom of laughter broke into her shriek. "Much better," he agreed, then spotting the handful of mud she was about to heave, he made a grab for her arm. "Oh, no, you don't!"

As he laughed, she shifted. Vance landed half on his chest, half on his side. With a muttered curse, he propped himself up, studying her out of narrowed eyes.

"City boy," she mocked on a whoop of appreciation. "Probably never been in a mud fight in your life." She was too pleased with her maneuver to see the next one coming.

In a flash, Vance had her by the shoulders. Rolling her over, he straddled her, holding a hand to the back of her head. Lying full length, Shane looked wide-eyed at the mud inches away from her face.

"Oh, Vance, you *wouldn't!*" The helpless laughter bubbled still as she struggled.

"The hell I wouldn't." He pushed her face an inch closer.

"Vance!" Though she was slippery as an eel by this time, Vance held her firmly, clamping his knees around her while his hand urged her down. As the distance between revenge and her nose lessened, Shane closed her eyes and held her breath.

"Give?" he demanded.

Cautiously, Shane opened one eye. She hesitated a moment, torn between the desire to win and the image of having her face pushed into the mud. She didn't doubt he'd do it. "Give," she said reluctantly.

Abruptly, Vance rolled her over so that she lay in his lap. "City boy, huh?"

"You wouldn't have won if I weren't out of practice," she told him. "It was just beginner's luck."

Her eyes were mocking him. Her face was streaked with mud from his own fingers. The hands pressed against his chest were slippery with it. The grip on the back of her neck lightened until it was a caress. The hand at her hip roamed absently down her thigh as he lowered his eyes to her mouth. Slowly, without any conscious thought of doing so, Vance began to draw her closer.

Shane saw the change in his eyes and was suddenly afraid. Did she really have the defenses she had bragged to Donna about? Now that she was certain she loved him, could there be any defense? It was too fast, she thought frantically. It was all happening too fast. Breathless from the race of her heart, she scrambled up.

"I'll beat you to the creek," she challenged, then was off in a flash.

Pondering her abrupt retreat, Vance watched her run around the side of the house. Normally, he would have considered it a ploy, but he found it didn't fit this time. Nothing about her fit, he concluded as he rose. Oddly, he realized he didn't seem to fit either. He hadn't realized he could find anything amusing or enjoyable about wrestling in the mud. Nor had he realized he could find a woman like Shane Abbott both intriguing and desirable. Trying to organize his thoughts, Vance walked around the side of the house to find her.

She had stripped off her boots and was wading knee-deep in the rushing creek water. "It's freezing!" she called out, then lowered herself to her waist. At the shock of cold, she sucked in her breath. "If it was warmer, we could walk down to Molly's Hole and take a quick swim."

"Molly's Hole?" Watching her, Vance sat on the grass to pull off his own boots.

"Right around the bend." She pointed vaguely in the direction of the main road. "Great swimming hole. Fishing too." Shivering a bit, she rubbed at the front of her shirt to help the water take off the worst of the mud. "We're lucky it rained, or else the creek wouldn't be high enough to do any good."

"If it hadn't rained, your car wouldn't have been stuck in the mud."

Shane shot him a grin. "That's beside the point." She watched him step into the water. "Cold?" she said sweetly when he winced.

"I should have pushed your face in," he decided. Stripping off his shirt, Vance tossed it on the grassy bank before scrubbing at his hands and arms.

"You'd have felt really bad if you had." Shane rubbed her face with creek water.

"No, I wouldn't have."

Glancing up, Shane laughed. "I like you, Vance. Gran would have called you a scoundrel."

He lifted a brow. "Is that praise?"

"Her highest," Shane agreed, rising to rub at the thighs of her jeans. They were plastered against her, molding her legs while her shirt clung wetly to her breasts. The cold had her nipples taut, straining against the thin cotton. Involved with cleaning off her clothes, she chattered, sublimely unaware they left her as good as naked.

"She loved scoundrels," Shane continued. "I suppose that's why she put up with me. I was always getting into one scrape or another."

"What kind?" Vance's torso was wet, cleaned of mud now, but he stayed where he was. Her body was exquisitely formed. He wondered how he hadn't noted before how perfectly scaled it was—small, round breasts, wasp-thin waist, narrow hips, lean thighs.

"I don't like to brag." Shane worked the mud from the slippery sleeves of her shirt. "But I can show you the best way into old man Trippet's orchard if you want to snitch a few green apples. And I used to have a great time riding Mr. Poffenburger's dairy cows." Shane sloshed over to him. "Here, you haven't got it all off your face." Cupping some water in her hand, she lifted it and began to clean his face herself. "I tore my britches on every farmer's fence for three miles," she went on. "Gran would patch them up saying she despaired of my being any more than a hooligan."

With one small, smooth hand, she methodically scrubbed Vance's face. The other she held balanced against his naked chest. He made no protest, but stood still, watching her.

"'That Abbott girl,' they'd say," Shane told him, rubbing at a spot on his jawline. "Now I have to convince them I'm an upstanding citizen so they'll forget I filched their apples and buy my antiques. No one takes a hooligan very seriously. There, that's better." Satisfied, Shane started to lower her hand. Vance caught it in his. Her eyes didn't waver from his, but she became very still.

Without speaking, he began to wash the few lingering traces of mud from her face. He worked in very slow, very deliberate circles, his eyes fixed on hers. Though his palm was rough, his touch was gentle. Shane's lips trembled apart. With something like curiosity, Vance took a damp finger to trace their shape. He felt her quick, convulsive shudder. Still slow, still inquisitive, he ran his fingertip along the inside of her bottom lip. Under his thumb, the pulse in her wrist began to hammer. The sun broke briefly through the clouds, so that the light shifted and brightened before it dimmed again. He watched it play over her face.

"You won't run away this time, Shane," he murmured, as if to himself.

She said nothing, afraid to speak while his finger lingered on her lips. Slowly, he traced it down, over her chin, over the throbbing pulse in her throat. He paused there a moment, as if gauging and enjoying her response to him. Then he allowed his fingertip to sweep up over the swell of her breast and lie lightly on the erect peak covered only by the thin wet shirt.

Heat and cold shot through her; her skin was chilled from the water; her blood flamed at his touch. Vance watched the color drain from her face while her eyes grew impossibly large and dark. Yet she didn't draw away or protest the intimacy. He heard the sharp intake of her breath, then the slow, ragged expulsion.

"Are you afraid of me?" he asked, bringing his hand up to cup the back of her neck.

"No," she whispered. "Of me."

Puzzled, he drew his brows together. For a moment he looked hard and very fierce. Though his eyes weren't cold, they were piercing—full of questions, full of suspicion. Still Shane felt no fear of him, only of the needs and longing running through her. "An odd answer, Shane," he murmured thoughtfully. "You're an odd woman." With his fingers, he kneaded the back of her neck while he searched her face for answers. "Is that why you excite me?"

"I don't know," she said, struggling for breath. "I don't want to know. Just kiss me."

He lowered his lips, but only tested hers with the same lightness as his fingertip. "I wonder," he said softly against her mouth, "what it is about you I can't quite shake. Your taste?" He dug his teeth almost experimentally into her bottom lip. A low moan of pleasure was wrenched from her. "Fresh as rain one minute and honey soaked the next." Lightly, languidly, he traced her lips with his tongue. "Is it the way you feel? That skin of yours . . . like the underside of a rose petal." He ran his hands down her arms, then up again, gradually bringing her to him until she was caught close. The thud of her heart sounded like thunder in her ears.

"Why do you have to know?" The question was low and shaky. "Feeling's enough." They might have been naked, pressed body to body with only wet clinging clothes between them. "Kiss me, Vance, just kiss me. It's enough."

"You smell like rain now," he murmured, telling himself to resist her but knowing he wouldn't. "Pure and honest.

When I look in your eyes, I'd swear there isn't a lie in you. Is there?" he demanded, but he crushed his mouth to hers before she could answer.

Shane reeled from the impact. Even as she gasped, his tongue was probing and exploring. The anger she had sensed in him before was now pure passion. Hunger, the rawness of his hunger, thrilled her. The water ran swiftly, grumbling as it hurried on its way to the river, but Shane heard only her own heartbeat. She no longer felt the stinging cold, only the warmth of his hand as it ran up her spine and down again.

He wasn't content with only her lips now, but took his own wild journey of her face. It was still wet, tasting of the cold freshness of the creek. But wherever his kisses wandered, he was drawn back again to the soft, sweet taste of her mouth. It seemed always to be waiting for him, ready to open, invite, demand. Beneath the pliancy, beneath the willingness was a passion as great as his own and a strength he was just beginning to measure.

Vance told himself he needed a woman. That was why he was so desperate for Shane. He needed a woman's softness and flavor, and she was here. There was no exclusivity to it. How could there be? Yet there was something about her slight body, her fascinatingly different taste that drove every other woman to some dark corner of his mind, leaving only Shane in the light.

He could take her now, on the bank of the creek, in the dim daylight on the rain-damp grass. As her mouth moved, moist and warm under his, Vance could imagine how it would be to take full possession of her body. Her energy and hunger would match his own. There would be no false, foolish pretense of seduction, but an honest meeting of desires.

Her small round breasts pressed into his naked chest. Vance thought he could feel the aching need in them—or was it his own need? It raged in him, drove at him, until she was

all he craved. Her mouth was small too, but avid, never re-
treating from the savageness of his. Instead, she matched it,
propelling him further and further, pulling him closer and
closer. All women or one woman, he was no longer certain,
but she was overpowering him.

Somehow he knew that if he took her, he would never walk
away easily. The reasons might not be fully clear yet, but she
wasn't like the other women he had known and bedded. He
was afraid her eager hands and mouth could hold him—and
he wasn't yet ready to chance it.

Vance drew her away, but Shane dropped her head on
his chest. There was something vulnerable in the gesture
though the arms around his waist were strong. The contrast
aroused him, as did the lightning fast beat of her heart. For
a moment, he stood holding her while the water ran cold and
fast around their legs and hazy sunlight drifted through the
trees.

She'd once told him that a snowfall had made her feel complete isolation. Vance felt it now. There might have been
nothing, no one beyond the rushing creek and fringe of
trees. And to his own confusion, he felt a need for none. He
wanted only her. Perhaps they were alone . . . The thought
both excited and disturbed him. Perhaps there was nothing
beyond that forgotten little spot, and no reason not to take
what he wanted.

Shane shivered, making him realize she must be chilled
to the bone. It brought him back to reality in a rush. His arms
dropped away from her.

"Come on," he muttered. "You should get inside." Vance
pulled her up the slippery bank.

Shane bent over to pick up her boots. When she was certain she could do so calmly, she met his eyes. "You're not
coming in." It wasn't a question. She had sensed all too well
his change of attitude.

"No." His tone was cool again though his blood still throbbed for her. "I'll go change, then come back and get started on the porch."

Shane had known he would bring her pain, but she hadn't thought it would be so soon. The old wounds of rejection opened again. "All right. If I'm not here, just do whatever you have to do."

Vance could feel the hurt, yet she met his eyes and her voice was steady. Recriminations he could have dealt with easily. Anger he would have welcomed. For the first time in years, he was completely baffled by a woman.

"You know what would happen if I came in now." The words were rough with impatience. Vance found himself wanting to shake her.

"Yes."

"Is that what you want?"

Shane said nothing for a moment. When she smiled, the light didn't reach her eyes. "It's not what you want," she said quietly. Turning, she started back to the house, but Vance caught her arm, spinning her around. He was furious now, all the more furious when he saw the effort her composure was costing her.

"Damn it, Shane, you're a fool if you think I don't want you."

"You don't want to want me," she returned evenly. "That's more important to me."

"What difference does it make?" he ground out impatiently. Frustrated by the calmness of her answer, he did shake her. How could she look at him with those big quiet eyes when she'd driven him to the wall only moments before? "You know how close I came to taking you right here on the ground. Isn't it enough to know you can push me to that? What more do you want?"

She gave him a long, searching look. "Push you to it," she repeated quietly. "Is that really how you see it?"

The conflict raged in him. He wanted badly to get away from her. "Yes," he said bitterly. "How else?"

"How else," she agreed with a shaky laugh that started a new ache moving in him. "I suppose for some that might be a compliment of sorts."

"If you like," he said curtly as he picked up his shirt.

"I don't," she murmured. "But then, you said I was odd." With a sigh, she stared into his eyes. "You've cut yourself off from your feelings, Vance, and it eats at you."

"You don't know a damn thing," he tossed back, only more enraged to hear her speak the truth.

As he glared at her, Shane heard a bird set up a strident song in the woods behind her. The high, piercing notes suited the air of tension and anger. "You're not nearly as hard or cold as you'd like to think," she said calmly.

"You don't know anything about me," he countered furiously, grabbing her arms again.

"And it infuriates you when the guard slips," Shane continued without breaking rhythm. "It infuriates you even more that you might actually feel something for me." His fingers loosened on her arms, and Shane drew away. "I don't push you, but something else certainly does. No, I don't know what it is, but you do." She took a long steadying breath as she studied him. "You've got to fight your own tug-of-war, Vance."

Turning, she walked to the house, leaving him staring after her.

CHAPTER 7

He couldn't stop thinking of her. In the weeks that passed, the mountains became a riot of color. The air took on the nip of fall. Twice, Vance spotted deer through his own kitchen window. And he couldn't stop thinking of her.

He split his time between the two houses. His own was taking shape slowly. Vance calculated he would be ready to start the more detailed inside work by winter.

Shane's was progressing more quickly. Between roofers and plumbers, the house had been bedlam for more than a week. The old kitchen had been gutted and stood waiting for new paint and trim. Shane had waited patiently for rain after the roof had been repaired. Then she had checked all the familiar spots for signs of leaks. Oddly, she found herself a trifle sad that she didn't have to set out a single pan or bucket.

The museum area was completely finished. While Vance worked elsewhere, Shane busied herself arranging and filling the display cases that had been delivered.

At times she would be gone for hours, hunting up treasures at auctions and estate sales. He always knew the moment she returned because the house would spring to life again. In the basement, she'd set up a workroom where she refinished certain pieces or stored others. He saw her dash out or dash in. He saw her carting tables, dragging packing boxes, climbing ladders. He never saw her idle.

Her attitude toward him was just as it had been from the first—friendly and open. Not once did she mention what had happened between them. It took all of his strength of will not to touch her. She laughed, brought him coffee and gave him amusing accounts of her adventures at auctions. He wanted her more every time he looked at her.

Now, as he finished up the trim on what had been the summer parlor, Vance knew she was downstairs. He went over his work critically, checking for flaws, while the simple awareness of her played havoc with his concentration. It might be wise, he thought, to take a trip back to Washington. So far, he had handled everything pertaining to his company by phone or mail. There was nothing urgent that required his attention, but he wondered if it wouldn't be wise to have a week of distance. She was haunting him. Plaguing him, Vance corrected. On a wave of frustration he packed his tools. The woman was trouble, he decided. Nothing but trouble.

Still, as he got ready to leave, Vance detoured to the basement steps. He hesitated, cursed himself, then started down.

Dressed in baggy cord jeans and a hip-length sweater, she was working on a tilt-top table. Vance had seen the table when Shane had first brought it in. It had been scarred and scratched and dull. Flushed with excitement, she had claimed to have bought it for a song, then had hustled it off to the basement. Now, the grain of mahogany gleamed through the thin coats of clear lacquer she had applied. She was industriously buffing it with paste wax. The basement smelled of tung oil and lemon.

Vance would have turned to go back upstairs, but Shane raised her head and saw him. "Hi!" Her smile welcomed him before she gestured him over. "Come take a look. You're the expert on wood." As he crossed the room, Shane stood back to survey her work. "The hardest thing now," she muttered as she twisted a curl around her finger, "is going to be parting with it. I'll make a nice profit. I only paid a fraction of its worth."

Vance ran a fingertip over the surface. It was baby smooth and flawless. His mother had a similar piece in the drawing room of her Washington estate. Since he had purchased it for her himself, he knew the value. He also knew the difference between an amateur job of refinishing and an expert one. This hadn't been done haphazardly. "Your time's worth something," he commented. "And your talent. It would have cost a good deal to have this done."

"Yes, but I enjoy it, so it doesn't count."

Vance lifted his eyes. "You're in business to make money, aren't you?"

"Yes, of course." Shane snapped the lid back on the can of paste wax. "I love the smell of this stuff."

"You won't make a lot of money if you don't consider your own time and labor."

"I don't need to make a lot of money." She placed the can on a shelf, then examined the ladder-back chair, which needed recaning. "I need to pay bills and stock my shop and have a bit left over to play with." Turning the chair upside down, she frowned at the frayed hole in the center of the seat. "I wouldn't know what to do with a lot of money."

"You'd find something," Vance said dryly. "Clothes, furs."

Shane glanced up, saw he was serious, then burst out laughing. "Furs? Oh, yes, I can see myself waltzing into the general store to buy milk in a mink. Vance, you're a riot."

"I've never known a woman who didn't appreciate a mink," he countered.

"Then you've known the wrong women," she said lightly as she set the chair upright again. "I know this man in

Boonsboro who does caning and rushing. I'll have to give him a call. Even if I had the time, I wouldn't know where to begin on this."

"What kind of woman are you?"

Shane's thoughts came back from her ladder-back chair. When she looked at him again, she noted that Vance's expression was cynical. She sighed. "Vance, why do you always look for complications?"

"Because they're always there," he returned.

She shook her head, keeping her hands on the top rung of the chair's back. "I'm exactly the kind of woman I seem to be. Perhaps that's too simple for you, but it's true."

"The kind who's content to work twelve hours a day just for enough money to get by on?" Vance demanded. "The kind who's willing to slave away hour after hour—"

"I don't slave," Shane interrupted testily.

"The hell you don't. I've watched you. Dragging furniture, lugging boxes, scrubbing on your hands and knees." Remembering only made him angrier. She was too small to labor the way he had seen over the past weeks. The fact that he wanted to insist she stop only infuriated him further. "Damn it, Shane, it's too much for you to handle by yourself."

"I know what I'm capable of," she tossed back, springing to her own defense. "I'm not a child."

"No, you're a woman who doesn't crave furs or all the niceties an attractive female can have if she plays her cards right." The words were cool with sarcasm.

Temper sprang into Shane's eyes. Struggling not to explode, she turned away from him. "Do you think everyone has a game to play, Vance?"

"And some play better than others" was his response.

"Oh, I feel sorry for you," she said tightly. "Really very sorry."

"Why?" he demanded. "Because I know that grabbing all

they can get is what motivates people? Only a fool settles for less."

"I wonder if you really believe that," she murmured. "I wonder if you really could."

"I wonder why you pretend to believe otherwise," he retorted.

"I'm going to tell you a little story." When she turned back, her eyes were dark with anger. "A man like you will probably find it corny and a bit boring, but you'll just have to listen anyway." Stuffing her hands into her pockets, she paced the low-ceilinged room until she was certain she could continue.

"Do you see these?" Shane demanded, indicating a row of shelves that held filled mason jars. "My grandmother—technically, she was my great-grandmother—canned these. Putting by, she always called it. She'd dig and hoe and plant and weed, then spend hours in a hot, steamy kitchen canning. Putting by," Shane repeated more quietly as she studied the colorful glass jars. "When she was sixteen, she lived in a mansion in southern Maryland. Her family was very wealthy. They still are," Shane added with a shrug. "The Bristols. The Leonardtown Bristols. You might have heard of them."

He had, and though his eyes registered surprise, he said nothing. Bristols Department Stores were scattered strategically all over the country. It was a very old, very prestigious firm that catered to the wealthy and the prominent. Even now, Vance's firm was contracted to build another branch in Chicago.

"In any case," Shane continued, "she was a young, beautiful, pampered girl who could have had anything. She'd been educated in Europe, and there were plans for her to be finished in Paris before a London debut. If she had followed her parents' plans, she would have married well, had her own mansion and her own staff of servants. The closest she would have come to planting would have been watching her gardener prune a rosebush."

Shane gave a little laugh as though the thought both amused and baffled her. "She didn't follow the plan, though. She fell in love with William Abbott, an apprentice mason who had been hired to do some stonework on the estate. Of course, her family would have none of it. They were already planning the groundwork for a marriage between Gran and the heir to some steel company. The moment they got wind of what was happening, they fired him. To keep it brief, Gran made her choice and married him. They disowned her. Very dramatic and Victorian. The I-have-no-daughter sort of thing you read in a standard Gothic."

Vance said nothing as she stared at him, almost daring him to comment. "They moved here, back with his family," Shane continued. "They had to share this house with his parents because there wasn't enough money for one of their own. When his father died, they cared for his mother. Gran never regretted giving up all the *niceties*. She had such tiny hands," she murmured, looking down at her own. "You wouldn't have thought they could be so strong." She shook off the mood and turned away. "They were poor by the standards she had grown up with. What horses they had were for pulling a plow. Some of your land was hers at one time, but with the taxes and no one to work it . . ." She trailed off, lifting down a mason jar, then setting it back. "The only gesture her parents ever made was when her mother left Gran the dining room set and a few pieces of china. Even that was done through lawyers after her mother had died." Shane plucked up her polishing cloth and began to run it through her hands.

"Gran had five children, lost two in childhood, another in the war. One daughter moved to Oklahoma and died childless about forty years ago. Her youngest son settled here, married and had one daughter. Both he and his wife were killed when the daughter was five." She paused a moment, brooding up at the small window set near the ceiling. Light poured through it to lie in a patch on the concrete floor. "I wonder if you can appreciate how a mother feels when she outlives every one of her children."

Vance said nothing, only continued to watch as Shane moved agitatedly around the room. "She raised her granddaughter, Anne. Gran loved her. Maybe part of the love was grief, I don't know. My mother was a beautiful child—there are pictures of her upstairs—but she was never content. The stories I've heard came mostly from people in town, though once or twice Gran talked to me. Anne hated living here, hated not having enough. She wanted to be an actress. When she was seventeen, she got pregnant."

Shane's voice altered subtly, but he heard the change. It was flat now, devoid of emotion. He'd never heard that tone from her before. "She didn't know—or wouldn't admit—who the father was," she said simply. "As soon as I was born, she took off and left me with Gran. From time to time, she came back, spent a few days and talked Gran out of more money. At last count she's been married three times. I've seen her in furs. They don't seem to make her happy. She's still beautiful, still selfish, still discontented."

Shane turned and looked at Vance for the first time since she had begun. "My grandmother only grabbed for one thing in her life, and that was love. She spoke French beautifully, read Shakespeare and tilled a garden. And she was happy. The only thing my mother ever taught me was that *things* meant nothing. Once you have a *thing*, you're too busy looking for the next one to be happy with it. You're too worried that someone might have a better one to be able to enjoy it. All the games my mother played never brought anything but pain to the people who loved her. I don't have the time or the skill for those games."

As she started to walk to the stairs, Vance stepped in front of her to bar her way. She lifted her chin to stare with eyes that glittered with anger and tears. "You should have told me to go to hell," he said quietly.

Shane swallowed. "Go to hell, then," she muttered, and tried to move past him again.

Vance took her shoulders, holding her firmly at arm's length. "Are you angry with me, Shane, or with yourself for telling me something that was none of my business?" he asked.

After taking a deep breath, Shane stared at him, dry-eyed. "I'm angry because you're cynical, and I've never been able to understand cynicism."

"Any more than I understand an idealist."

"I'm not an idealist," she countered. "I simply don't automatically assume there's someone waiting to take advantage of me." She felt calmer suddenly, and sadder. "I think you miss a lot more by not trusting people than you risk by trusting them."

"What happens when the trust is violated?"

"Then you pick up and go on," she told him simply. "You're only a victim if you choose to be."

His brows drew together. Is that what he considered himself? A victim? Was he continuing to allow Amelia to blight his life two years after she'd died? And how much longer would he look over his shoulder for the next betrayal?

Shane felt his fingers relax, saw the puzzled consideration on his face. She lifted a hand to touch his shoulder. "Were you hurt very badly?" she asked him.

Vance focused on her again, then released her. "I was . . . disillusioned."

"That's the worst kind of hurt, I think." In compassion, she laid a hand on his arm. "When someone you love or care for turns out to be dishonest, or an ideal turns to glass, it's difficult to accept. I always set my ideals high. If they're going to crumble, I'd just as soon take the long fall." She smiled, slipping her hand down so it linked with his. "Let's go for a drive."

His thoughts were so bound up in her words, it took him a moment to understand the suggestion. "A drive?" he repeated.

"We've been cooped up for weeks," Shane stated as she pulled him toward the stairs. "I don't know about you, but I haven't done anything but work until I tumbled into bed. It's a beautiful day, maybe the last of Indian summer." She shut the basement door behind them. "And I bet you haven't had a tour of the battlefield yet. Certainly not with an expert guide."

"Are you," he asked with the beginnings of a smile, "an expert guide?"

"The best," she said without modesty. As she had hoped, the tension went out of the fingers that were laced with hers. "There's nothing about the battle I can't tell you, or as some of my critics would claim, won't tell you."

"As long as I don't have to take a quiz afterward," Vance agreed as she pulled him out the back door.

"I'm retired," she reminded him primly.

* * *

The Battle of Antietam," Shane began as she drove down a narrow, winding road lined with monuments, "though claimed as a clear victory for neither side, resulted in the repulse of Lee's first effort to invade the North." Vance gave a quick grin at her faintly lecturing tone, but didn't interrupt. "Near Antietam Creek here in Sharpsburg," she continued, "on September 17, 1862, Lee and McClellan engaged in the bloodiest single day of the Civil War. That's Dunker Church." Shane pointed to a tiny white building set off the road. "Some of the heaviest fighting went on there. I have some pretty good prints for the museum."

Vance glanced back at the peaceful little spot as Shane drove by. "Looks quiet enough now," he commented, and earned a mild look.

"Lee divided his forces," she went on, ignoring him, "sending Jackson to capture Harper's Ferry. A Union soldier picked up a copy of Lee's orders, giving McClellan an advantage, but he didn't move fast enough. Even when he engaged Lee's much smaller army in Sharpsburg, he failed to smash through the line before Jackson returned with support. Lee lost a quarter of his army and withdrew. McClellan still didn't capitalize on his advantage. Even so, twenty-six thousand men were lost."

"For a retired schoolteacher, you don't seem to have forgotten the facts," Vance remarked.

Shane laughed, taking a bend in the road competently. "My ancestors fought here. Gran didn't let me forget it."

"For which side?"

"Both." She gave a small shrug. "Wasn't that the worst of it really? The choosing sides, the disintegration of families. This is a border state. Though it went for the North, sympathies this far south leaned heavily toward the Confederacy as well. It isn't difficult to imagine a number of people from this area cheering secretly or openly for the Stars and Bars."

"And with this section being caught between Virginia and West Virginia—"

"Exactly," she said, very much like a teacher approving of a bright student. Vance chuckled but she didn't seem to notice. Shane pulled off the side of the road into a small parking area. "Come on, let's walk. It's beautiful here."

Around them mountains circled in the full glory of fall. A few leaves whipped by—orange, scarlet, amber—to be caught by the wind and carried off. There were rolling hills, gold in the slanting sunlight, and fields with dried, withering stalks of corn. The air was cooler now as the sun dropped toward the peaks of the western mountains. Without thinking, Vance linked his hand with hers.

"Bloody Lane," Shane said, bringing his attention to a long, narrow trench. "Gruesome name, but apt. They came at each other from across the fields. Rebs from the north. Yanks from the south. Artillery set up there"—she pointed— "and there. This trench is where most of them lay after it was over. Of course, there were engagements all around—at the Burnside Bridge, the Dunker Church—but this . . ."

Vance shot her a curious look. "War really fascinates you, doesn't it?"

Shane looked out over the field. "It's the only true obscenity. The only time killing's glorified rather than condemned. Men become statistics. I wonder if there's anything more dehumanizing." Her voice became more thoughtful. "Haven't you ever found it odd that to kill one to one is considered man's ultimate crime, but the more a man kills during war, the more he's honored? So many of these were farm boys," she continued before Vance could form an answer. "Children who'd never shot at anything more than a weasel in the henhouse. They put on a uniform, blue or gray, and marched into battle. I doubt if a fraction of them had any idea what it was really going to be like. I'll tell you what fascinates me." Shane looked back at Vance, too wrapped up in her own thoughts to note how intensely he watched her. "Who were they really? The sixteen-year-old Pennsylvania farm boy who rushed across this field to kill a sixteen-year-old boy from a Georgia plantation—did they start out looking for adventure? Were they on a quest? How many pictured themselves sitting around a campfire like men and raising some hell away from their mothers?"

"A great many, I imagine," Vance murmured. Affected by the image she projected, he slipped an arm around her shoulders as he looked out over the field. "Too many."

"Even the ones who got back whole would never be boys again."

"Then why history, Shane, when it's riddled with wars?"

"For the people." She tossed back her head to look at him. The lowering sun shining on her eyes seemed to accentuate the tiny gold flecks that he sometimes couldn't see at all. "For the boy I can imagine who came across that field in September more than a hundred and twenty years ago. He was seventeen." She turned back to the field as if she could indeed see him. "He'd had his first whiskey, but not his first woman. He came running across that field full of terror and glory. The bugles were blaring, the shells exploding, so that the noise was so huge, he never heard his own fear. He killed an enemy that was so obscure to him it had no face. And when the battle was over, when the war was over, he went home a man, tired and aching for his own land."

"What happened to him?" Vance murmured.

"He married his childhood sweetheart, raised ten kids and told his grandchildren about his charge to Bloody Lane in 1862."

Vance drew her closer, not in passion, but in camaraderie. "You must have been a hell of a teacher," he said quietly.

That made Shane laugh. "I was a hell of a storyteller," she corrected.

"Why do you do that?" he demanded. "Why do you underrate yourself?"

She shook her head. "No, I know my capabilities and my limitations. And," she added, "I'm willing to stretch them both a bit to get what I want. It's much smarter than thinking you're something you're not." Before he could speak, she laughed, giving him a friendly hug. "No, no more philosophizing. I've done my share for the day. Come on, let's go up in the tower. The view's wonderful from there." She was off in a sprint, pulling Vance with her. "You can see for miles," she told him as they climbed the narrow iron steps.

The light was dim though the sun shot through the small slits set in the sides of the stone tower. It grew brighter as they climbed, then poured through the opening at the top. "This is the part I like best," she told him, while a few annoyed pigeons fluttered away from their roost in the roof. She leaned over the wide stone, pleased to let the wind buffet her face. "Oh, it's beautiful, the perfect day for it. Look at those colors!" She drew Vance beside her, wanting to share. "Do you see? That's our mountain."

Our mountain. Vance smiled as he followed the direction of her hand. The way she said it, it might have belonged to the two of them exclusively. Beyond the tree-thick hills, the more distant mountains were cast in blue from the falling afternoon light. Farmhouses and barns were set here and there, with the more closely structured surrounding towns quiet in the early evening hush. Just barely, he could hear the whiz of a car on the highway. As he looked over a cornfield, he saw three enormous crows take flight. They argued, taunting each other as they glided across the sky. The air was very still after they passed, so quiet he could hear the breeze whisper in the dry stalks of corn.

Then he saw the buck. It stood poised no more than ten yards from where Shane had parked her car. It was still as a statue, head up, ears pricked. Vance turned to Shane and pointed.

In silence, hands linked, they watched. Vance felt something move inside him, a sudden sense of belonging. He wouldn't have been amused now if Shane had said "our mountain." Remnants of bitterness washed from him as he realized his answer had been staring him in the face. He'd kept himself a victim, just as Shane had said, because it was easier to be angry than to let go.

The buck moved quickly, bounding over the grassy hill, taking a low stone fence with a graceful leap before he darted out of sight. Vance felt rather than heard Shane's long, slow sigh.

"I never get used to it," she murmured. "Every time I see one, I'm struck dumb."

Shane turned her face up to his. It seemed natural to kiss her here, with the mountains and fields around them, with the feeling of something shared still on both of them. Above their heads a pigeon cooed softly, content now that the intruders were quiet.

Here was the tenderness Shane had sensed but had not been sure of. His mouth was firm but not demanding, his hands strong but not bruising. Her heart seemed to flutter to her throat. Everything warm and sweet poured through her until she was limp and pliant in his arms. She had been waiting for this—this final assurance of what she knew he held trapped inside him: a gentle goodness she would respect as much as his strength and confidence. Her sigh was not of surrender, but of joy in knowing she could admire what she already loved.

Vance drew her closer, changing the angle of the kiss, reluctant to break the moment. Emotions seeped into him, through the cracks in the wall he had built so long ago. He felt the soft give of her mouth, tasted its moist generosity. With care, he let his fingertips reacquaint themselves with the texture of her skin.

Could she have been there all along, he wondered, waiting for him to stumble onto her through a curtain of bitterness and suspicion?

Vance drew her against his chest, holding her tightly with both arms as if she might vanish. Was it too late for him to fall in love? he wondered. Or to win a woman who already knew the worst of him and had no notion of his material advantages? Closing his eyes, he rested his cheek on her hair. If it wasn't too late, should he take the chance and tell her who and what he was? If he told her now, he might never be fully certain, if she came to him, that she came only to him. He needed that—to be taken for himself without the Riverton Banning fortune or power. He hesitated, torn and indecisive. That alone shook him. Vance was a man who ruled a multimillion-dollar company by being decisive. Now a slip of a woman whose hair curled chaotically under his cheek was changing the order of his life.

"Shane." Vance drew her away to kiss her brow.

"Vance." Laughing, she kissed him soundly, more like a friend than a lover. "You look so serious."

"Have dinner with me." It came out too swiftly, and he cursed himself. What had become of his finesse with women?

Shane pushed at her windblown hair. "All right. I can fix us something at the house."

"No, I want to take you out."

"Out?" Shane frowned, thinking of the expense.

"Nothing fancy," he told her, thinking she was worried about her bulky sweater and jeans. "As you said, neither of us has done anything but work in weeks." He brushed his knuckles over the back of her cheek. "Come with me."

She smiled, pleasing him. "I know a nice little place just over the border in West Virginia."

Shane chose the tiny, out-of-the-way restaurant because it was inexpensive and she had some fond memories of an abbreviated career as a waitress there. She'd worked the summer after her high school graduation in order to earn extra money for college.

After they had settled into a cramped booth with a sputtering candle between them, she shot him a grin. "I knew you'd love it."

Vance glanced around at the painted landscapes in vivid colors and plastic frames. The air smelled ever so faintly of onion. "Next time, I choose."

"They used to serve a great spaghetti here. It was Thursday's special, all you can eat for—"

"It's not Thursday," Vance pointed out, dubiously opening the plastic-coated menu. "Wine?"

"I think they probably have it." Shane smiled at him when he peered over the top of the menu. "We could go next door and get a whole bottle for two ninety-seven."

"Good vintage?"

"Just last week," she assured him.

"We'll take our chances here." He decided next time he would take her somewhere he could buy her champagne.

"I'll have the chili," Shane announced, bringing his thoughts back.

"Chili?" Vance frowned at the menu again. "Is it any good?"

"*Oh, no!*"

"Then why are you—" He broke off as he lowered his menu and saw Shane buried behind her own. "Shane, what—"

"They just came in," she hissed, turning her menu toward the entrance and peeping around the side of it.

Curiously, he glanced over. Vance spotted Cy Trainer with a trim brunette in a severely tailored tan suit and sensible pumps. His first reaction was annoyance; then, looking the woman over again and noting the way her hand rested on Cy's arm, he turned back to Shane. She was fully hidden behind the menu.

"Shane, I know it must upset you, but you're bound to run into him from time to time and . . ." He heard a muffled sound from behind the plastic-coated cardboard. Instinctively, Vance reached for her hand. "We could go somewhere else, but we can't leave now without his seeing you."

"It's Laurie MacAfee." She squeezed Vance's fingers convulsively. He returned the pressure, furious that she still had feelings for the man who had hurt her.

"Shane, you've got to face this and not let him see you make a fool of yourself."

"I know, but it's so hard." Cautiously, she tilted the menu to the side. With a jolt, Vance saw she was convulsed not with tears but with laughter. "As soon as he sees us," she began confidentially, "he's going to come over and be polite."

"I can see that's going to cause you a lot of pain."

"Oh, it is," she agreed. "Because you've got to promise to kick me under the table or stomp on my foot the minute you see I'm going to laugh."

"My pleasure," he assured her.

"Laurie used to keep her dolls lined up according to height, and she sewed little name tags on all their clothes," Shane explained, taking deep breaths to prepare herself.

"That certainly clears everything up."

"Okay, now, I'm going to put the menu down." She swallowed, lowering her voice a bit more. "Whatever you do, don't look at them."

"I wouldn't dream of it."

After a final cleansing breath, Shane set the menu on the table. "Chili?" she said in a normal tone. "Yes, it's always been good here. I believe I'll have it too."

"You're an idiot."

"Oh, yes, I agree." Smiling, she picked up her water glass. Out of the corner of her eye, she spotted Cy and Laurie crossing the room toward them. To kill the first bubble of laughter, she cleared her throat violently.

"Shane, how nice to see you."

Looking up, Shane managed to feign surprise. "Hello, Cy. Hello, Laurie. How've you been?"

"Very well," Laurie answered in her carefully modulated voice. She's really very pretty, Shane thought. Even if her eyes are just a fraction too close together.

"I don't think you know Vance," she continued. "Vance, this is Cy Trainer and Laurie MacAfee, old school friends of mine. Vance is my neighbor."

"Ah, of course, the old Farley place." Cy extended his hand. Vance found it soft. The grip was correctly firm and brief. "I hear you're fixing the place up."

"A bit." Vance allowed himself to study Cy's face. He was passable, Vance decided, considering he had a weak jaw.

"You must be the carpenter who's helping Shane set up her little shop," Laurie put in. Her glance slipped over his work clothes before it shifted to Shane's sweater. "I must say, I was surprised when Cy told me your plans."

Seeing Shane's lip quiver, Vance set his foot firmly on top of hers. "Were you?" Shane said as she reached for her water again. Her eyes danced with suppressed amusement as they met Vance's over the rim. "Well, I've always liked to surprise people."

"We couldn't imagine you with your own business, could we, Cy?" Laurie went on without giving him a chance to answer. "Of course, we wish you the very best of luck, Shane, and you can count on both of us to buy something to help you get started."

The laughter was a pain in her stomach. Shane had to press a hand against it while Vance increased the pressure on her foot. "Thank you, Laurie. I can't tell you what that means to me . . . I really can't."

"Anything for an old friend, right, Cy? You know we wish you every success, Shane. I'll be sure to tell everyone I know about your little shop. That should help bring a few people in. Though, of course," she sighed apologetically, "the sell-ing's up to you."

"Y-yes. Thank you."

"We'll just be running along now. We want to order be-fore it gets too crowded. So nice meeting you." Laurie sent Vance a brief smile and drew Cy away.

"Oh God, I think I'm going to burst!" Shane drank down the whole glass of water without a breath.

"Your boyfriend got just what he deserved," Vance mur-mured, glancing after them. "She'll regiment everything right down to their sex life." Thoughtfully, he looked after them. "Do you think they have one yet?"

"Oh, stop," Shane begged, savaging her lip in defense. "I'll be hysterical in a minute."

"Do you suppose she picked out that tie he's wearing?" Vance asked.

Giving up, Shane burst into laughter. "Oh, damn you, Vance," she whispered when Laurie turned her head. "I was doing so well too."

"Want to give them something to talk about over dinner?" Before she could answer, Vance pulled her across the nar-row booth and planted a long, lingering kiss on her lips. To keep Shane from ending it too soon, he caught her chin in his hand and held her still. He drew her away for only sec-onds, tilting her head, then pressing his mouth to hers again at a fresh angle. He heard her give a tiny moan of distress. Though she lifted a hand to his shoulder to push him away, when he deepened the kiss, she allowed it to lie unresisting until he took his lips from hers.

"Now you've done it," she said when she gathered her wits again. "By noon tomorrow it'll be all over Sharpsburg that we're lovers."

"Will it?" Smiling, he lifted her hand to his lips, then

slowly kissed her fingers one by one. It satisfied him to feel the faint tremor of arousal.

"Yes," Shane answered breathlessly, "and I don't . . ." she trailed off when he turned her palm up to press another long kiss in its center.

"Don't what?" he asked softly, taking his lips to the inside of her wrist. Her pulse pounded against the light trace of his tongue.

"Think it's—it's wise," she managed, forgetting the restaurant and Cy and Laurie and everything else.

"That we're lovers or that it's all over Sharpsburg?" Vance enjoyed the confusion in her eyes and the knowledge that he had put it there.

Her pulse beat jerkily. He was different. Reckless? she thought, and felt a fresh thrill race down her spine. Smooth? How could he be both at once? Yet he was. The recklessness was in his eyes, but the romantic moves were smooth with experience.

She hadn't been afraid of the hard, angry man she had met, but she felt a skip of fear for the one who even now traced his thumb over the speeding pulse at her wrist.

"I'm going to have to give that some thought," she murmured.

"Do that," he said agreeably.

CHAPTER 8

S hane opened the doors of Antietam Antiques and Museum the first week of December. As she had expected, for the first few days the shop and museum were crowded, for the most part with people she knew. They had come to buy or browse out of curiosity or affection. Others came to see what "that Abbott girl" had up her sleeve this time. It amused Shane to hear her past crimes discussed as though they had taken place the day before. Cy's name was dropped a time or two, causing her to force back a chuckle and change the subject. Still, after the initial novelty had worn off, she had a steady trickle of customers. That was enough to satisfy her.

As planned, she hired Donna's sister-in-law, Pat, on a part-time basis. The girl was eager and willing, and not opposed to giving Shane weekend hours. Shane considered the additional expense well worth it when Pat, flushed with triumph, rang up her first sale. With her coaching, and Pat's own enthusiastic studying, Shane's assistant had learned enough to classify certain articles in the shop and to handle questions in the museum section.

Shane found herself busier than ever, managing the shop, watching for ads for estate sales and overseeing the remodeling still under way on the second floor. The long, chaotic hours stimulated her, and helped her deal with the slow but steady loss of her grandmother's treasures. It was business, Shane reminded herself again and again as she sold a corner cabinet or candle holder. It was necessary. The bills in her desk had mounted over the weeks of preparation, and they had to be paid.

She saw Vance almost daily as he came to hammer and saw and trim on the second floor. Though he wasn't as withdrawn as he once had been, the intimacy they had shared for an afternoon and evening had faded. He treated her as a casual friend, not a woman whose palm he would kiss in a restaurant.

Shane concluded that he had taken on a loverlike aspect for Cy's benefit, and now it was back to business as usual. She wasn't discouraged. In fact, the man she had dined with had made her nervous and uncertain. She was more confident with Vance's temper than with soft words and tender caresses. Knowing herself well, Shane was aware it would be difficult not to make a fool of herself over him if he continued to treat her with gentleness. She had little defense against romance.

Daily, her love for him grew. It only made her more certain than ever that he was the only man for her. It would only be a matter of time, she decided, before he realized she was the woman for him.

It was late afternoon when Shane carried her latest acquisition up the new front steps and into the shop. She was flushed with cold and highly pleased with herself. She was learning to be ruthless when bargaining. After pushing the door open with her bottom, she carried the table through the entrance sideways.

"Just look what I've got!" she said to Pat before she closed the door behind her. "It's a Sheridan. Not a scratch on it either."

Pat stopped washing the glass on the display case. "Shane, you were supposed to take the afternoon off." Automatically she polished off a lingering smear before giving Shane her full attention. "You've got to take some time for yourself," she reminded her with a hint of exasperation. "That's why you hired me."

"Yes, of course," Shane said distractedly. "There's a mantel clock in the car and a complete set of cut glass saltcellars." Pat sighed, smart enough to know when she was being ignored, and followed Shane into the main showroom.

"Don't you ever quit?" she demanded.

"Uh-uh." After setting the table beside a Hitchcock chair, Shane stepped back to view the results. "I don't know," she said slowly. "It might look better in the front room, right under the window. Well, I want to polish it first anyway." She darted to the work counter, rummaging for the furniture polish. "How'd we do today?"

Pat shook her head. The first thing she had learned on the job was that Shane Abbott was a powerhouse. "I'll do that," she said, taking the polish and rag from Shane's hands. Shane grinned at Pat's weighty sigh but said nothing. "You had seven people come through the museum," Pat told her as she began to polish the Sheridan. "I sold some postcards and a print of the Burnside Bridge. A woman from Hagerstown bought the little table with the fluted edges."

Shane stopped unbuttoning her coat. "The rosewood piecrust?" It had sat in the summer parlor for as long as she could remember.

"Yes. And she was interested in the bentwood rocker." Pat tucked a strand of hair behind her ear while Shane struggled to be pleased. "I think she'll be back."

"Good."

"Oh, and you had a nibble on Uncle Festus."

"Really?" Shane grinned, thinking of the portrait of a dour Victorian man she'd been unable to resist. She had bought it because it amused her, though she had had little hope of selling it. "Well, I'll be sorry to lose him. He gives the place dignity."

"He gives me the creeps," Pat said baldly as Shane headed for the front door to fetch the rest of her new stock. "Oh, I nearly forgot. You didn't tell me you'd sold the dining room set."

"What?" Puzzled, Shane stopped with her hand on the knob.

"The dining room set with the heart-shaped chairs," Pat explained. "The Hepplewhite," she added, pleased that she was beginning to remember makes and periods. "I nearly sold it again."

"Again?" Shane released the knob and faced Pat fully. "What are you talking about?"

"There were some people in here a few hours ago who wanted it. It seems their daughter's getting married, and they were going to buy it as a wedding gift. They must be rich," she added with feeling. "The reception's going to be at a Baltimore country club . . . with an orchestra." She began to daydream about this a bit, but then she noted Shane's hard look. "Anyway," she continued quickly, "I'd nearly finalized the sale when Vance came downstairs and explained it was taken already."

Shane's eyes narrowed. "Vance? Vance said it was already sold?"

"Well, yes," Pat agreed, puzzled by the tone. If she had known Shane better, she would have recognized the beginnings of rage. Innocently, she continued. "It was a lucky thing too, or else they'd have bought it and arranged for the shipping right then and there. I guess you'd have been in a fix."

"A fix," Shane repeated between set teeth. "Yeah, somebody's in a fix all right." Abruptly, she turned to stride toward
the rear of the shop while Pat looked after her, wide-eyed.

"Shane? Shane, what's wrong?" Confused, she trotted
after her. "Where are you going?"

"To settle some business," she said tightly. "Get the rest
of the stuff out of my car, will you?" she called back without
slackening her pace. "And lock up. This might take a while."

"Sure, but . . ." Pat trailed off when she heard the back
door slam. She puzzled a moment, shrugged, then went to follow orders.

"A fix," Shane muttered as she crushed dead leaves underfoot. "Lucky thing he came down." Furiously, she kicked
at a fallen branch and sent it skidding ahead of her, waiting to be kicked again. Grinding her teeth, she stormed purposefully down the path between denuded trees. "Already
taken!" Enraged, she made a dangerous sound in her throat.
A hapless squirrel started across the path, then dashed in the
other direction.

Through the bare trees, she could see his house, with
smoke puffing from the chimney to struggle up into a hard
blue sky. Shane set her jaw and increased her pace. Into the
quiet came a steady thump, pause, thump. Without hesitation,
she skirted around to the back of the house.

Vance put another log on the tree stump he used as a chop-
ping block, then bore down with his axe to split it neatly in
two. Without a pause in rhythm, he set a new log. Shane
took no time to admire the precision or grace of the movement.

"You!" she spat, and stuck her fists on her hips.

Vance checked his next swing. Glancing over, he saw
Shane glaring at him with glittering eyes and a flushed face.
He thought idly that she looked her best when in a temper,
then followed through. The next log split to fall in two pieces

on either side of the stump. The generous pile was evidence that he had been working for some time.

"Hello, Shane."

"Don't you 'hello, Shane' me," she snapped, closing the distance between them in three quick strides. "How dare you?"

"Most people consider it an acceptable greeting," he countered as he bent down for another log. Shane knocked it off the stump with a sweep of her hand.

"You had no right to interfere, no right to cost me a sale. An important sale," she added furiously. Her breath puffed out visibly in the frigid air. "Just who the hell do you think you are, telling my customers something's already taken? Even if it had been, which it wasn't, it's hardly your place to add your two cents."

Calmly, Vance picked up the log again. He had been expecting her—and her anger. He had acted on impulse but didn't regret it. Very clearly, he could recall the look on her face when she had first shown him her grandmother's pride and joy. There was no way he was going to stand by and do nothing while she watched it being carted out the door.

"You don't want to sell it, Shane."

Her eyes only became more furious. "It's none of your business what I want to do. I have to sell it. I'm *going* to sell it. If you hadn't opened your big mouth, I *would* have sold it."

"And spent several hours hating yourself and crying over the invoice," he tossed back, slamming the blade of the axe into the stump before he faced her. "The money isn't worth it."

"Don't you tell me what it's worth," she retorted, and poked a finger into his chest. "You don't know how I feel. You don't know what I have to do. *I* do. I need the money, damn it."

With strained calm, he curled his hand around the finger that dug into his chest, held it aloft a moment, then let it drop. "You don't need it enough to give up something that's important to you."

"Sentiment doesn't pay bills." The color in her cheeks heightened. "I've got a desk full of them."

"Sell something else," he shouted back at her. Her face was lifted to his, her eyes glowing with anger. He felt conflicting urges to protect her and to throttle her. "You've got the damn place packed with junk as it is."

"*Junk!*" He had just declared war. "*Junk!*" Her voice rose.

"Unload some of the other stuff you've got piled in there," he advised with a coolness that would have rattled his business associates. A dangerous hissing sound escaped through Shane's teeth.

"You don't know the first thing about it," she fumed, poking him again so that he stepped back. "I stock the very best pieces I can find, and *you*"—she poked again—"you don't know a Hepplewhite from a—a piece of pressboard. You keep your city nose out of my affairs, Vance Banning, and play with your planes and drill bits. I don't need some flatlander to hand out empty advice."

"That's it," he said grimly. In one swift move, he swept Shane off her feet and dumped her over his shoulder.

"What the hell do you think you're doing?" she screamed, thrashing and pounding him with her fists.

"I'm taking you inside to make love to you," he stated between his teeth. "I've had enough."

In absolute astonishment, Shane stopped thrashing. "You're *what*?"

"You heard me."

"You're crazy!" More furious than frantic, she renewed her efforts to inflict pain wherever she could land a hit. Vance continued through the back door. "You're not taking me inside," she raged, even as he carted her through the kitchen. "I'm not going with you."

"You're going exactly where I take you," he countered.

"Oh, you're going to pay for this, Vance," she promised as she pounded against his back.

"I don't doubt that," he muttered, starting up the stairs.

"You put me down this minute. I'm not putting up with this."

Weary of being kicked, he pulled off her shoes, tossed them over the banister, then tightened an arm around the back of her knees. "You're going to put up with a hell of a lot more in a few minutes."

With her legs effectively pinned, she wiggled uselessly as he continued up the stairs. "I'm telling you, you're in big trouble. I'll get you for this," she warned, beating furiously against him as he strode down the hall and into a bedroom. "If you don't put me down this minute, *right this minute*, you're fired!" Shane let out a shriek as she tumbled through the air, then a whoosh as she thudded heavily on the bed. Breathless and infuriated, she scrambled to her knees. "You idiot!" she raged, puffing a bit. "Just what do you think you're doing?"

"I told you what I was doing." Vance stripped off his jacket and tossed it aside.

"If you think for one minute you can toss me over your shoulder like a bale of hay and get away with it, you're sadly mistaken." Shane watched with mounting fury as he unbuttoned his shirt. "And you stop that right now. You can't *make* me make love with you."

"Watch me." Vance peeled off his shirt.

"Oh, no, you don't." Though she stuck her hands on her hips, the indignant pose lost something as she knelt on the bed. "Just put that right back on."

Watching her coolly, Vance dropped it to the floor, then bent to pull off his boots.

Shane glared at him. "You think you can just dump me on the bed and that's all there is to it?"

"I haven't even started yet," he informed her as the second boot dropped with a clatter.

"You simpleminded clod," she returned, heaving a pillow at him. "I wouldn't let you touch me if—" She searched for something original and scathing but settled on the standby. "If you were the last man on earth!"

Vance sent her a long, glittering look before he unbuckled his belt.

"I told you to stop that." Shane pointed a warning finger. "I mean it. Don't you dare take another thing off. Vance!" she added threateningly as he reached for the snap of his jeans. "I'm serious." The word ended on a giggle. His hands paused; his eyes narrowed. "Put your clothes back on this minute," she ordered, but pressed the back of her hand to her mouth. Over it, her eyes were wide and brilliant with amusement.

"What the hell's so funny?" he demanded.

"Nothing, not a thing." With this, Shane collapsed on her back, helpless with laughter. "Funny? No, no, this is a very grave situation." Convulsed with giggles, she pounded her fists on the bed. "The man is standing there, pulling off his clothes and looking fit for murder. Nothing could be more serious."

Shane glanced over at him, then covered her mouth with both hands. "*That* is the face of a man overcome by lust and desire." She laughed until tears came to her eyes.

Damn her, Vance thought as a grin tugged at his mouth. He crossed to the bed; then, sitting beside her, he planted his hands on either side of her head. The harder she tried to control her amusement, the more her eyes laughed at him. "Glad you're having a good time," he commented.

She swallowed a chuckle. "Oh, no, I'm furious, absolutely furious, but it was *so* romantic."

"Was it?" His grin widened as he considered her.

"Oh, yes, why you just swept me off my feet." Her laughter rang through the room. "I don't know when I've been more *aroused*," she managed.

"Is that so?" Vance murmured as Shane gave herself wholly to mirth. Very deliberately, he lowered his lips to brush her chin.

"Yes, unless it was when Billy Huffman pushed me into the briars in second grade. Obviously I inflame males into violent seizures of passion."

"Obviously," Vance agreed, tucking her hair behind her ear. "I've had several since I tangled with you." Her fit of giggles ceased abruptly when he caught her earlobe between his teeth. "I think I'm bound to have several more," he murmured, moving down to her neck.

"Vance—"

"Soon," he added against her throat. "Any minute."

"I have to get back," she began breathlessly. As she attempted to sit up, he pressed a hand to her shoulder to keep her still.

"I wonder what else might arouse you." He nibbled at the cord of her neck. "This?"

"No, I . . ."

"No?" He gave a deep, quiet laugh, feeling her pulse hammer against his lips. "Something else then." Her coat was unzipped, and deftly he loosened the range of buttons on her blouse. "This?" Very gently, he touched the tip of her breast with his tongue.

On a gasp, Shane arched against him. Vance drew her nipple into his mouth to let her taste seep through him. He savored it a moment as Shane dug her nails into his bare shoulders. But when the heat shot into him, he knew he had to pull back before he took her too quickly. He'd been careful since the night they had dined together to keep some space between them. He hadn't wanted to rush her. Now that he had her in his bed, he intended to savor every moment.

Vance lifted his head and looked down at her. Her eyes were wide and fixed on his. For a moment, they both looked for answers. Very slowly, Shane smiled. "This," she whispered, and drew his mouth down to hers.

She hadn't been prepared for the sweetness of the kiss. His lips moved gently over hers. Their breath merged and matched rhythm. With light kisses he roamed her face, only to return over and over to her waiting mouth. To linger, to savor, to make each moment, each taste last; that was his only thought. The fiery needs were banked by the simple knowledge that she was his to touch, to kiss, to love. For the first time in his memory, he wanted to bring a woman pleasure much more than he wanted to take his own. He could give her that with the slow kisses that made his own blood thunder. Until he sensed she craved more, he used only his lips and tongue to arouse her.

Hardly touching her, Vance drew her jacket over her shoulders and arms, lifting her slightly to slip it from under her. His touch was so sure, so gentle, she remained unaware of his inner conflict between passion and tenderness. Without hurry, he drew off her shirt, following its progress over her shoulders with his lips. Shane sighed as his kisses ranged down her arm to nibble at the inside of her elbow. Fighting the growing need to rush, Vance trailed his lips down to her wrist.

If the wind still blew outside the windows, if leaves still rustled along the ground, Shane was unaware. There was only the play of Vance's fingertips, only the warm trace of his mouth. Content, almost sleepy, she ran her fingers through his thick mane of hair as his teeth tugged lightly at the cord of her neck. The lazy friction of his skin against hers had her pulse beating thickly. She felt she could stay forever, floating in a world halfway between passion and serenity.

He began the downward journey slowly, hardly seeming to move at all. With kisses and light love bites, he circled her breast, moving inward until he captured the peak. It grew hot and hard in his mouth while she began to move under him. He suckled, using his tongue to bring them both to the edge of delirium. Her breathing was as raspy as his. Now he could feel the energy flowing from her, pouring out in passion and urgency. Moaning his name, she pressed him closer to her.

But there was so much more to give, so much more to take. With deliberate care, Vance repeated the same aching journey around her other breast, feeling her shudders, listening to the storm of her heartbeat under his hungry, seeking lips.

"So soft," he murmured. "So beautiful." For a moment he merely buried his face against her breast, struggling to hang on to his control. On a moan of need, Shane reached for him as if to bring his mouth back to hers, but he slipped lower.

Taking her arching hips in his hands, Vance traced his tongue down her quivering skin. Shane felt her jeans loosen at the waist and shifted to help him. But he only pressed his mouth deep into the vee of exposed flesh. Again she shifted, curving her back to offer herself, but he lingered, tracing lazy circles with his tongue.

When he worked the jeans over her hips, she felt each searing brush of his fingers. Down her thighs he journeyed, pausing to caress their soft inner flesh, over her calves to nibble gently at the taut muscles, then to her ankles, sending a devastating flush of heat up her body with a quick flick of his tongue.

He found points of pleasure she had been unaware existed.

Then he was at the core of her, his tongue stabbing inside her to catapult her beyond all bounds of reason. She moaned his name, moving with him, moving for him, with mind and body tormented by dark, pulsing delights.

Vance heard his name come huskily through her lips and thrilled to it. Her energy, her wellspring of passion inflamed him, driving him to take her deeper before he took all. The sweet, sweet taste of her made him greedy. Somewhere in the back of his clouded mind he knew he was no longer gentle with her, but needs whipped at him.

Madness overcame him. His mouth roamed wildly over her body as his fingers took her from peak to staggering peak. Her breath was heaving when he found her breast. If she had been capable of words, Shane would have pleaded with him to take her. Her world was spinning at a terrifying speed, a speed far beyond the scope of her imagination. When his mouth crushed hers, she answered blindly. He thrust into her.

The flow of energy came from nowhere—a power, a strength that hurled her beyond the reasonable and into the impossible. One fed the other, driving higher and faster until they found the apex. Together, they clung to it, shuddering.

How long he lay still, Vance was unsure. Perhaps he even dozed. When his mind began to clear, he found his mouth nuzzled against Shane's throat, her arms wrapped around him. He was still inside her and could feel the light pulses of lingering passion deep within her. For a moment longer he kept his eyes closed, wondering how it was possible to be both sated and exhilarated. When he started to move, thinking of her comfort, Shane tightened her hold to keep him close.

"No," she murmured. "Just a little longer."

He laughed as his lips grazed her ear. "Can you breathe?"

"I'll breathe later."

Content, he snuggled back into the curve of her neck.

"I like the way you taste. I've had a problem with that since the first time I kissed you."

"A problem?" she said lazily, running experimental fingers over the muscles of his back. "That doesn't sound much like a compliment to me."

"Would you like one?" He pressed his mouth to her skin. "You're the most exquisite creature I've ever seen."

Shane received this news with a snort of laughter. "Your first compliment was a bit more credible."

Vance lifted his head and looked down at her. Though her eyes were still sleepy with passion, they were amused. "You really don't see it, do you?" he said thoughtfully. Did she really have no notion what big velvet eyes and satin skin could do to a man when combined with her kind of vivacity? Didn't she realize the kind of power there was in striking innocence when it was offset by a sensual mouth and an open, honest sexuality? "You might lose it if you did," he said half to himself. "What if I said I liked your nose?"

She eyed him warily for a moment. "If you say I'm cute, I'll hit you."

He chuckled, then kissed both dimpled cheeks. "Do you know how long I've wanted you like this?"

"From the first moment in the general store." She smiled when he lifted his head to stare down at her. "I felt it too. It was as though I'd been expecting you."

Vance laid his forehead on hers. "I was furious."

"I was stunned. I forgot my coffee."

They laughed before their mouths met. "You were terribly rude that day," she remembered.

"I meant to be." He lured her lips back to his. "I wanted to get rid of you."

"Did you really think you could?" Chuckling, she nipped at his bottom lip. "Don't you know a determined woman when you see one?"

"I *would* have gotten rid of you if I'd been able to close my eyes at night without seeing you."

"Did you really? Poor Vance." She gave him a sympathetic kiss.

"I'm sure you're very sorry I lost sleep over you."

She made a suspicious sound. Vance lifted his head again to see her bottom lip caught firmly between her teeth. "I would be sorry," she assured him, "if I didn't think it was wonderful."

"I often wanted to strangle you at three o'clock in the morning."

"I'm sure you did," she returned soberly. "Why don't you kiss me instead?"

He did, roughly, as banked passions began to smolder again. "That day when you sat in the mud, laughing like a fool, I wanted you so badly I hurt. Damn you, Shane, I haven't been able to think straight for weeks." His mouth crushed down on hers again with a touch of the anger she remembered. She soothed the back of his neck with her fingers.

When he lifted his head, their eyes met in a long, deep look. Shane lifted her palm to his cheek.

So much turbulence, she thought. So many secrets.

So much sweetness, he thought. So much honesty.

"I love you," they said together, then stared at each other in amazement. For a moment, they neither moved nor spoke. It seemed even their breathing had halted at the same instant. Then, as one, they reached out, clinging heart to heart, mouth to mouth. What started as a desperate meeting of lips softened, then sweetened, then promised.

Vance closed his eyes on waves of relief and towering pleasure. When he felt Shane's shudders, he drew his arms tighter around her. "You're trembling. Why?"

"It's too perfect," she said in a voice that shook. "It frightens me. If I were to lose you now—"

"Shh." He cut her off with a kiss. "It *is* perfect."

"Oh, Vance, I love you so much. I've been waiting all these weeks for you to love me back, and now . . ." She took his face in her hands and shook her head. "Now that you do, I'm scared."

Looking down at her, he felt a surge of passion and possession. She was his now; nothing was going to change it. No more mistakes, no more disillusionments. He heard her breath catch, then shudder.

"I love you," he said fiercely. "I'm going to keep you, do you understand? We belong together. We both know it. Nothing, by God, nothing's going to interfere with that."

He took her on a wild surge of need and desperation, ignoring the shadow of trepidation that watched over his shoulder.

CHAPTER 9

It was dark when Shane woke. She had no idea of time or place, only of deep inner contentment and security. The weight of an arm around her waist meant love; the quiet breathing near her ear meant her lover slept beside her. She needed nothing more.

Idly, she wondered how long they had slept. The sun had been setting when she had closed her eyes. The moon was up now. Its cool white light filtered in through the windows to slant across the bed. Shifting slightly, Shane tilted her head back to look at Vance's face. In the dim light, she could make out the sweep of cheekbone and outline of jaw, the strong straight nose. With a fingertip, she traced his mouth gently, not wanting to wake him. As long as he slept, she could look her fill.

It was a strong face, even a hard one, she mused, with its sharp angles and dark coloring. His mouth could be cruel, his eyes cold. Even in his loving there was a ruthless sort of power in him. While a woman might feel safe in his arms, she would never be completely comfortable. A life with him would be full of constant demands, arguments, passion.

And he loves me, Shane thought in a kind of terrified wonder.

In sleep, Vance shifted, drawing her closer. As their naked bodies pressed intimately close, a dull throb of need moved through her. Her skin heated against his, tingling with the contact. Against the slow, steady beat of his heart, hers began to thud erratically. Desire had never seemed more demanding, yet he did nothing more than lie quietly beside her, deep in his own dreams.

It would always be like this, she realized as she settled her head in the crook of his shoulder. He would give her very little peace. Though she was a woman who had always taken peace for granted, Shane would now forfeit it cheerfully. He was her fate; she had known it from the first instant. Now, she felt as bound to him as if she had been his wife for decades.

For a long time she lay awake, listening to him sleep, feeling the steady rise and fall of his chest against her breasts. This would never change, she told herself. This need to hold each other. She burrowed against him for a moment, filling herself with his scent. As long as she lived, Shane knew she would remember every second, every word spoken during their first time together. She would need no diary to remind her of young, churning fires when she was old. No passage of time would dull her memory or her feelings.

With a sigh, she brushed a whisper of a kiss over his lips. He didn't stir, but she wondered if he dreamed of her. She wanted him to, and closing her eyes, she willed him to. Carefully, she drew away from him, then moving lightly, slipped from the bed. Their clothes were in scattered heaps. Finding Vance's shirt, Shane slipped it on before she left the room.

Her scent lingered on the pillowcase. It was the first thing to penetrate Vance's senses as he drifted awake. It suited her so, the fresh, clean fragrance with a suggestion of lemon. Lazily, he allowed it to seep into him. Even in sleep, his mind was full of her. There was a slight stiffness in his shoulder where her head had rested. Vance flexed it before reaching out to bring her back to him. He found himself alone. Opening his eyes, Vance whispered her name.

He experienced the same sense of time disorientation that Shane had. The room was dim with moonlight, so that for a moment he thought he must have dreamed it all. But the sheets were still warm from her, and her scent still lingered. No dream. The relief he felt overwhelmed him. Softly, he called her name. It was then he smelled the bacon. In the dark, he grinned foolishly and settled back. As he lay quietly, he could just hear Shane's voice as she sang some silly popular song.

She was in the kitchen, he thought. Vance stayed where he was, listening. She was rooting through the cupboards, clattering something. Water was running. The scent of bacon grew stronger. How long, he wondered, had he waited to feel this way? *Complete.* He hadn't known he had been waiting, but he did know what he had found. She filled the emptiness that had nagged at him for years, healed an old, festering wound. She was all the answers to all the questions.

And what would he bring her? his conscience demanded. Vance closed his eyes. He knew himself too well to pretend he would give her a smooth, serene life. His temper was too volatile, his responsibilities too intrusive. Even with adjustments to both, he could paint her no soft pastoral scene. His life, past, present and future, had too many complications. Even this, their first night together, would have to be marred by one of his ghosts. He had to tell her about Amelia. There was a burst of rage followed by a prickle of fear.

No, he wouldn't accept the fear, he told himself as he rose quickly from the bed. Nothing, no one was going to interfere with him. No shadow of a dead wife or demands of a hungry business were going to take her from him. She was strong, he reminded himself, trying to override the apprehension. He could make her see his past as it was—something that had happened before her. It might shock her to learn he was president of a multimillion-dollar firm, but she could hardly be displeased once it was out in the open. He would tell Shane everything and wipe the slate clean. When it was done, he could ask her to marry him. If he had to make professional adjustments, he'd make them. He had sacrificed his own youthful dream for the good of the company, but he wouldn't sacrifice Shane.

As he pulled on his jeans, Vance tried to work out the best way to tell her and, perhaps more important, to explain why he had yet to tell her.

*　*　*

Shane added a dash of thyme to the canned soup she was heating. She rose on her bare toes to reach for a bowl on the shelf, the hem of Vance's shirt skimming her naked thighs. Her hair was tousled, her cheeks flushed. Vance stood for a moment in the doorway watching her.

Then in three strides, he was behind her, wrapping his arms around her waist and burying his face in the curve of her neck. "I love you," he murmured in a low, fierce whisper. "God, how I love you."

Before she could answer, he spun her around to take her mouth with his. Both stunned and aroused, Shane clung to him as her knees buckled. But she met the kiss with equal passion with soft, willing lips until he slowly drew her away. As the flame mellowed to a glow, Vance looked down at her and smiled.

"Any time you want to drive me crazy, just put on one of my shirts."

"If I'd known the kind of results I'd get, I'd have done it weeks ago." Returning his smile, Shane clasped her hands around his neck. "I thought you'd be hungry. It's after eight."

"I smelled food," he said with a grin. "That's why I came down."

"Oh." Shane lifted a brow. "Is that the only reason?"

"What else?"

Her retort ended on a laugh as he nuzzled her neck. "You could make something up," she suggested.

"If it makes you feel better, I could pretend it was because I couldn't keep away from you." He kissed her until she was limp and breathless. "That I woke up reaching for you, then lay listening to your clattering in the kitchen and knew I'd never been happier in my life. Will that do?"

"Yes, I . . ." She sighed as his hands slid down to caress beneath the loose shirt. Behind her, bacon popped and hissed. "If you don't stop, the food's going to burn."

"What food?" He chuckled, pleased that she was flushed and breathing unsteadily when she struggled away from him.

"My own specially doctored tomato soup and prize-winning BLTs."

He pulled her back to nuzzle her neck another moment. "Mmm, it does smell pretty good. So do you."

"It's your shirt," she claimed as she wiggled out of his arms again. "It smells like wood chips." Deftly, Shane took the sizzling bacon from the frying pan to let it drain. "If you want coffee, the water's still hot."

Vance watched her finish preparing the simple meal. She did more than fill the kitchen with the scents and sounds of cooking. He'd done that himself often enough in the past weeks. Shane filled it with life. He may have repaired and renovated and remodeled, but the house had always been empty. Vance realized now that without her, it would have always been unfinished.

There would be no living there without her—no living anywhere. Fleetingly, he thought of the large white house in an exclusive Washington suburb—the house he had bought for Amelia. There was an oval swimming pool sheltered by a white brick wall, a formal rose garden with flagstone paths, a clay tennis court. Two maids, a gardener and a cook. When Amelia had been alive, there had been yet another maid to tend to her personally. Her dressing room alone had been larger than the kitchen where Shane was now fixing soup and sandwiches. There was a parlor with a rosewood cabinet Shane would adore, and heavy damask drapes she would detest.

No, Vance thought, he wouldn't go back there now, nor would he ask Shane to share his ghosts. He had no right to ask her to cope with something he was only beginning to re-solve himself. But he would have to tell her something of his former marriage, and of his work, before yesterday could be buried.

"Shane . . ."

"Sit down," she ordered, busily pouring soup into bowls. "I'm starving. I skipped lunch this afternoon bargaining for this wonderful Sheridan table. I paid a bit more for the clock than I should have, but made it up on the table and the salt-cellars."

"Shane, I have to talk to you."

Deftly, she sliced a sandwich in half. "Okay, I can talk and eat at the same time. I'm going to have some milk. Even I can tell that instant coffee's dreadful."

She was bustling here and there, putting bowls and plates on the table, poking into the refrigerator. Vance was suddenly struck with the picture of his life before she had come into it—the rush, the demands, the work that had ultimately added up to nothing. If he lost her . . . He couldn't bear thinking about it.

"Shane." He stopped her abruptly, taking both of her arms in a strong grip. Looking up, she was surprised by the fierceness in his eyes. "I love you. Do you believe it?" His grip tightened painfully on the question, but she made no protest.

"Yes, I believe it."

"Will you take me just as I am?" he demanded.

"Yes." There was no hesitation in her, no wavering. Vance pulled her toward him.

A few hours, he thought, squeezing his eyes tight. Just a few hours with no questions, no past. It's not too much to ask.

"There are things I have to tell you, Shane, but not tonight." As the tension drained, he loosened his hold to a caress. "Tonight, I only want to tell you that I love you."

Sensing turmoil and wanting to soothe it, Shane tilted her face back to his. "Tonight it's all I need to know. I love you, Vance. Nothing you tell me will change that." She pressed her lips to his cheek and felt some of the tightness in his body loosen. Part of her wanted to coax him to tell her what caused the storm inside him, but she was conscious of the same need for isolation that Vance had. This was their night. Problems were for the practical, for the daytime. "Come on," she said lightly, "the food's getting cold." The fierce hug she gave him made him laugh. "When I fix a gourmet meal, I expect it to be properly appreciated."

"I do," he assured her, kissing her nose.

"Do what?"

"Appreciate it. And you." He dropped a second kiss on her mouth. "Let's go into the living room."

"Living room?" Her brow creased, then cleared. "Oh, I suppose it would be warmer."

"Exactly what I had in mind," he murmured.

"I tossed a couple of logs onto the fire when I came downstairs."

"You're a clever soul, Shane," Vance said admiringly as he took her arm and steered her from the room.

"Vance, we have to take the food."

"What food?"

Shane laughed and started to turn back, but he propelled her into the sparsely furnished, firelit room. "Vance, the soup'll have to be reheated in a minute."

"It'll be terrific," he told her as he began to unbutton the oversize shirt she wore.

"Vance!" Shane brushed his fingers away. "Be serious."

"I am," he said reasonably, even as he pulled her down on the oval braided rug. "Deadly."

"Well, *I'm* not going to reheat it," she promised huffily while he leaned on an elbow to undo the rest of the buttons.

"No one would blame you," he told her as he parted the shirt. "It'll be fine cold."

She gave a snort. "It'll be dreadful cold."

"Hungry?" he asked lightly, cupping her breast.

Shane looked up at him. He saw the dimples flash. "Yes!" In a quick move, she was lying across his chest, her mouth fixed greedily on his.

The verve and speed of her passion stunned him. He had meant to tease her, to stoke her desires slowly, but she was suddenly and completely in command. Her mouth was avid, demanding, with her small teeth nibbling, her quick tongue arousing him so quickly he would have rolled her over and taken her at once had his limbs not been so strangely weak. Her weight was nothing, yet he couldn't move her when she shifted to do clever, torturous things to his ear. Her hands were busy too, stroking through his hair, skimming over his shoulders and chest to find and exploit small, devastating points of pleasure.

He reached to pull off her shirt, too dazed to realize his

fingers shook, but he fumbled, dragging at it. High on her own power, Shane gave a quick, almost nervous laugh. "Too soon," she whispered into his ear. "Much too soon."

He swore, but the curse ended on a groan when she pressed her lips to his throat. She burned even as he did, but she was driven to heighten his pleasure to the fullest. It spun through her mind until she was giddy that her touch, her kisses were enough to make him weak and vulnerable. Under her roaming mouth, his skin grew hot and damp. He stroked her where he could reach, but there was something dreamlike in the touch, as though he had passed the first feeling of desperation. For all his strength and power, he had surrendered to hers.

The light shifted and jumped with the crackling of the fire. A log broke apart, crumbling in a shower of sparks. The wind picked up, pushing a sluggish puff of smoke back down the chimney so that it struggled halfheartedly into the room to vie with the lingering scent of fried bacon. Neither of them was aware.

Shane heard the thunderous beat of his heart under her ear, the shallow, ragged sound of his breathing. Taking his mouth again, she kissed him deeply, filling herself on him, knowing she drained him. She luxuriated in him, experimenting with angles, allowing her tongue to twine with his. Then she began the journey down his throat.

Once, he murmured her name as though he were dreaming. She grew bolder. With firm, quick kisses, she ranged down his chest to the taut, flat stomach. Vance jolted as though he had been scorched. Shane pressed her lips to the heated skin, wrenching a moan from him, then circled almost lazily with her tongue.

Her excitement was almost unbearable. He was hers, and she was learning his secrets. Her body felt weightless and capable of anything. The gnawing hunger in the pit of her stomach was growing, but the need to learn, to explore was greater. With a kind of greedy wonder, she took her hands and lips over him, reveling in a man's taste—*her* man's taste. The hair on his chest tapered down. Shane followed it.

Slowly, with a light touch, she loosened his jeans and began to draw them over his hips. Curious, Shane moved her lips over his hipbone and down to his thigh.

She heard him call out to her, hoarse, desperate, but she found the corded muscles of his thighs fascinating. So strong, she thought as her heart began to thud painfully. She ran fingers down his leg, aroused by the lean firmness and straining sinews. Testing, she replaced her fingers with her tongue, then her teeth. Vance shifted under her, murmuring something between his short, ragged breaths. His taste was everything male and mysterious. Shane felt she would never get her fill of him.

But he was on the point of madness. Her slender fingers, her curious tongue had him plunging down and rocketing up so that each breath he drew was an agony of effort. His body was alive with pleasure and pain, his blood swimming with passion that was both tantalized and frustrated. He wanted her to go on touching him, driving him mad. He wanted to take her quickly before he lost his mind. Then slowly, her small avid mouth roamed back up over his stomach, so that his skin quivered with fresh dampness. The heat was unbearable and more wonderful than anything he had ever known. Her breasts with their hard, erect points brushed over him, making him long to taste them. She gave him her mouth instead. Lying full length on his, her body was furnace hot and agile.

"Shane, in the name of God," he breathed, groping for her. Then she slid down, taking him inside her with a shuddering sigh of triumph.

His sanity shattered. Not knowing what he did, Vance

seized her shoulders, rolling her over roughly, driving inside her with all the fierce, desperate strength that was pent up in him. Passion hammered through his core. Need was delirium.

She cried out as her hips arched to meet him, but he was far beyond any control. Harder and faster he took her, never feeling the bite of her nails on his flesh, barely hearing her harsh, quick breathing. She dragged him closer when he could get no closer. He drove her, drove himself to a crest that was dangerously high. Even the plummet was a shattering thrill.

She was shuddering beneath him, dazed, weak, powerful. Experimentally, Vance ran a hand over her arm, then linked his fingers around it. His thumb and forefinger met. "You're so small," he murmured. "I didn't mean to be rough."

Shane brushed a hand through his hair. "Were you?"

His sigh ended on a chuckle. "Shane, you make me crazy. I don't usually toss women around."

"I don't think this is a good time to go into that," she said dryly.

Shifting, he supported himself on his elbow so he could look down at her. "Would it be better to tell you that you inflame me into violent seizures of passion?"

"Infinitely."

"It appears to be true," he murmured.

She smiled at him, running her hand down his shoulder to the arm taut with muscle. "Would you rather I didn't?"

"No," he said definitely, then covered her laughing lips with his.

"Actually," she began in a considering tone, "since you do the same to me, it's only fair."

He liked seeing her with the sleepy, just-loved look on her face. Her eyes were soft and heavy, her mouth slightly swollen. With shifting shadows and a red glow, firelight danced over her skin. "I like your logic." Gently, he traced the shape of her face with a fingertip, imagining what it would be like to wake beside her every morning. Shane captured his hand, pressing his palm to her lips.

"I love you," she said softly. "Will you get tired of hearing that?"

"No." He kissed her brow, then her temple. Slipping an arm under her, he drew her close. "No," he said again on a sigh.

Shane snuggled, running a casual hand over his chest. "The fire's getting low," she murmured.

"Mmm."

"We should put some more wood on."

"Mmm-hmm."

"Vance." She tilted her face to look up at him. His eyes were closed. "Don't you dare go to sleep. I'm hungry."

"God, the woman's insatiable." After a long sigh, he cupped her breast. "I might find the energy with the right incentive."

"I want my dinner," she said firmly, but made no move to stop his caressing hand. "*You're* going to reheat the soup."

"Oh." Vance considered that a moment, running a lazy finger over the peak of her breast. "Aren't you afraid I might interfere with that special touch you have?"

"No," she told him flatly. "I have every confidence in you."

"I thought you might," he said as he sat up to tug on his jeans. Leaning over, he planted a quick kiss on her mouth. "*You* can toss some logs in the fire."

But after he had gone to the kitchen, Shane lay dreaming a moment. The hiss of the fire was comforting. She drew the soft flannel of Vance's shirt closer around her, smiling as his scent stayed with her. Could it really be true that he needed her so much? she wondered sleepily. Love, yes, and desire, but she had a deep, innate knowledge that he very simply needed her. Not just for lovemaking, for holding, but to *be* there. Though she was unsure what it was, Shane knew there was something she had—or something she was—that Vance needed. Whatever she brought to him, it was enough to balance his anger, his mistrust. Fleetingly, she wondered again what had caused him to retreat behind cynicism. Disillusioned, he had said. Who or what had disillusioned him? A woman, a friend, an ideal?

Shane watched the sizzling red coals in the fire and wondered. The anger was still there. She had sensed it when he had demanded to know if she would take him just as he was. Patience, she told herself. She had to be patient until he was ready to share his secrets with her. But it was difficult for Shane to love and not try to help. Shaking her head, she sat up to rebutton her shirt. She'd promised him that love was enough for tonight; she had to abide by it. Tomorrow would be soon enough for problems. Expertly, she arranged more wood on the coals before she went to the kitchen.

"About time," Vance said coolly as she walked in. "There's nothing I hate more than having food get cold."

Shane shot him a look. "How inconsiderate of me."

After setting the bowls back on the table, Vance shrugged. "Well, no harm done," he told her in a forgiving tone. His eyes brimmed with amusement as Shane sat. "Coffee?"

"Not yours," she said witheringly. "It's terrible."

"I suppose if someone really cared, they'd see to it that I had decent coffee in the morning."

"You're right." Shane lifted her spoon. "I'll buy you a percolater." Grinning, she began to eat. The soup was hot and tangy, causing her to close her eyes in appreciation. "Good grief, I'm starving!"

"You should know better than to miss meals," Vance commented before applying himself to the meal. He quickly discovered he was famished.

"It was worth it." Shane shot him another grin. "The Sheridan I bought is fabulous." When he only lifted a brow, she chuckled. "Then I had intended to have an early dinner . . . but I was distracted."

Vance reached over to take her hand. Gently, he lifted it to his lips, then bit her knuckle. "Ow!" Shane snatched her hand away as he picked up his sandwich. "I didn't say it wasn't an enjoyable distraction," she added after a moment. "Even if you did make me furious."

"The feeling was mutual," he assured her mildly.

"At least I control my temper," she said primly. She eyed him coolly as he choked over his soup. "I *wanted* to punch you," she explained. "Hard."

"Again the feeling was mutual."

"You're not a gentleman," she accused with her mouth full.

"Good God, no," he agreed. For a moment, he hesitated, wanting to choose his words carefully. "Shane, will you hold off for a little while on that dining room set?"

"Vance," she began, but he took her hand again.

"Don't tell me I shouldn't have interfered. I love you."

Shane stirred her soup, frowning down at it. She didn't want to tell him how pressing her bills were. In the first place, she had every confidence that between her current stock and the small amount of capital she had left, she could straighten out her finances. And more, she simply didn't want to heap her problems on him.

"I know you did what you did because you cared," she began slowly. "I appreciate that, really. But it's important to me to make the shop work." She lifted her eyes now to meet the frown in his. "I didn't fail as a teacher, but I didn't succeed either. I have to make a go of this."

"By selling the one tangible thing you have left of your

grandmother's?" Immediately, he saw he had hit a nerve. He tightened his fingers around hers. "Shane . . ."

"No. It is hard for me. I won't pretend it isn't." Wearily, she let out a long breath. "I'm not basically a practical person, but in this case I have to be. I have no place to keep that set, and it's very valuable. The money it'll bring into the shop will keep me going for quite a while. And more than that . . ." She broke off with a little shake of her head. "If you can understand, it's more difficult for me having it there, knowing it has to be sold, than if it were already done."

"Let me buy it. I could—"

"No!"

"Shane, listen to me."

"*No!*" Pulling her hand from his, she rose to lean against the sink. For a moment she stared hard out the window at the trees splattered with moonlight. "Please, it's very sweet of you, but I couldn't allow it."

Frustrated, Vance rose. Taking her shoulders, he drew Shane back against him. And how, he wondered, was he going to begin to explain? "Shane, you don't understand. I can't bear watching you hurting, watching you work so hard when I could—"

"Please, Vance." Shane turned to him. Though her eyes were dry, they were eloquent. "I'm doing what I have to do, and what I want." She took his hands tightly in hers. "It's not that I don't love you even more for wanting to help. I do."

"Then let me help," he began. "If it's just a matter of the money right now—"

"It wouldn't make any difference if you were a millionaire," she said, giving him a little shake. "I'd still say no."

Not knowing whether to laugh or swear, Vance pulled her against him. "Stubborn little twit, I could make it easier for you. Let me try to explain."

"I don't want anyone, not even you, to make it easier." She

gave him a fierce squeeze. "Please understand. All of my life I've been cute little Shane Abbott, Faye's sweet, slightly odd granddaughter. I need to prove something."

Remembering how frustrating it had been to be known as Miriam Riverton Banning's son, Vance sighed. Yes, he understood. And the understanding made him keep his silence on how simple it would be for him to help. "Well," he said, wanting to hear her laugh, "you are kind of cute."

"Oh, Vance," she moaned.

"And sweet," he added, tilting her face up for a kiss. "And slightly odd."

"That's no way to endear yourself to me," she warned. "I'll wash, you dry."

"Wash what?"

"The dishes."

He pulled her closer, wrapping his arms firmly around her waist. "I don't see any dishes. You have wonderful eyes, just like a cocker spaniel."

"Watch it, Vance," she said threateningly.

"I like your freckles." He placed a light kiss on the bridge of her nose. "I've always thought that Becky Thatcher had freckles."

"You're heading for trouble," she told him, narrowing her eyes.

"And your dimples," he continued blithely. "She probably had dimples too, don't you think?"

Shane bit her lips to hold back a smile. "Shut up, Vance."

"Yes," he continued, beaming down at her, "I'd say that's definitely a cute little face."

"Okay, that does it." Putting a good deal of effort into it, Shane tried to wiggle out of his hold.

"Going somewhere?"

"Home," she told him grandly. "You can do your own dishes."

He sighed. "I guess I have to get tough again."

Anticipating him, Shane began to struggle in earnest. "If you throw me over your shoulder again, you really are fired!"

Hooking an arm behind her knees, Vance swept her up. "How's this?"

She circled his neck. "Better," she said grudgingly. The smile was becoming impossible to control.

"And this?" Softly, he placed his lips on hers, letting the kiss deepen until he heard her sigh.

"Much better," she murmured as he carried her from the room. "Where are we going?"

"Upstairs," he told her. "I want my shirt back."

CHAPTER 10

"Yes, of course you could convert it," Shane agreed, passing her fingertip over the porcelain base of a delicate oil lamp.

"That's just what I thought." Mrs. Trip, Shane's potential customer, nodded her carefully groomed white head. "And my husband's very handy with electrical things too."

Shane managed a smile for Mr. Trip's prowess. It broke her heart to think that the sweet little lamp would be tampered with. "You know," she began, trying another tactic, "an oil lamp is a smart thing to have around in case of power failure. I keep a couple myself."

"Well, yes, dear," Mrs. Trip said placidly, "but I have candles for that. This lamp's going to go right next to my rocker. That's where I do my crocheting."

Though she knew the value of a sale, Shane couldn't stop herself from adding, "If you really want an electric lamp, Mrs. Trip, you could buy a good reproduction much cheaper."

Mrs. Trip sent her a vague smile. "But it wouldn't be a real antique then, would it? Do you have a box I can carry it in?"

"Yes, of course," Shane murmured, seeing it was useless to repeat that converting the lamp would decrease both its value and its charm. Resigned, she wrote out the sales slip, comforting herself with the thought that the profit from the lamp would help pay her own electric bill.

"Oh my, I didn't see this!"

Glancing up, Shane noted that Mrs. Trip was admiring a tea set in cobalt blue. The sun slanting in the windows fell generously on the dark, rich glass. There was a contrast of delicate gold leaf painted around the rim of each cup and the edge of each saucer.

"It's lovely, isn't it," Shane agreed, though she bit the underside of her lip as the lady began to handle the sugar bowl. When she found the discreet price tag, she lifted a brow. "It goes as a complete set," Shane began, knowing the price would seem staggering to someone unacquainted with valuable glass. "It's late nineteenth century and . . ."

"I must have it," Mrs. Trip said decisively, cutting off Shane's explanation. "It's just the thing for my corner cabinet." She sent a surprised Shane a grin. "I'll tell my husband he's just bought me a Christmas present."

"I'll wrap it for you," Shane decided, as pleased as Mrs. Trip with the idea.

"You have a lovely shop," the woman told her as Shane began to box the glass. "I must say, I only stopped in because the sign at the bottom of the hill intrigued me. I wondered what in the world I would find. But it wasn't a big barn of a place with nonsense packed around like a yard sale." She pursed her lips, glancing around again. "You've done very well." Shane laughed at the description and thanked her. "And it's so nice to have the little museum too," Mrs. Trip went on. "A very clever idea, and so tidy. I believe I'll bring my nephew by the next time I'm in the area. Are you married, dear?"

Shane sent her a look of wary amusement. "No, ma'am."

"He's a doctor," Mrs. Trip disclosed. "Internal medicine."

Clearing her throat, Shane sealed the box. "That's very nice."

"A good boy," Mrs. Trip assured her as Shane adjusted the sales ticket to include the tea set. "Dedicated." She dug out her checkbook, pulling her wallet along with it. "I have a picture of him right here."

Politely, Shane examined the snapshot of a young, attractive man with serious eyes. "He's very good-looking," she told his aunt. "You must be proud of him."

"Yes," she said wistfully, tucking the wallet back into her purse. "Such a pity he hasn't found the right girl yet. I'm going to be sure to bring him by." Without a blink for the amount, Mrs. Trip wrote out a check.

It wasn't easy, but Shane maintained her composure until the door shut behind her customer. With a shout of laughter, she dropped into a button-back chair. Though she was uncertain if the nephew should be congratulated or pitied for having such a dedicated aunt, she did know what appealed to her sense of humor. Her next thought was how Vance would try not to grin when she told him of the lady's matchmaking attempts.

He'd lift a brow, Shane thought, and make some dry comment about her charming the old ladies so that they'd dangle their nephews under her nose. She was beginning to know him very well. Most of him, Shane corrected with a considering smile. The rest would come.

She checked her watch, finding herself impatient that two hours remained before he would be with her. She'd promised him dinner—a more elaborate dinner than the soup and sandwiches they had eaten the night before. Even now, the small rib roast was cooking gently in the oven upstairs. She considered closing early, calculating she had just about enough time to whip up some outrageous, elaborate dessert before he arrived. As the thought passed through her head, the door opened again.

Laurie MacAfee stepped in, buttoned to the neck in a long tan coat. "Shane," she said, observing her casual posture in the chair. "Not busy I see."

Though she smiled in greeting, some demon kept her seated. "Not at the moment. How are you, Laurie?"

"Just fine. I took off work early to go to the dentist, so I thought I'd drop by afterward."

Shane waited, half expecting Laurie to comment on her good checkup. "I'm glad you did," she said at length. "Would you like a tour?"

"I'd love to browse," Laurie told her, glancing around. "What sweet things you have."

Shane swallowed a retort and rose. "Thank you," she said with a humility Laurie never noticed. Shane thought again how well suited she was to Cy.

"I must say, the place looks so much different." In her slow, measured step, Laurie began to wander the old summer parlor. Though she hadn't expected to approve, she could find nothing to condemn in Shane's taste. The room was small, but light and airy with its ivory-toned walls, and the gleaming natural wood floor was scattered with hand-hooked rugs. Furniture was set to advantage, with accessories carefully arranged to give the appearance of a tidy, rather comfortable room instead of a store. Loosening the first few buttons of her coat, she roamed to the main showroom, then stood perusing it from the doorway.

"Why, you've hardly changed this at all?" she exclaimed. "Not even the wallpaper."

"No," Shane agreed, unable to keep her eyes from skimming over the dining room set. "I didn't want to. Of course, I had to set more stock in here, and widen the doorways, but I loved the room as it was."

"Well, I'll confess I'm surprised," Laurie commented as she wandered through to what had been the kitchen. "It's so organized, not jumbled up at all. Your bedroom was always a disaster."

"It still is," Shane replied dryly.

Laurie gave what passed for a laugh before continuing into the museum. "Yes, this I might have expected." She gave a quick nod. "You always were a whiz at this sort of thing. I could never understand it."

"Because I wasn't a whiz at anything else?"

"Oh, Shane." Laurie flushed, revealing how close Shane's words had been to her thoughts.

"I'm sorry." Immediately contrite, Shane patted her arm. "I was only teasing you. I'd show you the upstairs, Laurie, but it's not quite finished, and I shouldn't leave the shop in any case. Pat has classes this afternoon."

Mollified, Laurie strolled back into the shop. "I'd heard she was working for you. It was very kind of you to give her the job."

"She's been a big help. I couldn't manage it seven days a week all alone." Shane felt a twinge of impatience as Laurie began to browse again. There wasn't going to be time to whip up anything more than instant chocolate pudding at this rate.

"Oh well, this is very nice." Laurie's voice held the first true ring of admiration as she studied the Sheridan table Shane had bought the day before. "It doesn't look old at all."

That was too much for Shane. She gave a burst of appreciative laughter. "No, I'm sorry," she assured Laurie when she turned to frown at her. "You'd be surprised how many people think antiques should look moldy or dented. It's quite old, really, and it is lovely."

"And expensive," Laurie added, squinting at the price. "Still, it would look rather nice with the chair Cy and I just bought. Oh . . . ." Turning, she gave Shane a quick, guilty look.

"I wonder if you'd heard—that is, I'd been meaning to have a talk with you."

"About Cy?" Shane controlled the smile, noting Laurie was truly uncomfortable. "I know you're seeing quite a lot of each other."

"Yes." Hesitating, Laurie brushed some fictitious lint from her coat. "It's a bit more than that really. You see, we're—actually . . ." She cleared her throat. "Shane, we're planning to be married next June."

"Congratulations," Shane said so simply that Laurie's eyes widened.

"I hope you're not upset." Laurie began to twist the strap of her purse. "I know that you and Cy . . . Well, it was quite a few years ago, but still, you were . . ."

"Very young," Shane said kindly. "I really do wish you the best, Laurie." But a demon of mischief had her adding, "You suit him much better than I ever could."

"I appreciate your saying that, Shane. I was afraid you might . . ." She flushed again. "Well, Cy's such a wonderful man."

She means it, Shane noted with some surprise. She really loves him. Shane felt simultaneous tugs of shame and amusement. "I hope you're happy, Laurie, both of you."

"We will be." Laurie gave her a beaming smile. "And I'm going to buy this table," she added recklessly.

"No," Shane corrected her. "You're going to take the table as an early wedding present."

Comically, Laurie's mouth dropped open. "Oh, I couldn't! It's so expensive."

"Laurie, we've known each other a long time, and Cy was a very important part of my"—she searched for the proper phrase—"growing up years. I'd like to give it to both of you."

"Well, I—thank you." Such uncomplicated generosity baffled her. "Cy will be so pleased."

"You're welcome." Laurie's flustered appreciation made Shane smile. "Can I help you out to the car with it?"

"No, no, I can manage." Laurie lifted the small table, then paused. "Shane, I really hope you have a tremendous success here. I really do." She stood awkwardly at the door a moment. "Goodbye."

"Bye, Laurie."

Shane closed the door with a smile, then immediately put Laurie and Cy out of her mind. After a glance at her watch, she noted that she had barely more than an hour now before Vance would be there. She hurried around to lock up the museum entrance. If she moved fast, she would have time to . . . The sound of an approaching car had her swearing.

Business is business, she reminded herself, and unlocked the door again. If Vance wanted dessert, he'd have to settle for a bag of store-bought cookies. Hearing the sound of footsteps on the porch, she opened the door with a ready smile. It faded instantly, as did her color.

"Anne," she managed in a voice unlike her own.

"Darling!" Anne bent down for a quick brush of cheeks. "What a greeting. Anyone would think you weren't glad to see me."

It took only a few seconds to see that her mother was as lovely as ever. Her pale, heart-shaped face was unlined, her eyes the same deep china blue, her hair a glorious sweeping blond. She wore a casual, expensive blue fox stroller belted at the waist with black leather, and silk slacks unsuitable for an Eastern winter. Her beauty, as always, sent the same surges of love and resentment through her daughter.

"You look lovely, Anne."

"Oh, thank you, though I know I must look a wreck after that dreadful drive from the airport. This place is in the middle of nowhere. Shane, dear, when are you going to do something about your hair?" She cast a critical eye over it before breezing past. "I'll never understand why . . . Oh, my Lord, what *have* you done!"

Stunned, she gazed around the room, taking in the display cases, the shelves, the racks of postcards. With a trill of laughter, she set down her exquisite leather bag. "Don't tell me you've opened a Civil War museum right in the living room. I don't believe it!"

Shane folded her hands in front of her, feeling foolish. "Didn't you see the sign?"

"Sign? No—or perhaps I did but didn't pay any attention." Her eyes slid, sharp and amused around the room. "Shane, what *have* you been up to?"

Determined not to be intimidated, she straightened her shoulders. "I've started a business," she said boldly.

"*You?*" Delighted, Anne laughed again. "But, darling, surely you're joking."

Stabbed by the utter incredulity in Anne's voice, Shane angled her chin. "No."

"Well, for heaven's sake." She gave a pretty chuckle and eyed Shane's dented bugle. "But what happened to your teaching job?"

"I resigned."

"Well, I can hardly blame you for that. It must have been a terrible bore." She brushed away Shane's former career as a matter of indifference. "But why in God's name did you come back here and bury yourself in Hicksville?"

"It's my home."

With a mild *hmm* for the temper in Shane's eyes, Anne spun the rack of postcards. "Everyone to his own taste. Well, what have you done with the rest of the place?" Before Shane could answer, Anne swept through the doorway and into the shop. "Oh, no, don't tell me, an antique shop! Very quaint and tasteful. Shane, how clever of you." Her eye was sharp enough to recognize a few very good pieces. She began to wonder if her daughter wasn't quite the fool she'd always considered her. "Well . . ." Anne unbelted her fur and dropped it carelessly over a chair. "How long has this been going on?"

"Not long." Shane stood rigid, knowing part of herself was drawn, as it always was, to the strange, beautiful woman who was her mother. Knowing too that Anne was deadly.

"And?" Anne prompted.

"And what?"

"Shane, don't be difficult." Masking quick annoyance, Anne gave her daughter a charming smile. She was an actress. Though she had never made the splash she had hoped for, she wrangled a bit part now and again. She felt she knew her trade well enough to handle Shane with a friendly smile. "Naturally I'm concerned, darling. I only want to know how you're doing?"

Uncomfortable with her own manners, Shane unbent. "Well enough, though I haven't been open long. I wasn't happy with teaching. Not bored," she explained, "just not suited for it. I am happy with this."

"Darling, that's wonderful." She crossed her nylon-clad legs and looked around again. It occurred to her that Shane might be useful after all. It had taken brains and determination to set up this kind of establishment. Perhaps it was time she started to take a little more interest in the daughter she had always thought of as a mild annoyance. "It helps to know you're settling your life, especially since mine's such a mess at the moment." Noting the wariness in Shane's eyes, she sent her a sad smile. If memory served her, the girl was very susceptible to an unhappy story. "I divorced Leslie."

"Oh?" Shane only lifted a brow.

Momentarily set back by Shane's coolness, Anne continued. "I can't tell you how mistaken I was in him, how foolish it feels to know I was deceived into thinking he was a kind, charming man." She didn't add that he had failed, again and

again, to get her the kind of parts that would lead to the
fame she craved—or that she'd already begun to cultivate a
certain producer she felt would be more successful. In any
event, Leslie had begun to bore her to distraction. "There's
nothing more devastating than to have failed in love."

You've had practice, Shane thought, but held her tongue.

"These past few months," Anne added on a sigh, "haven't
been easy."

"For any of us," Shane agreed, understanding Anne too
well. "Gran died six months ago. You didn't even bother to
come to the funeral."

Anne had been ready for this. With a tiny sigh, she dropped
her eyes to her soft, pampered hands. "You must know
how badly I felt, Shane. I was finishing a film. I couldn't be
spared."

"You couldn't find the time for a card, a phone call?" Shane
asked. "You never even bothered to answer my letter."

As if on cue, Anne's lovely eyes filled with tears. "Darling, don't be cruel. I couldn't—I just couldn't put the words
down on a piece of paper." She drew a delicate swatch of silk
from her breast pocket. "Even though she was old, somehow
I felt she would just live forever, always be here." Mindful
of her mascara, she dabbed at the tears. "When I got your
letter telling me she was . . . I was so devastated." She lifted
beautifully drenched eyes to Shane's, waiting while a single
tear trickled gently down her cheek. "You of all people must
know how I feel. She raised me." A little sob caught in her
throat. "I still can't believe she's not in the kitchen, fussing
over the stove."

Because the image tore at her own grief, Shane knelt at
her mother's feet. She'd had no family to mourn with her, no
one to help her through the wrenching, aching hours after
the numbness had passed. If she had been unable to share
anything else with her mother throughout her life, perhaps

they could share this. "I know," she managed in a thick voice. "I still miss her terribly."

Anne began to think the little scene had a great deal of possibility. "Shane, please forgive me." Anne gripped her hands, concentrating on adding a tremor to her voice. "I know it was wrong of me not to come, wrong to make excuses. I just wasn't strong enough to face it. Even now, when I thought I could . . ." She trailed off, bringing Shane's hand to her damp cheek.

"I understand. Gran would have understood too."

"She was so good to me always. If I could only see her one more time."

"You mustn't dwell on it." Those very thoughts had haunted Shane's mind a dozen times after the funeral. "I felt the same way, but it's better to remember all the good times. She was so happy here in this house, doing her gardening, her canning."

"She did love the house," Anne murmured, casting a nostalgic eye around the old summer parlor. "And I imagine she'd have been pleased with what you're doing here."

"Do you think so?" Earnestly, Shane looked up into her mother's damp eyes. "I was so sure, but still sometimes . . ." Trailing off, she glanced at the freshly painted walls.

"Of course she would," Anne said briskly. "I suppose she left the house to you?"

"Yes." Shane was looking around the room, remembering how it had been.

"There was a will, then?"

"A will?" Distracted, Shane glanced back at her. "Yes, Gran had a will drawn up years ago. She had Floyd Arnette's son do it after he passed the bar. She was his first client." Shane smiled, thinking how proud Gran had been of the fancy legal terms that "sassy Arnette boy" had come up with.

"And the rest of the estate?" Anne prompted, attempting to curb her impatience.

"There was the house and land of course," Shane answered, still looking back. "Some stocks I sold to pay the taxes and the funeral expenses."

"She left everything to you?"

The tightness in Anne's voice didn't penetrate. "Yes. There was enough cash in her savings to handle most of the repairs on the place, and—"

"You're lying!" Anne shoved at her as she sprung to her feet. Shane grabbed the arm of the chair to keep from toppling; then, too stunned to move, she stayed on the floor. "She wouldn't have cut me off without a penny!" Anne exploded, glaring down at her.

The blue eyes were hard and glittery now, the lovely face white with fury. Once or twice before, Shane had seen her mother in this sort of rage—when her grandmother hadn't given her precisely what she had wanted. Slowly, Shane rose to face her. Anne's tantrums, she knew, had to be handled carefully before they turned violent.

"Gran would never have thought of it as cutting you off, Anne," Shane said with a calm she was far from feeling. "She knew you'd have no interest in the house or land, and there weren't that many extra pennies after taxes."

"What kind of fool do you think I am?" Anne demanded in a harsh, bitter voice. It was her temper more than a lack of talent that had snagged her career. Too often, she had let it rake over directors and other actors. Even now, when patience and the right words would have ensured success, she lashed out. "I know damn well she had money socked away, molding in some bank. I had to pry every penny I got out of her when she was alive. I'm going to have my share."

"She gave you what she could," Shane began.

"What the hell do you know? Do you think I'm so stupid

I don't know this property is worth a tidy sum on the market?" She glanced around once in disgust. "You want the place, keep it. Just give me the cash."

"There isn't any to give. She didn't—"

"Don't hand me that." Anne shoved her aside and strode toward the stairs.

For a moment, Shane stood still, caught in a turmoil of disbelief. How was it possible anyone could be so unfeeling? And how, she asked herself, was it possible for her to be taken in again and again? Well, she would end it this time, once and for all. On her own wave of fury, she raced after her mother.

She found Anne in her bedroom, pulling papers out of her desk. Without hesitation, Shane dashed across the room and slammed the desk lid shut. "Don't you touch my things," she said in a dangerous voice. "Don't you ever touch what belongs to me."

"I want to see the bankbooks, and this so-called will." Anne turned to leave the room, but Shane grabbed her arm in a surprisingly strong grip.

"You'll see nothing in this house. This is mine."

"There *is* money," Anne said furiously, then jerked away. "You're trying to hide it."

"I don't have to hide anything from you." Rage raced through Shane, fed by years of cast-aside love. "If you want to see the will and the status of the estate, get yourself a lawyer. But I own this house, and everything in it. I won't have you going through my papers."

"Well . . ." Anne's blue eyes became slits. "Not such a sweet simpleton after all, are you?"

"You've never known what I am," Shane said evenly. "You've never cared enough to find out. It didn't matter, because I had Gran. I don't need you." Though saying the words was a relief, they didn't bank her fury. "There were times I thought I did, when you came sweeping in, so beautiful I hardly believed you were real. That was closer to the truth than I knew, because there's nothing real about you. You never cared about her. She knew that, and she loved you anyway. But I don't." Her breathing was coming quickly, but she was unaware of how close it was to sobbing. "I can't even work up a hate. I just want to be rid of you."

Turning, she pulled open the desk and drew out her checkbook. Quickly, she wrote out a check for half of the capital she had left. "Here." She held it out to Anne. "Take it; consider it from Gran. You'll never get anything from me."

After snatching the check, Anne scanned the amount with a smirk. "If you think I'll be satisfied with this, you're wrong." Still, she folded the check neatly, then slipped it into her pocket. She knew better than to press her luck, and her own financial status was far from solid. "I'll get that lawyer," she promised, though she had no intention of wasting her money on the slim chance of getting more. "And I'll contest the will. We'll just see how much I get from you, Shane."

"Do what you like," Shane said wearily. "Just stay away from me."

Anne tossed back her hair with a harsh laugh. "Don't think I'll spend any more time in this ridiculous house than I have to. I've always wondered how the hell you could possibly be my daughter."

Shane pressed a hand to her throbbing temple. "So have I," she murmured.

"You'll hear from my lawyer," Anne told her. Turning on her heel, she glided from the room, exiting gracefully.

Shane stood beside the desk until she heard the slam of the front door. Bursting into tears, she crumpled into a chair.

CHAPTER 11

Vance sat in the one decent chair he had in the living room. Impatiently, he checked his watch. He should have been with Shane ten minutes ago. And would have been, he thought with a glance at the front door, if the phone hadn't caught him as he'd been leaving the house. Resigned, he listened to the problems listed by the manager of his Washington branch. Though it wasn't said in words, Vance was aware there was some grumbling in the ranks that the boss had taken a sabbatical.

"And with the union dispute, the construction on the Wolfe project is three weeks behind schedule," the manager continued. "I've been informed that there will be a delay in delivery of the steel on the Rheinstone site—possibly a lengthy one. I'm sorry to bother you with this, Mr. Banning, but as these two projects are of paramount importance to the firm, particularly with the bids going out on the shopping mall Rheinstone is planning, I felt . . ."

"Yes, I understand." Vance cut off what promised to be a detailed explanation. "Put a double shift on the Wolfe project until we're back on schedule."

"A double shift? But—"

"We contracted for completion by April first," Vance said

mildly. "The increase in payroll will be less than the payment
of the penalty clause, or the damage to the firm's reputation."

"Yes, sir."

"And have Liebewitz check into the steel delivery. If it's
not taken care of satisfactorily by Monday, I'll handle it from
here." Picking up a pencil, Vance made a scrawled note on
a pad. "As to the Rheinstone bid, I looked it over myself last
week. I see no problem." He scowled at the floor a moment.
"Set up a meeting with the department heads for the end of
next week. I'll be in. In the meantime," he added slowly,
"send someone . . . Masterson," he decided, "up here to scout
out locations for a new branch."

"New branch? Up there, Mr. Banning?"

The tone had a smile tugging at his mouth. "Have him
concentrate on the Hagerstown area and give me a report. I
want a list of viable locations in two weeks." He checked his
watch again. "Is there anything else?"

"No, sir."

"Good. I'll be in next week." Without waiting for a reply,
Vance broke the connection.

His last orders, he thought ruefully, would put them into
quite a stir. Well, he reflected, Riverton had expanded before;
it was going to expand again. For the first time in years, the
company was going to bring him some personal happiness.
He would be able to settle down with the woman he loved,
where he chose to settle down, and still keep a firm rein
on his business. If he had to justify the new branch to the
board, which he would certainly have to do, he would point
out that Hagerstown was the largest city in Maryland. There
was also its proximity to Pennsylvania to consider . . . and
to West Virginia. Yes, he mused, the expansion could be
justified to the board easily enough. His track record would
go a long way toward swaying them.

Rising, Vance shrugged back into his coat. All he had

left to do now was to talk to Shane. Not for the first time, he speculated on her reaction. She was bound to be a bit stunned when he told her he wasn't precisely the unemployed carpenter she had taken him for. And he hadn't discounted the possibility that she might be angry with him for allowing her to go on believing him to be one. Vance felt a slight tug of apprehension as he stepped out into the cold, clear night.

There was a stiff breeze whipping in from the west. It sent stiff, dead leaves scattering and smelled faintly of snow. With his mind fully occupied, Vance never noticed the old stag fifty yards to his right, scenting the air and watching him.

He'd never set out to deceive her, he reminded himself. When they had first met, it had been none of Shane's business who he was. More, he added thoughtfully, he had simply wanted to shake loose of his company title for a while and be exactly what she had perceived him to be. Had there been any way of knowing she would become more important to him than anything else in his life? Could he have guessed that weeks after he met her he would be planning to ask her to marry him, finding himself ready to toss his company into a frenzy of rush and preparation so that she wouldn't have to give up her home or the life she had chosen for herself?

Once he'd explained the circumstances, Vance told himself as he crunched through frosted leaves, she'd understand. One of Shane's most endearing qualities was understanding. And she loved him. If he was sure of nothing else, he was sure of that. She loved him without questions, without demands. No one had ever given him so much for so little. He intended to spend the rest of his life showing her just what that meant to him.

He imagined that once the surprise of what he had to tell her had worn off, she would laugh. The money, the position he could offer her would mean nothing. She would probably find it funny that the president of Riverton had cut and hammered the trim in her kitchen.

Telling her about Amelia would be more difficult, but it would be done—completely. He wouldn't pass over his first marriage, but would tell her everything and rely on her to understand. He wanted to tell her that she had been responsible for softening his guilt, lightening his bitterness. Loving her was the only genuine emotion he'd felt in years. Tonight, he would open up his past long enough to let the air in; then he would ask Shane to share his future.

Still, Vance felt a twinge of apprehension as he approached her house. He might have ignored it if it hadn't been for the sudden realization that all the windows were dark. It was odd, he thought, unconsciously increasing his pace. She was certainly home, not only because her car was there, but because he knew she was expecting him. But why in God's name, he wondered, wasn't there a single light on? Vance tried to push away a flood of pure anxiety as he reached the back door.

It was unlocked. Though he entered without knocking, he called her name immediately. The house remained dark and silent. Hitting a switch, Vance flooded the rear showroom with light. A quick glance showed him nothing amiss before he continued through the first floor.

"Shane?"

The quiet was beginning to disturb him even more than the darkness. After making a quick circle of the lower floor, he went upstairs. At once he caught the scent of cooking. But the kitchen was empty. Absently turning off the oven, Vance went back into the hall. The thought struck him that she might have lain down after closing the shop and had simply fallen asleep. Amused more than concerned now, he walked quietly into her bedroom. All the amusement fled when he saw her curled up in the chair.

Though the room was in darkness, there was enough moonlight to make her out clearly. She wasn't asleep, but was curled up tightly with her head resting on the arm of the chair. He'd never seen her like that. His first thought was that she looked lost; then he corrected himself. Stricken. There was no innate vivacity in her eyes, and her face glowed palely in the silvery light of the moon. He might have thought her ill, but something told him that even in illness Shane wouldn't lose all of her spark. The thought ran through his mind in only seconds before he crossed the room to her. She made no sign that she saw him, nor was there any response when he spoke her name again. Vance knelt in front of her and took her chilled hands.

"Shane."

For a moment, she stared at him blankly. Then, as though a dam had burst, desperate emotion flooded her eyes. "Vance," she said brokenly, throwing her arms around his neck. "Oh, Vance."

She trembled violently but didn't weep. The tears were dry as stone inside her. With her face pressed into his shoulder, she clung to him, breaking out of the numbed shock that had followed her earlier bout of tears. It was the warmth of him that made her realize how cold she had been. Without questions, with both strength and sweetness he held her to him.

"Vance, I'm so glad you're here. I need you."

The words struck him more forcibly than even her declaration of love. Up to that moment he had been almost uncomfortably aware that his needs far outweighed hers. Now it seemed there was something he could do for her, if it was only to listen.

"What happened, Shane?" Gently he drew her away only far enough to look into her eyes. "Can you tell me?"

She drew a raw breath, making him eloquently aware of the effort it cost her to speak. "My mother."

With his fingertips, he brushed the tousled hair from her cheeks. "Is she ill?"

"No!" It was a quick, furious explosion. The violence of the denial surprised him, but he took her agitated hands in his.

"Tell me what happened."

"She came," Shane managed, then fought to compose herself.

"Your mother came here?" he prompted.

"Near closing time. I didn't expect . . . She didn't come for the funeral or answer my letter." Her hands twisted in his, but Vance kept them in a gentle grip.

"This is the first time you've seen her since your grandmother died?" he asked. His voice was calm and quiet. Shane's eyes were still for a moment as she met his eyes directly.

"I haven't seen Anne in over two years," she said flatly. "Since she married her publicity agent. They're divorced now, so she came back." Shaking her head, Shane drew in a breath. "She almost made me believe she cared. I thought we could talk to each other. Really talk." She squeezed her eyes shut. "It was all an act, all the tears and grief. She sat there begging me to understand, and I believed—" Breaking off again, she shuddered with the effort of continuing. "She didn't come because of Gran or because of me." When she opened her eyes again, Vance saw they were dull with pain. With a savage effort he kept his voice calm.

"Why did she come, Shane?"

Because her breathing was jerky again, she took a moment to answer. "Money," she said flatly. "She thought there would be money. She was furious that Gran left everything to me, and she wouldn't believe me when I told her how little there had been. I should have known!" she said in a quick rage, which then almost immediately subsided. "I did know."

Her shoulders slumped as though she bore an intolerable weight. "I've always known. She's never cared about anyone. I'd hoped there might be some feeling in her for Gran, but . . . When she came running up here to paw through my papers, I said horrible things. I can't be sorry that I did." Tears sprang to her eyes, only to be swiftly controlled. "I gave her half of what's left and made her leave."

"You gave her money?" Vance demanded, incredulous enough to interrupt.

Shane gave him a weary look. "Gran would have given it to her. She's still my mother."

Disgust and rage rose in his throat. It took all the willpower he had not to give in to it. His anger wouldn't help Shane. "She's not your mother, Shane," he said matter-of-factly. When she opened her mouth to speak, he shook his head and continued. "Biologically, yes, but you're too smart to think that means anything. Cats have kittens too, Shane." He tightened his grip when he saw the flicker of pain on her face. "I'm sorry. I don't want to hurt you."

"No. No, you're right." Her hands went limp again as she let out a sigh. "The truth is, I very rarely think of her. Whatever feelings I have for her are mostly because Gran loved her. And yet . . ."

"And yet," he finished, "you make yourself sick with guilt."

"How can it be natural to want her to stay away?" Shane demanded in a rush. "Gran—"

"Your grandmother might have felt differently, might have given her money out of a sense of obligation. But think, who did she leave everything to? Everything important to her?"

"Yes, yes, I know, but . . ."

"When you think of the meaning of 'mother,' Shane, who comes to your mind?"

She stared at him. This time when the tears gathered, they brimmed over. Without a word, she dropped her head back onto his shoulder. "I told her I didn't love her. I meant it, but . . ."

"You don't owe her anything." He drew her closer. "I know something about guilt, Shane, about letting it tear at you. I won't let you do that to yourself."

"I told her to stay away from me." She gave a long, weary sigh. "I don't think she will."

Vance remained silent for a moment. "Is that what you want?"

"Oh God, yes."

He pressed his lips to her temple before lifting her into his arms. "Come on, you're exhausted. Lie down for a while and sleep."

"No, I'm not tired," she lied as her lids fluttered down. "I just have a headache. And dinner's—"

"I turned off the oven," he told her as he carried her to the bed. "We'll eat later." After flipping down the quilt, he bent to lay Shane between the cool sheets. "I'll go get you some aspirin." He slipped off her shoes, but as he started to pull the quilt over her, Shane took his hand.

"Vance, would you just . . . stay with me?"

Touching the back of his hand to her cheek, he smiled at her. "Sure." As soon as he had pulled off his boots, he slipped into bed beside her. "Try to sleep," he murmured, gathering her close. "I'll be right here."

He heard her long, quiet sigh, then felt the feather brush of her lashes against his shoulder as her eyes shut.

How long they lay still, he had no idea. Though the grand-father clock that stood in Shane's sitting room struck the hour once, Vance paid no attention. She wasn't trembling anymore, nor was her skin chilled. Her breathing was slow and even. The fingers that absently soothed at her temple were gentle, but his thoughts were not.

No one, nothing, was ever going to put that look on Shane's

face again. He would see to it. He lay staring at the ceiling as he thought out the best way to deal with Anne Abbott. He'd let the money go, because that's the way Shane wanted it. But he couldn't resign himself to allowing her to deal with a constant emotional drain. Nothing had ever wrenched at him like the sight of her pale, shocked face or pain-filled eyes.

He should have known that anyone with as open a heart as Shane's could be hurt just as deeply as she could be made happy. And how, he wondered, could anyone who had dealt with that kind of pain since childhood be so generous and full of joy? The trial of a careless mother, the embarrassment and hurt of a broken engagement, the loss of the one constant family member she had known—none of it had broken her spirit or her simple kindness.

But tonight she needed an arm around her. It would be his tonight—and whenever she needed him. Unconsciously he drew her closer as if to shield her from anything and everything that could hurt.

"Vance."

He thought she spoke his name in sleep and brushed a light kiss over her hair.

"Vance," Shane said again, so that he looked down to see the glint of her eyes against the darkness. "Make love with me."

It was a quiet, simple request that asked for comfort rather than passion. The love he already thought infinite tripled. So did his concern that he might not be gentle enough. Very softly, cupping the shape of her face in one hand, he touched his lips to hers.

Shane let herself float. She was too physically and emotionally drained to feel stinging desire, but he seemed to know what she asked for. Never had she felt such tenderness from him. His mouth was warm and softer than she had thought possible. Minute after minute, he kissed her—and only kissed her. His fingers stroked soothingly over her face, then moved to the base of her neck as if he knew the dull, throbbing ache that centered there. Lovingly, patiently, he drew the quiet response from her, never asking for more than she could give. She relaxed and let him guide her.

With slow care, he roamed her face with kisses, touching his lips lightly to her closed lids as he shifted the gentle massage to her shoulders. There was a concentrated sweetness in his touch that was more kind than loverlike. When his mouth came back to hers, he used only the softest pressure, taking the kiss deep without fire or fury. With a sigh, she answered it, letting her needs pour out.

Passively, she let him undress her. His hands were deft and slow and undemanding. With a sensitivity neither of them had been aware he possessed, he made no attempt to arouse. Even when they were naked, he did nothing more than kiss her and hold her close. She knew she was taking without giving any in return and, murmuring, reached for him.

"Shh." He kissed her palm before turning her gently onto her stomach. With his fingertips only at first, he stroked and soothed, running them down her back, over her shoulders. She hadn't known love could be so compassionate or unselfish. With a sigh, she closed her eyes again and let her mind empty.

He was drawing out the pain, bringing back the warmth. As she lay quietly, Shane felt herself settle and balance. There was no need to think, and no need to feel anything but Vance's strong, sure hands. All of her trust was his. Knowing this, he took even more care not to abuse it.

The old bed swayed slightly as he bent to kiss the back of her neck. Shane felt the first stir of desire. It was mild and wonderfully easy. Content, she remained still to allow herself the full enjoyment of being treasured. He was treating her like something fragile and precious. She wallowed in the new experience as he ranged soft kisses down her spine. Tension and tears were a world away from the Jenny Lind bed with a sagging mattress and worn linen sheets. The only reality now was Vance's sweet loving and the growing response of her pampered body.

He heard the subtle change in her breathing, the faint quickening, which meant relaxation was becoming desire. Still, he kept his hands easy, not wanting to rush her. The clock in the sitting room struck the hour again with low, ponderous bongs. Creakily the house settled around them with moans and groans. Vance heard little but Shane's deepening breathing.

The moonlight shivered over her skin, seeming to chase after his roaming hands. It only made him see more clearly how slender her back was, how slight the flare of her hips. Pressing his lips to her shoulder, he could smell the familiar lemon tang of her hair mixed with the lavender sachet lingering on the sheets. The room was washed in shadows.

Her cheek rested on the pillow, giving him a clear view of her profile. She might have been sleeping had it not been for the breath hurrying between her lips and the subtle movements her body was beginning to make. Still gentle, he turned her onto her back to press his mouth to hers.

Shane moaned, so lost in him she noticed no sound, no scent that didn't come from him. But his pace never altered, remaining slow and unhurried. He wanted her, God, yes, but felt no fierce, consuming drive. Love, much more than desire, pulled him to her. When he lowered his mouth to her breast, it was with such infinite tenderness that she felt a warmth, half glow, half ache, pour into her. His tongue began to turn the warmth into heat. She rose up but seemed to take the journey on a cloud.

With the same infinite care, he took his lips and hands over her. Her skin hummed at his touch but softly. There was no sweet pain in the passion he brought her, but such pleasure, such comfort, she desired him all the more. Her thoughts became wholly centered on her own body and the quiet delights he had awakened.

Though his lips might stray from hers to taste her neck or her cheek, they returned again and again. Her mindless answer, the husky breath that trembled into his mouth, had the fires roaring inside him. But he banked them. Tonight, she was porcelain. She was as fragile as the moonlight. He wouldn't allow his own passion and needs to overtake him, then find he had treated her roughly. Tonight he would forget her energy and strength and only think of her frailty.

And when he took her, the tenderness made her weep.

CHAPTER 12

In a thick, steady curtain, the snow fell. Already the road surface was slick. Trees had been quickly transformed from dark and stark to glittery. Vance's windshield wipers swept back and forth with the monotonous swish of rubber on glass. The snow brought him neither annoyance nor pleasure. He barely noticed it.

With a few phone calls and casual inquiries, he had learned enough about Anne Abbott—or Anna Cross, as she called herself professionally—to make his anger of the night before intensify. Shane's description had been too kind.

Anne had been through three turbulent marriages. Each had been a contact in the film industry. She had coolly bled each husband for as much as she could get before jumping into the next relationship. Her latest, Leslie Stuart, had proven a bit too clever for her—or his attorney had. She'd come out of her last marriage with nothing more than she had gone into it. And, as she had a penchant for the finer things, she was already badly in debt.

She worked sporadically—bit parts, walk-ons, an occasional commercial. Her talent was nominal, but her face had earned her a few lines in a couple of legitimate films. It might

have earned her more had her temper and self-importance
not interfered. She was tolerated more than liked by Holly-
wood society. Even the tolerance, it seemed, was due more
to her various husbands and intermittent lovers than to herself. Vance's contacts had painted a picture of a beautiful,
scheming woman with a streak of viciousness. He felt he already knew her.

As he drove through the rapidly falling snow, his thoughts
centered on Shane. He'd held her through the night, soothing her when she became restless, listening when she needed
to talk. The shattered expression in her eyes would remain
with him for a long time to come. Even that morning, though
she had tried to be cheerful, there'd been an underlying list-
lessness. And he sensed her unspoken fear that Anne would
come back and put her through another emotional storm.
Vance couldn't change what had happened, but he could take
steps to protect her in the future. That was precisely what he
intended to do.

Vance turned into the lot of the roadside motel and parked.
For a moment, he only sat, watching the snow accumulate on
the windshield. He had considered telling Shane he intended
to see her mother, then had rejected the idea. She'd been so
pale that morning. In any case, he didn't doubt she would
have been against it—even violently opposed to it. She was
a woman who insisted on solving her own problems. Vance
respected that, even admired it, but in this instance he was
going to ignore it.

Stepping out of the car, he walked across the slippery
parking lot to find the office and the information he needed.
Ten minutes later, he knocked on Anne Abbott's door.

The crease of annoyance between her brows altered into
an expression of consideration when she saw Vance. He was
certainly a very pleasant surprise. Vance eyed her coolly, dis-
covering that Shane's description hadn't been exaggerated.

She was lovely. Her face had a delicacy of bone and complex-
ion complemented by the very deep blue eyes and mane of
blond hair. Her body, clad in a clinging pink dressing gown,
was ripe and rounded. Though her glittery fairness was the
direct opposite of Amelia's sultry beauty, Vance knew instantly they were women of the same mold.

"Well, hello." Her voice was languid and sulky, her eyes
amused and appraising. Though he looked for it, Vance found
not the slightest resemblance to her daughter. Overcoming a
wave of disgust, he smiled in return. He had to get in the door.

"Hello, Ms. Cross."

He saw instantly that the use of her stage name had been
a wise move. She flashed him the full-power smile that was
one of her best tools. "Do I know you?" She touched the pink
tip of her tongue to her top lip. "There is something familiar
about you, but I can't believe I'd forget your face."

"Vance Banning, Ms. Cross," he said, keeping his eyes on
hers. "We have some mutual friends, the Hourbacks."

"Oh, Tod and Sheila!" Though she couldn't abide them,
Anne infused her voice with rich pleasure. "Isn't that marvelous! Oh, but you must come in. It's freezing out there. Ap-
palling Eastern weather." She closed the door behind him,
then stood leaning back against it a moment. Perhaps, she
mused, the hometown visit wouldn't be so boring after all.
This was the best-looking thing to knock at her door for quite
some time. And, if he knew the stuffy Hourbacks, chances
were he'd have a few dollars as well. "Well, well, isn't it a
small world," she murmured, gently tucking a strand of delicate blond hair behind her ear. "How are Tod and Sheila? I
haven't seen them for an age."

"Fine when I last spoke to them." Well aware where her
thoughts were traveling, Vance smiled again, this time with
cold amusement. "They mentioned that you were in town. I
couldn't resist looking you up, Ms. Cross."

"Oh, Anna, please," she said graciously. With a sigh, she gave the room a despairing glance. "I must apologize for my accommodations, but I have some business nearby, and . . ." She gave a tiny shrug. "I'm forced to make do. I can offer you a drink, however, if you'll take bourbon."

It was barely eleven, but Vance answered smoothly, "If it's not too much trouble."

"None at all." Anne glided to a small table. She felt particularly grateful that she had packed the silk dressing gown and hadn't yet drummed up the energy to change. It was, she knew, both becoming and alluring. A quick glance in the mirror as she poured assured her she looked perfect. Thank God she'd just finished putting on her makeup. "But tell me, Vance," she continued, "what in the world are you doing in this dull little place? You're not a hometown boy, are you?"

"Business," he said simply, nodding his thanks as she handed him a neat bourbon.

Anne's eyes narrowed a moment, then widened. "Oh, of course. How could I be so foolish!" She beamed at him as the wheels began to spin in her head. "I've heard Tod speak of you. Riverton Construction, right?"

"Right."

"My, my, I am impressed." Her tongue ran lightly over her teeth as she considered. "It's about the biggest in the country."

"So I'm told," he answered mildly, watching her eye him over the rim of her glass. Without much interest, he wondered how much bait she would toss out before she tried to reel him in. If it hadn't been for Shane, he might have enjoyed letting her make a fool of herself.

With her carefully languid grace, Anne sat on the edge of the bed. As she sipped again, she wondered how soon he would try to sleep with her and how much resistance she should feign before she obliged him. "Well, Vance, what can I do for you?"

Vance swirled the bourbon without drinking. He sent her a cool, direct stare. "Leave Shane alone."

The change in her expression might have been comical under any other circumstances. She forgot herself long enough to gape at him. "What are you talking about?"

"Shane," he repeated. "Your daughter."

"I know who Shane is," Anne said sharply. "What has she to do with you?"

"I'm going to marry her."

Shock covered her face, then dissolved with her burst of laughter. "Little Shane? Oh, that's too funny. Don't tell me my cute little daughter caught herself a live one! I've underestimated her." Tossing her head, she sent Vance a shrewd glance. "Or I overestimated you."

Though his fingers tightened on the glass, he controlled his temper. When he spoke, his voice was dangerously mild. "Be careful, Anne."

The look in his eye checked her laughter. "Well," she continued with an unconcerned shrug, "so you want to marry Shane. What's that to me?"

"Not a damn thing."

Masking both apprehension and irritation, Anne rose gracefully. "I suppose I should go congratulate my little girl on her luck."

Vance took her arm. Though he applied no pressure, the meaning was very clear. "You'll do nothing of the kind. What you're going to do is pack your bags and get out."

Enraged, Anne jerked away from him. "Who the hell do you think you are? You can't order me to leave."

"Advise," Vance corrected. "You'd be wise to take the suggestion."

"I don't like the tone of your suggestion," she retorted. "I intend to see my daughter—"

"Why?" Vance stopped her cold without raising his voice. "You won't get another dime, I promise you."

"I haven't any idea what you're talking about," Anne claimed with frigid dignity. "I don't know what nonsense Shane's been telling you, but—"

"You'd be wise to think carefully before you say any more," Vance warned quietly. "I saw Shane shortly after you left her last night. She had to tell me very little before I got the picture." He gave her a long, hard look. "I know you, Anne, every bit as well as you know yourself. There'll be no more money," he continued when Anne fell silent. "You'd be smarter to cut your losses and go back to California. It would be a simple matter to stop payment on the check she's already given you."

That annoyed her. Anne cursed herself for not getting up early and cashing the check before Shane thought better of it. "I have every intention of seeing my daughter." She gave him a glittering smile. "And when I do, I'll have a few words to say to her about her choice of lovers."

His eyes neither heated nor chilled, but became faintly bored. Nothing could have infuriated her more. "You won't see Shane again," he corrected.

Under the silk, her lovely bust heaved. "You can't keep me from seeing my own daughter."

"I can," Vance countered, "and I will. If you contact her, if you try to wheedle another dollar out of her or hurt her in any way, I'll deal with you myself."

Anne felt the first prickle of physical fear. Warily, she stepped back from him. "You wouldn't dare touch me."

Vance gave a mirthless laugh. "Don't be too sure. I don't think it'll come to that though." Casually, he set down the glass of liquor. "I have a number of contacts in the movie industry, Anne. Old friends, business associates, clients. A few words in the right ears, and what little career you have is out the window."

"How dare you threaten me," she began, both furious and afraid.

"Not a threat," he assured her. "A promise. Hurt Shane again, and you'll pay for it. You're getting the best of the deal, Anne," he added. "She doesn't have anything you want."

Smoldering, she took a step toward him. "I have a right to my share. Whatever my grandmother had should be split fifty-fifty between Shane and me."

He lifted a brow in speculation. "Fifty-fifty," he said thoughtfully. "You must be desperate if you're willing to settle for that." Without pity, he shrugged off her problems. "I won't waste my time arguing legalities with you, much less morals or ethics. Just accept that what Shane gave you yesterday is all you'll ever get." With this he turned toward the door. In a last-ditch effort, Anne sank down on the bed and began to weep.

"Oh, Vance, you can't be so cruel." She lifted an already tear-drenched face to his. "You can't mean to keep me from seeing my own daughter, my only child."

He studied the beautiful, tragic face, then gave a slight nod of approval. "Very good," he commented. "You're a better actress than they give you credit for." As he pulled the door to behind him, he heard the sound of smashing glass on the wood.

Springing up, Anne grabbed the second glass, then hurled it as well. No one, *no one*, she determined, was going to threaten her. Or mock her, she fumed, remembering the cool amusement in his eyes. She'd see he paid for it. Sitting back on the bed, she clenched her fists until she could bring her temper to order. She had to think. There had to be a way to get to Vance Banning. Riverton Construction, she reflected, closing her eyes as she concentrated. Had there been any scandal connected with the firm? Frustrated, she hurled her pillow across the room. She could think of nothing. What did she know about a stupid firm that built shopping centers and hospitals? It was all so boring, she thought furiously.

Grabbing the second pillow, she started to toss it as well when a sudden glimmer of memory arrested her. Scandal, she repeated. But not about the firm. There had been something . . . something a few years back. Just a few whispers at a party or two. *Damn!* she swore silently when her recollection took her no further. Sheila Hourback, Anne thought, tightening her lips. Maybe the stuffy old bird could be useful. Scrambling over the unmade bed, Anne reached for the phone.

* * *

Shane was busy detailing a skirmish of the Battle of Antietam for three eager boys when Vance walked in. She smiled at him, and he heard enthusiasm in her voice as she spoke, but she was still pale. That alone brushed away any doubts that he had done the right thing. She'd bounce back, he told himself as he wandered into the antique shop, because it was her nature to do so. But even someone as intrinsically strong as Shane could take only so much. Spotting Pat dusting glassware, he went over to her.

"Hi, Vance." She sent him a quick, friendly grin. "How're you doing?"

"I'm fine." He cast a look over his shoulder to be certain Shane was still occupied. "Listen, Pat, I wanted to talk to you about that dining room set."

"Oh yeah. There was some mix-up about that. I still haven't gotten it straight. Shane said—"

"I'm going to buy it."

"*You?*" Her initial surprise turned into embarrassment. Vance grinned at her, however, and her cheeks cooled.

"For Shane," he explained. "For Christmas."

"Oh, that's so sweet!" The romance of it appealed to her immediately. "It was her grandmother's, you know. She just loves it."

"I know, and she's determined to sell it." Idly, he picked up a china demitasse cup. "I'm just as determined to buy it for her. She won't let me." He gave Pat a conspirator's wink. "But she can hardly turn down a Christmas present, can she?"

"No." Appreciating his cleverness, Pat beamed at him. So the rumors were true, she thought, pleased and interested. There was something going on between them. "She sure couldn't. It'll mean so much to her, Vance. It just about kills her to have to sell some of these things, but that's the hardest. It's . . . ah, it's awfully expensive though."

"That's all right. I'm going to give you a check for it today." It occurred to him that it would soon be all over town that he had a great deal of money to spend. He would have to talk to Shane very soon. "Put a sold sign on it." He glanced back again, seeing Shane's three visitors were preparing to leave. "Just don't say anything to her unless she asks."

"I won't," Pat promised, pleased to be in on the surprise. "And if she does, I'll just say the person who bought it wants it held until Christmas."

"Clever girl," he complimented. "Thanks."

"Vance." She lowered her voice to a whisper. "She looks kind of down today. Maybe you could take her out for a while and cheer her up. Oh, Shane," she continued quickly in a normal tone, "how did you manage to keep those little monsters quiet for twenty minutes? Those are Clint Drummond's boys," she explained to Vance with a shudder. "I nearly ran out the back door when they came in."

"They were thrilled that school was called off because of

the snow." Instinctively, Shane reached for Vance's hand as she came in. "What they wanted was to work out the fine details of a few engagements so they could have their own Battle of Antietam with snowballs."

"Get your coat," Vance told her, planting a kiss on her brow.

"What?"

"And a hat. It's cold outside."

Laughing, Shane gave his hand a squeeze. "I know it's cold outside, fool. There's already six inches of snow."

"Then we'd better get started." He gave her a friendly swat on the seat. "You'll need boots too, I suppose. Just don't take all day."

"Vance, it's the middle of the day. I can't leave."

"It's business," he told her gravely. "You have to get your Christmas tree."

"Christmas tree?" With a chuckle, she picked up the duster Pat had set down. "It's too early in the season."

"Early?" Vance sent Pat a grin. "You've got just over two weeks until Christmas, and no tree. Most self-respecting stores are decked out by Thanksgiving."

"Well, I know, but—"

"But nothing," he interrupted, taking the duster from her and handing it back to Pat. "Where's your holiday spirit? Not to mention your sales strategy. According to the most recent poll, people spend an additional twelve and a half percent in a store decorated for the holidays."

Shane gave him a narrow glance. "What poll?"

"The Retail Sale and Seasonal Atmosphere Survey," he said glibly.

The first genuine laugh in nearly twenty-four hours burst from her. "That's a terrible lie."

"Certainly not," he disagreed. "It's a very good one. Now go get your coat."

"But, Vance—"

"Oh, don't be silly, Shane," Pat interrupted, giving her a push toward the stairs. "I can handle the shop. We're not likely to have customers pouring in with all this snow. Besides," she added, shrewd enough to know her employer, "I'd really love a tree. I'll make a place for it right in front of this window." Without waiting for a reply, Pat began to rearrange furniture.

"Gloves too," Vance added as Shane hesitated.

"All right," she said, surrendering. "I'll be back in a minute."

In little more than ten, she was sitting beside Vance in the cab of his small pickup. "Oh, it's beautiful out here!" she exclaimed, trying to look everywhere at once. "I love the first snow. Look, there're the Drummond boys."

Vance glanced in the direction she indicated and saw three boys pelting each other violently with snow.

"The battle's under way," he murmured.

"General Burnside's having his problems," Shane observed, then turned back to Vance. "By the way, what did you and Pat have your heads together about when I went upstairs to get my things?"

Vance lifted a brow. "Oh," he said complacently, "I was trying to make a date with her. She's cute."

"Really?" Shane drew out the word as she eyed him. "It would be a shame for her to be fired this close to Christmas."

"I was only trying to develop good employee relations," he explained, pulling up at a stop sign. Taking her by surprise, he pulled her into his arms and kissed her thoroughly. "I love that little choking sound you make when you try not to laugh. Do it again."

Breathless, she pulled away from him. "Firing a trusted employee is no laughing matter," she told him primly, and adjusted her ski hat. "Turn right here." Instead of obeying, he kissed her again. The rude blast of a horn had her struggling out of his arms a second time. "Now you've done it." She ruined the severity of the lecture with a smothered chuckle. "The sheriff's going to arrest you for obstructing traffic."

"One disgruntled man in a Buick isn't traffic," Vance disagreed as he made a right turn. "Do you know where you're going?"

"Certainly. There's a place a few miles down where you can dig your own tree."

"Dig?" Vance repeated, shooting her a look. Shane met it placidly.

"Dig," she repeated. "According to the latest conservation poll—"

"Dig," he agreed, cutting her off.

Laughing, Shane leaned over to kiss his shoulder. "I love you, Vance."

By the time they arrived at the tree farm, the snow had slowed to a gentle mist. Shane dragged him from tree to tree, examining each one minutely before rejecting it. Though he knew the color in her face was a result of the cold, the spark was back. Even if he sensed some of the energy was a product of nerves, he was satisfied that she was bouncing back. The simple pleasure of choosing a Christmas tree was enough to put the laughter back in her eyes.

"This one!" Shane exclaimed, stopping in front of a short-needle pine. "It's exactly right."

"It doesn't look much different from the other five hundred trees we've looked at," Vance grumbled, slicing the point of his shovel into the snow.

"That's because you don't have a connoisseur's eye," she said condescendingly. He scooped up a handful of snow and rubbed it into her face. "Be that as it may," Shane continued with remarkable aplomb, "this is the one. Dig," she instructed, and stepping back, folded her arms.

"Yes, ma'am," he said meekly, bending to the task. "You know," he said a few moments later, "it suddenly occurs to me that you're going to expect me to dig a hole to put this thing in after Christmas."

Shane sent him a guileless smile. "What a good idea. I know just the place too. You'll probably need a pick though. There are an awful lot of rocks." Ignoring Vance's rude rejoinder, she waved over an attendant. With the roots carefully wrapped in burlap and the tree itself paid for—by Shane over Vance's objection—they headed home.

"Damn it, Shane," he said in exasperation. "I wanted to buy the tree for you." The truck rumbled over the narrow wooden bridge.

"The tree's for the shop," she pointed out logically as they pulled in front of the house. "So the shop bought the tree. Just as it buys the stock and pays the electric bill." Noting that he was annoyed, Shane walked around the truck to kiss him. "You're sweet, Vance, and I do appreciate it. Buy me something else."

He gave her a long, considering look. "What?"

"Oh, I don't know. I've always had a fancy for something frivolous and extravagant . . . like chinchilla earmuffs."

With difficulty, he maintained his gravity. "It would serve you right if I did buy you some. Then you'd have to wear them."

She rose on her toes, inviting another kiss. As he bent down, Shane slipped the handful of snow she'd been holding down his back. When he swore pungently, she made a dash for safety. Shane fully expected the snowball that bashed into the back of her head, but she didn't expect to be agilely tackled so that she landed facedown in the snow.

"Oh! You really aren't a gentleman," she muttered, hampered by a mouthful of snow. Vance sat back, roaring with laughter while she struggled to sit up, wiping at her face.

"Snow looks even better on you than mud," he told her.

Shane lunged at him, catching him off-balance so that he toppled onto his back. She landed with a soft thud on his chest. Before she could deposit the snow she held in his face, he rolled her over and pinned her. Resigned, she closed her eyes and waited. Instead of the cold shock of snow, she felt his lips crush down on hers. In immediate response, she pulled him closer, answering hungrily.

"Give?" he demanded.

"No," she said firmly, and dragged him back again.

The urgency of her response made him forget they were lying in the snow in the middle of the afternoon. He no longer felt the wet flakes that drifted down the back of his neck, though he could taste others on her skin. He fretted against the bulky clothes that kept the shape of her from him, against the gloves that prevented him from feeling the softness of her skin. But he could taste, and he did so greedily.

"God, I want you," he murmured, savaging her small, avid mouth again and again. "Right here, right now." Lifting his head, he looked down on her, but whatever he would have said was cut off by the sound of an approaching car. "If I'd had any sense I'd have taken you to my house," he mumbled, then helped her to her feet.

Hugging him, she whispered in his ear, "I close in two hours."

While Shane dealt with a straggle of customers who touched everything and bought nothing, Vance made himself useful by setting up the tree. Pat's lighthearted chatter helped cool the blood Shane had so quickly heated. Following Shane's instructions, he found the boxes of ornaments in the dusty attic.

Dusk was falling before they were alone again. Because she was still looking pale, Vance bullied her into a quick meal before they began to sort through the ornaments. They made do with cold meat from the rib roast neither of them had touched the night before.

But as well as alleviating her hunger, the meal reminded her forcibly of her mother's visit. She struggled to push away the depression, or at least to conceal it. Her chatter was bright and mindless and entirely too strained.

Vance caught her hand, stopping her in midsentence. "Not with me, Shane," he said quietly.

Not bothering to pretend she didn't understand, Shane squeezed his hand. "I'm not dwelling on it, Vance. It just sneaks up on me sometimes."

"And when it does, I'm here. Lean on me, Shane, when you need to." He lifted her hand to his lips. "God knows, I'll lean on you."

"Now," she said shakily. "Just hold me a minute."

He drew her into his arms, pressing her head to his heart. "As long as you want."

She sighed, relaxing again. "I hate being a fool," she murmured. "I suppose I hate that worse than anything."

"You're not being a fool," he said, then drew her away as he came to a decision. "Shane, I went to see your mother this morning."

"What?" The word came out in a whisper.

"You can be angry if you like, but I won't stand by and watch you be hurt again. I made it very clear that if she bothered you again, she'd have me to deal with."

Shaken, she turned away from him. "You shouldn't—"

"Don't tell me what I shouldn't have done," he interrupted angrily. "I love you, damn it. You can't expect me to do nothing while she puts you through the wringer."

"I can deal with it, Vance."

"No." Taking her shoulders, he turned her around. "With

an amazing number of things, yes, but not with this. She turns you inside out." His grip lightened to a caress. "Shane, if it had been me hurting, what would you have done?"

She opened her mouth to speak, but only released a pent-up breath. Taking his face in her hands, she pulled it down to hers. "I hope I'd have done the same thing. Thank you," she said, kissing him gently. "I don't want to know what was said," she added with more firmness. "No more problems tonight, Vance."

He shook his head, acknowledging another delay in making everything known to her. "All right, no more problems."

"We'll trim the tree," she stated decisively. "Then you're going to make love to me under it."

He grinned. "I suppose I could do that." He allowed her to pull him down the stairs. "What if I make love to you under it, then we trim it?"

"There's nothing festive in that," she said gravely as she began unpacking ornaments.

"Wanna bet?"

She laughed, but shook her head. "Absolutely not. There's an order to these things, you know. Lights first," she announced, pulling out a neatly coiled string.

It took well over an hour as Shane shared her memories about nearly every ornament she unpacked. As she took out a red felt star, she recalled the year she had made it for her grandmother. It brought both a sting and a warmth. She'd been dreading Christmas. It hadn't seemed possible to celebrate the holiday in that house without the woman who had always shared it with her. Gran would have reminded her that there was a cycle, but Shane knew she would have found a tree and tinsel unbearable had she been alone.

She watched Vance carefully arranging a garland. How Gran would have loved him, she thought with a smile. And he her. Somehow she found it didn't matter that the two people she loved most in the world had never met. She knew both of them, and the link was formed. Shane was ready to give herself to him completely.

If he doesn't ask me to marry him soon, she mused, I'll just have to ask him. When he glanced over, she sent him a saucy smile.

"What are you thinking?" he demanded.

"Oh, nothing," she said innocently, stepping back to view the results. "It's perfect, just as I knew it would be." She gave a satisfied nod before taking out the old silver star that would adorn the top.

Vance accepted it from her, then eyed the top branch. "I'm not going to be able to get this on there without knocking half of everything else off. We need a ladder."

"Oh no, that's okay. Let me up on your shoulders."

"There's a stepladder upstairs," he began.

"Oh, don't be so fussy." Shane jumped nimbly onto his back, hooking her legs around his waist for balance. "I'll be able to reach it without any trouble," she assured him, then began scooting up to his shoulders. Vance felt every line of her body as if he'd run his hands over it. "There," she said, settled. "Hand it to me, and I'll stick it on."

He obliged, then gripped her knees as she leaned forward. "Damn it, Shane, not so far; you're going to fall into the tree."

"Don't be silly," she said lightly as she secured the star. "I have terrific balance. There!" Putting her hands on her hips, she surveyed the results. "Step back a bit so I can see the whole thing." When he had, Shane gave a long sigh, then kissed the top of his head. "It's beautiful, isn't it? Just smell the pine." Carelessly, she linked her ankles against his chest.

"It'll look better with the overhead lights off." Still carrying her, he moved to flick the wall switch. In the dark, the colored lights on the tree seemed to jump into life. They shimmered against garland and tinsel, glowed warmly against pine.

"Oh yes," Shane breathed. "Just perfect."

"Not quite yet," Vance disagreed.

With a deft move, he pulled her around into his arms as she slid down from his shoulders. "This," he told her as he laid her on the rug, "is perfect."

The lights danced on her face as she smiled up at him. "It certainly is."

His hands weren't patient tonight, but neither were hers. They undressed each other quickly, laughing and swearing a bit at buttons or snaps. But when they were naked, the urgency only intensified. Their hands sought to touch, their mouths hurried to taste—everywhere. She marveled again at his taut, corded muscles. He filled himself again on the flavor and fragrance of her skin. They paid no more notice to the warmth of the lights or the tang of pine than they had to the chill of the snow. They were alone. They were together.

CHAPTER 13

It wasn't easy for Shane to keep her mind on her work the next day. Though she made several sales, among them the tilt-top table she had so painstakingly refinished, she was distracted throughout the morning. Distracted enough that she never noticed the discreet sold sign Pat had attached to the Hepplewhite set in lieu of a price tag. She could think of little else but Vance. Once or twice during the morning, she caught herself glancing at the Christmas tree and remembering. In all of her dreams, in all of her wishes, she had never imagined it could be this way. Each time they made love it was different, a new adventure. Yet somehow it was as though they had been together for years.

Every time she touched him it was like making a fresh discovery, and still Shane felt she had known him for a lifetime rather than a matter of three short months. When he kissed her, it was just as thrilling and novel as the first time. The recognition she had felt the instant she had seen him had deepened into something much more abiding. Faith.

Without doubt, she was certain that the excitement and the learning would go on time after time over the comfortable core of honest love. There was no need to romanticize what was real. She had only to look at him to know what they shared was special and enduring. With another glance at the tree, she realized she'd never been happier in her life.

"Miss!" The customer considering the newly caned ladder-back chair called impatiently for Shane's attention.

"Yes, ma'am, I'm sorry." If the smile Shane gave her was a bit dreamy, the woman didn't seem to notice. "It's a lovely piece, isn't it? The seat's just been redone." Calling herself to order, Shane turned the chair over to show off the workmanship.

"Yes, I'm interested." The woman poked at the caning a moment. "But the price . . ."

Recognizing the tone, Shane settled down to bargain.

It was just past noon when things began to quiet down. The morning's profits weren't extraordinary, but solid enough to help Shane stop worrying over the large chunk of her capital that she had given to her mother. The wolf wasn't at the door yet, she told herself optimistically. And with luck—and the Christmas rush—she could hold him off for quite some time. Two or three good sales would keep her books from dipping too deeply into the red. Professionally, she wanted little more at the moment than to calmly tread water. Personally, she knew precisely what she wanted, and she had every intention of seeing to it quickly.

She was going to marry Vance, and it was time she told him so. If he was too proud to ask her because he didn't yet have a steady job, she would simply have to persuade him to see things differently. Shane had made up her mind to take a firm stand that very day. There was an excitement bubbling inside her, a sense of purpose. Today, she thought, almost giddy from it, nothing could hurt her. She was going to propose to the man she loved. And she wasn't going to take no for an answer.

"Pat, can you handle things if I go out for an hour?"

"Sure, it's slow now anyway." Pat glanced up from the table she was polishing. "Are you going to another auction?"

"No," Shane told her blithely. "I'm going on a picnic."

Leaving Pat staring behind her, Shane raced upstairs.

It took her less than ten minutes to fill the wicker basket. There was a cold bottle of Chablis inside it, which she had splurged on madly. It might be a bit rich for the peanut butter sandwiches, but Shane's mind wasn't on proprieties. As she raced out the back door, she was already picturing spreading the checked tablecloth in front of Vance's living room fire.

Wet, slushy snow sloshed over her boots as she stepped off the porch onto the lawn. The perfect day for a picnic, she decided, letting the hamper swing. The air was absolutely still. Melted snow dripped from the roof with a musical patter. The fast water in the creek broke through thin sheets of ice with an excited hissing and bubbling. Shane paused to listen a moment, enjoying the mixture of sounds. The feeling of euphoria built. She found it the most exquisite of days, with the sky coldly blue, the snow-laced mountains rising and the naked trees slick with wet.

Then the low purr of an engine intruded. She looked back, then stopped as she recognized Anne pulling up in the drive. All of her joy in the afternoon slipped quietly away. She hardly noticed the fingers of tension that crept up to the base of her neck.

With her faultless grace, Anne picked her way over the melting snow in calfskin boots. She wore a trim fox-fur hat now to match her coat, and a small, smug smile. There were ruby studs, or clever imitations, glinting at her ears. Though her daughter stood rigid as a stone, she glided up to greet her with the customary brush of cheeks. Without speaking, Shane set the hamper down on the bottom step of the porch.

"Darling, I had to drop by before I left." Anne beamed at her with a cold gleam in her eye.

"Going back to California?" Shane asked flatly.

"Yes, of course, I have the most marvelous script. Of course, I'll probably be weeks on location, but . . ." She gave a gay shrug. "But that's not why I dropped by."

Shane studied her, marveling. It was as though the ugly scene between them had never taken place. She has no feelings, Shane realized abruptly. It meant less than nothing to her. "Why did you come by, Anne?"

"Why, to congratulate you, of course!"

"Congratulate me?" Shane lifted a brow. It was easier somehow knowing that the woman in front of her was simply a stranger. A few shared genes didn't make a bond. It was love that did that, or affection. Or at the very least, respect.

"I admit I didn't think you had it in you, Shane, but I'm pleasantly surprised."

Shane then surprised both of them by giving an impatient sigh, "Will you get to the point, Anne? I was on my way out."

"Oh, now, don't be cross," she said placatingly. "I'm really thrilled for you, catching yourself a man like that."

Shane's eyes chilled. "I beg your pardon?"

"Vance Banning, darling." She gave a slow, appreciative smile. "What a catch!"

"Strange, I never thought about it quite that way." Bending, Shane prepared to pick up the hamper again.

"The president of Riverton Construction isn't just a mild triumph, sweetheart; it's a downright *coup*."

Shane's fingers froze on the handle. Straightening, she looked Anne dead in the eye. "What are you talking about?"

"Only your fantastic luck, Shane. After all, the man's *rolling* in it. I imagine you'll be able to turn this little shop of yours into an antique palace if you want a hobby." She gave a quick, brittle laugh. "Leave it to cute little Shane to land herself a millionaire the first time around. If I had a bit more time, darling, I'd insist on hearing the details of how you managed it."

"I don't know what you're talking about." Cold panic was beginning to rush through her. She wanted to turn and run away, but her legs were stiff and unyielding.

"God knows why he decided to dump himself in this town," Anne went on mildly. "But it's your good fortune he did, and right next door too. I suppose he means to keep it for a little hideaway once the two of you move to D.C." *A fabulous house,* she thought on a flash of envy. *Servants, parties.* Carefully, she kept her tone gay. "I can't tell you how thrilled I was to learn you'd hooked up with the man who owns virtually the biggest construction firm in the country."

"Riverton," Shane repeated numbly.

"Very prestigious, darling Shane. It does give me cause to wonder how you'll fit in, but . . ." She shrugged this off and aimed her coup de grâce. "It's a shame about that nasty scandal though." Shane merely shook her head and stared at Anne blankly. "His first wife, you know. A terrible tangle."

"Wife?" Shane repeated faintly. She felt the nausea rising in her stomach. "Vance's wife?"

"Oh, Shane, don't tell me he didn't mention it!" It was exactly what she'd hoped for. Anne shook her head and sighed. "That's disgraceful of him, really. Isn't it just like a man to expect some wide-eyed girl to take everything on face value." She clucked her tongue in disapproval, thinking with inner appreciation that Vance Banning was going to take his knocks on this one. She didn't think of Shane at all.

"Well, the very least he might have done was tell you he was married before," she continued primly. "Even if he didn't go into the nasty business."

"I don't . . ." Shane managed to swallow the sickness and continue. "I don't understand."

"A spicy little scandal," Anne told her. "His wife was a

raving beauty, you know. Perhaps too much so." Anne paused delicately. "One of her lovers put a bullet in her heart. At least that's what the Bannings would have everyone believe." The shock in Shane's eyes gave Anne another surge of gratification. Oh yes, she thought grimly, Vance Banning was going to get back some of his own now. "Hushed it up rather quickly too," she added, then brushed the matter away with the back of an elegantly gloved hand. "An odd business. Well, I must run, don't want to miss my plane. *Ciao*, darling, and don't let that handsome gold mine slip away from you. There are plenty of women just dying to catch him." Pausing, she touched Shane's cap of curls with a finger. "For God's sake, Shane, find a decent hairdresser. I suppose he thinks you're . . . refreshing. Get the ring on your finger before he gets bored." She brushed Shane's cold cheek with hers, then dashed off, satisfied she'd paid Vance back for his threats.

Shane stood perfectly still, staring after her. But she didn't see her. She saw nothing. Trapped in the ice of shock, the pain was dormant. That would have surprised Anne had she given it any thought. As a woman who knew nothing of emotional pain, she would assume Shane would feel only fury. But the fury was surrounded by pain, and the pain lay waiting to spring out.

The sun bounced glaringly off the melting snow. A breeze, chill and sharp, whipped through her carelessly unbuttoned coat. In a flash of scarlet, a cardinal swooped over the ground to roost comfortably on a low branch. Shane stood absolutely still, noticing nothing. Sluggishly, her mind began to work.

It wasn't true, she told herself. Anne had made it up for some unexplainable purpose of her own. *President of Riverton?* No, he said he was a carpenter. He *was*, she thought desperately. She'd seen his work herself . . . He'd . . . he'd worked for her. Taken the job she had offered. Why would he—how could he—if he was everything Anne had said? *His first wife.*

Shane felt the first stab of pain. No, it couldn't be, he would have told her. Vance loved her. He wouldn't lie or pretend. He wouldn't make a fool of her by letting her think he was out of work when he was the head of one of the biggest construction firms in the country. He wouldn't have said he loved her without telling her who he really was. *His first wife.* Shane heard a soft, despairing moan without realizing it was hers.

When she saw him coming down the path, she stared blankly. As she watched him, her whirling thoughts came to a sudden halt. She knew then she'd been a fool.

Spotting her, Vance smiled in greeting and increased his pace. He was still several yards away when he recognized the expression on her face. It was the same stricken look he'd seen in the moonlight only a few nights before.

"Shane?" He came to her quickly, reaching for her. Shane stepped back.

"Liar," she said in a broken whisper. "All lies." Her eyes both accused and pleaded. "Everything you said."

"Shane—"

"No, don't!" The panic in her voice was enough to halt the hand he held out to her. He knew that somehow she had learned everything before he could tell her himself.

"Shane, let me explain."

"Explain?" She dragged shaking fingers through her hair. "Explain? How? How can you explain why you let me think you were something you're not? How can you explain why you didn't bother to tell me you were president of Riverton, that you—that you'd been married before? I *trusted* you," she whispered. "God, how could I have been such a fool!"

Anger he could have met and handled. Vance faced despair without any notion of how to cope with it. Impotently he thrust his hands into his pockets to keep from touching her. "I would have told you, Shane. I intended—"

"Would have?" She gave a quick, shaky laugh. "When? After you'd gotten bored with the joke?"

"There was never any joke," he said furiously, then clamped down on his panic. "I wanted to tell you, but every time—"

"No joke?" Her eyes glittered now with the beginnings of anger, the beginnings of tears. "You let me give you a job. You let me pay you six dollars an hour, and you don't think that's funny?"

"I didn't want your money, Shane. I tried to tell you. You wouldn't listen." Frustrated, he turned away until he had himself under control. "I banked the checks in an account under your name."

"How dare you!" Wild with pain, she shouted at him, blind and deaf to everything but the sense of betrayal. "How dare you play games with me! *I believed you.* I believed everything. I thought—I thought I was helping you, and all the time you were laughing at me."

"Damn it, Shane, I never laughed at you." Pushed beyond endurance, he grabbed her shoulders. "You know I never laughed at you."

"I wonder how you managed not to laugh in my face. God, you're clever, Vance." She choked on a sob, then swallowed it.

"Shane, if you'd try to understand why I came, why I didn't want to be connected with the company for a little while . . ." None of the words he needed would come to him. "It had nothing to do with you," he told her fiercely. "I didn't expect to get involved."

"Did it keep you from being bored?" she demanded, struggling against his hold. "Amusing yourself with a stupid little country girl who was so gullible she'd believe anything you

said? You could play the poor working man and be entertained."

"It was never like that." Enraged by the words, he shook
her. "You don't really believe that."

The tears gushed out passionately, strangling her voice.
"And I was so willing to fall into bed with you. You knew
it!" She sobbed, pushing desperately at him. "Right from the
first I had no secrets from you."

"I had them," he admitted in a tight voice. "I had reasons
for them."

"You knew how much I loved you, how much I wanted
you. You *used* me!" On a moan, she covered her face with
her hands. "Oh God, I left myself wide open."

She wept with the same honest abandon he'd seen when
she laughed. Unable to do otherwise, he crushed her against
him. He thought if he could only calm her down, he could
make her understand. "Shane, please, you have to listen
to me."

"No, no, I don't." She pulled in breath after jerky breath
as she struggled for release. "I'll never forgive you. I'll never
believe anything you say again. Damn you, let me go."

"Not until you stop this and hear what I have to say."

"No! I won't listen to any more lies. I won't let you make
a fool of me again. All this time, all this time when I was
giving you everything, you were lying and laughing at me. I
was just something to keep the nights from being dull while
you were on vacation."

He jerked her back, his face rigid with fury. "Damn it,
Shane, you know better than that."

Her struggles ceased abruptly. As he watched, the tears
seemed to turn to ice. Without expression, she stared up at
him. Nothing she had said so far had struck him to the core
like that one cool look.

"I don't know you," she said quietly.

"Shane—"

"Take your hands off me." The command was devoid
of passion. Vance felt his stiff fingers loosen. Freed, Shane
stepped back until they were no longer touching. "I want you
to go away and leave me alone. Stay away from me," she
added flatly, still looking directly into his eyes. "I don't want
to see you again."

Turning, she walked up the steps and to the door. After
its final click came absolute silence.

*   *   *

Far beneath the window, the streets were packed with
traffic. The steady fall of snow increased the confusion.
Beneath the overhang of the department store across the
street, a red-cheeked Santa rang his bell, ho-hoing when
someone dropped a coin into his bucket. The scene below
was played in pantomime. The thick glass of the window and
well-constructed walls allowed no street sounds to intrude.
Vance kept his back to his plush, spacious office and continued to watch.

He'd made his obligatory appearance at the company
Christmas party. It was still going on, with enthusiasm, in a
large conference room on the third floor. When it broke up,
everyone would go home to spend Christmas Eve with their
families or friends. He'd refused more than a dozen invita-
tions for the evening since his return to Washington. It was
one thing to do his duty as the head of the company, and
another to put himself through hours of small talk and cel-
ebrating. *She wouldn't be there,* he thought, staring down at
the snowy sidewalk.

Two weeks. In two weeks, Vance had managed to straighten
out a few annoying contractual tangles, plot out a bid for a
new wing to a hospital in Virginia and head a heated board

meeting. He'd dealt with paperwork and some minor corporate intrigue he might have found amusing if he'd been sleeping properly. But he wasn't sleeping properly any more than he was forgetting. Work wasn't an elixir this time. As she had from the very first moment, Shane haunted him.

Turning from the window, Vance took his place behind the massive oak desk. It was clear of papers. In a fury of frustrated energy, he'd taken care of every letter, memo and contract, putting his secretary and assistants through an orgy of work over the last two weeks. Now, he had nothing but an empty desk and a clear calendar. He considered the possibility of flying to Des Moines to supervise the progress of a condominium development. That would throw the Iowa branch into a panic, he thought with a quick laugh. Hardly fair to upset their applecart because he was restless. He brooded at the far wall, wondering what Shane was doing.

He hadn't left in anger. It would have been easier for Vance if that had been the case. He had left because Shane had wanted it. He didn't blame her, and that too made it impossibly frustrating. Why should she listen to him or understand? There had been enough truth in what she had flung at him to make the rest difficult to overturn. He had lied, or at the very least, he hadn't been honest. To Shane, one was the same as the other.

He'd hurt her. He had put that look of helpless despair on her face. That was unforgivable. Vance pushed away from the desk to pace over the thick stone-colored carpet. But damn it, if she'd just listened to him! If she'd only given him a moment. Going to the window again, he scowled out. Laughed at her? Made fun of her? No, he thought with the first true fury he'd felt in two weeks. No, by God, he'd be damned if he'd stand quietly aside while she turned the most important thing in his life into a joke.

She'd had her say, Vance told himself as he headed for the door. Now he was going to have his.

* * *

S hane, don't be stubborn." Donna followed her through the doorway from the museum into the shop.

"I'm not being stubborn, Donna, I really have a lot to do." To prove her point, Shane leafed through a catalog to price and date her latest stock. "With the Christmas rush, I've really fallen behind on the paperwork. I've got invoices to file, and if I don't get the books caught up before the quarter, I'm going to be in a jam."

"Baloney," Donna said precisely, flipping the catalog closed.

"Donna, please."

"No, I don't please." She stuck her hands on her hips. "And it's two against one," she added, indicating Pat with a jerk of her head. "We're not having you spend Christmas Eve alone in this house, and that's all there is to it."

"Come on, Shane." Pat joined ranks with her sister-in-law. "You should see Donna and Dave chase after Benji when he heads for the tree. And as Donna's putting on a little weight," she added, grinning at the expectant mother, "she isn't as fast as she used to be."

Shane laughed, but shook her head. "I promise I'll come by tomorrow. I've got a very noisy present for Benji. You'll probably never speak to me again."

"Shane." Firmly, Donna took her by the shoulders. "Pat's told me how you've been moping around. And," she continued, ignoring the annoyed glance Shane shot over her shoulder at the informant, "anyone can take one look at you and see you're worn-out and miserable."

"I'm not worn-out," Shane corrected.

"Just miserable?"

"I didn't say—"

Donna gave her a quick affectionate shake. "Look, I don't know what happened between you and Vance—"

"Donna . . ."

"And I'm not asking," she added. "But you can't expect me to stand by while my best friend is unhappy. How much fun can I have, thinking about you here all alone?"

"Donna." Shane gave her a fierce hug then drew away. "I appreciate it, really I do, but I'm lousy company now."

"I know," Donna agreed mercilessly.

That made Shane laugh and hug her again. "Please, take Pat and go back to your family."

"So speaks the martyr."

"I'm not—" Shane began furiously, then broke off, seeing the gleam in Donna's eyes. "That won't work," she told her. "If you think you can make me mad so I'll come just to prove you wrong—"

"All right." Donna settled herself in a rocker. "Then I'll just sit here. Of course, poor Dave will spend Christmas Eve without me, and my little boy won't understand where his mother could be, but . . ." She sighed and folded her hands.

"Oh, Donna, really." Shane dragged her hand through her hair, caught between laughter and tears. "Talk about martyrs."

"I'm not complaining for myself," she said in a long-suffering tone. "Pat, run along and tell Dave I won't be home. Dry little Benji's tears for me."

Pat gave a snort of laughter, but Shane rolled her eyes. "I'll be sick in a minute," she promised. "Donna, go home!" she insisted. "I'm closing the shop."

"Good, go get your coat. I'll drive."

"Donna, I'm not . . ." She trailed off as the shop door

opened. Seeing her friend pale, Donna turned her head to watch Vance walk in.

"Well, we have to run," she stated, springing quickly to her feet. "Come on, Pat, Dave's probably at his wit's end keeping Benji from pulling over the tree. Merry Christmas, Shane." She gave Shane a quick kiss before grabbing her coat.

"Donna, wait . . ."

"No, we just can't stay," she claimed, making the reversal without blinking an eye. "I've got a million things to do. Hi, Vance, nice to see you. Let's go, Pat." They were out the door before Shane could fit in another word.

Vance lifted a brow at the hasty exit but made no comment. Instead, he studied Shane as the silence grew long and thick. The anger that had driven him there melted. "Shane," he murmured.

"I—I'm closing."

"Fine." Vance turned and flicked the lock on the door. "Then we won't be disturbed."

"I'm busy, Vance. I have . . ." She searched desperately for something important. "Things to do," she finished lamely. When he neither spoke nor moved, she sent him a look of entreaty. "Please go away."

Vance shook his head. "I tried that, Shane. I can't." He slipped off his coat and dropped it on the chair Donna had vacated. Shane stared at him, thrown off-balance by his appearance in a trimly tailored suit and silk tie. It brought it home to her again that she didn't know him. And, God help her, she loved him anyway. Turning, she began to fiddle with an arrangement of cut glass.

"I'm sorry, Vance, but I have a few things to finish up here before I leave. I'm supposed to go to Donna's tonight."

"She didn't seem to expect you," he commented as he walked to her. Gently, he laid his hands on her shoulders. "Shane—"

She stiffened immediately. "Don't!"

Very slowly, he took his hands from her, then dropped them to his sides. "All right, damn it, I won't touch you." The words came out savagely as he whirled away.

"Vance, I told you I'm busy."

"You said that you loved me."

Shane spun around, white with anger. "How can you throw that in my face?"

"Was it a lie?" he demanded.

She opened her mouth but closed it again before any impetuous words could be spoken. Lifting her chin, she looked at him steadily. "I loved the man you pretended to be."

He winced, but he didn't back away. "Direct hit, Shane," he said quietly. "You surprise me."

"Why, because I'm not as stupid as you thought I was?"

Anger flashed into his eyes, then dulled. "Don't."

Shaken by the pain in the single word, she turned away. "I'm sorry, Vance. I don't want to say spiteful things. It would be better for both of us if you just went away."

"The hell it would, if you've been half as miserable as I've been. Have you been able to sleep, Shane? I haven't."

"Please," she whispered.

He took a deep breath as his hands clenched into fists. He'd come prepared to fight with her, to bully her, to plead with her. Now, it seemed he could do nothing but try to fumble through an explanation. "All right, I'll go, but only if you listen to me first."

"Vance," she said wearily, "what difference will it make?"

The finality of her tone had fear twisting in his stomach. With a strong effort, he kept his voice calm. "If that's true, it won't hurt you to listen."

"All right." Shane turned back to face him. "All right, I'll listen."

He was quiet for a moment, then began to pace as though

whatever ran through him wouldn't allow him to keep still. "I came here because I had to get away, maybe even hide. I'm not sure anymore. I was still very young when I took over the company. It wasn't what I wanted." He stopped for a moment to send her a direct look. "I'm a carpenter, Shane, that was the truth. I'm president of Riverton because I have to be. *Why* doesn't really matter at this point, but a title, a position, doesn't change who I am." When she said nothing, he began to pace again.

"I was married to a woman you'd recognize very quickly. She was beautiful, charming and pure plastic. She was totally self-consumed, emotionless, even vicious." Shane's brows drew together as she thought of Anne. "Unfortunately, I didn't recognize the last of those qualities until it was too late." He stopped because the next words were difficult. "I married the woman she pretended to be." Because his back was to her, Vance didn't see the sudden change in Shane's expression. Pain rushed into her eyes, but it wasn't for herself. It was all for him.

"For all intents and purposes, the marriage was over very soon after it had begun. I couldn't make a legal break at first because too many things were involved. So, we lived together in mutual distaste for several years. I involved myself in the company to the point of obsession, while she began to take lovers. I wanted her out of my life more than I wanted anything. Then, when she was dead, I had to live with the knowledge that I'd wished her dead countless times."

"Oh, Vance," Shane murmured.

"That was over two years ago," he continued. "I buried myself in work . . . and bitterness. I'd come to a point where I didn't even recognize myself anymore. That's why I bought the house and took a leave of absence. I needed to separate myself from what I'd become, try to find out if that was all there was to me." He dragged an agitated hand through his hair. "I brought the bitterness with me, so that when you popped up and started haunting my mind, I wanted nothing more than to be rid of you. I looked . . . I searched," he corrected, turning to her again, "for flaws in you. I was afraid to believe you could really be so . . . generous. The truth was, I didn't want you to be because I'd never be able to resist the woman you are." His eyes were suddenly very dark and very direct on hers. "I didn't want you, Shane, and I wanted you so badly I ached. I loved you, I think, from the very first minute."

On a long breath, he moved away again to stare at the flickering lights of the tree. "I could have told you—should have—but at first I had a need for you to love me without knowing. Unforgivably selfish."

She remembered the secrets she had seen in his eyes. Remembered too, telling herself they were his until he shared them with her. Still, she felt the hurt of not being trusted. "Did you really think any of it would have mattered to me?"

Vance shook his head. "No."

"Then why did you hide it all from me?" Confused, she lifted her hands palms up.

"I never intended to. Circumstances—" He broke off, no longer sure he could make her understand. "The first night we were together, I was going to tell you, but I didn't want any past that night. I told myself it wasn't too much to ask and that I'd explain things to you the next day. God, Shane, I swear to you I would have." He took a step toward her, then stopped himself. "You were so lost, so vulnerable after Anne had left, I couldn't. How could I have dumped all this on you when you already had that to deal with?"

She remained silent, but he knew she listened very carefully. He didn't know she was remembering very clearly the things he had said to her their first night together, the tension in him, the hints of things yet to be told. And she remembered too his compassion the next evening.

"You needed my support that night, not my problems," Vance went on. "From the very first, you gave everything to me. You brought me back, Shane, and I knew that I took much more than I gave. Until that night, you'd never asked me for anything."

She gave him a puzzled look. "I never gave you anything."

"Nothing?" he countered with a baffled shake of his head. "Trust, understanding. You made me laugh at myself again. Maybe you don't see just how important that is because you've never lost it. If I could give you nothing else, I thought that for a few days I could give you some peace of mind. I tried to tell you again when we argued about that damned dining room set." Pausing, he sent her a narrowed look. "I bought it anyway."

"You—"

"There's not a thing you can do about it," he stated, cutting off her astonished exclamation. "It's done."

She met the angry challenge in his eyes. "I see."

"Do you?" He let out a quick, rough laugh. "Do you really? The only thing you see when you lift your chin up like that is your own pride." He watched her mouth open, then close again. "It's just as well," he murmured. "It would be difficult if you were perfect." He moved to her then but was careful not to touch her. "I never set out to deceive you, but I deceived you nonetheless. And now I have to ask you to forgive me, even if you can't accept who and what I am."

Shane lowered her eyes to her hands a moment. "It's not accepting so much as understanding," she said quietly. "I don't know anything about the president of Riverton. I knew the man who bought the old Farley place, you see." She lifted her eyes again. "He was rude, and nasty, with a streak of kindness he did his best to overcome. I loved him."

"God knows why," Vance replied, thinking over her description. "If that's who you want, I can promise I'm still rude and nasty."

With a small laugh, she turned away. "Vance, it's all hit me, you see. Maybe if I had time to get used to it, to think it through . . . I don't know. When I thought you were just . . ." She made an uncharacteristically helpless gesture with her hands. "It all seemed so easy."

"Did you only love me because you thought I was out of work?"

"No!" Frustrated, she tried to explain herself. "I haven't changed though," she added thoughtfully. "I'm still exactly what I seem. What would the president of Riverton do with me? I can't even drink martinis."

"Don't be absurd."

"It's not absurd," she corrected. "Be honest. I don't fit in. I'd never be elegant if I had years to practice."

"What the hell's wrong with you?" Suddenly angry, he spun her around. "*Elegant!* In the name of God, Shane, what kind of nonsense is that? I had my share of elegance the way you mean. I'll be damned if you're going to put me off because you've got some twisted view of the life I lead. If you can't accept it, fine. I'll resign."

"W-what?"

"I said I'll resign."

She studied him with wide, astonished eyes. "You mean it," she said wonderingly. "You really do."

He gave her an impatient shake. "Yes, I mean it. Can you really believe the company means more to me than you do? God, you're an idiot!" Furious, he gave her an unlover-like shove and strode away. "You don't yell at me for anything I've done. You don't demand to hear all the filthy details of my first marriage. You don't make me crawl as I was damn well ready to do. You start spouting nonsense about martinis and elegance." After swearing rudely, he stared out the window.

Shane swallowed a sudden urge to laugh. "Vance, I—"

"Shut up," he ordered. "You drive me crazy." With a quick jerk, he pulled his coat from the chair. Shane opened her mouth, afraid he was about to storm out, but he only pulled an envelope out of the pocket before he flung the coat down again. "Here." He stuck it out to her.

"Vance," she tried again, but he took her hand and slapped the envelope into her palm.

"Open it."

Deciding a temporary retreat was advisable, Shane obeyed. She stared in silent astonishment at two round-trip tickets to Fiji.

"Someone told me it was a good place for a honeymoon," Vance stated with a bit more control. "I thought she might still think so."

Shane looked up at him with her heart in her eyes. Vance needed nothing more to pull her into his arms, crushing the envelope and its contents between them as he found her mouth.

Shane's answer was wild and unrestricted. She clung to him even as she demanded, yielded even as she aroused. She couldn't get enough of him, so that the desperate kisses incited only more urgent needs. "Oh, I've missed you," she murmured. "Make love to me, Vance. Come upstairs and make love to me."

He buried his face against her neck. "Uh-uh. You haven't said you're taking me to Fiji yet." But his hands were already searching under her sweater. As his fingers skimmed over her warm, soft skin, he groaned, pulling her to the floor.

"Oh, Vance, your suit!" Laughing breathlessly, Shane struggled against him. "Wait until we go upstairs."

"Shut up," he suggested, then assured himself of her

obedience by crushing his mouth on hers. It only took a moment to realize her trembling came from laughter, not from passion. Lifting his head, Vance studied her amused eyes. "Damn you, Shane," he said in exasperation. "I'm trying to make love to you."

"Well, then at least take off that tie," she suggested, then buried her face against his shoulder and laughed helplessly. "I'm sorry, Vance, but it just seems so funny. I mean, there you are asking if I'll take you to Fiji before I've even gotten around to asking you to marry me, and—"

"*You* asking *me*?" he demanded, eyeing her closely.

"Yes," she continued blithely. "I've been meaning to, though I thought I'd have to overcome some silly ego thing. You know, I thought you were out of work."

"Ego thing," he repeated.

"Yes, and of course, now that I know you're such an important person . . . Oh, this tie is *silk*!" she exclaimed after she had begun to struggle with the knot.

"Yes." He allowed her to finger it curiously. "And now that you know I'm such an important person?" he prompted.

"I'd better snap you up quick."

"Snap me up?" He bit her ear painfully.

Shane only giggled and linked her arms around his neck. "And even if I refuse to drink martinis or be elegant, I'll make an extremely good wife for a . . ." She paused a moment, lifting a brow. "What are you?"

"Insane."

"A corporate president," Shane decided with a nod. "No, I don't suppose you could do any better. You're making a pretty good deal now that I think about it." She gave him a noisy kiss. "When do we leave for Fiji?"

"Day after tomorrow," he informed her before he rose and dumped her over his shoulder.

"Vance, what are you doing?"

"I'm taking you upstairs to make love with you."

"Vance," she began with a half laugh. "I told you before I won't be carted around this way. This is no way for the fiancée of the president of Riverton to be treated."

"You haven't seen anything yet," he promised her.

Exasperated, Shane gave him a hearty thump on the back. "Vance, I mean it, put me down!"

"Am I fired?"

He heard the telltale choke of laughter. "Yes!"

"Good." He tucked his arm firmly around her knees and carried her up the stairs.

Less of a Stranger

CHAPTER 1

He watched her coming. Though she wore jeans and a jacket, with a concealing helmet over her head, Katch recognized her femininity. She rode a small Honda motorcycle. He drew on his thin cigar and appreciated the competent way she swung into the market's parking lot.

Settling the bike, she dismounted. She was tall, Katch noted, perhaps five feet eight, and slender. He leaned back on the soda machine and continued to watch her out of idle curiosity. Then she removed the helmet. Instantly, his curiosity was intensified. She was a stunner.

Her hair was loose and straight, swinging nearly to her shoulders, with a fringe of bangs sweeping over her forehead. It was a deep, rich brunette that showed glints of red and gold from the sun. Her face was narrow, the features sharp and distinct. He'd known models who'd starved themselves to get the angles and shadows that were in this woman's face. Her mouth, however, was full and generous.

Katch recognized the subtleties of cosmetics and knew that none had been used to add interest to the woman's features. She didn't need them. Her eyes were large, and even with the distance of the parking lot between them, he caught the

depth of dark brown. They reminded him of a colt's eyes—
deep and wide and aware. Her movements were unaffected.
They had an unrefined grace that was as coltish as her eyes.
She was young, he decided, barely twenty. He drew on the
cigar again. She was definitely a stunner.

"Hey, Megan!"

Megan turned at the call, brushing the bangs from her eyes
as she moved. Seeing the Bailey twins pull to the curb in their
Jeep, she smiled.

"Hi." Clipping the helmet onto a strap on her bike, Megan
walked to the Jeep. She was very fond of the Bailey twins.

Like herself, they were twenty-three and had golden,
beach-town complexions, but they were petite, blue-eyed and
pertly blond. The long, baby-fine hair they shared had been
tossed into confusion by the wind. Both pairs of blue eyes
drifted past Megan to focus on the man who leaned against
the soda machine. In reflex, both women straightened and
tucked strands of hair behind their ears. Tacitly, they agreed
their right profile was the most comely.

"We haven't seen you in a while." Teri Bailey kept one eye
cocked on Katch as she spoke to Megan.

"I've been trying to get some things finished before the
season starts." Megan's voice was low, with the gentle flow
of coastal South Carolina. "How've you been?"

"Terrific!" Jeri answered, shifting in the driver's seat.
"We've got the afternoon off. Why don't you come shopping
with us?" She, too, kept Katch in her peripheral vision.

"I'd like to—" Megan was already shaking her head "—
but I've got to pick up a few things here."

"Like the guy over there with terrific gray eyes?" Jeri demanded.

"What?" Megan laughed.

"And shoulders," Teri remarked.

"He hasn't taken those eyes off her, has he, Teri?" Jeri

remarked. "And we spent twelve-fifty for this blouse." She fingered the thin strap of the pink camisole top which matched her twin's.

"What," Megan asked, totally bewildered, "are you talking about?"

"Behind you," Teri said with a faint inclination of her fair head. "The hunk by the soda machine. Absolutely gorgeous." But as Megan began to turn her head, Teri continued in a desperate whisper, "Don't turn around, for goodness sake!"

"How can I see if I don't look?" Megan pointed out reasonably as she turned.

His hair was blond, not pale like the twins', but dusky and sun-streaked. It was thick and curled loosely and carelessly around his face. He was lean, and the jeans he wore were well faded from wear. His stance was negligent, completely relaxed as he leaned back against the machine and drank from a can. But his face wasn't lazy, Megan thought as he met her stare without a blink. It was sharply aware. He needed a shave, certainly, but his bone structure was superb. There was the faintest of clefts in his chin, and his mouth was long and thin.

Normally, Megan would have found the face fascinating—strongly sculpted, even handsome in a rough-and-ready fashion. But the eyes were insolent. They were gray, as the twins had stated, dark and smoky. And, Megan decided with a frown, rude. She'd seen his type before—drifters, loners, looking for the sun and some fleeting female companionship. Under her bangs, her eyebrows drew together. He was openly staring at her. As the can touched his lips, he sent Megan a slow wink.

Hearing one of the twins giggle, Megan whipped her head back around.

"He's adorable," Jeri decided.

"Don't be an idiot." Megan swung her hair back with a toss of her head. "He's typical."

The twins exchanged a look as Jeri started the Jeep's engine. "Too choosy," she stated. They gave Megan mirror smiles as they pulled away from the curb. "Bye!"

Megan wrinkled her nose at them, but waved before she turned away. Purposefully ignoring the man who loitered beside the concessions, Megan walked into the market.

She acknowledged the salute from the clerk behind the counter. Megan had grown up in Myrtle Beach. She knew all the small merchants in the five-mile radius around her grandfather's amusement park.

After choosing a basket, she began to push it down the first aisle. Just a few things, she decided, plucking a quart of milk from a shelf. She had only the saddle-bags on the bike for transporting. If the truck hadn't been acting up . . . She let her thoughts drift away from that particular problem. Nothing could be done about it at the moment.

Megan paused in the cookie section. She'd missed lunch and the bags and boxes looked tempting. Maybe the oatmeal . . .

"These are better."

Megan started as a hand reached in front of her to choose a bag of cookies promising a double dose of chocolate chips. Twisting her head, she looked up into the insolent gray eyes.

"Want the cookies?" He grinned much as he had outside.

"No," she said, giving a meaningful glance at his hand on her basket. Shrugging, he took his hand away but, to Megan's irritation, he strolled along beside her.

"What's on the list, Meg?" he asked companionably as he tore open the bag of cookies.

"I can handle it alone, thanks." She started down the next aisle, grabbing a can of tuna. He walked, Megan noted, like

a gunslinger—long, lanky strides with just a hint of swag-
ger.

"You've got a nice bike." He bit into a cookie as he strolled
along beside her. "Live around here?"

Megan chose a box of tea bags. She gave it a critical glance
before tossing it into the basket. "It lives with me," she told
him as she moved on.

"Cute," he decided and offered her a cookie. Megan ignored him and moved down the next aisle. When she
reached for a loaf of bread, however, he laid a hand on top
of hers. "Whole wheat's better for you." His palm was hard
and firm on the back of her hand. Megan met his eyes indignantly and tried to pull away.

"Listen, I have . . ."

"No rings," he commented, lacing his fingers through hers
and lifting her hand for a closer study. "No entanglements.
How about dinner?"

"No way." She shook her hand but found it firmly locked
in his.

"Don't be unfriendly, Meg. You have fantastic eyes." He
smiled into them, looking at her as though they were the only
two people on earth. Someone reached around her, with an
annoyed mutter, to get a loaf of rye.

"Will you go away?" she demanded in an undertone. It
amazed her that his smile was having an effect on her even
though she knew what was behind it. "I'll make a scene if
you don't."

"That's all right," he said genially, "I don't mind scenes."

He wouldn't, she thought, eyeing him. He'd thrive on
them. "Look," she began angrily, "I don't know who you are,
but . . ."

"David Katcherton," he volunteered with another easy
smile. "Katch. What time should I pick you up?"

"You're not going to pick me up," she said distinctly. "Not

now, not later." Megan cast a quick look around. The market was all but empty. She couldn't cause a decent scene if she'd wanted to. "Let go of my hand," she ordered firmly.

"The Chamber of Commerce claims Myrtle Beach is a friendly town, Meg." Katch released her hand. "You're going to give them a bad name."

"And stop calling me Meg," she said furiously. "I don't know you."

She stomped off, wheeling the basket in front of her.

"You will." He made the claim quietly, but she heard him.

Their eyes met again, hers dark with temper, his assured. Turning away, she quickened her pace to the check-out counter.

You wouldn't believe what happened at the market." Megan set the bag on the kitchen table with a thump.

Her grandfather sat at the table, on one of the four matching maple chairs, earnestly tying a fly. He grunted in acknowledgment but didn't glance up. Wires and feathers and weights were neatly piled in front of him.

"This man," she began, pulling the bread from the top bag. "This incredibly rude man tried to pick me up. Right in the cookie section." Megan frowned as she stored tea bags in a canister. "He wanted me to go to dinner with him."

"Hmm." Her grandfather meticulously attached a yellow feather to the fly. "Have a nice time."

"Pop!" Megan shook her head in frustration, but a smile tugged at her mouth.

Timothy Miller was a small, spare man in his mid-sixties. His round, lined face was tanned, surrounded by a shock of white hair and a full beard. The beard was soft as a cloud and carefully tended. His blue eyes, unfaded by the years, were settled deeply into the folds and lines of his face. They missed little. Megan could see he was focused on his lures. That he had heard her at all was a tribute to his affection for his granddaughter.

Moving over, she dropped a kiss on the crown of his head. "Going fishing tomorrow?"

"Yessiree, bright and early." Pop counted out his assortment of lures and mentally reviewed his strategy. Fishing was serious business. "The truck should be fixed this evening. I'll be back before supper."

Megan nodded, giving him a second kiss. He needed his fishing days. The amusement parks opened for business on weekends in the spring and fall. In the three summer months they worked seven days a week. The summer kept the town alive; it drew tourists, and tourists meant business. For one-fourth of the year, the town swelled from a population of thirteen or fourteen thousand to three hundred thousand. The bulk of those three hundred thousand people had come to the small coastal town to have fun.

To provide it, and make his living, her grandfather worked hard. He always had, Megan mused. It would have been a trial if he hadn't loved the park so much. It had been part of her life for as long as she could remember.

Megan had been barely five when she had lost her parents. Over the years, Pop had been mother, father and friend to her. And Joyland was home to her as much as the beach-side cottage they lived in. Years before, they had turned to each other in grief. Now, their love was bedrock firm. With the exclusion of her grandfather, Megan was careful with her emotions, for once involved, they were intense. When she loved, she loved totally.

"Trout would be nice," she murmured, as she gave him a last, quick hug. "We'll have to settle for tuna casserole tonight."

"Thought you were going out."

"Pop!" Megan leaned back against the stove and pushed her hair from her face with both hands. "Do you think I'd spend the evening with a man who tried to pick me up with a bag of chocolate chip cookies?" With a jerk of her wrist, she flicked on the burner under the teakettle.

"Depends on the man." She saw the twinkle in his eye as he glanced up at her. Megan knew she finally had his full attention. "What'd he look like?"

"A beach bum," she retorted, although she knew the answer wasn't precisely true. "With a bit of cowboy thrown in." She smiled then in response to Pop's grin. "Actually, he had a great face. Lean and strong, very attractive in an unscrupulous sort of way. He'd do well in bronze."

"Sounds interesting. Where'd you meet him again?"

"In the cookie section."

"And you're going to fix tuna casserole instead of having dinner out?" Pop gave a heavy sigh and shook his head. "I don't know what's the matter with this girl," he addressed a favored lure.

"He was cocky," Megan claimed and folded her arms. "And he *leered* at me. Aren't grandfathers supposed to tote shotguns around for the purpose of discouraging leerers?"

"Want to borrow one and go hunting for him?"

The shrill whistling of the kettle drowned out her response. Pop watched Megan as she rose to fix the tea.

She was a good girl, he mused. A bit too serious about things at times, but a good girl. And a beauty too. It didn't surprise him that a stranger had tried to make a date with her. He was more surprised that it hadn't happened more often. But Megan could discourage a man without opening her mouth, he recalled. All she had to do was aim one of her "I beg your pardon" looks and most of them backed off. That seemed to be the way she wanted it.

Between the amusement park and her art, she never

seemed to have time for much socializing. Or didn't make time, Pop amended thoughtfully. Still, he wasn't certain that he didn't detect more than just annoyance in her attitude toward the man in the market. Unless he missed his guess, she had been amused and perhaps a touch attracted. Because he knew his granddaughter well, he decided to let the subject ride for the time being.

"The weather's supposed to hold all weekend," he commented as he carefully placed his lures in his fishing box. "There should be a good crowd in the park. Are you going to work in the arcade?"

"Of course." Megan set two cups of tea on the table and sat again. "Have those seats been adjusted on the Ferris wheel?"

"Saw to it myself this morning." Pop blew on his tea to cool it, then sipped.

He was relaxed, Megan saw. Pop was a simple man. She'd always admired his unassuming manner, his quiet humor, his lack of pretensions. He loved to watch people enjoy. More, she added with a sigh, than he liked to charge them for doing so. Joyland never made more than a modest profit. He was, Megan concluded, a much better grandfather than businessman.

To a large extent, it was she who handled the profit-and-loss aspect of the park. Though the responsibility took time away from her art, she knew it was the park that supported them. And, more important, it was the park that Pop loved.

At the moment, the books were teetering a bit too steeply into the red for comfort. Neither of them spoke of it at any length with the other. They mentioned improvements during the busy season, talked vaguely about promoting business during the Easter break and over Memorial Day weekend.

Megan sipped at her tea and half listened to Pop's rambling about hiring summer help. She would see to it when the time came. Pop was a whiz in dealing with cranky machines and sunburned tourists, but he tended to overpay and underwork his employees. Megan was more practical. She had to be.

I'll have to work full-time myself this summer, she reflected. She thought fleetingly of the half-completed sculpture in her studio over the garage. It'll just have to wait for December, she told herself and tried not to sigh. There's no other way until things are on a more even keel again. Maybe next year . . . it was always next year. There were things to do, always things to do. With a small shrug, she turned back to Pop's monologue.

"So, I figure we'll get some of the usual college kids and drifters to run the rides."

"I don't imagine that'll be a problem," Megan murmured. Pop's mention of drifters had led her thoughts back to David Katcherton.

Katch, she mused, letting his face form in her mind again. Ordinarily, she'd have cast his type as a drifter, but there had been something more than that. Megan prided herself on her observations, her characterizations of people. It annoyed her that she wasn't able to make a conclusive profile on this man. It annoyed her further that she was again thinking of a silly encounter with a rude stranger.

"Want some more tea?" Pop was already making his way to the stove when Megan shook herself back.

"Ah . . . yeah, sure." She scolded herself for dwelling on the insignificant when there were things to do. "I guess I'd better start dinner. You'll want an early night if you're going fishing in the morning."

"That's my girl." Pop turned the flame back on under the kettle as he glanced out the window. He cast a quick look at his unsuspecting granddaughter. "I hope you've got enough for three," he said casually. "It looks like your beach-cowboy found his way to the ranch."

"What?" Megan's brows drew together as she stood up.

"A perfect description, as usual, Megan," Pop complimented her as he watched the man approach, loose-limbed with a touch of a swashbuckler, a strong, good-looking face. Pop liked his looks. He turned with a grin as Megan walked to the window to stare out. Pop suppressed a chuckle at her expression.

"It *is* him," she whispered, hardly believing her eyes as she watched Katch approach her kitchen door.

"I thought it might be," Pop said mildly.

"Of all the nerve," she muttered darkly. "Of all the *incredible* nerve!"

CHAPTER 2

Before her grandfather could comment, Megan took the few strides necessary to bring her to the kitchen door. She swung it open just as Katch stepped up on the stoop. There was a flicker, only a flicker, of surprise in the gray eyes.

"You have a nerve," she said coolly.

"So I've been told," he agreed easily. "You're prettier than you were an hour ago." He ran a finger down her cheek. "There's a bit of rose under the honey now. Very becoming." He traced the line of her chin before dropping his hand. "Do you live here?"

"You know very well I do," she retorted. "You followed me."

Katch grinned. "Sorry to disappoint you, Meg. Finding you here's just a bonus. I'm looking for Timothy Miller. Friend of yours?"

"He's my grandfather." She moved, almost imperceptibly, positioning herself between Katch and the doorway. "What do you want with him?"

Katch recognized the protective move, but before he could comment, Pop spoke from behind her.

"Why don't you let the man in, Megan? He can tell me himself."

"I'm basically human, Meg," Katch said quietly. The tone of his voice had her looking at him more closely.

She glanced briefly over her shoulder, then turned back to Katch. The look she gave him was a warning. Don't do anything to upset him.

She noticed something in his eyes she hadn't expected— gentleness. It was more disconcerting than his earlier arrogance. Megan backed into the kitchen, holding open the door in silent invitation.

Katch smiled at her, casually brushing a strand of hair from her cheek as he walked by and into the kitchen. Megan stood for a moment, wondering why she should be so moved by a stranger's touch.

"Mr. Miller?" She heard the unaffected friendliness in Katch's voice and glanced over as he held out a hand to her grandfather. "I'm David Katcherton."

Pop nodded in approval. "You're the fellow who called me a couple of hours ago." He shot a look past Katch's shoulder to Megan. "I see you've already met my granddaughter."

His eyes smiled in response. "Yes. Charming."

Pop chuckled and moved toward the stove. "I was just about to make some more tea. How about a cup?"

Megan noticed the faint lift of his brow. Tea, she thought, was probably not his first choice.

"That'd be nice. Thanks." He walked to the table and sat, Megan decided, as if his acquaintance were long-standing and personal. Half reluctant, half defiant, she sat next to him. Her eyes asked him questions behind Pop's back.

"Did I tell you before that you have fabulous eyes?" he murmured. Without waiting for her answer, he turned his attention to Pop's tackle box. "You've got some great lures here," he observed to Pop, picking up a bone squid, then a wood plug painted to simulate a small frog. "Do you make any of your own?"

"That's half the sport," Pop stated, bringing a fresh cup to the table. "Have you done much fishing?"

"Here and there. I'd guess you'd know the best spots along the Grand Strand."

"A few of them," Pop said modestly.

Megan scowled into her tea. Once the subject of fishing had been brought up, Pop could go on for hours. And hours.

"I thought I'd do some surf casting while I'm here," Katch mentioned offhandedly. Megan was surprised to catch a shrewdly measuring expression in his eyes.

"Well now—" Pop warmed to the theme "—I might just be able to show you a spot or two. Do you have your own gear?"

"Not with me, no."

Pop brushed this off as inconsequential. "Where are you from, Mr. Katcherton?"

"Katch," he corrected, leaning back in his chair. "California originally."

That, Megan decided, explained the beachboy look. She drank her cooling tea with a casual air while studying him over the rim.

"You're a long way from home," Pop commented. He shifted comfortably, then brought out a pipe he saved for interesting conversations. "Do you plan to be in Myrtle Beach long?"

"Depends. I'd like to talk with you about your amusement park."

Pop puffed rapidly on his pipe while holding a match to the bowl. The tobacco caught, sending out cherry-scented smoke. "So you said on the phone. Funny, Megan and I were just talking about hiring on help for the summer. Only about six weeks before the season starts." He puffed and let the smoke waft lazily. "Less than three until Easter. Ever worked rides or a booth?"

"No." Katch sampled his tea.

"Well . . ." Pop shrugged his inexperience away. "It's simple enough to learn. You look smart." Again, Megan caught the flash of Katch's grin. She set down her cup.

"We can't pay more than minimum to a novice," she said dampeningly.

He made her nervous, she was forced to admit. With any luck, she could discourage him from Joyland so that he'd try his luck elsewhere. But something nagged at her. He didn't look the type to take a job running a roller coaster or hawking a pitch-and-toss for a summer. There were hints of authority in his face, touches of casual power in his stance. Yet there was something not altogether respectable in his raffish charm.

He met her stare with a complete lack of self-consciousness. "That seems reasonable. Do you work in the park, Meg?"

She bit back a retort to his familiarity. "Often," she said succinctly.

"Megan's got a good business head," Pop interjected. "She keeps me straight."

"Funny," Katch said speculatively. "Somehow I thought you might be a model. You've the face for it." There was no flirtatiousness in his tone.

"Megan's an artist," Pop said, puffing contentedly at his pipe.

"Oh?"

She watched Katch's eyes narrow and focus on her. Uncomfortable, she shifted in her chair. "We seem to be drifting away from the subject," she said crisply. "If you've come about a job—"

"No."

"But . . . didn't you say—"

"I don't think so," he cut her off again and added a smile.
He turned to Pop now, and Megan recognized a subtle change
in his manner. "I don't want a job in your park, Mr. Miller.
I want to buy it."

Both men were intent on each other. Pop was surprised,
unmistakably so, but there was also a look of consideration
in his eyes. Neither of them noticed Megan. She stared at
Katch, her face open and young, and just a little frightened.
She wanted to laugh and say he was making a foolish joke,
but she knew better. Katch said exactly what he meant.

She'd recognized the understated authority and power
beneath the glib exterior. This was business, pure and simple. She could see it on his face. There was a flutter of panic
in her stomach as she looked at her grandfather.

"Pop?" Her voice was very small, and he made no sign that
he heard her.

"You're a surprise," the old man said eventually. Then he
began to puff on his pipe again. "Why my park?"

"I've done some research on the amusements here." Katch
shrugged off the details. "I like yours."

Pop sighed and blew smoke at the ceiling. "I can't say I'm
interested in selling out, son. A man gets used to a certain
way of life."

"With the offer I'm prepared to make, you might find it
easy to get used to another."

Pop gave a quiet laugh. "How old are you, Katch?"

"Thirty-one."

"That's just about how long I've been in this business. How
much do you know about running a park?"

"Not as much as you do." Katch grinned and leaned back
again. "But I could learn fast with the right teacher."

Megan saw that her grandfather was studying Katch carefully. She felt excluded from the conversation and resented

it. Her grandfather was capable of doing this very subtly. She recognized that David Katcherton had the same talent. Megan sat silently; natural courtesy forbade her interrupting private conversation.

"Why do you want to own an amusement park?" Pop asked suddenly. Megan could tell he was interested in David Katcherton. A warning bell began to ring in her head. The last thing she wanted was for her grandfather to become too involved with Katch. He was trouble, Megan was sure of it.

"It's good business," Katch answered Pop's question after a moment. "And fun." He smiled. "I like things that put fun into life."

He knows how to say the right thing, Megan acknowledged grudgingly, noting Pop's expression.

"I'd appreciate it if you'd think about it, Mr. Miller," Katch continued. "We could talk about it again in a few days."

And how to advance and retreat, she thought.

"I can't refuse to think about it," Pop agreed, but shook his head. "Still, you might take another look around. Megan and I've run Joyland for a good many years. It's home to us." He looked to his granddaughter teasingly. "Weren't you two going out to dinner?"

"No!" She flashed him a scowl.

"Exactly what I had in mind," Katch said smoothly. "Come on, Meg, I'll buy you a hamburger." As he rose, he took her hand, pulling her to her feet. Feeling her temper rise with her, Megan attempted to control it.

"I can't tell you how I hate to refuse such a charming invitation," she began.

"Then don't," Katch cut her off before turning to Pop. "Would you like to join us?"

Pop chuckled and motioned them away with the back of his hand. "Go on. I've got to get my gear together for the morning."

"Want company?"

Pop studied Katch over the bowl of his pipe. "I'm leaving at five-thirty," he said after a moment. "I have extra gear."

"I'll be here."

Megan was so astonished that she allowed Katch to lead her outside without making another protest. Pop never invited anyone along on his fishing mornings. They were his relaxation, and he enjoyed his solitude too much to share it.

"He never takes anyone with him," she murmured, thinking aloud.

"Then I'm flattered."

Megan noticed that Katch still had her hand, his fingers comfortably laced with hers.

"I'm not going out with you," she said positively and stopped walking. "You might be able to charm Pop into taking you fishing, but—"

"So you think I'm charming?" His smile was audacious as he took her other hand.

"Not in the least," she said firmly, repressing an answering smile.

"Why won't you have dinner with me?"

"Because," she said, meeting his eyes directly, "I don't like you."

His smile broadened. "I'd like the chance to change your mind."

"You couldn't." Megan started to draw her hands away, but he tightened his fingers.

"Wanna bet?" Again, she squashed the desire to smile. "If I change your mind, you'll go to the park with me Friday night."

"And if I don't change my mind?" she asked. "What then?"

"I won't bother you anymore." He grinned, as persuasive, she noted, as he was confident.

Her brow lifted in speculation. It might, she reflected, it just might be worth it.

"All you have to do is have dinner with me tonight," Katch continued, watching Megan's face. "Just a couple of hours."

"All right," she agreed impulsively. "It's a deal." She wriggled her fingers, but he didn't release them. "We could shake on it," she said, "but you still have my hands."

"So I do," he agreed. "We'll seal it my way then."

With a quick tug, he had her colliding against his chest. She felt a strength there which wasn't apparent in the lean, somewhat lanky frame. Before she could express annoyance, his mouth had taken hers.

He was skillful and thorough. She never knew whether she had parted her lips instinctively or if he had urged her to do so with the gently probing tip of his tongue.

From the instant of contact, Megan's mind had emptied, to be filled only with thoughts she couldn't center on. Her body dominated, taking command in simple surrender. She was melted against him, aware of his chest hard against her breasts . . . aware of his mouth quietly savaging hers. There was nothing else. She found there was nothing to hold on to. No anchor to keep her from veering off into wild water. Megan gave a small, protesting moan and drew away.

His eyes were darker than she'd thought, and too smoky to read clearly. Why had she thought them so decipherable? Why had she thought him so manageable? Nothing was as she had thought it had been minutes before. Her breath trembled as she fought to collect herself.

"You're very warm," Katch said softly. "It's a pity you struggle so hard to be remote."

"I'm not. I don't . . ." Megan shook her head, wishing desperately for her heartbeat to slow.

"You are," he corrected, "and you do." Katch gave her

hands a companionable squeeze before releasing one of them. The other he kept snugly in his as he turned toward his car.

Panic was welling up inside Megan, and she tried to suppress it. *You've been kissed before,* she reminded herself. This was just unexpected. It just caught you off guard. Even as the excuse ran through her mind, she knew it for a lie. She'd never been kissed like that before. And the situation was no longer under her control.

"I don't think I'll go after all," she told him in calmer tones.

Katch turned, smiling at her as he opened the car door. "A bet's a bet, Meg."

CHAPTER 3

Katch drove a black Porsche. Megan wasn't surprised. She wouldn't have expected him to drive anything ordinary. It wasn't difficult to deduce that David Katcherton could afford the best of everything.

He'd probably inherited his money, she decided as she settled back against the silver gray seat cushion. He'd probably never worked a day in his life. She remembered the hard, unpampered feel of his palm. Probably a whiz at sports, she thought. Plays tennis, squash, sails his own yacht. Never does anything worthwhile. Only looks for pleasure. *And finds it,* she thought.

Megan turned to him, pushing her swinging hair back behind her shoulders. His profile was sharply attractive, with the dusky blond hair curling negligently over his ear.

"See something you like?"

Megan flushed in annoyance, aware that she'd been caught staring.

"You need a shave," she said primly.

Katch turned the rearview mirror toward him as if to check her analysis. "Guess I do." He smiled as they merged into the traffic. "On our next date I'll be sure to remember. Don't say anything," he added, feeling her stiffen at his side.

"Didn't your mother ever tell you not to say anything if you couldn't say something pleasant?"

Megan stifled a retort.

Katch smiled as he merged into traffic. "How long have you lived here?"

"Always." With the windows down, Megan could hear the outdoor noises. The music from a variety of car radios competed against each other and merged into a strange sort of harmony. Megan liked the cluttered, indefinable sound. She felt herself relaxing and straightened her shoulders and faced Katch again.

"And what do you do?"

He caught the thread of disdain in the question, but merely lifted a brow. "I own things."

"Really? What sort of things?"

Katch stopped at a red light, then turned, giving her a long, direct look. "Anything I want." The light changed and he deftly slid the car into the parking lot.

"We can't go in there," Megan told him with a glance at the exclusive restaurant.

"Why not?" Katch switched off the ignition. "The food's good here."

"I know, but we're not dressed properly, and—"

"Do you like doing things properly all the time, Meg?"

The question stopped her. She searched his face carefully, wondering if he was laughing at her, and unsure of the answer.

"Tell you what." He eased himself out of the car, then leaned back in the window. "Think about it for a few minutes. I'll be back."

Megan watched him slide through the elegant doors of the restaurant and shook her head. They'll boot him out, she thought. Still, she couldn't help admiring his confidence. There was something rather elusive about it. She crossed her arms over. "Still, I don't really *like* him," she muttered.

Fifteen minutes later, she decided she liked him even less. How impossibly rude! she fumed as she slammed out of his car. Keeping me waiting out here all this time!

She decided to find the nearest phone booth and call her grandfather to ask him to come pick her up. She searched the pockets in her jeans and her jacket. Not a dime, she thought furiously. Not one thin dime to my name. Taking a deep breath, she stared at the doors of the restaurant. She'd have to borrow change, or beg their permission to use the house phone. Anything was better than waiting in the car. Just as she pulled open the door of the restaurant, Katch strolled out.

"Thanks," he said casually and moved past her.

Megan stared after him. He was carrying the biggest picnic basket she'd ever seen. After he'd opened the trunk and settled it inside, he glanced back up at her.

"Well come on." He slammed the lid. "I'm starving."

"What's in there?" she asked suspiciously.

"Dinner." He motioned for her to get in the car. Megan stood beside the closed door on the passenger side.

"How did you get them to do that?"

"I asked. Are you hungry?"

"Well, yes . . . But how—"

"Then let's go." Katch dropped into the driver's seat and started the engine. The moment she sat beside him, he swung out of the parking lot. "Where's your favorite place?" he demanded.

"My favorite place?" she repeated dumbly.

"You can't tell me you've lived here all your life and don't have a favorite place." Katch turned the car toward the ocean. "Where is it?"

"Toward the north end of the beach," she said. "Not many people go there, except at the height of the season."

"Good. I want to be alone with you."

The simple directness had butterflies dancing in her stomach. Slowly, she turned to look at him again.

"Anything wrong with that?" The smile was back, irreverent and engaging. Megan sighed, feeling like she was just climbing the first hill of a roller coaster.

"Probably," she murmured.

T he beach was deserted but for the crying gulls. She stood for a moment facing west, enjoying the rich glow of the dying sun.

"I love this time of day," she said softly. "Everything seems so still. As if the day's holding its breath." She jumped when Katch's hands came to her shoulders.

"Easy," he murmured, kneading the suddenly tense muscles as he stood behind her. He looked over her head to the sunset. "I like it just before dawn, when the birds first start to sing and the light's still soft.

"You should relax more often," he told her. He slid his fingers lazily up her neck and down again. The pleasure became less quiet and more demanding. When she would have slipped away, Katch turned her to face him.

"No," she said immediately, "don't." Megan placed both her hands on his chest. "Don't."

"All right." He relaxed his hold but didn't release her for a moment. Then he stooped for the picnic basket and pulled out a white tablecloth saying briskly, "Besides, it's time to eat." Megan took it from him, marveling that the restaurant had given him their best linen.

"Here you go." With his head still bent over the basket, he handed her the glasses.

And they're crystal, she thought, dazed as she accepted the elegant wineglasses. There was china next, then silver.

"Why did they give you all this?"

"They were low on paper plates."

"Champagne?" She glanced at the label as he poured. "You must be crazy!"

"What's the matter?" he returned mildly. "Don't you like champagne?"

"Actually I do, though I've only had American."

"Here's to the French." Katch held out a glass to her.

Megan sipped. "It's wonderful," she said before experimenting with another sip. "But you didn't have to . . ." she gestured expansively.

"I decided I wasn't in the mood for a hamburger." Katch screwed the bottle down into the sand. He placed a small container on the cloth, then dived back into the basket.

"What's this?" Megan demanded as she opened it. She frowned at the shiny black mass inside. He placed toast points on a plate. "Is it . . ." She paused in disbelief and glanced at him. "Is this caviar?"

"Yeah. Let me have some, will you? I'm starving." Katch took it from her and spread a generous amount on a piece of toast. "Don't you want any?" he asked her as he took a bite.

"I don't know." Megan examined it critically. "I've never tasted it before."

"No?" He offered her his piece. "Taste it." When she hesitated, Katch grinned and held it closer to her mouth. "Go on, Meg, have a bite."

"It's salty," she said with surprise. She plucked the toast from his hand and took another bite. "And it's good," she decided, swallowing.

"You might've left me some," he complained when Megan finished off the toast. She laughed and, heaping caviar onto another piece, handed it to him. "I wondered how it would sound." Katch took the offering, but his attention was on Megan.

"What?" Still smiling, she licked a bit of caviar from her thumb.

"Your laugh. I wondered if it would be as appealing as your face." He took a bite now, still watching her. "It is."

Megan tried to calm her fluttering pulse. "You didn't have to feed me caviar and champagne to hear me laugh." With a casual shrug, she moved out of his reach. "I laugh quite a bit."

"Not often enough."

She looked back at him in surprise. "Why do you say that?"

"Your eyes are so serious. So's your mouth." His glance swept over her face. "Perhaps that's why I feel compelled to make you smile."

"How extraordinary." Megan sat back on her heels and stared at him. "You barely know me."

"Does it matter?"

"I always thought it should," she murmured as he reached into the hamper again. Megan watched, no longer surprised as he drew out lobster tails and fresh strawberries. She laughed again and, pushing back her hair, moved closer to him.

"Here," she said. "Let me help."

The sun sank as they ate. The moon rose. It shot a shimmering white line across the sea. Megan thought it was like a dream—the china and silver gleaming in the moonlight, the exotic tastes on her tongue, the familiar sound of surf and the stranger beside her, who was becoming less of a stranger every minute.

Already Megan knew the exact movement of his face when he smiled, the precise tonal quality of his voice. She knew the exact pattern of the curls over his ear. More than once, bewitched by moonlight and champagne, she had to restrain her fingers from reaching for them, experimenting with them.

"Aren't you going to eat any cheesecake?" Katch gestured with a forkful, then slid it into his mouth.

"I can't." Megan brought her knees up to her chest and rested her chin on them. She watched his obvious enjoyment with dessert. "How do you do it?"

"Dedication." Katch took the last bite. "I try to see every project through to the finish."

"I've never had a picnic like this," she told him with a contented sigh. Leaning back on her elbows, she stretched out her legs and looked up at the stars. "I've never tasted anything so wonderful."

"I'll give Ricardo your compliments." Katch moved to sit beside her. His eyes moved from the crown of her head down the slender arch of her neck. Her face was thrown up to the stars.

"Who's Ricardo?" she asked absently. There was no thought of objection when Katch tucked her hair behind her ear with his fingertip.

"The chef. He loves compliments."

Megan smiled, liking the way the sound of his voice mixed with the sound of the sea. "How do you know?"

"That's how I lured him away from Chicago."

"Lured him away? What do you mean?" It took only an instant for the answer to come to her. "You own that restaurant?"

"Yes." He smiled at the incredulity in her face. "I bought it a couple of years ago."

Megan glanced at the white linen cloth scattered with fine china and heavy silver. She recalled that a little more than two years before, the restaurant had been ready to go under. The food had been overpriced and the service slack. Then it had received a face-lift. The interior had been redesigned, boasting, she was told, a mirrored ceiling. Since its reopening, it had maintained the highest of reputations in a town which prided itself on its quality and variety of restaurants.

She shifted her attention back to him. "*You* bought it?"

"That's right." Katch smiled at her. He sat cross-legged, facing her as she leaned back on her elbows. "Does that surprise you?"

Megan looked at him carefully: the careless toss of curls, the white knees of his jeans, the frayed sneakers. He was not her conception of a successful businessman. Where was the three-piece suit, the careful hairstyling? And yet . . . she had to admit there was something in his face.

"No," she said at length. "No, I suppose it doesn't." Megan frowned as he shifted his position. In a moment he was close, facing the sea as she did. "You bought it the same way you want to buy Joyland."

"I told you, that's what I do."

"But it's more than owning things, isn't it?" she insisted, not satisfied with his offhand answers. "It's making a success of them."

"That's the idea," he agreed. "There's a certain satisfaction in succeeding, don't you think?"

Megan sat up and turned to him. "But you can't have Joyland, it's Pop's whole life. You don't understand . . ."

"Maybe not," he said easily. "You can explain it to me later. Not tonight." He covered her hand with his. "This isn't a night for business."

"Katch, you have to—"

"Look at the stars, Meg," he suggested as he did so himself. "Have you ever tried to count them?"

Her eyes were irresistibly drawn upward. "When I was little. But—"

"Star counting isn't just for kids," he instructed in a voice warm and laced with humor. "Do you come here at night?"

The stars were brilliant and low over the sea. "Sometimes," she murmured. "When a project isn't going well and I need to clear my head, or just be alone."

"What sort of artist are you?" His fingers trailed over her knuckles. "Do you paint seascapes? Portraits?"

She smiled and shook her head. "No, I sculpt."

"Ah." He lifted her hand, then examined it—one side, then the other—while she watched him. "Yes, I can see that. Your hands are strong and capable." When he pressed his lips to the center of her palm, she felt the jolt shoot through her entire body.

Carefully, Megan drew her hand away; then, bringing her knees up to her chest, wrapped her arms around them. She could feel Katch smile without seeing it.

"What do you work in? Clay, wood, stone?"

"All three." Turning her head, she smiled again.

"Where did you study?"

"I took courses in college." With a shrug, she passed this off. "There hasn't been much time for it." She looked up at the sky again. "The moon's so white tonight. I like to come here when it's full like this, so that the light's silvery."

When his lips brushed her ear, she would have jerked away, but he slipped an arm around her shoulders. "Relax, Meg." His voice was a whisper at her cheek. "There's a moon and the ocean. That's all there is besides us."

With his lips tingling on her skin, she could almost believe him. Her limbs were heavy, drugged with wine and the magic of his touch. Katch trailed his mouth down to her throat so that she moaned with the leap of her pulse.

"Katch, I'd better go." He was tracing her jaw with light kisses. "Please," she said weakly.

"Later," he murmured, going back to nuzzle her ear. "Much, much later."

"No, I . . ." Megan turned her head, and the words died.

Her lips were no more than a breath from his. She stared at him, eyes wide and aware as he bent closer. Still his mouth didn't touch hers. It hovered, offering, promising. She moaned again, lids lowering as he teased the corners of her lips. His hands never touched her. He had moved his arm so that their only contact was his mouth and tongue on her skin and the mingling of their breath.

Megan felt her resistance peel away, layer by layer until there was only need. She forgot to question the dangers, the consequences. She could only feel. Her mouth sought his. There was no hesitation or shyness now but demand, impatient demand, as she hungered to feel what she had felt before—the delicious confusion, the dark awareness.

When he still didn't touch her, Megan slipped her arms around him. She pulled him close, enjoying his soft sound of pleasure as the kiss deepened. Still, he let her lead, touching her now, but lightly, his fingers in her hair. She could barely hear the hissing of the surf over the pounding of her heart. Finally, she drew away, pulling in a deep breath as their lips separated.

But he wouldn't let her go. "Again?" The question was quiet and seemed to shout through the still night.

Refusal trembled on Megan's tongue. She knew the ground beneath her was far from solid. His hand on the back of her neck brought her a whisper closer.

"Yes," she said, and went into his arms.

This time he was less passive. He showed her there were many ways to kiss. Short and light, long and deep. Tongue and teeth and lips could all bring pleasure. Together, they lowered themselves to the sand.

It was a rough blanket, but she felt only the excitement of his lips on her skin as they wandered to her throat. She ran her fingers through his hair. His mouth returned to hers, harder now, more insistent. She was ready for it, answering it. Craving it.

When his hand took the naked skin of her breast, she murmured in resistance. She hadn't felt him release the zipper of her jacket or the buttons of her shirt. But his hand was gentle, persuasive. He let his fingers trail over her, a whispering touch. Resistance melted into surrender, then heated into passion. It was smoldering just under her skin, threatening to explode into something out of her control. She moved under him and his hands became less gentle.

There was a hunger in the kiss now. She could taste it, a flavor sharper than any she'd known. It was more seductive than soft words or champagne, and more frightening.

"I want you." Katch spoke against her mouth, but the words were not in his easygoing tone. "I want to make love with you."

Megan felt control slipping from her grasp. Her need for him was overpowering, her appetite ravenous. She struggled to climb back to reality, to remember who they were. Names, places, responsibilities. There was more than the moon and the sea. And he was a stranger, a man she barely knew.

"No." Megan managed to free her mouth from his. She struggled to her feet. "No." The repetition was shaky. Quickly, she began to fumble with the buttons of her shirt.

Katch stood and gathered the shirttail in his hands. Surprised, Megan looked up at him. His eyes were no longer calm, but his voice was deadly so. "Why not?"

Megan swallowed. There wasn't lazy arrogance here, but a hint of ruthlessness. She had sensed it, but seeing it was much more potent. "I don't want to."

"Liar," he said simply.

"All right." She nodded, conceding his point. "I don't know you."

Katch inclined his head in agreement but tugged on the tails of her shirt to bring her closer. "You will," he assured her. He kissed her then, searingly. "But we'll wait until you do."

She fought to steady her breathing and stabilize her pulse. "Do you think you should always get what you want?" she demanded. The defiance was back, calming her.

"Yes," he said and grinned. "Of course."

"You're going to be disappointed." She smacked his hands from her shirt and began doing the buttons. Her fingers were unfaltering. "You can't have Joyland and you can't have me. Neither of us is for sale."

The roughness with which he took her arm had her eyes flying back to his face. "I don't buy women." He was angry, his eyes dark with it. The appealing voice had hardened like flint. The artist in her was fascinated by the planes of his face, the woman was uneasy with his harsh tone. "I don't have to. We're both aware that with a bit more persuasion I'd have had you tonight."

Megan pulled out of his hold. "What happened tonight doesn't mean I find you irresistible, you know." She zipped up her jacket with one quick jerk. "I can only repeat, you can't have Joyland and you can't have me."

Katch watched her a moment as she stood in the moonlight, her back to the sea. The smile came again, slowly, arrogantly. "I'll have you both, Meg," he promised quietly. "Before the season begins."

CHAPTER 4

The afternoon sun poured into Megan's studio. She was oblivious to it, and to the birdsong outside the windows. Her mind was focused on the clay her hands worked with, or, more precisely, on what she saw in the partially formed mound.

She had put her current project aside, something she rarely did, to begin a new one. The new subject had haunted her throughout the night. She would exorcise David Katcherton by doing a bust of him.

Megan could see it clearly, knew precisely what she wanted to capture: strength and determination behind a surface affability.

Though she had yet to admit it, Katch had frightened her the night before. Not physically—he was too intelligent to use brute force, she acknowledged—but by the force of his personality. Angrily, she stabbed at the clay. Obviously, this was a man who got what he wanted. But she was determined that this time he would not have his way. He would soon find out that she couldn't be pushed around any more than Pop could. Slowly and meticulously, her fingers worked to mold the planes of his face. It gave her a certain satisfaction to have control over him—if only vicariously with the clay.

Almost without thinking, she shaped a careless curl over the high brow. She stepped back to survey it. Somehow, she had caught a facet of his nature. He was a rogue, she decided. The old-fashioned word suited him. She could picture him with boots and six-guns, dealing cards for stud poker in a Tucson saloon; with a saber, captaining a ship into the Barbary Coast. Her fingers absently caressed the clay curls. He would laugh in the face of the wind, take treasure and women where he found them. *Women.* Megan's thoughts zeroed in on the night before . . . . On the feel of his lips on hers, the touch of his hand on her skin. She could remember the texture of the sand as they had lain together, the scent and sounds of the sea. And she remembered how the moonlight had fallen on his hair, how her hands had sought it while his lips had wandered over her. How thick and soft it had felt. How . . .

Megan stopped, appalled. She glanced down to see her fingers in the clay replica of Katch's hair. She swore, and nearly, very nearly, reduced the clay to a formless mass. Controlling herself, she rose, backing away from the forming bust. I should never allow myself to be distracted from my work by petty annoyances, she thought. Her evening with Katch belonged in that category. Just a petty annoyance. Not important.

But it was difficult for Megan to convince herself this was true. Both her intuition and her emotions told her that Katch was important, far more important than a stranger should be to a sensible woman.

And I *am* sensible, she reminded herself. Taking a long breath, she moved to the basin to rinse the clay from her hands. She had to be sensible. Pop needed someone around to remind him that bills had to be paid. A smile crept across her mouth as she dried her hands. Megan thought, as she did from time to time, that she had been almost as much of a savior to her grandfather as he had been to her.

In the beginning, she'd been so young, so dependent upon him. And he hadn't let her down. Then, as she had grown older, Megan had helped by assuming the duties her grandfather had found tiresome: accounts and bank reconciliations. Often, Megan suppressed her own desires in order to fulfill what she thought of as her duty. She dealt with figures, the unromantic process of adding and subtracting. But she also dealt with the illusionary world of art. There were times, when she was deep in her work, that she forgot the rules she had set up for day-to-day living. Often she felt pulled in two directions. She had enough to think about without David Katcherton.

Why a man virtually unknown to her should so successfully upset the delicate balance of her world, she didn't know. She shook her head. Instead of dwelling on it, she decided, she would work out her frustration by finishing the bust. When it was done, perhaps she would be able to see more clearly exactly how she perceived him. She returned to her work.

The next hour passed quickly. She forgot her irritation with Katch for going fishing with her grandfather. How annoying to have seen him so eager and well rested when she had peeked through her bedroom curtain at five-thirty that morning! She'd fallen back into her rumpled bed to spend another hour staring, heavy-eyed, at the ceiling. She refused to remember how appealing his laugh had sounded in the hush of dawn.

The planes of his face were just taking shape under her hands when she heard a car drive up. Katch's laugh was followed by the more gravelly tones of her grandfather's.

Because her studio was above the garage, Megan had a bird's-eye view of the house and drive. She watched as Katch lifted their fishing cooler from the back of the pickup. A grin was on his face, but whatever he said was too low for Megan to hear. Pop threw back his head, his dramatic mane of white flying back as he roared his appreciation. He gave Katch a companionable slap on the back. Unaccountably, Megan was miffed. They seemed to be getting along entirely too well.

She continued to watch the men as they unloaded tackle boxes and gear. Katch was dressed much as he had been the day before. The pale blue T-shirt had lettering across the chest, but the words were faded and the distance was too great for Megan to read them. He wore Pop's fishing cap, another source of annoyance for Megan. She was forced to admit the two of them looked good together. There was the contrast between their ages and their builds, but both seemed to her to be extraordinarily masculine men. Their looks were neither smooth nor pampered. She became engrossed with the similarities and differences between them. When Katch looked up, spotting her at the window, Megan continued to stare down, oblivious, absorbed with what she saw in them.

Katch grinned, pushing the fishing cap back so that he had a clearer view. The window was long, the sill coming low at her knees. It had the effect of making Megan seem to be standing in a full-size picture frame. As was her habit when working, she had pulled her hair back in a ribbon. Her face seemed younger and more vulnerable, her eyes wider. The ancient shirt of Pop's she used as a smock dwarfed her.

Her eyes locked on Katch's, and for a moment she thought she saw something flash in them—something she'd seen briefly the night before in the moonlight. A response trembled along her skin. Then his grin was arrogant again, his eyes amused.

"Come on down, Meg." He gestured before he bent to lift the cooler again. "We brought you a present." He turned to carry the cooler around the side of the house.

"I'd rather have emeralds," she called back.

"Next time," Katch promised carelessly, before turning to carry the cooler around the side of the house.

She found Katch alone, setting up for the cleaning of the catch. He smiled when he saw her and set down the knife he held, then pulled her into his arms and kissed her thoroughly, to her utter astonishment. It was a kiss of casual ownership rather than passion, but it elicited a response that surprised her with its force. More than a little shaken, Megan pushed away.

"You can't just . . ."

"I already did," he pointed out. "You've been working," Katch stated as if the searing kiss had never taken place. "I'd like to see your studio."

It was better, Megan decided, to follow his lead and keep the conversation light. "Where's my grandfather?" she asked as she moved to the cooler and prepared to lift the lid.

"Pop's inside stowing the gear."

Though it was the habit of everyone who knew him to refer to Timothy Miller as Pop, Megan frowned at Katch.

"You work fast, don't you?"

"Yes, I do. I like your grandfather, Meg. You of all people should understand how easy that is to do."

Megan regarded him steadily. She took a step closer, as if testing the air between them. "I don't know if I should trust you."

"You shouldn't." Katch grinned again and ran a finger down the bridge of her nose. "Not for a second." He tossed open the lid of the cooler, then gestured to the fish inside. "Hungry?"

Megan smiled, letting herself be charmed despite the warnings of her sensible self. "I wasn't. But I could be. Especially if I don't have to clean them."

"Pop told me you were squeamish."

"Oh, he *did,* did he?" Megan cast a long, baleful look over her shoulder toward the house. "What else did he tell you?"

"That you like daffodils and used to have a stuffed elephant named Henry."

Megan's mouth dropped open. "He told you that?"

"And that you watch horror movies, then sleep with the blankets over your head."

Megan narrowed her eyes as Katch's grin widened. "Excuse me," she said crossly, pushing Katch aside before racing through the kitchen door. She could hear Katch's laughter behind her.

"Pop!" She found him in the narrow room off the kitchen where he stored his fishing paraphernalia. He gave her an affectionate smile as she stood, hands on hips, in the doorway.

"Hi, Megan. Let me tell you, that boy knows how to fish. Yessiree, he knows how to fish."

His obvious delight with Katch caused Megan to clench her teeth. "That's the best news I've had all day," she said, stepping into the room. "But exactly why did you feel it necessary to tell *that boy* that I had a stuffed elephant and slept with the covers over my head?"

Pop lifted a hand, ostensibly to scratch his head. It wasn't in time, however, to conceal the grin. Megan's brows drew together.

"Pop, really," she said in exasperation. "Must you babble about me as if I were a little girl?"

"You'll always be my little girl," he said maddeningly, and kissed her cheek. "Did you see those trout? We'll have a heck of a fish fry tonight."

"I suppose," Megan began and folded her arms, "*he's* going to eat with us."

"Well, of course." Pop blinked his eyes. "After all, Meg, he caught half the fish."

"That's just peachy."

"We thought you might whip up some of your special blueberry tarts." He smiled ingenuously.

Megan sighed, recognizing defeat.

Within minutes, Pop heard the thumping and banging of pans. He grinned, then slipped out of the room, moving noiselessly through the house and out the front door.

"Whip up some tarts," Megan muttered later as she cut shortening into the flour. *"Men."*

She was bending over to slip the pastry shells into the oven when the screen door slammed shut behind her. Turning, she brushed at the seat of her pants and met the predictable grin.

"I've heard about your tarts," Katch commented, setting the cleaned, filleted fish on the counter. "Pop said he had a few things to see to in the garage and to call him when dinner's ready."

Megan glared through the screen door at the adjoining building. "Oh, he did, did he?" She turned back to Katch. "Well, if you think you can just sit back and be waited on, then you're in for a disappointment."

"You didn't think I'd allow you to cook my fish, did you?" he interrupted.

She stared at his unperturbed face.

"I always cook my own fish. Where's the frying pan?"

Silently, still eyeing him, Megan pointed out the cabinet. She watched as he squatted down to rummage for it.

"It's not that I don't think you're a good cook," he went on as he stood again with the cast-iron skillet in his hand. "It's that I know I am."

"Are you implying I couldn't cook those pathetic little sardines properly?"

"Let's just say I just don't like to take chances with my dinner." He began poking into cupboards. "Why don't you make a salad," he suggested mildly, "and leave the fish to me?" There was a grunt of approval as he located the cracker meal.

Megan watched him casually going through her kitchen cupboards. "Why don't you," she began, "take your trout and . . ."

Her suggestion was interrupted by the rude buzz of the oven timer.

"Your tarts." Katch walked to the refrigerator for eggs and milk.

With supreme effort, Megan controlled herself enough to deal with the pastry shells. Setting them on the rack to cool, she decided to create the salad of the decade. It would put his pan-fried trout to shame.

For a time there were no words. The hot oil hissed as Katch added his coated trout. Megan tore the lettuce. She sliced raw vegetables. The scent from the pan was enticing. Megan peeled a carrot and sighed. Hearing her, Katch raised a questioning eyebrow.

"You had to be good at it, didn't you?" Megan's smile was reluctant. "You had to do it right."

He shrugged, then snatched the peeled carrot from her hand. "You'd like it better if I didn't?" Katch took a bite of the carrot before Megan could retrieve it. Shaking her head, she selected another.

"It would have been more gratifying if you'd fumbled around and made a mess of things."

Katch tilted his head as he poked at the sizzling fish with a spatula. "Is that a compliment?"

Megan diced the carrot, frowning at it thoughtfully. "I don't know. It might be easier to deal with you if you didn't seem so capable."

He caught her off guard by taking her shoulders and turning her around to face him. "Is that what you want to do?" His fingers gently massaged her flesh. "Deal with me?" When she felt herself being drawn closer, she placed her hands on his chest. "Do I make you nervous?"

"No." Megan shook her head with the denial. "No, of course not." Katch only lifted a brow and drew her closer. "Yes," she admitted in a rush, and pulled away. "Yes, blast it, you do." Stalking to the refrigerator, she yanked out the blueberry filling she had prepared. "You needn't look so pleased about it," she told him, wishing she could work up the annoyance she thought she should feel.

"Several things make me nervous." Megan moved to the pastry shells and began to spoon in the filling. "Snakes, tooth decay, large unfriendly dogs." When she heard him chuckle, Megan turned her head and found herself grinning at him. "It's difficult to actively dislike you when you make me laugh."

"Do you have to actively dislike me?" Katch flipped the fish expertly and sent oil sizzling.

"That was my plan," Megan admitted. "It seemed like a good idea."

"Why don't we work on a different plan?" Katch suggested, searching through a cupboard again for a platter. "What do you like? Besides daffodils?"

"Soft ice cream," Megan responded spontaneously. "Oscar Wilde, walking barefoot."

"How about baseball?" Katch demanded.

Megan paused in the act of filling the shells. "What about it?"

"Do you like it?"

"Yes," she considered, smiling. "As a matter of fact, I do."

"I knew we had something in common." Katch grinned. He turned the flame off under the pan. "Why don't you call Pop? The fish is done."

There was something altogether too cozy about the three of them sitting around the kitchen table eating a meal each of them had a part in providing, Megan thought. She could sense the growing affection between the two men and it worried her. She was sure that Katch was still as determined as ever to buy Joyland. Yet Pop was so obviously happy in his company. Megan decided that, while she couldn't trust Katch unreservedly, neither could she maintain her original plan. She couldn't dislike him or keep him from touching their lives. She thought it best not to dwell on precisely how he was touching hers.

"Tell you what." Pop sighed over his empty plate and leaned back in his chair. "Since the pair of you cooked dinner, I'll do the dishes." His eyes passed over Megan to Katch. "Why don't you two go for a walk? Megan likes to walk on the beach."

"Pop!"

"I know you young people like to be alone," he continued shamelessly.

Megan opened her mouth to protest, but Katch spoke first. "I'm always willing to take a walk with a beautiful woman, especially if it means getting out of KP," he said.

"You have such a gracious way of putting things," Megan began.

"Actually, I'd really like to see your studio."

"Take Katch up, Megan," Pop insisted. "I've been bragging about your pieces all day. Let him see for himself."

After a moment's hesitation, Megan decided it was simpler to agree. Certainly she didn't mind showing Katch her work. And, there was little doubt that it was safer to let him putter around her studio than to walk with him on the beach.

"All right." She rose. "I'll take you up."

As they passed through the screen door, Katch slipped his arm over her shoulders. "This is a nice place," he commented. He looked around the small trim yard lined with azalea shrubs. "Very quiet and settled."

The weight of his arm was pleasant. Megan allowed it to remain as they walked toward the garage. "I wouldn't think you'd find something quiet and settled terribly appealing."

"There's a time for porch swings and a time for roller coasters." Katch glanced down at her as she paused at the foot of the steps. "I'd think you'd know that."

"I do," she said, knowing her involvement with him was beginning to slip beyond her control. "I wasn't aware you did." Thoughtfully, Megan climbed the stairs. "It's rather a small-scale studio, I suppose, and not very impressive. It's really just a place to work where I won't disturb Pop and he won't disturb me."

Megan opened the door, flicking on the light as the sun was growing dim.

There was much less order here than she permitted herself in other areas of her life. The room was hers, personally, more exclusively than her bedroom in the house next door. There were tools—calipers, chisels, gouges, and an assortment of knives and files. There was the smock she'd carelessly thrown over a chair when Katch had called her downstairs. Future projects sat waiting inside, untouched slabs of limestone and chunks of wood. There was a precious piece of marble she hoarded like a miser. Everywhere, on shelves, tables and even the floor, were samples of her work.

Katch moved past her into the room. Strangely, Megan felt a flutter of nerves. She found herself wondering how to react if he spoke critically, or worse, offered some trite compliment. Her work was important to her and very personal. To her surprise she realized that she cared about his opinion. Quietly, she closed the door behind her, then stood with her back against it.

Katch had gone directly to a small walnut study of a young girl building a sand castle. She was particularly pleased with the piece, as she had achieved exactly the mood she had sought. There was more than youth and innocence in the child's face. The girl saw herself as the princess in the castle tower. The half-smile on her face made the onlooker believe in happy endings.

It was painstakingly detailed, the beginnings of a crenellated roof and the turrets of the castle, the slender fingers of the girl as she sculpted the sand. Her hair was long, falling over her shoulders and wisping into her face as though a breeze teased it. Megan had felt successful when the study had been complete, but now, watching Katch turn it over in his hands, his mouth oddly grave, his eyes intent, she felt a twinge of doubt.

"This is your work?" Because the silence had seemed so permanent, Megan jerked when Katch spoke.

"Well, yes." While she was still searching for something more to say, Katch turned away to prowl the room.

He picked up piece after piece, examining, saying nothing. As the silence dragged on, minute upon minute, Megan became more and more tense. If he'd just say something, she thought. She picked up the discarded smock and folded it, nervously smoothing creases as she listened to the soft sound of his tennis shoes on the wood floor.

"What are you doing here?"

She whirled, eyes wide. Whatever reaction she had expected, it certainly hadn't been anger. And there was anger on his face, a sharp, penetrating anger which caused her to grip the worn material of the smock tighter.

"I don't know what you mean." Megan's voice was calm, but her heart had begun to beat faster.

"Why are you hiding?" he demanded. "What are you afraid of?"

She shook her head in bewilderment. "I'm not hiding, Katch. You're not making any sense."

"I'm not making sense?" He took a step toward her, then

stopped, turning away to pace again. She watched in fascination. "Do you think it makes sense to create things like this and lock them up in a room over a garage?" He lifted polished limestone which had been formed into a head-and-shoulders study of a man and a woman in each other's arms. "When you've been given talent like this, you have an obligation. What are you going to do, continue to stack them in here until there isn't any more room?"

His reaction had thrown Megan completely off-balance. She looked around the room. "No, I . . . I take pieces into an art gallery downtown now and then. They sell fairly well, especially during the season, and—"

Katch's pungent oath cut her off. Megan gave her full attention back to him. Was this furious, disapproving man the same one who had amiably prepared trout in her kitchen a short time ago?

"I don't understand why you're so mad." Annoyed with herself for nervously pleating the material of the smock, Megan tossed it down.

"Waste," he said tersely, placing the limestone back on the shelf. "Waste infuriates me." He came to her, taking her deliberately by the shoulders. "Why haven't you done anything with your work?" His eyes were direct on hers, demanding answers, not evasions.

"It's not as simple as that," she began. "I have responsibilities."

"Your responsibilities are to yourself, to your talent."

"You make it sound as though I've done something wrong." Confused, Megan searched his face. "I've done what I know how to do. I don't understand why you're angry. There are things, like time and money, to be considered," she went on. "A business to run. And reality to face." Megan shook her head. "I can hardly cart my work to a Charleston art gallery and demand a showing."

"That would make more sense than cloistering it up here."
He released her abruptly, then paced again.

He was, Megan discovered, much more volatile than her
first impression had allowed. She glanced at the clay wrapped
in the damp towel. Her fingertips itched to work while fresh
impressions were streaming through her brain.

"When's the last time you've been to New York?" Katch
demanded, facing her again. "Chicago, L.A.?"

"We can't all be globetrotters," she told him. "Some are
born to other things."

He picked up the sand-castle girl again, then strode over
to the limestone couple. "I want these two," he stated. "Will
you sell them to me?"

They were two of her favorites, though totally opposite in
tone. "Yes, I suppose. If you want them."

"I'll give you five hundred." Megan's eyes widened.
"Apiece."

"Oh, no, they're not worth—"

"They're worth a lot more, I imagine." Katch lifted the
limestone. "Have you got a box I can carry them in?"

"Yes, but, Katch." Megan paused and pushed the bangs
from her eyes. "A thousand dollars?"

He set down both pieces and came back to her. He was
still angry; she could feel it vibrating from him. "Do you
think it's safer to underestimate yourself than to face up to
your own worth?"

Megan started to make a furious denial, then stopped. Uncertain, she made a helpless gesture with her hands. Katch
turned away again to search for a box himself. She watched
him as he wrapped the sculptures in old newspapers. The
frown was still on his face, the temper in his eyes.

"I'll bring you a check," he stated, and was gone without
another word.

CHAPTER 5

There was a long, high-pitched scream. The roller coaster rumbled along the track as it whipped around another curve and tilted its passengers. Lights along the midway were twinkling, and there was noise. Such noise. There was the whirl and whine of machinery, the electronic buzz and beeps from video games, the pop of arcade rifles and the call of concessionaires.

Tinny music floated all over, but for the most part, there was the sound of people. They were laughing, calling, talking, shouting. There were smells: popcorn, peanuts, grilled hot dogs, machine oil.

Megan loaded another clip into the scaled-down rifle and handed it to a would-be Wyatt Earp. "Rabbits are five points, ducks ten, deer twenty-five and the bears fifty."

The sixteen-year-old sharpshooter aimed and managed to bag a duck and a rabbit. He chose a rubber snake as his prize, to the ensuing screams and disgust of his girl.

Shaking her head, Megan watched them walk away. The boy slipped his arm around the girl's shoulders, then pursued the romance by dangling the snake in front of her face. He earned a quick jab in the ribs.

The crowd was thin tonight, but that was to be expected in

the off-season. Particularly, Megan knew, when there were so many other parks with more rides, live entertainment and a more sophisticated selection of video games. She didn't mind the slack. Megan was preoccupied, as she had been since the evening Katch had seen her studio. In three days, she hadn't heard a word from him. At first, she had wanted badly to see him, to talk about the things he'd said to her. He had made her think, made her consider a part of herself she had ignored or submerged most of her life.

Her desire to speak with Katch had faded as the days had passed, however. After all, what right did he have to criticize her lifestyle? What right did he have to make her feel as if she'd committed a crime? He'd accused, tried and condemned her in the space of minutes. Then, he'd disappeared.

Three days, Megan mused, handing another hopeful deadeye a rifle. Three days without a word. And she'd watched for him—much to her self-disgust. She'd waited for him. As the days had passed, Megan had taken refuge in anger. Not only had he criticized and scolded her, she remembered, but he'd walked out with two of her favorite sculptures. A thousand dollars my foot, she mused, frowning fiercely as she slid a fresh clip into an empty rifle. Just talk, that's all. Talk. He does that very well. It was probably all a line, owning that restaurant. *But why?* Men like that don't need logical reasons, she decided. It's all ego.

"Men," she muttered as she handed a rifle to a new customer.

"I know what you mean, honey." The plump blond woman took the rifle from Megan with a wink.

Megan pushed her bangs back and frowned deeper. "Who needs them?" she demanded.

The woman shouldered the rifle. "We do, honey. That's the problem."

Megan let out a long sigh as the woman earned 125 points.

"Nice shooting," she congratulated. "Your choice on the second row."

"Let me have the hippo, sweetie. It looks a little like my second husband."

Laughing, Megan plucked it from the shelf and handed it over. "Here you go." With another wink, the woman tucked the hippo under her arm and waddled off.

Megan settled back while two kids tried their luck. The exchange had been typical of the informality enjoyed by people in amusement parks. She smiled, feeling less grim, if not entirely mollified by the woman's remarks. But she doesn't know Katch, Megan reflected, again exchanging a rifle for a quarter. And neither, she reminded herself, do I.

Automatically, Megan made change when a dollar bill was placed on the counter. "Ten shots for a quarter," she began the spiel. "Rabbits are five, ducks ten . . ." Megan pushed three quarters back as she reached for a rifle. The moment the fingers pushed the change back to her, she recognized them.

"I'll take a dollar's worth," Katch told her as she looked up in surprise. He grinned, then leaned over to press a quick kiss to her lips. "For luck," he claimed when she jerked away.

Before Megan had pocketed the quarters, Katch had bull's-eyed every one of the bears.

"Wow!" The two boys standing next to Katch were suitably impressed. "Hey, mister, can you do it again?" one asked.

"Maybe." Katch turned to Megan. "Let's have a reload." Without speaking, she handed him the rifle.

"I like the perfume you're wearing," he commented as he sighed. "What is it?"

"Gun oil."

He laughed, then blasted the hapless bears one by one. The two boys gave simultaneous yelps of appreciation. A crowd began to gather.

"Hey, Megan." She glanced up to see the Bailey twins leaning over the counter. Both pairs of eyes drifted meaningfully to Katch. "Isn't he the . . ."

"Yes," Megan said shortly, not wanting to explain.

"Delicious," Teri decided quietly, giving Katch a flirtatious smile when he straightened.

"Mmm-hmm," Jeri agreed with a twin smile.

Katch gave them a long, appreciative look.

"Here." Megan shoved the rifle at him. "This is your last quarter."

Katch accepted the rifle. "Thanks." He hefted it again. "Going to wish me luck?"

Megan met his eyes levelly. "Why not?"

"Meg, I'm crazy about you."

She dealt with the surge his careless words brought her as he picked off his fourth set of bears. Bystanders broke into raucous applause. Katch set the rifle on the counter, then gave his full attention to Meg.

"What'd I win?"

"Anything you want."

His grin was a flash, and his eyes never left her face. She blushed instantly, hating herself. Deliberately, she stepped to the side and gestured toward the prizes.

"I'll take Henry," he told her. When she gave him a puzzled look, he pointed. "The elephant." Glancing up, Megan spotted the three-foot lavender elephant. She lifted it down from its perch. Even as she set it on the counter for him, Katch took her hands. "And you."

She made her voice prim. "Only the items on display are eligible prizes."

"I love it when you talk that way," he commented.

"Stop it!" she hissed, flushing as she heard the Bailey twins giggle.

"We had a bet, remember?" Katch smiled at her. "It's Friday night."

Megan tried to tug her hands away, but his fingers interlocked with hers. "Who says I lost the bet?" she demanded. The crowd was still milling around the stand so she spoke in an undertone, but Katch didn't bother.

"Come on, Meg, I won fair and square. You're not going to welch, are you?"

"Shh!" She glanced behind him at the curious crowd. "I never welch," she whispered furiously. "And even if I did lose, which I never said I did, I can't leave the stand. I'm sure you can find somebody else to keep you company."

"I want you."

She struggled to keep her eyes steady on his. "Well, I can't leave. Someone has to run the booth."

"Megan." One of the part-timers slipped under the counter. "Pop sent me to relieve you." He smiled innocently when she gave him a disgusted look.

"Perfect timing," she mumbled, then stripped off the change apron and stuffed it in his hands. "Thanks a lot."

"Sure, Megan."

"Hey, keep this back there for me, will you?" Katch dumped the elephant into his arms and captured Megan's hands again as she ducked under the counter. As she straightened, he tugged, tumbling her into his arms.

The kiss was long and demanding. When Katch drew her away, her arms were around his neck. She left them there, staring up into his face with eyes newly aware and darkened.

"I've wanted to do that for three days," he murmured, and rubbed her nose lightly with his.

"Why didn't you?"

He lifted a brow at that, then grinned when her blush betrayed the impetuousness of her words.

"I didn't mean that the way it sounded," Megan began, dropping her arms and trying to wriggle away.

"Yes you did," he countered. Katch released her but dropped a friendly arm over her shoulder. "It was nice, don't spoil it." He took a sweeping glance of the park. "How about a tour?"

"I don't know why you want one. We're not selling."

"We'll see about that," he said, as maddeningly confident as ever. "But in any case, I'm interested. Do you know why people come here? To a place like this?" He gestured with his free arm to encompass the park.

"To be entertained," Megan told him as she followed the movement of his arm.

"You left out two of the most important reasons," he added. "To fantasize and to show off."

They stopped to watch a middle-aged man strip out of his jacket and attempt to ring the bell. The hammer came down with a loud thump, but the ball rose only halfway up the pole. He rubbed his hands together and prepared to try again.

"Yes, you're right." Megan tossed her hair back with a move of her head, then smiled at Katch. "You ought to know."

He tilted his head and shot her a grin. "Want me to ring the bell?"

"Muscles don't impress me," she said firmly.

"No?" He guided her away with his arm still around her. "What does?"

"Poetry," Megan decided all at once.

"Hmm." Katch rubbed his chin and avoided a trio of teenagers. "How about a limerick? I know some great limericks."

"I bet you do." Megan shook her head. "I think I'll pass."

"Coward."

"Oh? Let's ride the roller coaster, then we'll see who's a coward."

"You're on." Taking her hand, he set off in a sprint. He stopped at the ticket booth, and gratefully she caught her breath.

I might as well face it, she reflected as she studied his face. I enjoy him. There isn't any use in pretending I don't.

"What are you thinking?" Katch demanded as he paid for their ride.

"That I could learn to like you—in three or four years. For short periods of time," she added, still smiling.

Katch took both her hands and kissed them, surprising Megan with the shock that raced up her arms. "Flatterer," he murmured, and his eyes laughed at her over their joined hands.

Distressed by the power she felt rushing through her system, Megan tried to tug her hands from his. It was imperative, for reasons only half-formed in her brain, that she keep their relationship casual.

"You have to hold my hand." Katch jerked his head toward the roller coaster. "I'm afraid of heights."

Megan laughed. She let herself forget the tempestuous instant and the hint of danger. She kept her hand in his.

Katch wasn't satisfied with only the roller coaster. He pulled Megan to ride after ride. They were scrambled on the Mind Maze, spooked in the Haunted Castle and spun lazily on the Ferris wheel.

From the top of the wheel, they watched the colored lights of the park, and the sea stretching out to the right. The wind tossed her hair into her face. Katch took it in his hand as they rose toward the top again. When he kissed her, it felt natural and right . . . a shared thing, a moment which belonged only to them. The noise and people below were of another world. Theirs was only the gentle movement of the wheel and the dance of the breeze. And the touch of mouth on mouth. There was no demand, only an offering of pleasure.

Megan relaxed against him, finding her head fit naturally in the curve of his shoulder. Held close beside him, she watched the world revolve. Above, the stars were scattered and few. A waning moon shifted in and out of the clouds. The air was cool with a hint of the sea. She sighed, utterly content.

"When's the last time you did this?"

"Did what?" Megan tilted her head to look at him. Their faces were close, but she felt no danger now, only satisfaction.

"Enjoyed this park." Katch had caught the confusion on her face. "Just enjoyed it, Megan, for the fun."

"I . . ." The Ferris wheel slowed, then stopped. The carts rocked gently as old passengers were exchanged for new. She remembered times when she had been very young. When had they stopped? "I don't know." Megan rose when the attendant lifted the safety bar.

This time, as she walked with Katch, she looked around thoughtfully. She saw several people she knew; locals out for an evening's entertainment mixed with tourists taking a pre-season vacation.

"You need to do this more often," Katch commented, steering her toward the east end of the park. "Laugh," he continued as she turned her head to him. "Unbend, relax those restrictions you put on yourself."

Megan's spine stiffened. "For somebody who barely knows me, you seem remarkably certain of what's good for me."

"It isn't difficult." He stopped at a concession wagon and ordered two ice-cream cones. "You haven't any mysteries, Meg."

"Thank you very much."

With a laugh, Katch handed her a cone. "Don't get huffy, I meant that as a compliment."

"I suppose you've known a lot of sophisticated women."

Katch smiled, then his arm came around her as they began to walk again. "There's one, her name's Jessica. She's one of the most beautiful women I know."

"Really?" Megan licked at the soft swirl of vanilla.

"That blond, classical look. You know, fair skin, finely chiseled features, blue eyes. Terrific blue eyes."

"How interesting."

"Oh, she's all of that," he continued. "And more: intelligent, a sense of humor."

"You sound very fond of her." Megan gave the ice cream her undivided attention.

"A bit more than that actually. Jessica and I lived together for a number of years." He dropped the bomb matter-of-factly. "She's married now and has a couple of kids, but we still manage to see each other now and again. Maybe she can make it down for a few days, then you can meet her."

"Oh, really!" Megan stopped, incensed. "Flaunt your relationship somewhere else. If you think I want to meet your— your . . ."

"Sister," Katch supplied, then crunched into his cone. "You'd like her. Your ice cream's dripping, Meg."

They walked to the entrance gates of the park.

"It's a very nice park," Katch murmured. "Small but well set up. No bored-faced attendants." He reached absently in his pocket and pulled out a slip of paper.

"I forgot to give you your check."

Megan stuffed it into her pocket without even glancing at it. Her eyes were on Katch's face. She was all too aware of the direction his thoughts had taken. "My grandfather's devoted his life to this park," she reminded him.

"So have you," Katch said.

"Why do you want to buy it?" she asked. "To make money?"

Katch was silent for a long moment. By mutual consent, they cut across the boardwalk and moved down the sloping sand toward the water. "Is that such a bad reason, Megan? Do you object to making money?"

"No, of course not. That would be ridiculous."

"I wondered if that was why you haven't done anything with your sculpting."

"No. I do what I'm capable of doing, and what I have time for. There are priorities."

"Perhaps you have them wrong." Before she could comment, he spoke again. "How would it affect the park's business if it had some updated rides and an expanded arcade?"

"We can't afford . . ."

"That wasn't my question." He took her by the shoulders and his eyes were serious.

"Business would improve, naturally," Megan answered. "People come here to be entertained. The more entertainment provided, the slicker, the faster the entertainment, the happier they are. And the more money they spend."

Katch nodded as he searched her face. "Those were my thoughts."

"It's academic because we simply haven't the sort of money necessary for an overhaul."

"Hmm?" Though he was looking directly at her, Megan saw that his attention had wandered. She watched it refocus.

"What are you thinking?" she demanded.

The grip on her shoulder altered to a caress. "That you're extraordinarily beautiful."

Megan pulled away. "No, you weren't."

"It's what I'm thinking now." The gleam was back in his eyes as he put his hands to her waist. "It's what I was thinking the first time I saw you."

"You're ridiculous." She made an attempt to pull away, but he caught her closer.

"I've never denied that. But you can't call me ridiculous for finding you beautiful." The wind blew her hair back, leaving her face unframed. He laid a soft, unexpected kiss on her forehead. Megan felt her knees turn to water. She placed her hands on his chest both for support and in protest. "You're an artist." He drew her fractionally closer, and his voice lowered. "You recognize beauty when you see it."

"Don't!" The protest was feeble as she made no attempt to struggle out of his gentle hold.

"Don't what? Don't kiss you?" Slowly, luxuriously, his mouth journeyed over her skin. "But I have to, Meg." His lips touched hers softly, then withdrew, and her heart seemed to stop. The flavor of his lips as they brushed against hers overwhelmed her. They tempted, then ruled. With a moan of pleasure, Megan drew him close against her.

Something seemed to explode inside her as the kiss deepened. She clung to him a moment, dazed, then terrified by the power of it. Needs, emotions and new sensations tumbled together too quickly for her to control them. As panic swamped her, Megan struggled in his arms. She would have run, blindly, without direction, but Katch took her arms and held her still.

"What is it? You're trembling." Gently, he tilted her chin until their eyes met. Hers were wide, his serious. "I didn't mean to frighten you. I'm sorry."

The gentleness was nearly her undoing. Love, so newly discovered, hammered for release. She shook her head, knowing her voice would be thick with tears if she spoke. Swallowing, Megan prayed she could steady it.

"No, it's . . . I have to get back. They're closing." Behind him, she could see the lights flickering off.

"Meg." The tone halted her. It was not a demand this time, but a request. "Have dinner with me."

"No—"

"I haven't even suggested an evening," he pointed out mildly. "How about Monday?"

Megan stood firm. "No."

"Please."

Her resolution dissolved on a sigh. "You don't play fair," she murmured.

"Never. How about seven?"

"No picnics on the beach," she compromised.

"We'll eat inside, I promise."

"All right, but just dinner." She stepped away from him. "Now, I have to go."

"I'll walk you back." Katch took her hand and kissed it before she could stop him. "I have to get my elephant."

CHAPTER 6

Megan held Katch's face in her hands. With totally focused absorption, she formed his cheekbones. She had thought when she had first begun to work on this bust that morning that it would be good therapy. To an extent, she'd been right. The hours had passed peacefully, without the restless worry of the past two nights. Her mind was centered on her work, leaving no spaces for the disturbing thoughts that had plagued her all weekend.

She opened and closed her hands slowly, using the muscles until the cramping was a dull ache. A glance at her watch told her she had worked for longer than she'd intended. Late afternoon sun poured through the windows. Critically, as she pulled on each finger to soothe it, Megan studied her work.

The model was good, she decided, with just the proper touches of roughness and intelligence she had aimed for. The mouth was strong and sensuous, the eyes perceptive and far too aware. The mobility of the face which Megan found fascinating could only be suggested. It was a face that urged one to trust against better judgment and common sense.

Narrowing her eyes, she studied the clay replica of Katch's face. There are certain men, she thought, who make a career out of women—winning them, making love to them, leaving them. There are other men who settle down and marry, raise families. How could she doubt what category Katch fell into?

Megan rose to wash her hands. Infatuation, she reflected. It's simply infatuation. He's different, and I can't deny he's exciting. I wouldn't be human if I weren't flattered that he's attracted to me. I've overreacted, that's all. She dried her hands on a towel and tried to convince herself. A person doesn't fall in love this quickly. And if they do, it's just a surface thing, nothing lasting. Megan's eyes were drawn to the clay model. Katch's smile seemed to mock all her sensible arguments. She hurled the towel to the floor.

"It can't happen this fast!" she told him furiously. "Not this way. Not to me." She swung away from his assured expression. "I won't let it."

It's only the park he wants, she reminded herself. Once he's finally convinced he can't have it, he'll go away. The ache was unexpected, and unwelcome. That's what I want, she thought. For him to go away and leave us alone. She tried not to remember the new frontiers she had glimpsed while being held in his arms.

With a brisk shake of her head, Megan pulled the tie from her hair so that it tumbled back to brush her shoulders. I'll start in wood tomorrow, she decided, and covered the clay model. Tonight, I'll simply enjoy a dinner date with an attractive man. It's that simple.

With a great deal more ease than she was feeling, Megan took off her work smock and left her studio.

H i, sweetheart." Pop pulled the truck into the driveway just as Megan reached the bottom step.

She noticed the weariness the moment he climbed from

the cab. Knowing he hated fussing, she said nothing, but walked over and slipped an arm around his waist.

"Hi, yourself. You've been gone a long time."

"A problem or two at the park," he told her as they moved together toward the house.

That explained the weariness, Megan thought as she pushed open the back door. "What sort of problem?" Megan waited for him to settle himself at the kitchen table before she walked to the stove to brew tea.

"Repairs, Megan, just repairs. The coaster and the Octopus and a few of the smaller rides." He leaned back in his chair as Megan turned to face him.

"How bad?"

Pop sighed, knowing it was better to tell her outright than to hedge. "Ten thousand, maybe fifteen."

Megan let out a long, steady breath. "Ten thousand dollars." She ran a hand under her bangs to rub her brow. There was no purpose in asking if he was sure. If he'd had any doubt, he'd have kept the matter to himself.

"Well, we can come up with five," she began, lumping the check she had just received from Katch into their savings. "We'll have to have a more exact amount so we can decide how big a loan we'll need."

"Banks take a dim view of lending great lumps of money to people my age," Pop murmured.

Because she saw he was tired and discouraged, she spoke briskly. "Don't be silly." She walked back to the stove to set on the kettle. "In any case, they'd be lending it to the park, wouldn't they?" She tried not to think of tight money and high interest rates.

"I'll go see a few people tomorrow," he promised, reaching for his pipe as if to indicate their business talk was over. "You're having dinner with Katch tonight?"

"Yes." Megan took out cups and saucers.

"Fine young man." He puffed pleasantly on his pipe. "I like him. Has style."

"He has style all right," she grumbled as the kettle began to sing. Carefully, she poured boiling water into cups.

"Knows how to fish," Pop pointed out.

"Which, of course, makes him a paragon of virtue."

"Well, it doesn't make me think any less of him." He spoke genially, smiling into Megan's face. "I couldn't help noticing the two of you on the wheel the other night. You looked real pretty together."

"Pop, really." Feeling her cheeks warm, Megan walked back to fiddle with the dishes in the sink.

"You seemed to like him well enough then," he pointed out before he tested his tea. "I didn't notice any objections when he kissed you." Pop sipped, enjoying. "In fact, you seemed to like it."

"Pop!" Megan turned back, astonished.

"Now, Meg, I wasn't spying," he said soothingly, and coughed to mask a chuckle. "You were right out in public, you know. I'd wager a lot of people noticed. Like I said, you looked real pretty together."

Megan came back to sit at the table without any idea of what she should say. "It was just a kiss," she managed at length. "It didn't mean anything."

Pop nodded twice and drank his tea.

"It didn't," Megan insisted.

He gave her one of his angelic smiles. "But you do like him, don't you?"

Megan dropped her eyes. "Sometimes," she murmured. "Sometimes I do."

Pop covered her hand with his and waited until she looked at him again. "Caring for someone is the easiest thing in the world if you let it be."

"I hardly know him," she said quickly.

"I trust him," Pop said simply.

Megan searched his face. "Why?"

After a shrug, Pop drew on his pipe again. "A feeling I have, a look in his eyes. In a people business like mine, you get to be a good judge of character. He has integrity. He wants his way, all right, but he doesn't cheat. That's important."

Megan sat silently for a moment, not touching her cooling tea. "He wants the park," she said quietly.

Pop looked at her through a nimbus of pipe smoke. "Yes, I know. He said so up front. He doesn't sneak around either." Pop's expression softened a bit as he looked into Megan's eyes. "Things don't always stay the same in life, Megan. That's what makes it work."

"I don't know what you mean. Do you . . . are you thinking of selling him the park?"

Pop heard the underlying hint of panic and patted her hand again. "Let's not worry about that now. The first problem is getting the rides repaired for the Easter break. Why don't you wear the yellow dress I like tonight, Meg? The one with the little jacket. It makes me think of spring."

Megan considered questioning him further, then subsided. There was no harder nut to crack than her grandfather when he had made up his mind to close a subject. "All right. I think I'll go up and have a bath."

"Megan." She turned at the door and looked back at him. "Enjoy yourself. Sometimes it's best to roll with the punches."

When she walked away, he looked at the empty doorway and thoughtfully stroked his beard.

An hour later, Megan looked at herself in the yellow dress. The shade hinted at apricot and warmed against her skin. The lines were simple, suiting her willow-slim figure and height. Without the jacket, her arms and shoulders were bare but for wispy straps. She ran a brush through her hair in long, steady strokes. The tiny gold hoops in her ears were her only jewelry.

"Hey, Megan!"

The brush paused in midair as she watched her own eyes widen in the mirror. He wasn't really standing outside shouting for her!

"Meg!"

Shaking her head in disbelief, Megan went to the window. Katch stood two stories down. He lifted a hand in salute when she appeared in the window.

"What are you doing?" she demanded.

"Open the screen."

"Why?"

"Open it," he repeated.

"If you expect me to jump, you can forget it." Out of curiosity, she leaned out the window.

"Catch!"

Her reflexes responded before she could think. Megan reached for the bundle he tossed up to her, and found her hands full of daffodils. She buried her face in the bouquet.

"They're beautiful." Her eyes smiled over the blooms and down at him. "Thank you."

"You're welcome," he returned. "Are you coming down?"

"Yes." She tossed her hair behind her shoulder. "Yes, yes, in a minute."

Katch drove quickly and competently, but not toward Restaurant Row as Megan had anticipated. He turned toward the ocean and headed north. She relaxed, enjoying the quieting light of dusk and his effortless driving.

She recognized the area. The houses there were larger, more elaborate than those in and on the very outskirts of

town. There were tall hedges to assure privacy both from
other houses and the public beaches. There were neatly
trimmed lawns, willows, blossoming crepe myrtle, and as-
phalt drives. Katch pulled into one set well away from the
other homes and bordered by purplish shrubbery.

The house was small by the neighborhood standards, and
done in the weathered wood Megan invariably found attractive. It was a split-level building, with an observation deck
crowning the upper story.

"What's this?" she asked, liking the house immediately.

"This is where I live." Katch leaned across her to unlatch
her door, then slid out his own side.

"You live here?"

Katch smiled at the surprised doubt in her voice. "I have
to live somewhere, Meg."

She wandered farther along the stone path that led to the
house. "I suppose I really didn't think about you buying a
house here. It suggests roots."

"I have them," he told her. "I just transplant them easily."

She looked at the house, the widespread yard. "You've
picked the perfect spot."

Katch took her hand, interlocking fingers. "Come inside,"
he invited.

"When did you buy this?" she asked as they climbed the
front steps.

"Oh, a few months ago when I came through. I moved in
last week and haven't had a lot of time to look for furniture."
The key shot into the lock. "I've picked up a few things here
and there, and had others sent down from my apartment in
New York."

It was scantily furnished, but with style. There was a low,
sectional sofa in biscuit with a hodgepodge of colored pillows
and a wicker throne chair coupled with a large hanging ivy
in a pottery dish. A pair of étagères in brass and glass held a

collection of shells; on the oak planked floor lay a large sisal rug.

The room was open, with stairs to the right leading to the second level, and a stone fireplace on the left wall. The quick survey showed Megan he had not placed her sculptures in the main room. She wondered fleetingly what he had done with them.

"It's wonderful, Katch." She wandered to a window. The lawn sloped downward and ended in tall hedges that gave the house comfortable privacy. "Can you see the ocean from the top level?"

When he didn't answer, she turned back to him. Her smile faded against the intensity of his gaze. Her heart beat faster. This was the part of him she had to fear, not the amiable gallant who had tossed her daffodils.

She tilted her head back, afraid, but wanting to meet him equally. He brought his hands to her face, and she felt the hardness of his palms on her skin. He brushed her hair back from her face as he brought her closer. He lowered his mouth, pausing only briefly before it claimed hers, as if to ascertain the need mirrored in her eyes. The kiss was instantly deep, instantly seeking.

She had been a fool—a fool to believe she could talk herself out of being in love with him. A fool to think that reason had anything to do with the heart.

When Katch drew her away, Megan pressed her cheek against his chest, letting her arms wind their way around his waist. His hesitation was almost too brief to measure before he gathered her close. She felt his lips in her hair and sighed from the sheer joy of it. His heartbeat was quick and steady in her ear.

"Did you say something?" he murmured.

"Hmm? When?"

"Before." His fingers came up to massage the back of her neck. Megan shivered with pleasure as she tried to remember the world before she had been in his arms.

"I think I asked if I could see the ocean from the top level."

"Yes." Again he took his hands to her face to tilt it back for one long, searing kiss. "You can."

"Will you show me?"

The grip on her skin tightened and her eyes closed in anticipation of the next kiss. But he drew her away until only their hands were touching. "After dinner."

Megan, content with looking at him, smiled. "Are we eating here?"

"I hate restaurants," Katch said, leading her toward the kitchen.

"An odd sentiment from a man who owns one."

"Let's say there are times when I prefer more intimate surroundings."

"I see." He pushed open the door to the kitchen and Megan glanced around at efficiency in wood and stainless steel. "And who's doing the cooking this time?"

"We are," he said easily, and grinned at her. "How do you like your steak?"

There was a rich, red wine to accompany the meal they ate at a smoked-glass table. A dozen candles flickered on a sideboard behind them, held in small brass holders. Megan's mood was as mellow as the wine that waltzed in her head. The man across from her held her in the palm of his hand. When she rose to stack the dishes, he took her hand. "Not now. There's a moon tonight."

Without hesitation, she went with him.

They climbed the stairs together, wide, uncarpeted stairs which were split into two sections by a landing. He led her through the main bedroom, a room dominated by a large bed with brass head- and footboards. There were long glass doors which led to a walkway. From there, stairs ascended to the observation deck.

Megan could hear the breakers before she moved to the rail. Beyond the hedgerow, the surf was turbulent. White water frothed against the dark. The moon's light was thin, but was aided by the power of uncountable stars.

She took a long breath and leaned on the rail. "It's lovely here. I never tire of looking at the ocean." There was a click from his lighter, then tobacco mixed pleasantly with the scent of the sea.

"Do you ever think about traveling?"

Megan moved her shoulders, a sudden, restless gesture. "Of course, sometimes. It isn't possible right now."

Katch drew on the thin cigar. "Where would you go?"

"Where would I go?" she repeated.

"Yes, where would you go if you could?" The smoke from his cigar wafted upward and vanished. "Pretend, Meg. You like to pretend, don't you?"

She closed her eyes a moment, letting the wine swim with her thoughts. "New Orleans," she murmured. "I've always wanted to see New Orleans. And Paris. When I was young I used to dream about studying in Paris like the great artists." She opened her eyes again. "You've been there, I suppose. To New Orleans and to Paris?"

"Yes, I've been there."

"What are they like?"

Katch traced the line of her jaw with a fingertip before answering. "New Orleans smells of the river and swelters in the summer. There's music at all hours from open nightclubs and street musicians. It moves constantly, like New York, but at a more civilized pace."

"And Paris?" Megan insisted, wanting to see her wishes through his eyes. "Tell me about Paris."

"It's ancient and elegant, like a grand old woman. It's not very clean, but it never seems to matter. It's best in the spring; nothing smells like Paris in the spring. I'd like to take you there." Unexpectedly he took her hair in his hand. His eyes were intense again and direct on hers. "I'd like to see the emotions you control break loose. You'd never restrict them in Paris."

"I don't do that." Something more than wine began to swim in her head.

He tossed the cigar over the rail, then his free hand came to her waist to press her body against his. "Don't you?" There was a hint of impatience in his voice as he began to slide the jacket from her shoulders. "You've passion, but you bank it down. It escapes into your work, but even that's kept closed up in a studio. When I kiss you, I can taste it struggling to the surface."

He freed her arms from the confines of the jacket and laid it over the rail. Slowly, deliberately, he ran his fingers over the naked skin, feeling the warmth of response. "One day it's going to break loose. I intend to be there when it does."

Katch pushed the straps from her shoulders and replaced them with his lips. Megan made no protest as the kisses trailed to her throat. His tongue played lightly with the pulse as his hand came up to cup her breast. But when his mouth came to hers, the gentleness fled, and with it her passivity. Hunger incited hunger.

When he nipped her bottom lip, she gasped with pleasure. His tongue was avid, searching while his hands began a quest of their own. He slipped the bodice of her dress to her waist, murmuring with approval as he found her naked breasts taut with desire. Megan allowed him his freedom, riding on the crest of the wave that rose inside her. She had no knowledge to guide her, no experience. Desire ruled and instinct followed.

She trailed her fingers along the back of his neck, kneading the warm skin, thrilling to the response she felt to her touch. Here was a power she had never explored. She slipped her hands under the back of his sweater. Their journey was slow, exploring. She felt the muscles of his shoulders tense as her hands played over them.

The quality of the kiss changed from demanding to urgent. His passion swamped her, mixing with her own until the combined power was more than she could bear. The ache came from nowhere and spread through her with impossible rapidity. She hurt for him. Desire was a pain as sharp as it was irresistible. In surrender, in anticipation, Megan swayed against him.

"Katch." Her voice was husky. "I want to stay with you tonight."

She was crushed against him for a moment, held so tightly, so strongly, there was no room for breath. Then, slowly, she felt him loosen his hold. Taking her by the shoulders, Katch looked down at her, his eyes dark, spearing into hers. Her breath was uneven; shivers raced along her skin. Slowly, with hands that barely touched her skin, he slipped her dress back into place.

"I'll take you home now."

The shock of rejection struck her like a blow. Her mouth trembled open, then shut again. Quickly, fighting against the tears that were pressing for release, she fumbled for her jacket.

"Meg." He reached out to touch her shoulders, but she backed away.

"No. No, don't touch me." The tears were thickening her voice. She swallowed. "I won't be patted on the head. It appears I misunderstood."

"You didn't misunderstand anything," he tossed back. "And don't cry, damn it."

"I have no intention of crying," she said. "I'd like to go

home." The hurt was in her eyes, shimmering behind the tears she denied.

"We'll talk." Katch took her hand, but she jerked it away.

"Oh, no. No, we won't." Megan straightened her shoulders and looked at him squarely. "We had dinner—things got a bit beyond what they should have. It's as simple as that, and it's over."

"It's not simple or over, Meg." Katch took another long look into her eyes. "But we'll drop it for now."

Megan turned away and walked back down the stairs.

CHAPTER 7

Amusement parks lose their mystique in the light of day. Dirt, scratched paint and dents show up. What is shiny and bright under artificial light is ordinary in the sunshine. Only the very young or the very young-hearted can believe in magic when faced with reality.

Megan knew her grandfather was perennially young. She loved him for it. Fondly, she watched him supervising repairs on the Haunted Castle. His ghosts, she thought with a smile, are important to him. She walked beside the track, avoiding her own ghost along the way. It had been ten days since Pop had told her of the repair problems. Ten days since she had seen Katch. Megan pushed thoughts of him from her mind and concentrated on her own reality—her grandfather and their park. She was old enough to know what was real and what was fantasy.

"Hi," she called out from behind him. "How are things going?"

Pop turned at the sound of her voice, and his grin was expansive. "Just fine, Megan." The sound of repairs echoed around his words. "Quicker than I thought they would. We'll be rolling before the Easter rush." He swung an arm around her shoulder and squeezed. "The smaller rides are already back in order. How about you?"

She made no objection when he began to steer her outside. The noise made it difficult to hear. "What about me?" she replied. The sudden flash of sunlight made her blink. The spring day had all the heat of midsummer.

"You've that unhappy look in your eyes. Have had, for more than a week." Pop rubbed his palm against her shoulder as if to warm her despite the strength of the sun. "You know you don't hide things from me, Megan. I know you too well."

She was silent a moment, wanting to choose her words carefully. "I wasn't trying to hide anything, Pop." Megan shrugged, turning to watch the crew working on the roller coaster. "It's just not important enough to talk about, that's all. How long before the coaster's fixed?"

"Important enough to make you unhappy," he countered, ignoring her evasion. "That's plenty important to me. You haven't gotten too old to talk to me about your problems now, have you?"

She turned dark, apologetic eyes on him. "Oh no, Pop, I can always talk to you."

"Well," he said simply, "I'm listening."

"I made a mistake, that's all." She shook her head and would have walked closer to inspect the work crew had he not held her to him with a firm hand.

"Megan." Pop placed both hands on her shoulders and looked into her eyes. As they were nearly the same height, their eyes were level. "I'm going to ask you straight," he continued. "Are you in love with him?"

"No," she denied quickly.

Pop raised an eyebrow. "I didn't have to mention any names, I see."

Megan paused a moment. She had forgotten how shrewd her grandfather could be. "I thought I was," she said more carefully. "I was wrong."

"Then why are you so unhappy?"

"Pop, please." She tried to back away, but again his broad hands held her steady.

"You've always given me straight answers, Meg, even when I've had to drag them out of you."

She sighed, knowing evasions and half-truths were useless when he was in this mood. "All right. Yes, I'm in love with him, but it doesn't matter."

"Not a very bright statement from a bright girl like you," he said with a gentle hint of disapproval. Megan shrugged. "Why don't you explain why being in love doesn't matter," he invited.

"Well, it certainly doesn't work if you're not loved back," Megan murmured.

"Who says you're not?" Pop wanted to know. His voice was so indignant, she felt some of the ache subside.

"Pop." Her expression softened. "Just because you love me doesn't mean everyone else does."

"What makes you so sure he doesn't?" her grandfather argued. "Did you ask him?"

"No!" Megan was so astonished, she nearly laughed at the thought.

"Why not? Things are simpler that way."

Megan took a deep breath, hoping to make him understand. "David Katcherton isn't a man who falls in love with a woman, not seriously. And certainly not with someone like me." The broad gesture she made was an attempt to enhance an explanation she knew was far from adequate. "He's been to Paris, he lives in New York. He has a sister named Jessica."

"That clears things up," Pop agreed, and Megan made a quick sound of frustration.

"I've never been anywhere." She dragged a hand through her hair. "In the summer I see millions, literally millions of people, but they're all transient. I don't know who they are. The only people I really know are ones who live right here. The farthest I've been away from the beach is Charleston."

Pop brushed a hand over her hair to smooth it. "I've kept you too close," he murmured. "I always told myself there'd be other times."

"Oh no, Pop, I didn't mean it that way." She threw her arms around him, burying her face in his shoulder. "I didn't mean to sound that way. I love you, I love it here. I wouldn't change anything. That was hateful of me."

He laughed and patted her back. The subtle scent of her perfume reminded him forcefully that she was no longer a girl but a woman. The years had been incredibly quick. "You've never done a hateful thing in your life. We both know you've wanted to see a bit of the world, and I know you've stuck close to keep an eye on me. Oh yes," he said, anticipating her objection. "And I was selfish enough to let you."

"You've never done anything selfish," she retorted and drew away. "I only meant that Katch and I have so little common ground. He's bound to see things differently than I do. I'm out of my depth with him."

"You're a strong swimmer, as I recall." Pop shook his head at her expression and sighed. "All right, we'll let it lie awhile. You're also stubborn."

"Adamant," she corrected, smiling again. "It's a nicer word."

"Just a fancy way of saying pigheaded," Pop said bluntly, but his eyes smiled back at her. "Why aren't you back in your studio instead of hanging around an amusement park in the middle of the day?"

"It wasn't going very well," she confessed, thinking of the half-carved face that haunted her. "Besides, I've always had a thing for amusement parks." She tucked her arm in his as they began to walk again.

"Well, this one'll be in apple-pie order in another week," Pop said, looking around in satisfaction. "With luck, we'll have a good season and be able to pay back a healthy chunk of that ten thousand."

"Maybe the bank will send us some customers so they'll get their money faster," Megan suggested, half listening to the sound of hammer against wood as they drew closer to the roller coaster.

"Oh, I didn't get the money from the bank, I got it from—" Pop cut himself off abruptly. With a cough and a wheeze, he bent down to tie his shoe.

"You didn't get the money from the bank?" Megan frowned at the snowy white head in puzzlement. "Well, where in the world did you get it then?"

His answer was an unintelligible grunt.

"You don't know anybody with that kind of money," she began with a half-smile. "Where . . ." The smile flew away. "No. No, you didn't." Even as she denied it, Megan knew it had to be the truth. "You didn't get it from him?"

"Oh now, Megan, you weren't to know." Distress showed in his eyes and seemed to weaken his voice. "He especially didn't want you to know."

"Why?" she demanded. "Why did you do it?"

"It just sort of happened, Meg." Pop reached out to pat her hand in his old, soothing fashion. "He was here, I was telling him about the repairs and getting a loan, and he offered. It seemed like the perfect solution." He fiddled with his shoestrings. "Banks poke around and take all that time for paperwork, and he isn't charging me nearly as much interest. I thought you'd be happy about that . . ." He trailed off.

"Is everything in writing?" she asked, deadly calm.

"Of course." Pop assumed a vaguely injured air. "Katch

said it didn't matter, but I know how fussy you are, so I had papers drawn up, nice and legal."

"Didn't matter," she repeated softly. "And what did you use as collateral?"

"The park, naturally."

"Naturally," she repeated. Fury bubbled in the single word. "I bet he loved that."

"Now, don't you worry, Megan. Everything's coming along just fine. The repairs are going well, and we'll be opening right on schedule. Besides," he added with a sigh, "you weren't even supposed to know. Katch wanted it that way."

"Oh, I'm sure he did," she said bitterly. "I'm sure he did."

Turning, she darted away. Pop watched her streak out of sight, then hauled himself to his feet. She had the devil's own temper when she cut loose, that girl. Brushing his hands together, he grinned. That, he decided, pleased with his own maneuvering, should stir up something.

Megan brought the bike to a halt at the crest of Katch's drive, then killed the engine. She took off her helmet and clipped it on the seat. He was not, she determined, going to get away with it.

Cutting across the lawn, she marched to the front door. The knock was closer to a pound but still brought no response. Megan stuffed her hands into her pockets and scowled. Her bike sat behind his black Porsche. Ignoring amenities, she tried the knob. When it turned, she didn't hesitate. She opened the door and walked inside.

The house was quiet. Instinct told her immediately that no one was inside. Still, she walked through the living room looking for signs of him.

A watch, wafer-thin and gold, was tossed on the glass shelves of the étagère. A Nikon camera sat on the coffee table, its back open and empty of film. A pair of disreputable tennis shoes were half under the couch. A volume of John Cheever lay beside them.

Abruptly, she realized what she had done. She'd intruded where she had no right. She was both uncomfortable and fascinated. An ashtray held the short stub of a thin cigar. After a brief struggle with her conscience, she walked toward the kitchen. She wasn't prying, she told herself, only making certain he wasn't home. After all, his car was here and the door had been unlocked.

There was a cup in the sink and a half pot of cold coffee on the stove. He had spilled some on the counter and neglected to wipe it up. Megan curtailed the instinctive move to reach for a dish towel. As she turned to leave, a low mechanical hum from outside caught her attention. She walked to the window and saw him.

He was coming from the south side of the lawn, striding behind a power mower. He was naked to the waist, with jeans low and snug at his hips. He was tanned, a deep honey gold that glistened now with the effort of manual labor. She admired the play of muscles rippling down his arms and across his back.

Stepping back from the window with a jerk, she stormed through the side kitchen door and raced across the lawn.

The flurry of movement and a flash of crimson caught his eye. Katch glanced over as Megan moved toward him in a red tailored shirt and white jeans. Squinting against the sun, he wiped the back of his hand across his brow. He reached down and shut off the mower as she came to him.

"Hello, Meg," he said lightly, but his eyes weren't as casual.

"You have nerve, Katcherton," she began. "But even I didn't think you'd take advantage of a trusting old man."

He lifted a brow and leaned against the mower's handle. "Once more," he requested, "with clarity."

"You're the type who has to poke your fingers into other people's business," she continued. "You just had to be at the park, you just had to make a magnanimous offer with your tidy little pile of money."

"Ah, a glimmer of light." He stretched his back. "I didn't think you'd be thrilled the money came from me. It seems I was right."

"You knew I'd never allow it," she declared.

"I don't believe I considered that." He leaned on the mower again, but there was nothing restful in the gesture. "You don't run Pop's life from what I've seen, Meg, and you certainly don't run mine."

She did her best to keep her tone even. "I have a great deal of interest in the park and everything that pertains to it."

"Fine, then you should be pleased that you have the money for the repairs quickly, and at a low rate of interest." His tone was cool and businesslike.

"Why?" she demanded. "Why did you lend us the money?"

"I don't," Katch said after a long, silent moment, "owe you any explanation."

"Then I'll give you one," Megan tossed back. There was passion in her voice. "You saw an opportunity and grabbed it. I suppose that's what people do in your sort of world. Take, without the least thought of the people involved."

"Perhaps I'm confused." His eyes were slate, opaque and unreadable. His voice matched them. "I was under the impression that I gave something."

"*Lent* something," Megan corrected. "With the park as collateral."

"If that's your problem, take it up with your grandfather." Katch bent down, reaching for the cord to restart the mower.

"You had no right to take advantage of him. He trusts everyone."

Katch released the cord again with a snap. "A shame it's not an inherited quality."

"I've no reason to trust you."

"And every reason, it appears, to mistrust me since the first moment." His eyes had narrowed as if in speculation. "Is it just me or a general antipathy to men?"

She refused to dignify the question with an answer. "You want the park," she began.

"Yes, and I made that clear from the beginning." Katch shoved the mower aside so that there was no obstacle between them. "I still intend to have it, but I don't need to be devious to get it. I still intend to have you." She stepped back but he was too quick. His fingers curled tightly around her upper arm. "Maybe I made a mistake by letting you go the other night."

"You didn't want me. It's just a game."

"Didn't want you?" She made another quick attempt to pull away and failed. "No, that's right, I didn't want you." He pulled her against him and her mouth was crushed and conquered. Her mind whirled with the shock of it. "I don't want you now." Before she could speak, his mouth savaged hers again. There was a taste of brutality he had never shown her. "Like I haven't wanted you for days." He pulled her to the ground.

There was none of the teasing persuasion he had shown her before, no light arrogance. These were primordial demands, eliciting primordial responses from her. He would take what he wanted, his way. He plundered, dragging her with him as he raced for more. Then his lips left hers, journeying to her throat before traveling downward. Megan felt she was suffocating, suffused with heat. Her breath caught in her lungs, emerging in quick gasps or moans. His fingers ran a bruising trail over her quivering flesh. He ran his thumb over the point of her breast, back and forth, until she was beyond fear, beyond thought. His mouth came back to hers, fever hot, desperate. She murmured mindlessly, clinging to him as her body shuddered with waves of need.

Katch lifted his head, and his breath was warm and erratic on her face. Megan's lids fluttered open, revealing eyes dazed with passion, heavy with desire. Silently, she trembled. If words had been hers, she would have told him that she loved him. There was no pride in her, no shame, only soaring need and a love that was painful in its strength.

"This isn't the place for you." His voice was rough as he rolled over on his back. They lay there a moment, side by side, without touching. "And this isn't the way."

Her mind was fogged, and her blood surging. "Katch," Megan managed his name and struggled to sit up. His eyes lingered on her form, then slid up slowly to brood on her face. It was flushed and aware. She wanted to touch him but was afraid.

For a moment their eyes met. "Did I hurt you?"

She shook her head in denial. Her body ached with longing.

"Go home then." He rose, giving her a last, brief glance. "Before I do." He turned and left her.

Megan heard the slam of the kitchen door.

CHAPTER 8

It was difficult for Megan to cope with the two-week influx of tourists and sun seekers. They came, as they did every Easter, in droves. It was a preview of what the summer would hold. They came to bake on the beach and impress those left at home with a spring tan. They came to be battered and bounced around by the waves. They came to have fun. And what better place to find it than on white sand beaches or in an ocean with a gentle undertow and cresting waves? They came to laugh and sought their entertainment on spiraling water slides, in noisy arcades or crowded amusement parks.

For the first time in her life, Megan found herself resenting the intrusion. She wanted the quiet, the solitude that went with a resort town in its off-season. She wanted to be alone, to work, to heal. It seemed her art was the only thing she could turn to for true comfort. She was unwilling to speak of her feelings to her grandfather. There was still too much to be sorted out in her own mind. Knowing her, and her need for privacy, Pop didn't question.

The hours she spent at the park were passed mechanically. The faces she saw were all strangers. Megan resented it. She resented their enjoyment when her own life was in such turmoil. She found solace in her studio. If the light in her studio burned long past midnight, she never noticed the time. Her energy was boundless, a nervous, trembling energy that kept her going.

It was afternoon at the amusement park. At the kiddie cars Megan was taking tickets and doing her best to keep the more aggressive youngsters from trampling others. Each time the fire engines, race cars, police cruisers and ambulances were loaded, she pushed the lever which sent the caravan around in its clanging, roaring circle. Children grinned fiercely and gripped steering wheels.

One toddler rode as fire chief with eyes wide with stunned pleasure. Even though she'd been on duty nearly four hours, Megan smiled.

"Excuse me." Megan glanced over at the voice, prepared to answer a parental question. The woman was an exquisite blonde, with a mane of hair tied back from a delicately molded face. "You're Megan, aren't you? Megan Miller?"

"Yes. May I help you?"

"I'm Jessica Delaney."

Megan wondered that she hadn't seen it instantly. "Katch's sister."

"Yes." Jessica smiled. "How clever of you—but Katch told me you were. There is a family resemblance, of course, but so few people notice it unless we're standing together."

Megan's artist eyes could see the similar bone structure beneath the surface differences. Jessica's eyes were blue, as Katch had said, and the brows above them more delicate than his, but there were the same thick lashes and long lids.

"I'm glad to meet you." Megan reached for something to say. "Are you visiting Katch?" She didn't look like a woman who would patronize amusement parks, more likely country clubs or theaters.

"For a day or so." Jessica gestured to the adjoining ride where children flew miniature piper cubs in the inevitable circle. "My family's with me. Rob, my husband." Megan smiled at a tall man with a straight shock of dark hair and an attractive, angular face. "And my girls, Erin and Laura." She nodded to the two caramel-haired girls of approximately four and six riding double in a plane.

"They're beautiful."

"We like them," Jessica said comfortably. "Katch didn't know where I might find you in the park, but he described you very accurately."

"Is he here?" Megan asked, trying without much success to sound offhanded even as her eyes scanned the crowd.

"No, he had some business to attend to."

The timer rang, signaling the ride's end. "Excuse me a moment," Megan murmured. Grateful for the interruption, she supervised the unloading and loading of children. It gave her the time she needed to steady herself. Her two final customers were Katch's nieces. Erin, the elder, smiled at her with eyes the identical shade of her uncle's.

"I'm driving," she said positively as her sister settled beside her. "She only rides."

"I do not." Laura gripped the twin steering wheel passionately.

"It runs in the family," Jessica stated from behind her. "Stubbornness." Megan hooked the last safety belt and returned to the controls. "You've probably noticed it."

Megan smiled at her. "Yes, once or twice." The lights and noise spun and circled behind her.

"I know you're busy," Jessica stated, glancing at the packed vehicles.

Megan gave a small shrug as she followed her gaze. "It's mostly a matter of making certain everyone stays strapped in and no one's unhappy."

"My little angels," Jessica said, "will insist on dashing off to the next adventure the moment the ride's over." She paused. "Could we talk after you're finished here?"

Megan frowned. "Well, yes, I suppose . . . I'm due relief in an hour."

"Wonderful." Jessica's smile was as charming as her brother's. "I'd like to go to your studio, if that suits you. I could meet you in an hour and a half."

"At my studio?"

"Wonderful!" Jessica said again and patted Megan's hand. "Katch gave me directions."

The timer rang again, recalling Megan to duty. As she started yet another round of junior rides she wondered why Jessica had insisted on a date in her studio.

With a furrowed brow, Megan studied herself in the bedroom mirror. Would a man who admired Jessica's soft, delicate beauty be attracted to someone who seemed to be all planes and angles? Megan shrugged her shoulders as if it didn't matter. She twirled the stem of the brush idly between her fingers. She supposed that he, like the majority of people who came here, was looking for some passing entertainment.

"You are," she said softly to the woman in the glass, "such a fool." She closed her eyes, not wanting to see the reflected accusation. Because you can't let go, her mind continued ruthlessly. Because it doesn't really matter to you why he wanted you with him, just that he wanted you. And you wish, you wish with all your heart that he still did.

She shook her head, disturbing the work she had done with the brush. It was time to stop thinking of it. Jessica Delaney would be arriving any moment.

Why? Megan set down her brush and frowned into middle

distance. Why was she coming? What could she possibly want? Megan still had no sensible answer. I haven't heard from Katch in two weeks, she reflected. Why should his sister suddenly want to see me?

The sound of a car pulling into the drive below interrupted her thoughts. Megan walked to the window in time to see Jessica get out of Katch's Porsche.

Megan reached the back stoop before Jessica, as she had been taking a long, leisurely look at the yard. "Hello." Megan felt awkward and rustic. She hesitated briefly before stepping away from the door.

"What a lovely place." Jessica's smile was so like Katch's that Megan's heart lurched. "How I wish my azaleas looked like yours."

"Pop—my grandfather babies them."

"Yes." The blue eyes were warm and personal. "I've heard wonderful things about your grandfather. I'd love to meet him."

"He's still at the park." Her sense of awkwardness was fading. Charm definitely ran in the Katcherton family. "Would you like some coffee? Tea?"

"Maybe later. Let's go up to the studio, shall we?"

"If you don't mind my asking, Mrs. Delaney—"

"Jessica," she interrupted cheerfully and began to climb the open back stairs.

"Jessica," Megan agreed, "how did you know I had a studio, and that it was over the garage?"

"Oh, Katch told me," Jessica said breezily. "He tells me a great many things." She stood to the side of the door and waited for Megan to open it. "I'm very anxious to see your work. I dabble in oil from time to time."

"Do you?" Jessica's interest now made more sense. Artistic kinship.

"Badly, I'm afraid, which is a constant source of frustration to me." Again the Katcherton smile bloomed on her face.

Megan's reaction was unexpectedly sharp and swift. She fumbled for the doorknob. "I've never had much luck on canvas," she said quickly. She needed words, lots of words to cover what she feared was much too noticeable. "Nothing seems to come out the way I intend," she continued as they entered the studio. "It's maddening not to be able to express yourself properly. I do some airbrushing during the summer rush, but . . ."

Jessica wasn't listening. She moved around the room much the same way her brother had—intently, gracefully, silently. She fingered a piece here, lifted a piece there. Once, she studied a small ivory unicorn for so long, Megan fidgeted with nerves.

What was she doing? she wondered. *And why?*

Sunlight stippled the floor. Dust motes danced in the early evening light. Too late, Megan recalled the bust of Katch. One slanted beam of sun fell on it, highlighting the planes the chisel had already defined. Though it was still rough hewn and far from finished, it was unmistakably Katch. Feeling foolish, Megan walked over to stand in front of it, hoping to conceal it from Jessica's view.

"Katch was right," Jessica murmured. She still held the unicorn, stroking it with her fingertips. "He invariably is. Normally that annoys me to distraction, but not this time." The resemblance to Katch was startling now. Megan's fingers itched to make a quick sketch even as she tried to follow the twisting roads in Jessica's conversation.

"Right about what?"

"Your extraordinary talent."

"What?" Meg's eyes widened.

"Katch told me your work was remarkable," she went on, giving the unicorn a final study before setting it down. "I agreed when I received the two pieces he sent up to me, but they were only two, after all." She picked up a chisel and tapped it absently against her palm while her eyes continued to wander. "This is astonishing."

"He sent you the sculptures he bought from me?"

"Yes, a few weeks ago. I was very impressed." Jessica set down the chisel with a clatter and moved to a nearly completed study in limestone of a woman rising from the sea. It was the piece Megan had been working on before she had set it aside to begin Katch's bust. "This is fabulous!" Jessica declared. "I'm going to have to have it as well as the unicorn. The response to the two pieces Katch sent me has been very favorable."

"I don't understand what you're talking about." Try as she might, Megan couldn't keep up with Jessica's conversation. "Whose response?"

"My clients'," said Jessica. "At my gallery in New York." She gave Megan a brilliant smile. "Didn't I tell you I run my own gallery?"

"No," Megan answered. "No, you didn't."

"I suppose I thought Katch did. I'd better start at the beginning then."

"I'd really appreciate it if you would," Megan told her, and waited until she had settled herself in the small wooden chair beside her.

"Katch sent me two of your pieces a few weeks ago," Jessica began briskly. "He wanted a professional opinion. I may only be able to dabble in oil, but I know art." She spoke with a confidence that Megan recognized. "Since I knew I'd never make it as a working artist, I put all the years of study to good use. I opened a gallery in Manhattan. *Jessica's.* Over the past six years, I've developed a rather nice clientele." She smiled.

"So naturally, when my wandering brother saw your work, he sent it off to me. He always has his instincts verified by an expert, then plunges along his own way notwithstanding." She sighed indulgently. "I happen to know he was advised against building that hospital in Central Africa last year but he did it anyway. He does what he wants to."

"Hospital." Megan barely made the jump to Jessica's new train of thought.

"Yes, a children's hospital. He has a soft spot for kids." Jessica tried to speak teasingly, but the love came through. "He did some astonishing things for orphaned refugees after Vietnam. And there was the really fabulous little park he built in New South Wales."

Megan sat dumbly. Could they possibly be speaking about the same David Katcherton? Was this the man who had brashly approached her in the local market?

She remembered with uncomfortable clarity that she had accused him of trying to cheat her grandfather. She had told herself that he was an opportunist, a man spoiled by wealth and good looks. She'd tried to tell herself he was irresponsible, undependable, a man in search of his own pleasure.

"I didn't know," she murmured. "I didn't know anything about it."

"Oh, Katch keeps a low profile when he chooses," Jessica told her. "And he chooses to have no publicity when he's doing that sort of thing. He has incredible energy and outrageous self-confidence, but he's also very warm." Her gaze slipped beyond Megan's shoulder. "But then, you appear to know him well."

For a moment, Megan regarded Jessica blankly. Then she twisted her head and saw Katch's bust. In her confusion, she had forgotten her desire to conceal it. Slowly, she turned her head back, trying to keep her voice and face passive.

"No. No, really I don't think I know him at all. He has a fascinating face. I couldn't resist sculpting it."

She noted a glint of understanding in Jessica's eyes. "He's a fascinating man," Jessica murmured.

Megan's gaze faltered.

"I'm sorry," Jessica said immediately. "I've intruded, a bad habit of mine. We won't talk about Katch. Let's talk about your showing."

Megan lifted her eyes again. "My what?"

"Your showing," Jessica repeated, dashing swiftly up a new path. "When do you think you'll have enough pieces ready? You certainly have a tremendous start here, and Katch mentioned something about a gallery in town having some of your pieces. I think we can shoot for the fall."

"Please, Jessica, I don't know what you're talking about." A note of panic slipped into Megan's voice. It was faint, almost buried, but Jessica detected it. She reached over and took both of Megan's hands. The grip was surprisingly firm.

"Megan, you have something special, something powerful. It's time to share it." She rose then, urging Megan up with her. "Let's have that coffee now, shall we? And we'll talk about it."

An hour later, Megan sat alone in the kitchen. Darkness was encroaching, but she didn't rise from the table to switch on the light. Two cups sat, her own half-filled with now cold coffee, Jessica's empty but for dregs. She tried to take her mind methodically over what had happened in the last sixty minutes.

A showing at Jessica's, an art gallery in Manhattan. New York. A public show. Of her work.

It didn't happen, she thought. I imagined it. Then she looked down at the empty cup across from her. The air still smelled faintly of Jessica's light, sophisticated scent.

Half-dazed, Megan took both cups to the sink and automatically began rinsing them. *How did she talk me into it?*
she wondered. *I was agreeing to dates and details before I
had agreed to do the showing. Does anyone ever say no to a
Katcherton?* She sighed and looked down at her wet hands.
I have to call him. The knowledge increased the sense of
panic. *I have to.*

Carefully, she placed the washed cups and saucers in
the drainboard. *I have to thank him.* Nerves fluttered in her
throat, but she made a pretense, for herself, of casually dry-
ing her damp hands on the hips of her jeans. She walked to
the wall phone beside the stove.

"It's simple," she whispered, then bit her lip. She cleared
her throat. "All I have to do is thank him, that's all. It'll only
take a minute." Megan reached for the phone, then drew her
hand away. Her mind raced on with her heartbeat.

She lifted the receiver. She knew the number. Hadn't she
started to dial it a dozen times during the past two weeks?
She took a long breath before pushing the first digit. It would
take five minutes, and then, in all probability, she'd have no
reason to contact him again. It would be better if they erased
the remnants of their last meeting. It would be easier if their
relationship ended on a calmer, more civilized note. Megan
pressed the last button and waited for the click of connection,
the whisper of transmitters and the ring.

It took four rings—four long, endless rings before he
picked up the phone.

"Katch." His name was barely audible. She closed her eyes.

"Meg?"

"Yes, I . . ." She fought herself to speak. "I hope I'm not
calling you at a bad time." *How trite,* she thought desperately.
How ordinary.

"Are you all right?" There was concern in the question.

"Yes, yes, of course." Her mind fretted for the simple, casual words she had planned to speak. "Katch, I wanted to talk to you. Your sister was here—"

"I know, she got back a few minutes ago." There was a trace of impatience in his tone. "Is anything wrong?"

"No, nothing's wrong." Her voice refused to level. Megan searched for a quick way to end the conversation.

"Are you alone?"

"Yes, I . . ."

"I'll be there in ten minutes."

"No." Megan ran a frustrated hand through her hair. "No, please—"

"Ten minutes," he repeated and broke the connection.

CHAPTER 9

Megan stared at the dead receiver for several silent moments. How had she, in a few uncompleted sentences, managed to make such a mess of things? She didn't want him to come. She never wanted to see him again. *That is a lie.*

Carefully, Megan replaced the receiver. I do want to see him, she admitted, have wanted to see him for days. It's just that I'm afraid to see him. Turning, she gazed blindly around the kitchen. The room was almost in complete darkness now. The table and chairs were dark shadows. She walked to the switch, avoiding obstacles with the knowledge of years. The room flooded with brightness. That's better, she thought, more secure in the artificial light. Coffee, she decided, needing something, anything, to occupy her hands. I'll make fresh coffee.

Megan went to the percolator and began a step-by-step preparation, but her nerves continued to jump. In a few moments, she hoped, she'd be calm again. When he arrived, she would say what she needed to say, and then they would part.

The phone rang, and she jolted, juggling the cup she held and nearly dropping it. Chiding herself, Megan set it down and answered the call.

"Hello, Megan." Pop's voice crackled jovially across the wire.

"Pop . . . are you still at the park?" What time is it? she wondered distractedly and glanced down at her watch.

"That's why I called. George stopped by. We're going to have dinner in town. I didn't want you to worry."

"I won't." She smiled as the band of tension around her head loosened. "I suppose you and George have a lot of fish stories to exchange."

"His have gotten bigger since he retired," Pop claimed. "Hey, why don't you run into town, sweetheart? We'll treat you."

"You two just want an audience," she accused and her smile deepened with Pop's chuckle. "But I'll pass tonight, thanks. As I recall, there's some leftover spaghetti in the fridge."

"I'll bring you back dessert." It was an old custom. For as long as Megan could remember, if Pop had dinner without her, he'd bring her back some treat. "What do you want?"

"Rainbow sherbet," she decided instantly. "Have a good time."

"I will, darling. Don't work too late."

As she hung up the phone, Megan asked herself why she hadn't told her grandfather of Katch's impending visit. Why hadn't she mentioned Jessica or the incredible plans that had been made? It has to wait until we can talk, she told herself. Really talk. It's the only way I'll be certain how he really feels—and how everything will affect him.

It's probably a bad idea. Megan began to fret, pushing a hand through her hair in agitation. It's a crazy idea. How can I go to New York and—

Her thoughts were interrupted by the glaring sweep of headlights against the kitchen window. She struggled to compose herself, going deliberately to the cupboard to close it before heading to the screen door.

Katch stepped onto the stoop as she reached for the handle. For a moment, in silence, they studied each other through the mesh. She heard the soft flutter of moths' wings on the outside light.

Finally he turned the knob and opened the door. After he had shut it quietly behind him, he reached up to touch her cheek. His hand lingered there while his eyes traveled her face.

"You sounded upset."

Megan moistened her lips. "No, no, I'm fine." She stepped back so that his palm no longer touched her skin. Slowly, his eyes on hers, Katch lowered his hand. "I'm sorry I bothered you—"

"Megan, stop it." His voice was quiet and controlled. Her eyes came back to his, a little puzzled, a little desperate. "Stop backing away from me. Stop apologizing."

Her hands fluttered once before she could control the movement. "I'm making coffee," she began. "It should be ready in a minute." She would have turned to arrange the cups and saucers, but he took her arm.

"I didn't come for coffee." His hand slid down until it encircled her wrist. Her pulse vibrated against his fingers.

"Katch, please, don't make this difficult."

Something flared in his eyes while she watched. Then it was gone, and her hand was released. "I'm sorry. I've had some difficulty the past couple of weeks dealing with what happened the last time I saw you." He noted the color that shot into her cheeks, but she kept her eyes steady. He slipped his hands into his pockets. "Megan, I'd like to make it up to you."

Megan shook her head, disturbed by the gentleness in his voice, and turned to the coffee pot.

"Don't you want to forgive me?"

The question had her turning back, her eyes darkened with distressed confusion. "No . . . that is, yes, of course."

"Of course you don't want to forgive me?" There was a

faint glimmer of a smile in his eyes and the charm was around his mouth. She could feel herself sinking.

"Yes, of course I forgive you," she corrected and this time did turn to the coffee. "It's forgotten." He laid his hands on her shoulders, and she jumped.

"Is it?" Katch turned her until they were again face-to-face. The glimpse of humor in his eyes was gone. "You can't seem to abide my touching you. I don't much like thinking I frighten you."

She made a conscious effort to relax under his hands. "You don't frighten me, Katch," Megan murmured. "You confuse me. Constantly."

She watched his brow lift in consideration. "I don't have any intention of confusing you. I am sorry, Megan."

"Yes." She smiled, recognizing the simple sincerity. "I know you are."

He drew her closer. "Can we kiss and make up then?"

Megan started to protest, but his mouth was already on hers, light and gentle. Her heart began to hammer in her throat. He made no attempt to deepen the kiss. His hands were easy on her shoulders. Against all the warnings of her mind, she relaxed against him, inviting him to take whatever he chose. But he took no more.

Katch drew her away, waiting until her heavy lids fluttered open before he touched her hair. Without speaking, he turned and paced to the window. Megan struggled to fill the new gap.

"I wanted to talk to you about your sister." She busied her hands with the now noisy percolator. "Or, more accurately, about what Jessica came to see me about."

Katch turned his head, watching her pour the coffee into the waiting cups. He walked to the refrigerator and took out the milk.

"All right." Standing beside her now, he poured milk into one cup and, at her nod, into the second.

"Why didn't you tell me you were sending my work to your sister?"

"I thought it best to wait until I had her opinion." Katch sat beside Megan and cradled the cup in both hands. "I trust her. . . . And I thought you'd trust her opinion more than mine. Are you going to do the showing? Jessica and I didn't have time to talk before you called."

She shifted in her chair, studied her coffee, then looked directly at him. "She's very persuasive. I was agreeing before I realized it."

"Good," Katch said simply and drank.

"I want to thank you," Meg continued in a stronger voice, "for arranging things."

"I didn't arrange anything," he responded. "Jessica makes her own decisions, personal and professional. I simply sent her your sculptures for an opinion."

"Then I'll thank you for that, for making a move I might never have made for the hundreds of reasons which occurred to me five minutes after she'd left."

Katch shrugged. "All right, if you're determined to be grateful."

"I am," she said. "And I'm scared," she continued, "really terrified at the thought of putting my work on public display." Megan let out a shaky breath at the admission. "I may despise you when all this is over and art critics stomp all over my ego, so you'd better take the gratitude now."

Katch crossed to her, and her heart lifted dizzily, so sure was she that he would take her into his arms. He merely stroked her cheek with the back of his hand. "When you're a smashing success, you can give it to me again." He smiled at her, and the world snapped into sharp focus. Until that moment, she hadn't realized how dull everything had been without him.

"I'm so glad you came," she whispered and, unable to resist, slipped her arms around him, pressing her face into his shoulder. After a moment, he rested his hands lightly at her waist. "I'm sorry for the things I said . . . about the loan. I didn't mean any of it really, but I say horrible things when I lose my temper."

"Is this your turn to be penitent?"

He made her laugh. "Yes." She smiled and tilted back her head. Her arms stayed around him. He kissed her and drew away. Reluctantly, she let him slip out of her arms. Then he stood silently, staring down at her.

"What are you doing?" she asked with a quick, self-conscious smile.

"Memorizing your face. Have you eaten?"

She shook her head, wondering why it should come as a surprise that he continued to baffle her. "No, I was going to heat up some leftovers."

"Unacceptable. Want a pizza?"

"*Mmm,* I'd love it, but you have company."

"Jessica and Rob took the kids to play miniature golf. I won't be missed." Katch held out his hands. "Come on."

His eyes were smiling, and her heart was lost. "Oh wait," she began even as she put her hand into his. Quickly, Megan scrawled a message on the chalkboard by the screen door.

OUT WITH KATCH

It was enough.

CHAPTER 10

Katch drove along Ocean Boulevard so they could creep along in the traffic filled with tourists and beachers. Car radios were turned up high and windows rolled down low. Laughter and music poured out everywhere. The lights from a twin Ferris wheel glittered red and blue in the distance. People sat out on their hotel balconies, with colorful beach towels flapping over the railings, as they watched the sluggish flow of cars and pedestrians. To the left, there were glimpses of the sea in between buildings.

Sleepily content after pizza and Chianti, Megan snuggled deeper into the soft leather seat. "Things'll quiet down after this weekend," she commented. "Until Memorial Day."

"Do you ever feel as though you're being invaded?" Katch asked her with a gesture at the clogged traffic.

"I like the crowds," she said immediately, then laughed. "And I like the winter when the beaches are deserted. I suppose there's something about the honky-tonk that appeals to me, especially since I know I'm going to have a few isolated months in the winter."

"That's your time," Katch murmured, glancing back at her. "The time you give yourself for sculpting."

She shrugged, a bit uncomfortable with the intense look.

"I do some in the summer too—when I can. Time's something I forgot when Jessica was talking about a showing and making all those plans . . ." Megan trailed off, frowning. "I don't know how I can possibly get things ready."

"Not backing out, are you?"

"No, but—" The look in his eyes had her swallowing excuses. "No," she said more firmly. "I'm not backing out."

"What're you working on now?"

"I, ah . . ." Megan looked fixedly out the window, thinking of the half-formed bust of Katch's head. "It's just . . ." She shrugged and began to fiddle with the dial of the radio. "It's just a wood carving."

"Of what?"

Megan made a few inarticulate mumbles until Katch turned to grin at her. "A pirate," she decided as the light from a street lamp slanted over his face, throwing it into planes and shadows. "It's the head of a pirate."

His brow lifted at the sudden, narrow-eyed concentration with which she was studying him. "I'd like to see it."

"It's not finished," she said quickly. "I've barely got the clay model done. In any case, I might have to put it off if I'm going to get the rest of my pieces organized for your sister."

"Meg, why don't you stop worrying and just enjoy it?"

Confused, she shook her head and stared at him. "Enjoy it?"

"The show," he said, ruffling her hair.

"Oh, yes." She fought to get her thoughts back into some kind of order. "I will . . . after it's over," she added with a smile. "Do you think you'll be in New York, then?"

As the rhythm of the traffic picked up, he shifted into third. "I'm considering it."

"I'd like you to be there if you could arrange it." When he laughed, shaking his head, she continued, "It's just that I'm going to need all the friendly faces I can get."

"You're not going to need anything but your sculptures," Katch corrected, but the amusement was still in his eyes. "Don't you think I'd want to be around the night of your opening so that I can brag I discovered you?"

"Let's just hope we both don't live to regret it," Megan muttered, but he only laughed again. "You just can't consider the possibility that you might have made a mistake," she accused testily.

"You can't consider the possibility that you might be successful," he countered.

Megan opened her mouth, then shut it again. "Well," she said after a moment, "we're both right." Waiting until they were stopped in traffic again, Megan touched his shoulder. "Katch?"

"Hmm?"

"Why did you build a hospital in Central Africa?"

He turned to her then, a faint frown between his brows. "It was needed," he said simply.

"Just that?" she persisted, though she could see he wasn't pleased with her question. "I mean, Jessica said you were advised against it, and—"

"As it happens, I have a comfortable amount of money." He cut her off with an annoyed movement of his shoulder. "I do what I choose with it." Seeing her expression, Katch shook his head. "There are things I want to do, that's all. Don't canonize me, Meg."

She relaxed again and found herself brushing at the curls over his ear. "I wouldn't dream of it." He'd rather be thought of as eccentric than benevolent, she mused. And how much simpler it was to love him, knowing that one small secret. "You're much easier to like than I thought you'd be when you made a nuisance of yourself in the market."

"I tried to tell you," he pointed out. "You were too busy pretending you weren't interested."

"I wasn't interested," Megan insisted, "in the least." He turned to grin at her and she found herself laughing. "Well, not very much anyway." When he swung the car onto a side street, she looked back at him in question. "What are you doing?"

"Let's go out on the boardwalk." Expertly, he slid the Porsche into a parking space. "Maybe I'll buy you a souvenir." He was already out of the car—primed, impatient.

"Oh, I love rash promises," Megan crowed as she joined him.

"I said maybe."

"I didn't hear that part. And," she added as she laced her fingers with his, "I want something extravagant."

"Such as?" They jaywalked, maneuvering around stopped cars.

"I'll know when I see it."

The boardwalk was crowded, full of people and light and noise. The breeze off the ocean carried the scent of salt to compete with the aroma of grilling meat from concessions. Instead of going into one of the little shops, Katch pulled Megan into an arcade.

"Big talk about presents and no delivery," Megan said in disgust as Katch exchanged bills for tokens.

"It's early yet. Here." He poured a few tokens into her hand. "Why don't you try your luck at saving the galaxy from invaders?"

With a smirk, Megan chose a machine, then slipped two tokens into the slot. "I'll go first." Pressing the start button, she took the control stick in hand and began systematically to vaporize the enemy. Brows knit, she swung her ship right and left while the machine exploded with color and noise with each hit. Amused, Katch dipped his hands into his pockets and watched her face. It was a more interesting show than the sophisticated graphics.

She chewed her bottom lip while maneuvering into position, narrowing her eyes when a laser blast headed her way. Her breath hissed through her teeth at a narrow escape. But all the while, her face held that composed, almost serious expression that was so much a part of her. Fighting gamely to avoid being blown up in cross fire, Megan's ship at last succumbed.

"Well," Katch murmured, glancing at her score as she wiped her hands on the back of her jeans. "You're pretty good."

"You have to be," Megan returned soberly, "when you're the planet's last hope."

With a chuckle, he nudged her out of the way and took the control.

Megan acknowledged his skill as Katch began to blast away the invaders with as much regularity as she had, and a bit more dash. He likes to take chances, she mused as he narrowly missed being blown apart by laser fire in order to zap three ships in quick succession. As his score mounted, she stepped a bit closer to watch his technique.

At the brush of her arm against his, Megan noticed a quick, almost imperceptible break in his rhythm. Now, that was interesting, she reflected. Feeling an irrepressible surge of mischief, she edged slightly closer. There was another brief fluctuation in his timing. Softly, she touched her lips to his shoulder, then smiled up into his face. She heard rather than saw the explosion that marked his ship's untimely end.

Katch wasn't looking at the screen either, but at her. She saw something flash into his eyes—something hot, barely suppressed, before his hand released the control to dive into her hair.

"Cheat," he murmured.

For a moment, Megan forgot the cacophony of sound, forgot the crowds of people that milled around them. She was lost somewhere in those smoky gray eyes and her own giddy sense of power.

"Cheat?" she repeated, and her lips stayed slightly parted. "I don't know what you mean."

The hand on her hair tightened. He was struggling, she realized, surprised and excited. "I think you do," Katch said quietly. "And I think I'm going to have to be very careful now that you know just what you can do to me."

"Katch." Her gaze lowered to his mouth as the longings built. "Maybe I don't want you to be careful anymore."

Slowly, his hand slid out of her hair, over her cheek, then dropped. "All the more reason I have to be," he muttered. "Come on." He took her arm and propelled her away from the machine. "Let's play something else."

Megan flowed with his mood, content just to be with him. They pumped tokens into machines and competed fiercely—as much with each other as with the computers. Megan felt the same lighthearted ease with him that she'd experienced that night at the carnival. Spending time with him was much like a trip on one of the wild, breathless rides at the park. Quick curves, fast hills, unexpected starts and stops. No one liked the windy power of a roller coaster better than Megan.

Hands on hips, she stood back as he consistently won coupons at Skee Ball. She watched another click off on the already lengthy strip as he tossed the ball neatly into the center hole.

"Don't you ever lose?" she demanded.

Katch tossed the next ball for another forty points. "I try not to make a habit of it. Wanna toss the last two?"

"No." She brushed imaginary lint from her shirt. "You're having such a good time showing off."

With a laugh, Katch dumped the last two balls for ninety

points, then leaned over to tear off his stream of coupons. "Just for that, I might not turn these in for your souvenir."

"These?" Megan gave the ream of thin cardboard an arched-brow look. "You were supposed to *buy* me a souvenir."

"I did." He grinned, rolling them up. "Indirectly." Slipping an arm companionably around her shoulder, he walked to the center counter where prizes were displayed. "Let's see . . . I've got two dozen. How about one of those six-function pen-knives?"

"Just who's this souvenir for?" Megan asked dryly as she scanned the shelves. "I like that little silk rose." She tapped the glass counter to indicate a small lapel pin. "I have all the tools I need," she added with an impish grin.

"Okay." Katch nodded to the woman behind the counter, then tore off all but four of the tickets. "That leaves us these. Ah . . ." With a quick scan of the shelves, he pointed. "That."

Thoughtfully, Megan studied the tiny shell figure the woman lifted down. It seemed to be a cross between a duck and a penguin. "What're you going to do with that?"

"Give it to you." Katch handed over the rest of the tickets. "I'm a very generous man."

"I'm overwhelmed," she murmured. Megan turned it over in the palm of her hand as Katch pinned the rose to the collar of her shirt. "But what is it?"

"It's a mallard." Draping his arm over her shoulder again, he led her out of the arcade. "I'm surprised at your attitude. I figured, as an artist, you'd recognize its aesthetic value."

"Hmm." Megan took another study, then slipped it into her pocket. "Well, I do recognize a certain winsome charm. And," she added, rising on her toes to kiss his cheek, "it was sweet of you to spend all your winnings on me."

Smiling, Katch ran a finger down her nose. "Is a kiss on the cheek the best you can do?"

"For a shell penguin it is."

"It's a mallard," he reminded her.

"Whatever." Laughing, Megan slipped an arm around his waist as they crossed the boardwalk and walked down the slope to the beach.

The moon was only a thin slice of white, but the stars were brilliant and mirrored in the water. There was a quiet swish of waves flowing and ebbing over the sand. Lovers walked here and there, arm in arm, talking quietly or not speaking at all. Children dashed along with flashlights bobbing, searching the sand and the surf for treasures.

Bending, Megan slipped out of her shoes and rolled up the hem of her jeans. In silent agreement, Katch followed suit. The water lapped cool over their ankles as they began to walk north, until the laughter and music from the boardwalk was only a background echo.

"Your sister's lovely," Megan said at length. "Just as you said."

"Jessica was always a beauty," he agreed absently. "A little hardheaded, but always a beauty."

"I saw your nieces at the park." Megan lifted her head so that the ocean breeze caught at her hair. "They had chocolate all over their faces."

"Typical." He laughed, running a hand up and down her arm as they walked. Megan felt the blood begin to hum beneath her flesh. "Before they left tonight, they were out digging for worms. I've been drafted to take them fishing tomorrow."

"You like children."

He twisted his head to glance down at her, but Megan was looking out to sea. "Yes. They're a constant adventure, aren't they?"

"I see so many of them in the park every summer, yet they never cease to amaze me." She turned back then with her slow, serious smile hovering on her lips. "And I see a fair number of harassed or long-suffering parents."

"When did you lose yours?"

He saw the flicker of surprise in her eyes before she looked down the stretch of beach again. "I was five."

"It's difficult for you to remember them."

"Yes. I have some vague memories—impressions really, I suppose. Pop has pictures, of course. When I see them, it always surprises me how young they were."

"It must have been hard on you," Katch murmured. "Growing up without them."

The gentleness in his voice had her turning back to him. They'd walked far down the beach so that the only light now came from the stars. His eyes caught the glitter of reflection as they held hers. "It would have been," Megan told him, "without Pop. He did much more than fill in." She stopped to take a step farther into the surf. The water frothed and bubbled over her skin. "One of my best memories is of him struggling to iron this pink organdy party dress. I was eight or nine, I think." With a shake of her head, she laughed and kicked the water. "I can still see him."

Katch's arms came around her waist, drawing her back against him. "So can I."

"He was standing there, struggling with frills and flounces—and swearing like a sailor because he didn't know I was there. I still love him for that," she murmured. "For just that."

Katch brushed his lips over the top of her hair. "And I imagine you told him not long afterward that you didn't care much for party dresses."

Surprised, Megan turned around. "How did you know that?"

"I know you." Slowly, he traced the shape of her face with his fingertip.

Frowning, she looked beyond his shoulder. "Am I so simple?"

"No." With his fingertip still on her jaw, he turned her face back to his. "You might say I've made a study of you."

She felt her blood begin to churn. "Why?"

Katch shook his head and combed his fingers through her hair. "No questions tonight," he said quietly. "I don't have the answers yet."

"No questions," she agreed, then rose on her toes to meet his mouth with hers.

It was a soft, exploring kiss—a kiss of renewal. Megan could taste the gentleness. For the moment, he seemed to prize her, to find her precious and rare. He held her lightly, as though she would break at the slightest pressure. Her lips parted, and it was she who entered his mouth first, teasing his tongue with hers. His sound of pleasure warmed her. The water swayed, soft and cool, on her calves.

She ran her hands up his back, letting her strong, artist's fingers trail under his hair to caress the nape of his neck. There was tension there, and she murmured against his lips as if to soothe it. Megan felt both his resistance and the tightening of his fingers against her skin. Her body pressed more demandingly into his.

Passion began to smolder quietly. Megan knew she was drawing it from him without his complete consent. The wonder of her own power struck her like a flash. He was holding back, letting her set the pace, but she could feel the near-violence of need in him. It tempted her. She wanted to undermine his control as he had undermined hers. She wanted to make him need as blindly as she needed. It wasn't possible to make him love her, but she could make him want. If it was all she could have from him, then she would be satisfied with his desire.

Megan felt his control slipping. His arms tightened around

her, drawing her close so they were silhouetted as one. The kiss grew harder, more urgent. He lifted a hand to her hair, gripping it, pulling her head back as if now he would take command. There was fire now, burning brightly. Heat rose in her, smoking through her blood. She caught his bottom lip between her teeth and heard his quiet moan. Abruptly, he drew her away.

"Meg."

She waited, having no idea what she wanted him to say. Her head was tossed back, her face open to his, her hair free to the breeze. She felt incredibly strong. His eyes were nearly black, searching her face deeply. She could feel his breath feather, warm and uneven, on her lips.

"Meg." He repeated her name, bringing his hands back to her shoulders slowly. "I have to go now."

Daring more than she would have believed possible, Megan pressed her lips to his again. Hers were soft and hungry and drew instant response from him. "Is that what you want?" she murmured. "Do you want to leave me now?"

His fingers tightened on her arms convulsively, then he pulled her away again. "You know the answer to that," he said roughly. "What are you trying to do, make me crazy?"

"Maybe." Desire still churned in her. It smoldered in her eyes as they met his. "Maybe I am."

He caught her against him, close and tight. She could feel the furious race of his heart against hers. His control, she knew, balanced on a razor's edge. Their lips were only a whisper apart.

"There'll be a time," he said softly, "I swear it, when it'll just be you and me. Next time, the very next time, Meg. Remember it."

It took no effort to keep her eyes level with his. The power was still flowing through her. "Is that a warning?"

"Yes," he told her. "That's just what it is."

CHAPTER 11

It took two more days for Megan to finish the bust of Katch. She tried, when it was time, to divorce herself from emotion and judge it objectively.

She'd been right to choose wood. It was warmer than stone. With her tongue caught between her teeth, she searched for flaws in her workmanship. Megan knew without conceit it was one of her better pieces. Perhaps the best.

The face wasn't stylishly handsome, but strong and compelling. Humor was expressed in the tilt of the brows and mouth. She ran her fingertips over his lips. An incredibly expressive mouth, she mused, remembering the taste and texture. I know just how it looks when he's amused or angry or aroused. And his eyes. Hers drifted up to linger. I know how they look, how they change shades and expression with a mood. Light for pleasure, turning smoky in anger, darker in passion.

I know his face as well as my own . . . but I still don't know his mind. That's still a stranger. With a sigh she folded her arms on the table and lowered her chin to them.

Would he ever permit me to know him? she wondered. Tenderly, she touched a lock of the disordered hair. Jessica knows him, probably better than anyone else. If he loved someone . . .

What would happen if I drew up the courage to tell him that I love him? What would happen if I simply walked up to him and said *I love you?* Demanding nothing, expecting nothing. Doesn't he perhaps have the right to know? Isn't love too special, too rare to be closed up? Then Megan imagined his eyes with pity in them.

"I couldn't bear it," she murmured, lowering her forehead to Katch's wooden one. "I just couldn't bear it." A knock interrupted her soul-searching. Quickly, Megan composed her features and swiveled in her chair. "Come in."

Her grandfather entered, his fishing cap perched jauntily on his mane of white hair. "How do you feel about fresh fish for supper?" His grin told her that his early morning expedition had been a success. Megan cocked her head.

"I could probably choke down a few bites." She smiled, pleased to see his eyes sparkling and color in his cheeks. She sprang up and wound her arms around his neck as she had done as a child. "Oh, I love you, Pop!"

"Well, well." He patted her hair, both surprised and pleased. "I love you too, Megan. I guess I should bring you home trout more often."

She lifted her face from the warm curve of his neck and smiled at him. "It doesn't take much to make me happy."

His eyes sobered as he tucked her hair behind her ear. "No. . . . It never has." His wide, blunt hand touched her cheek. "You've given me so much pleasure over the years, Megan, so much joy. I'm going to miss you when you're in New York."

"Oh, Pop." She buried her face again and clung. "It'll only be for a month or two, then I'll be home." She could smell the cherry-flavored scent of the tobacco he carried in his breast pocket. "You could even come with me—the season'll be over."

"Meg." He stopped her rambling and drew her up so that their eyes met. "This is a start for you. Don't put restrictions on it."

Shaking her head, Megan rose to pace nervously. "I'm not. I don't know what you mean . . ."

"You're going to make something of yourself, something important. You have talent." Pop glanced around the room at her work until his eyes rested on the bust of Katch. "You've got a life to start. I want you to go after it at full speed."

"You make it sound as if I'm not coming home." Megan turned and, seeing where his eyes rested, clasped her hands together. "I've just finished that." She moistened her lips and struggled to keep her voice casual. "It's rather good, don't you think?"

"Yes, I think it's very good." He looked at her then. "Sit down, Megan, I need to talk to you."

She recognized the tone and tensed. Without a word, she obeyed, going to the chair across from him. Pop waited until she was settled, then studied her face carefully.

"Awhile back," he began, "I told you things change. Most of your life, it's been just the two of us. We needed each other, depended on each other. We had the park to keep a roof over our heads and to give us something to work for." His tone softened. "There hasn't been one minute in the eighteen years I've had you with me that you've been a burden. You've kept me young. I've watched you through all the stages of grow-ing up, and each time, you've made me more proud of you. It's time for the next change."

Because her throat was dry as dust, Megan swallowed. "I don't understand what you're trying to tell me."

"It's time you moved out into the world, Megan, time I let you." Pop reached in the pocket of his shirt and took out carefully folded papers. After spreading them out, he handed them to Megan.

She hesitated before accepting them, her eyes clinging to his. The instant she saw the papers, she knew what they were. But when she read, she read each sentence, each word, until the finish. "So," she said, dry-eyed, dry-voiced. "You've sold it to him."

"When I sign the papers," Pop told her, "and you witness it." He saw the look of devastation in her eyes. "Megan, hear me out. I've given this a lot of thought." Pop took the papers and set them on the table, then gripped her hands. "Katch isn't the first to approach me about selling, and this isn't the first time I've considered it. Everything didn't fit the way I wanted before—this time it does."

"What fits?" she demanded, feeling her eyes fill.

"It's the right man, Meg, the right time." He soothed her hands, hating to watch her distress. "I knew it when all those repairs fell on me. I'm ready to let it go, to let someone younger take over so I can go fishing. That's what I want now, Megan, a boat and a rod. And he's the man I want taking over." He paused, fumbling in his pocket for a handkerchief to wipe his eyes. "I told you I trusted him and that still holds. Managing the park for Katch won't keep me from my fishing, and I'll have the stimulation without the headaches. And you," he continued, brushing tears from her cheeks, "you need to cut the strings. You can't do what you're meant to do if you're struggling to balance books and make payroll."

"If it's what you want," Megan began, but Pop cut her off.

"No, it has to be what you want. That's why the last lines are still blank." He looked at her with his deep-set eyes sober and quiet. "I won't sign it, Megan, unless you agree. It has to be what's best for both of us."

Megan stood again, and he released her hands to let her

walk to the window. At the moment, she was unable to understand her own feelings. She knew agreeing to do a show in New York was a giant step away from the life she had led. And the park was a major part of that life. She knew in order to pursue her own career, she couldn't continue to tie herself to the business end of Joyland.

The park had been security—her responsibility, her second home—as the man behind her had been both mother and father to her. She remembered the look of weariness on his face when he had come to tell her that the park needed money. Megan knew the hours and endless demands that summer would bring.

He was entitled to live his winter years as he chose, she decided. With less worry, less responsibility. He was entitled to fish, and to sleep late and putter around his azaleas. What right did she have to deny him that because she was afraid to cut the last tie with her childhood? He was right, it was time for the change.

Slowly, she walked to her workbox and searched out a pen. Going to Pop, Megan held it out to him. "Sign it. We'll have champagne with the trout."

Pop took the pen, but kept his eyes on her. "Are you sure, Meg?"

She nodded, as sure for him as she was uncertain for herself. "Positive." She smiled and watched the answering light in his eyes before he bent over the paper.

He signed his name with a flourish, then passed her the pen so that she could witness his signature. Megan wrote her name in clear, distinct letters, not allowing her hand to tremble.

"I suppose I should call Katch," Pop mused, sighing as though a weight had been lifted. "Or take the papers to him."

"I'll take them." Carefully, Megan folded them again. "I'd like to talk to him."

"That's a good idea. Take the pickup," he suggested as she headed for the door. "It looks like rain."

Megan was calm by the time she reached Katch's house. The papers were tucked securely in the back pocket of her cutoffs. She pulled the truck behind his car and climbed out.

The air was deadly still and heavy, nearly shimmering with restrained rain. The clouds overhead were black and bulging with it. She walked to the front door and knocked as she had many days before. As before, there was no answer. She walked back down the steps and skirted the house.

There was no sign of him in the yard, no sound but the voice of the sea muffled by the tall hedges. He'd planted a willow, a young, slender one near the slope which led to the beach. The earth was still dark around it, freshly turned. Unable to resist, Megan walked to it, wanting to touch the tender young leaves. It was no taller than she, but she knew one day it would be magnificent . . . sweeping, graceful, a haven of shade in the summer. Instinct made her continue down the slope to the beach.

Hands in his pockets, he stood, watching the swiftly incoming tide. As if sensing her, he turned.

"I was standing here thinking of you," he said. "Did I wish you here?"

She took the papers and held them out to him. "It's yours," she told him calmly. "Just as you wanted."

He didn't even glance down at the papers, but she saw the shift of expression in his eyes. "I'd like to talk to you, Meg. Let's go inside."

"No." She stepped back to emphasize her refusal. "There really isn't anything more to say."

"That might be true for you, but I have a great deal to say. And you're going to listen." Impatience intruded into his tone. Megan heard it as she felt the sudden gust of wind which broke the calm.

"I don't want to listen to you, Katch. This is what Pop wants, too." She thrust the papers into his hands as the first spear of lightning split the sky. "Take them, will you?"

"Megan, wait." He grabbed her arm as she turned to go. The thunder all but drowned out his words.

"I will not wait!" she tossed back, jerking her arm free. "And stop grabbing me. You have what you wanted—you don't need me anymore."

Katch swore, thrust the papers in his pocket and caught her again before she'd taken three steps. He whirled her back around. "You're not that big an idiot."

"Don't tell me how big an idiot I am." She tried to shake herself loose.

"We have to talk. I have things to say to you. It's important." A gust of wind whipped violently across Megan's face.

"Don't you understand a simple no?" she shouted at him, her voice competing with pounding surf and rising wind. She struggled against his hold. "I don't want to talk. I don't want to hear what you have to say. I don't *care* about what you have to say."

The rain burst from the clouds and poured over them. Instantly, they were drenched.

"Tough," he retorted, every bit as angry as she. "Because you're going to hear it. Now, let's go inside."

He started to pull her across the sand, but she swung violently away and freed herself. Rain gushed down in torrents, sheeting around them. "No!" she shouted. "I won't go inside with you."

"Oh yes you will," he corrected.

"What are you going to do?" she demanded. "Drag me by the hair?"

"Don't tempt me." Katch took her hand again only to have her pull away. "All right," he said. "Enough." In a swift move that caught her off guard, he swept her up into his arms.

"Put me down." Megan wriggled and kicked, blind with fury. He ignored her, dealing with her struggles by shifting her closer and climbing the slope without any apparent effort. Lightning and thunder warred around them. "Oh, I hate you!" she claimed as he walked briskly across the lawn.

"Good. That's a start." Katch pushed open the door with his hip, then continued through the kitchen and into the living room. A trail of rain streamed behind them. Without ceremony, he dumped her on the sofa. "Sit still," he ordered before she could regain her breath, "and just be quiet a minute." He walked to the hearth. Taking a long match, he set fire to the paper waiting beneath kindling and logs. Dry wood crackled and caught almost instantly.

Regaining her breath, Megan rose and bounded for the door. Katch stopped her before her fingers touched the knob. He held her by the shoulders with her back to the door. "I warn you, Meg, my tolerance is at a very low ebb. Don't push me."

"You don't frighten me," she told him, impatiently flipping her dripping hair from her eyes.

"I'm not trying to frighten you. I'm trying to reason with you. But you're too stubborn to shut up and listen."

Her eyes widened with fresh fury. "Don't you talk to me that way! I don't have to take that."

"Yes, you do." Deftly, he reached in her right front pocket and pulled out the truck keys. "As long as I have these."

"I can walk," she tossed back as he pocketed them himself.

"In this rain?"

Megan hugged her arms as she began to shiver. "Let me have my keys."

Instead of answering, he pulled her across the room in front of the fire. "You're freezing. You'll have to get out of those wet clothes."

"I will not. You're crazy if you think I'm going to take off my clothes in your house."

"Suit yourself." He stripped off his own sopping T-shirt and tossed it angrily aside. "You're the most hardheaded, single-minded, stubborn woman I know."

"Thanks." Barely, Megan controlled the urge to sneeze. "Is that all you wanted to say?"

"No." He walked to the fire again. "That's just the beginning—there's a lot more. Sit down."

"Then maybe I'll have my say first." Chills were running over her skin, and she struggled not to tremble. "I was wrong about you in a lot of ways. You're not lazy or careless or glory-seeking. And you were certainly honest with me." She wiped water from her eyes, a mixture of rain and tears. "You told me up front that you intended to have the park, and it seems perhaps for the best. What happened between then and now is my fault for being foolish enough to let you get to me." Megan swallowed, wanting to salvage a little pride. "But then you're a difficult man to ignore. Now you have what you wanted, and it's over and done."

"I only have part of what I wanted." Katch came to her and gathered her streaming hair in his hand. "Only part, Meg."

She looked at him, too tired to argue. "Can't you just let me be?" she asked.

"Let you be? Do you know how many times I've walked that beach at three in the morning because wanting you kept me awake and aching? Do you know how hard it was for me to let you go every time I had you in my arms?" The fingers in her hair tightened, pulled her closer.

Her eyes were huge now while chills shivered over her skin. *What was he saying?* She couldn't risk asking, couldn't risk wondering. Abruptly, he cursed her and dragged her into his arms.

Thin wet clothes were no barrier to his hands. He molded her breasts even while his mouth ravished hers. She made no protest when he lowered her to the floor, as his fingers worked desperately at the buttons of her blouse. Her chilled wet skin turned to fire under his fingertips. His mouth was hungry, hot as it roamed to her throat and downward.

There was only the crackle of wood and the splash of rain on the windows to mix with their breathing. A log shifted in the grate.

Megan heard him take a long, deep breath. "I'm sorry. I wanted to talk—there are things I need to tell you. But I need you. I've kept it pent up a long time."

Need. Her mind centered on the word. Need was infinitely different from want. Need was more personal—still apart from love—but she let her heart grip the word.

"It's all right." Megan started to sit up, but he leaned over her. Sparks flicked inside her at the touch of naked flesh to naked flesh. "Katch . . ."

"Please, Meg. Listen to me."

She searched his face, noting the uncharacteristically grave eyes and mouth. Whatever he had to say was important to him. "All right," she said, quieter now, ready. "I'll listen."

"When I first saw you, the first minute, I wanted you. You know that." His voice was low, but without its usual calm. Something boiled just under the surface. "The first night we were together, you intrigued me as much as you attracted me. I thought it would be a simple matter to have you . . . a casual, pleasant affair for a few weeks."

"I know," she spoke softly, trying not to be wounded by the truth.

"No—shh." He lay a finger over her lips a moment. "You don't know. It stopped being simple almost immediately. When I had you here for dinner, and you asked to stay . . ." He paused, brushing wet strands of hair from her cheeks. "I couldn't let you, and I wasn't completely sure why. I wanted you—wanted you more than any woman I'd ever touched, any woman I'd ever dreamed about—but I couldn't take you."

"Katch . . ." Megan shook her head, not certain she was strong enough to hear the words.

"Please." She had closed her eyes, and Katch waited until she opened them again before he continued. "I tried to stay away from you, Meg. I tried to convince myself I was imagining what was happening to me. Then you were charging across the lawn, looking outraged and so beautiful I couldn't think of anything. Just looking at you took my breath away." While she lay motionless, he lifted her hand and pressed it to his lips. The gesture moved her unbearably.

"Don't," she murmured. "Please."

Katch stared into her eyes for a long moment, then released her hand. "I wanted you," he went on in a voice more calm than his eyes. "Needed you, was furious with you because of it." He rested his forehead on hers and shut his eyes. "I never wanted to hurt you, Meg—to frighten you."

Megan lay still, aware of the turmoil in him. Firelight played over the skin on his arms and back.

"It seemed impossible that I could be so involved I couldn't pull away," he continued. "But you were so tangled up in my thoughts, so wound up in my dreams. There wasn't any escape. The other night, after I'd taken you home, I finally admitted to myself I didn't want an escape. Not this time. Not from you." He lifted his head and looked down at her again. "I have something for you, but first I want you to know I'd decided against buying the park until your grandfather came to me last night. I didn't want that between us, but it was what he wanted. What he thought was best for you and for himself. But if it hurts you, I'll tear the papers up."

"No." Megan gave a weary sigh. "I know it's best. It's just

like losing someone you love. Even when you know it's the best thing, it still hurts." The outburst seemed to have driven out the fears and the pain. "Please, I don't want you to apologize. I was wrong, coming here this way, shouting at you. Pop has every right to sell the park, and you have every right to buy it." She sighed, wanting explanations over. "I suppose I felt betrayed somehow and didn't want to think it all through."

"And now?"

"And now I'm ashamed of myself for acting like a fool." She managed a weak smile. "I'd like to get up and go home. Pop'll be worried."

"Not just yet." When Katch leaned back on his heels to take something from his pocket, Megan sat up, pushing her wet, tangled hair behind her. He held a box, small and thin. Briefly, he hesitated before offering it to her. Puzzled, both by the gift and by the tension she felt emanating from him, Megan opened it. Her breath caught.

It was a dark, smoky green emerald, square cut and exquisite in its simplicity. Stunned, Megan stared at it, then at Katch. She shook her head wordlessly.

"Katch." Megan shook her head again. "I don't understand . . . I can't accept this."

"Don't say no, Meg." Katch closed his hand over hers. "I don't handle rejection well." The words were light, but she recognized, and was puzzled by, the strain in the tone. A thought trembled in her brain, and her heart leaped with it.

She tried to be calm and keep her eyes steady on his. "I don't know what you're asking me."

His fingers tightened on hers. "Marry me. I love you."

Emotions ran riot through her. He must be joking, she thought quickly, though no hint of amusement showed in his eyes. His face was so serious, she reflected, and the words so simple. Where were the carelessly witty phrases, the glib charm? Shaken, Megan rose with the box held tightly in her hand. She needed to think.

Marriage. Never had she expected him to ask her to share a lifetime. What would life be like with him? *Like the roller coaster.* She knew it instantly. It would be a fast, furious ride, full of unexpected curves and indescribable thrills. And quiet moments too, she reflected. Precious, solitary moments which would make each new twist and turn more exciting.

Perhaps he had asked her this way, so simply, without any of the frills he could so easily provide because he was as vulnerable as she. What a thought that was! She lifted her fingers to her temple. David Katcherton vulnerable. And yet . . . Megan remembered what she had seen in his eyes.

I love you. The three simple words, words spoken every day by people everywhere, had changed her life forever. Megan turned, then walking back, knelt beside him. Her eyes were as grave, as searching as his. She held the box out, then spoke quickly as she saw the flicker of desperation.

"It belongs on the third finger of my left hand."

Then she was caught against him, her mouth silenced bruisingly. "Oh, Meg," he murmured her name as he rained kisses on her face. "I thought you were turning me down."

"How could I?" She wound her arms around his neck and tried to stop his roaming mouth with her own. "I love you, Katch." The words were against his lips. "Desperately, completely. I'd prepared myself for a slow death when you were ready to walk away."

"No one's going to walk away now." They lay on the floor again, and he buried his face in her rain-scented hair. "We'll go to New Orleans. A quick honeymoon before you have to come back and work on the show. In the spring, we'll go to Paris." He lifted his face and looked down on her. "I've thought about you and me in Paris, making love. I want to see your face in the morning when the light's soft."

She touched his cheek. "Soon," she whispered. "Marry me soon. I want to be with you."

He picked up the box that had fallen beside them. Drawing out the ring, he slipped it on her finger. Then, gripping her hand with his, he looked down at her.

"Consider it binding, Meg," he told her huskily. "You can't get away now."

"I'm not going anywhere." She lifted her mouth to meet his kiss.

EPILOGUE

Nervously, Megan twisted the emerald on her finger and tried to drink the champagne Jessica had pushed into her hand. She felt as though the smile had frozen onto her face. People, she thought. She'd never expected so many people. What was she doing, standing in a Manhattan gallery pretending she was an artist? What she wanted to do was creep into the back room and be very, very sick.

"Here now, Meg." Pop strolled over beside her, looking oddly distinguished in his best—and only—black suit. "You should try one of these—tasty little things." He held out a canapé.

"No." Megan felt her stomach roll and shook her head. "No, thanks. I'm so glad you flew up for the weekend."

"Think I'd miss my granddaughter's big night?" He ate the canapé and grinned. "How about this turnout?"

"I feel like an impostor," Megan murmured, smiling gamely as a man in a flowing cape moved past her to study one of her marble pieces.

"Never seen you look prettier." Pop plucked at the sleeve of her dress, a swirl of watercolored silk. " 'Cept maybe at your wedding."

"I wasn't nearly as scared then." She made a quick scan of the crowd and found only strangers. "Where's Katch?"

"Last time I saw him he was cornered by a couple of ritzy-looking people. Didn't I hear Jessica say you were supposed to mingle?"

"Yes." Megan made a small, frustrated sound. "I don't think I can move."

"Now, Meg, I've never known you to be chicken-hearted."

With her mouth half-opened in protest, she watched him walk away. *Chicken-hearted,* she repeated silently. Straightening her shoulders, she drank some champagne. All right then, she decided, she wouldn't stand there cowering in the corner. If she was going to be shot down, she'd face it head on. Moving slowly, and with determined confidence, Megan walked toward the buffet.

"You're the artist, aren't you?"

Megan turned to face a striking old woman in diamonds and black silk. "Yes," she said with a fractional lift of her chin. "I am."

"Hmmm." The woman took Megan in with a long, sweeping glance. "I noticed the study of the girl with the sand castle isn't for sale."

"No, it's my husband's." After two months, the words still brought the familiar warmth to her blood. *Katch, my husband.* Megan's eyes darted around the room to find him.

"A pity," the woman in black commented.

"I beg your pardon?"

"I said it's a pity—I wanted it."

"You—" Stunned, Megan stared at her. "You wanted it?"

"I've purchased 'The Lovers,'" she went on as Megan only gaped. "An excellent piece, but I want to commission you to do another sand castle. I'll contact you through Jessica."

"Yes, of course." *Commission?* Megan thought numbly as

she automatically offered her hand. "Thank you," she added as the woman swept away.

"Miriam Tailor Marcus," a voice whispered beside her ear. "A tough nut to crack."

Megan half turned and grabbed Katch's arm. "Katch, that woman, she—"

"Miriam Tailor Marcus," he repeated and bent down to kiss her astonished mouth. "And I heard. I've just been modestly accepting compliments on my contribution to the art world." He touched the rim of his glass to hers. "Congratulations, love."

"They like my work?" she whispered.

"If you hadn't been so busy trying to be invisible, you'd know you're a smashing success. Walk around with me," he told her as he took her hand. "And look at all the little blue dots under your sculptures that mean SOLD."

"They're buying?" Megan gave a wondering laugh as she spotted sale after sale. "They're really buying them?"

"Jessica's frantically trying to keep up. Three people've tried to buy the alabaster piece she bought from you herself—at twice what you charged her. And if you don't talk to a couple of the art critics soon, she's going to go crazy."

"I can't believe it."

"Believe it." He brought Megan's hand to his lips. "I'm very proud of you, Meg."

Tears welled up, threatening to brim over. "I have to get out of here for a minute," she whispered. "Please."

Without a word, Katch maneuvered his way through the crowd, taking Megan into the storage room and shutting the door behind them.

"This is silly," she said immediately as the tears rolled freely down her cheeks. "I'm an idiot. I have everything I've ever dreamed of and I'm crying in the back room. I'd have handled failure better than this."

"Megan." With a soft laugh, he gathered her close. "I love you."

"It doesn't seem real," she said with a quaver in her voice. "Not just the showing . . . it's everything. I see your ring on my finger and I keep wondering when I'm going to wake up. I can't believe that—"

His mouth silenced her. With a low, melting sigh, she dissolved against him. Even after all the days of her marriage, and all the intimate nights, he could still turn her to putty with only his mouth. The tears vanished as her blood began to swim. Pulling him closer, she let her hands run up the sides of his face and into his hair.

"It's real," he murmured against her mouth. "Believe it." Tilting his head, he changed the angle of the kiss and took her deeper. "It's real every night when you're in my arms, and every morning when you wake there." Katch drew her away slowly, then kissed both her damp cheeks until her lashes fluttered up. "Tonight," he said with a smile, "I'm going to make love to the newest star in the New York art world. And when she's still riding high over the reviews in the morning papers, I'm going to make love to her all over again."

"How soon can we slip away?"

Laughing, he caught her close for a hard kiss. "Don't tempt me. Jessica'd skin us both if we didn't stay until the gallery closes tonight. Now, fix your face and go bask in the admiration for a while. It's good for the soul."

"Katch." Megan stopped him before he could open the door. "There's one piece I didn't put out tonight."

Curious, he lifted a brow. "Oh?"

"Yes, well . . ." A faint color rose to her cheeks. "I was afraid things might not go well, and I thought I could handle the criticism. But this piece—I knew I couldn't bear to have anyone say it was a poor attempt or amateurish."

Puzzled, he slipped his hands into his pockets. "Have I seen it?"

"No." She shook her head, tossing her bangs out of her eyes. "I'd wanted to give it to you as a wedding present, but everything happened so fast and it wasn't finished. After all," she added with a grin, "we were only engaged for three days."

"Two days longer than if you'd agreed to fly to Vegas," he pointed out. "All in all, I was very patient."

"Be that as it may, I didn't have time until later to finish it. Then I was so nervous about the showing that I couldn't give it to you." She took a deep breath. "I'd like you to have it now, tonight, while I'm feeling—really feeling like an artist."

"Is it here?"

Turning around, Megan reached up on the shelf where the bust was carefully covered in cloth. Wordlessly, she handed it to him. Katch removed the cloth, then stared down into his own face.

Megan had polished the wood very lightly, wanting it to carry that not-quite-civilized aura she perceived in the model. It had his cockiness, his confidence and the warmth the artist had sensed in him before the woman had. He stared at it for so long, she felt the nerves begin to play in her stomach again. Then he looked up, eyes dark, intense.

"Meg."

"I don't want to put it out on display," she said hurriedly. "It's too personal to me. There were times," she began as she took the bust from him and ran a thumb down a cheekbone, "when I was working on the clay model, that I wanted to smash it." With a half-laugh, she set it down on a small table. "I couldn't. When I started it, I told myself the only reason I kept thinking about you was because you had the sort of face I'd like to sculpt." She lifted her eyes then to find his fixed on hers. "I fell in love with you sitting in my studio, while my hands were forming your face." Stepping forward, Megan lifted her hands and traced her fingers over the planes and bones under his flesh. "I thought I couldn't love you more than I did then. I was wrong."

"Meg." Katch brought his hands to hers, pressing her palms to his lips. "You leave me speechless."

"Just love me."

"Always."

"That just might be long enough." Megan sighed as she rested her head against his shoulder. "And I think I'll be able to handle success knowing it."

Katch slipped an arm around her waist as he opened the door. "Let's go have some more champagne. It's a night for celebrations."

THE BRAND NEW NOVEL
from the *New York Times* bestselling author

NORA ROBERTS

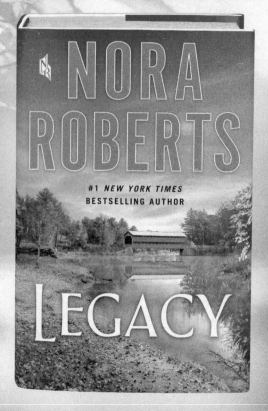

A tale of family tragedy, healing love,
and unnerving suspense.

AVAILABLE WHEREVER BOOKS ARE SOLD